RICH

P9-CEG-035

THE LAST COWGIRL

Riding in the Shadows of Saints:
A Woman's Story of Motorcycling the Mormon Trail

THE LAST COWGIRL

 JANA RICHMAN

wm

WILLIAM MORROW

An Imprint of HarperCollinsPublishers

The poetry that appears on page 171 is written by Brad Richman and is used with permission.

This book is a work of fiction. References to real people, events, establishments, organizations, or locales are intended only to provide a sense of authenticity, and are used fictitiously. All other characters, and all incidents and dialogue, are drawn from the author's imagination and are not to be construed as real.

FIRST EDITION

Designed by Gretchen Achilles

Library of Congress Cataloging-in-Publication Data
Richman, Jana, 1956–
    The last cowgirl : a novel / Jana Richman. — 1st ed.
        p. cm.
    ISBN 978-0-06-125718-6
        1. Middle-aged women—Fiction.   2. Homecoming—Fiction.   3. Ranch life—Utah—Fiction.   4. Family—Fiction.   5. Psychological fiction.   I. Title.
    PS3618.I348L37 2008
    813'.6—dc22
                                                                            2007032341

08 09 10 11 12 WBC/RRD 10 9 8 7 6 5 4 3 2 1

FOR STEVE

THE LAST COWGIRL

CHAPTER ONE

I was seven when my father decided to be a cowboy. At the time it seemed to happen with a jarring abruptness, my summer attire went from sunsuits and Keds to snap-button shirts and boots faster than my sister, Annie, could pick up jacks, and Annie held our neighborhood's title as Queen of Jacks. Since then—nearly forty-six years ago—I've blamed anything that needed blaming on what Annie refers to as Dad's "Gil Favor complex." This system of culpability has been a reliable one, comfortably accommodating every failure in my life, including the ultimate failure—to get married and spawn offspring—so I find no reason to abandon it now. Especially when I am in desperate need. My brother, Heber, is dead. Poisoned by nerve gas. And, if anyone cares to do the footwork, I am quite sure the path will lead directly back to a surprisingly frigid spring day in 1962 when Grandpa Sinfield keeled over from a heart attack and left my father nothing but an old bay horse named Rangy.

I pinpoint that event as the rock that dropped into the puddle of our family and splattered us Sinfields out of a collective life of ordinariness into five separate pieces scrambling for a soft place to land. But Annie says Dad's cowboy dreams had been sizzling and popping for years before that, sort of like a cheap aluminum coffeepot left on the stove long after the liquid had boiled away. Grandpa Sinfield was a hired hand for a cattle company in Blacksmith Fork Canyon in the Bear River Range of Utah's Rocky Mountains, a place where cold, clear trout-filled streams wound through tall wheatgrass, ponderosa pine, and quakin' asp' trees. Dad never had much to say about the days he spent as a boy riding alongside his father on horseback. But Aunt Alma, Dad's older sister and only sibling, told us those old stories as if they would explain everything we'd ever need to know about Dad, like why he wore cowboy boots with dress slacks and what caused him to spit forth a string of profanity upon little provocation. Alma said that during those shaded summer days, when Dad knew every fork in every canyon and any place a lost cow or calf might be found, the world made more sense to young George Sinfield than it ever had once he stepped outside the deep gorges of Blacksmith Fork.

He wasn't more than six years old the first time Frank Clark, an old sheepherder in Righthand Fork, told him the story of how he trapped and killed Old Ephraim, the last of the great grizzlies to wander the Bear River Range, with nothing but a .30-30 rifle and a prayer. Frank showed the boy the path Old Ephraim had taken from the wallow that held the trap directly into Frank's camp, still evident years later from gouges on aspen trees made by an angry grizzly dragging a twenty-three-pound trap chained to a large log. From that point forward through the next twelve years, every time George stood at Old Ephraim's grave site, excitement and reverence gushed through his veins and caught him just below the Adam's apple. So when, upon high school graduation, his father presented him with the cash he'd been stuffing in an unused saddlebag over the last eighteen years to get his son an education and an occupation that would garner more respect than that of hired hand, George initially balked. It was only the look of pride in his father's eyes that pulled the boy out of the mountains and deposited him onto a college campus. As a consequence, it was nothing but an old man's idea of generational betterment that led to my and my siblings' birth in the small town of Ganoa, two hundred miles southwest of Blacksmith Fork Canyon in Utah's west desert, where Dad, fresh out of college, took a job as an elementary school teacher, giving Grandpa bragging rights among the other hands—his son wore a tie and had a retirement plan. But ten years stuck in a class-room, where a cross breeze had to be coaxed through six-inch window openings, could not shake loose the sound of shivering aspen trees running through Dad's head like a melody.

George Sinfield married Ruth Pace as quickly as he could talk her into it—two years and eight months after they graduated from high school. As soon as he entered college she set her intentions to marry him—she was attracted to an educated man—but after high school she had a Salt Lake City apartment and a job behind the lunch coun-ter at Kress's waiting for her, an experience she wasn't going to miss. Once that romance wore itself out, she married George.

She kept her job while George finished college, and their early years of marriage were filled with weekends of loading eight or ten friends into a car and driving out to Saltair at the Great Salt Lake to dance on the bouncing, spring-loaded floor to the sound of the big bands playing their way to the West Coast. Mom would swoon and swirl when she recounted those stories, and Dad would smile while he leaned against the doorjamb watching her until she'd put on a record and they'd dance their way around the loop that incorporated the kitchen and living room in our Ganoa house. Mom said both the dancing and the friends disappeared as soon as Heber was born. I un-derstood that to mean it was unequivocally Heber's fault. Had Annie or I been born first, our lives would have been filled with music, danc-ing, and laughter, and Dad would have always carried the untroubled look that fell over his face every time Mom started humming "Star-dust."

Alma followed her brother to Ganoa, bought a cinderblock house about three blocks from ours, and took a job as a lunchroom lady in the same school where George taught. For the most part Aunt Alma, Mom, and Dad sort of came as a set. Ruth Pace didn't so much em-brace motherhood as simply resign herself to the role, unable to imagine—growing up in the Mormon religion as she did—any viable alternatives, so she generously shared all aspects of the position with

Aunt Alma. Annie, Heber, and I always took her presence in our lives for granted.

We lived in a cookie-cutter neighborhood of rectangular lawns, right-angle sidewalks, curbs and gutters, and chain-link fences. Immediately following Grandpa's death in '62, Rangy had a new home in some rented corrals at the end of a dusty road on the outskirts of Ganoa about two miles from the house. Shortly after that, Dad came home with Pug. "A good kids' horse," Dad had said, "not so high-headed he can't be handled but not so docile the kids don't learn a damn thing."

Aunt Alma says when Grandpa willed my father that old bay horse, Dad took the act as an apology and a mandate that he set about fulfilling with a frightening exuberance none of us had ever seen before. Seems like one Saturday I was roller-skating down a finely paved road past the rosebushes that lined our yard, and the next Rangy and Pug pranced in that very spot. Before I could come down with a convenient childhood illness or some other suitable excuse, I found myself being hefted—in full western regalia—onto Pug's back, alarmed at the distance between me and the smooth pavement I loved so dearly.

The neighbors treated my father's Saturday trail rides as a weekly spectator event, rushing from their kitchens and backyards to congregate on our front lawn as soon as they heard the clacking of hooves on pavement. My best friend, Holly Hamilton, lived up the street and arrived early on the day of my first ride. She donned my new straw cowboy hat and pranced higher than the horses while she stepped up fearlessly to stroke their necks and nuzzle their noses.

"Careful," Heber warned her in a drawl that materialized somewhere between the boots he never took off his feet and the hat pulled down so tight on his head he could no longer raise his eyebrows. Horse ownership had forthwith made him a nine-year-old authority on all things western. "They're both a bit skittish just now. One of em steps on you, it'll break every bone in yer foot."

Holly glared at him and went right on stroking Rangy, who stood motionlessly with his head hung low. Pug, however, with his ears back flat and his eyes wide, swung his head in one direction and his rear end in the other with every sound of slamming screen doors and tishing sprinklers.

"Darlene, put your damn feet in the stirrups," Dad said.

He always spoke like that—as if he'd given you the instruction twenty times already. Mom said his nouns felt naked to him without an adjective attached, and that we shouldn't pay it much attention. He was the only one who ever called me by my given name. I was named after my mother, Ruth Darlene, at my father's insistence, even though my mother hated the name. Everyone else called me Dickie, a nickname my mother gave me shortly after I was born. As far as nicknames go, I think she might have thought on that a bit longer. I guess she had her reasons, but she never shared them with me. Every time she called me Dickie, my father took it as a personal insult and maybe it was.

I stuck my right foot through the stirrup until it encircled my ankle and Dad pulled it back out. "Not like that—your feet are supposed to rest in the damn stirrups, not hang in them. How do those feel?" I shrugged, having no idea how they were supposed to feel.

"Where the hell is your hat?" he asked at the same time he snatched it off Holly's head. When I put it on, the pink toilet paper that had been stuffed inside to make it fit snuggly enough to cause a headache straggled down the left side of my face just in front of my ear, but I wasn't giving up my two-handed grip on the saddle horn long enough to fix it.

"Put your feet into the stirrups all the way up to the heel of your boot," Heber instructed, "but not any further. If this horse bucks you off, you don't want to be hung up and dragged with your head knocking along the road."

"Those need to be shortened," Dad said. He grasped my right ankle and pulled my foot out of the stirrup and Heber yanked on my left ankle at precisely the same moment the neighbors pulled into their driveway, beeping their horn at the spectacle and grinning like idiots, causing Pug to fly around, break from the crowd, and start down the street at a fast trot, reins swinging in front of him. As Pug turned, I toppled off the left side over my arms, my hands still clasped onto the saddle horn, as easily as if I were doing a somersault on the lawn. The upside-down world moved like a slow comedy as my head dangled toward the road. My father's belt buckle—a tiny gold calf roper dismounting from a horse—slid past my eyes like pictures in a zoetrope. As Mom and Alma ran toward me, their movement sent Pug spinning in the opposite direction. The cowboy hat stuck on my head and with each turn I caught a glimpse of pink toilet paper. As Pug trotted past the pudgy knees—two smushed little faces—of LaRee, the next-door neighbor, my grip gave way.

I opened my eyes to find Holly sitting cross-legged and wearing my cowboy hat—elbows propped on knees, chin propped on hands—looking as if she were waiting for me to take my turn at checkers.

"Where am I?"

"Well, your head's in the gutter, your feet're in the road."

"How long have I been here?"

"Well, about a minute."

"What's going on?"

"Well, your mom and dad are fighting, your aunt Alma is trying to referee, and everybody else is choosing up sides."

"What about?"

"Well, your mom wants to call an ambulance."

I tipped my chin upward to see Mom's slim, tan calves and slender ankles sticking out from a pair of lime-green pedal pushers, shifting around Dad's shiny cowboy boots, one pant leg of his Levi's pulled tight around his ankle, the other bunched up three inches from the top of his boot.

"She's awake," Heber yelled.

I sat up next to Holly, pushed my butt against the curb, and crossed my legs. Mom sat on the other side running her hands over my head and repeating, "That hurt? That hurt?" as she pressed on various points. I answered yes to all of them, although the hat served a purpose after all—nothing really hurt all that much.

I milked that episode for all it was worth over the following weeks, feigning headaches and fainting spells whenever my father talked about rescheduling our trail ride, thinking if I could hold out long enough I could turn my boots in for a pair of flip-flops. I was wrong. By the time my fake headaches had become fake brain hemorrhages, Dad had moved us to Clayton, Utah, a cluster of ranches at the southern end of Ganoa County, twenty miles beyond the reach of Ganoa's paved streets and sidewalks. I gave up hope and settled into despair.

"WHEN'S HEBER'S FUNERAL?" Michael asks, moving around me to wipe down the counter and clean the sink before carefully slipping the knife from my hands. "You've pretty much chopped everything in the house. What is it you're making?"

I give up the knife and turn my attention to the refrigerator. "No body, no funeral," I tell him. "Haven't decided yet. Maybe some sort of stew."

Out of the corner of my eye I see his eyebrows arch as he inspects the cutting board. Carrots, onions, potatoes, leeks, cabbage— anything I could find—all diced beyond recognition. I hate that, the way he raises his eyebrows to imply I've lost my mind.

"Is that apple peel I see in there?" he asks.

"Could be."

"What is it you're searching for?" He pulls me away from the open refrigerator and closes the door.

"Good piece of meat would be nice."

"Well, you know you won't find one in there. You must have a funeral. People expect it."

"What the hell is your problem with meat?"

"It's bloody. And messy. And we agreed to never have this conversation again."

"Death in the family; all bets off. A hater of messy foods. You and George have a lot in common. Except the funeral business. George doesn't care what people expect. He likes burials. Nothing to bury; no funeral."

"Your father and I have absolutely nothing in common. I wish you'd stop pointing out how much we have in common."

"If it's there, I have to point it out."

"Why can't your father have a memorial service without an interment?"

"Because George Sinfield is a better husband and father to the dead than he is to the living and he knows it. He never once gave Mom flowers when she was alive, but every time I go to her grave there's a bunch of purple iris there. And they'd be on Heber's grave, too, if he had one. There's something about a deep, dark hole that allows George to love in a way he can't otherwise do. I don't think the army should deprive him of that, do you?"

"Well, it doesn't much matter what I think. If there's no body, there's no body. What's George going to do about it?"

"Probably dig in and spend the rest of his life sulking and generally being a pain in the ass. In other words, nothing different than he's been doing the last forty years."

Michael pulls me toward him and tries to wrap his arms around me. I push him away.

"You're upset about your brother's death."

"Brilliant deduction, Professor."

"It's okay to cry, you know."

"I don't feel like crying. I feel like chopping." I take up the knife again but find no satisfaction in the mush of vegetables forming before me. "And I feel like eating a rare slab of beef swimming in its own blood. I'm going home."

"Dickie . . ." He grabs my arm as I start out the back door. "I'll be here."

I gently pull away from him. "I know you will, Michael."

I stride across Michael's brick patio in the growing darkness knowing that nothing will be out of place to trip me up, then dip through a
hole in the wood fence into my own backyard. Michael never comes
through the hole. He would prefer to have it repaired but hasn't because early on he recognized it as a relatively simple way to show his
love for me. I know this because Michael strategically placed a large
steel sculpture between the hole and his kitchen window, so that when
he stands at the sink doing dishes his eyes fall upon something that
looks like a womb holding a man's head instead of a fence in disrepair.
To get to my house he goes out his front door and down his winding
slate sidewalk lined with scarlet Oriental poppies growing up through
bird's-foot ivy. He then takes a sharp right turn on the cement strip in
front of our houses and comes up my crumbling uneven walk—with
eyebrows fully raised every single time—to my front door.

It was the gaping hole that instigated my first encounter with
Michael twelve years ago. A thriving zucchini plant had flattened
three rotting slats in the fence of my Salt Lake City home and found
untangled freedom on his orderly patio. Seemingly within minutes of
my zucchini's trespass, I found on my front porch a gray-haired gentleman wearing perfectly pressed khaki pants and a blue button-down
cotton shirt with a canary-yellow sweater tied jauntily over his shoulders. My first thought was that an Eddie Bauer catalog left in the
mailbox had sprung to life. He held an eleven-inch zucchini as if offering a gift.

"I believe this belongs to you," he said.

"Keep it. I have plenty."

"Yes, well, I appreciate the offer, but the overspill just won't do."
He peered past me into the living room with obvious concern that
the books and newspapers scattered about the floor might any minute
push through the east wall of my house and spill into his.

"The overspill just won't do? Did I hear you right?" I burst out
laughing. His face tightened.

"Yes, and you are not the first to find my ways a laughing matter."

He turned to leave, still cradling the zucchini with both hands as if it deserved his tender care for as long as it remained in his possession.

"Wait. I'm sorry. I'm a jerk, and you're not the first to notice that about me." He stopped and turned back. I stuck out my hand. "I'm Dickie, ashamed owner of an irreverent garden."

"I'm Dr. Wilson—Michael—your new neighbor."

"Well, Dr. Wilson Michael, come in. I'll put on a pot of tea and we'll talk zucchinis and overspill." He stood frozen to the spot. "No, no!" I said. "I'm not mocking. Really. This shit just comes out of me. It's unstoppable. Like my zucchinis! Like my newspapers!"

I swept my arm across the living room to prove my point. His narrow lips formed a barely perceptible smile and he stepped inside the door nudging a book aside with his foot.

"If you think there's room."

"Ah, there you go. A right jab. Now we're on firm ground."

Since then Michael and I have called ourselves a couple, although the classification baffles many and often elicits throat clearings among our friends and coworkers. Michael pretends not to notice and I pretend not to care. We never discuss it. In fact, we discuss very little of an intimate nature. We instead have great, raucous debates about politics, history, philosophy, and religion. We do this during long walks around our neighborhood and into the foothills of the Wasatch Mountains or in Michael's kitchen as we cook elaborate meals for ourselves. If a discussion is infused with enough passion, pot, and wine, it might sometimes lead to sex. Most often it does not.

The fact that we both love to argue makes it easy for us to justify our relationship, but that's not the reason we've been together twelve years. What Michael and I recognized in each other immediately—as we cleared a space at my kitchen table and shared a pot of tea—was a safe place to rest, a place free of inquisition, accusation, and explanation. That's where our loyalty to each other lies and we both trust it exhaustively.

• • •

BEFORE DAD DECIDED to be a cowboy, us Sinfields were just a normal Ganoa family. Of course I didn't find out for many years that normal in Ganoa, Utah, probably wasn't so normal in any other part of the country. From the air, one would think the Great Salt Lake and the Oquirrh Mountains separated Ganoa County's five thousand residents from Salt Lake City. Actually the United States military, not the geography, deserves credit for Ganoa's isolation. Three army bases form a large triangle around Ganoa anchored by the colossal Dugway Proving Grounds, a full one million lonely square acres near Clayton in the far west desert of the county. The army marked its territory with ten-foot chain-link fences topped with a few rows of concertina wire, so if you were new to the county, it might not always be clear whether you were on the inside or the outside.

Like most of its residents, Ganoa was born into farming, grew up in mining, milling, and smelting, then handed itself over to God and country. During World War II, the federal government discovered the west desert to be an ideal place to set off bombs, test nerve gas, and generally play around with chemical concoctions designed to annihilate large subsections of the human species. After brewing and testing, the potions were buried in bunkerlike igloos that rose up from the desert floor like giant prairie-dog mounds. From the early forties onward, chests in the county were puffed out so far folks could barely shake hands. After all, not everybody got chosen to be the keepers of democracy and freedom. It might have been a misdemeanor in Ganoa County not to own an American flag, and quite possibly a felony not to have one prominently displayed on appropriate days. The American dream thrived in Ganoa, as exhibited by kids on shiny new bicycles, Easter egg hunts, county fairs, and Fourth of July parades—Mayberry, military style.

The three army bases in Ganoa County were about 95 percent civilian-staffed, providing a job and two weeks of paid vacation to pretty much anyone who could make it into Building 595 at Ganoa Army Base under their own initiative and fill out a legible application. That promise alone kept Stony Westman, Ganoa High School's only college counselor, free enough to double as the football coach. As a senior, I walked into his office one day and requested help filling out a college application form, sending him and three linemen into knee-slapping hysterics.

Although Ganoa sat only sixty miles from Salt Lake City, Ganoans prided themselves on being self-contained. Doctors' appointments provided the only legitimate occasion for a trip to Salt Lake City because Ganoa County Clinic had a reputation for dredging the bottom of the reservoir of graduating medical students, and stories of livers being mistaken for kidneys abounded. A person could justifiably stop at Auerbach's Department Store on the way out of Salt Lake City providing your doctor's location forced you to drive right by there anyway, and many a doctor was chosen by this criterion.

Shoppng at Ganoa Merc, where you could find everything from Buster Browns to toasters, increasingly distressed Annie, who, at the beginning of each school year, begged for a trip to Auerbach's to prevent her from showing up on the first day of school wearing the exact same dress five other girls wore. My sister walked an absolutely perfect line at school between fitting in and setting trends, and she tended to it right down to the ideal fold at the top of her socks. Mom said she stood out simply by her talent for fitting in. The possibility of showing up in the same dress as some girl in a lower social stratum mortified Annie, although even in the first grade she was adept at accessorizing in a way that made the other girls look silly in their identical dresses. I, on the other hand, escaped Annie's predicament on two levels: one, from my first day of kindergarten I had been in the lowest possible social stratum available; and two, I always went to school in one of Annie's old dresses. Fashion wasn't something I was ever going to be noticed for anyway, so I didn't give it much of my worrying time. I had plenty of other things to keep me stirred up.

Like every small Utah town, Ganoa was mapped out according to Mormon wards, and life there could be summed up in three words: church, government, and family. Pretty much every household except ours held at least one federal government employee and possibly a member of the Mormon bishopric—a trio of volunteer laymen tapped to run each ward. Compared to other small Utah towns, though, Ganoa prided itself on "diversity," meaning we tolerated the Catholics and Greek Orthodox left over from Ganoa's early mining days.

Clayton, on the other hand, did not. It was settled by Mormons in the mid-1800s and, like most of rural Utah, fiercely protected its heritage. You could go to church or not, drink coffee or stick to milk, no one really much cared. But unless you came from good Mormon pioneer stock, chances are you wouldn't find Clayton a hospitable place to live although the folks there didn't mind Gentiles stopping in for short visits. Fortunately for us, both Ruth and George could pull genealogy charts with maternal and paternal lines that charted their Mormonness back five generations to the days of Joseph Smith. So even though Dad was a bona fide jack-Mormon—the beer-drinking, swearing Mormons who didn't like handing 10 percent of their hard-earned cash over to the church but still hoped to reap the benefits of eternal salvation by sending their children to Sunday service—the fine people of Clayton knew he came by it honestly. In fact, a good portion of the two hundred or so people who called Clayton home weren't entirely opposed to a cold beer on a hot summer day themselves if no one was looking, which kept the jack-Mormons' favorite joke circulating: Why do you always take two Mormons fishing with you? Because if you only take one he'll drink all your beer.

There were two distinct kinds of Mormon women in Ganoa County—those who dropped babies like chickens laying eggs and didn't see any reason to fix up in between, and those who used the Relief Society, the women's branch of the church, to exchange the fashion magazines around which they patterned their clothing, hair, and living rooms. Mom set out to be a Mormon wife and mother of the stylish set. Since us kids got an equal mix of Mormon and jack-Mormon ideology, we were sent to church but otherwise left to our own devices when it came to religious philosophy. Heber drifted decidedly toward jack-Mormonism because he liked to swear, Annie leaned toward the chic devout, and I remained confused.

ONCE ON MY SIDE of the fence, which has since done a relatively admirable job of keeping my zucchinis out of Michael's unforgiving yard, I sit cross-legged on a rock and survey my garden, reaching down to snap the stems of asparagus spears poking up amid the arugula and red lettuce. The rock that holds me is a flat piece of granitic from the west desert, which—according to Heber when he delivered it one day with a load of cedar firewood—is some mix of granite and quartz.

"How do you know that?" I had asked him. He said it was only right that a person know what kind of rocks he's been in the company of for more than fifty years. I told him if he was so smart about the rocks, he might want to educate himself about those junipers he kept calling cedar trees. He just grinned and said that would make him sound like "one a you damn city slickers" and might get him kicked off the Clayton City Council.

"Clayton has a city council? It's not even a town."

"Well, that's fine cause we're not exactly elected anyway. Me and Stump are the only two members and we have a hard time reaching a majority decision on any given issue, so not much new legislation gets passed."

As always it strikes—like a deflating puncture wound—before I have time to deflect it. No matter how often I hear his name, I'm ill-prepared.

"And how is Stumpy?"

"Fine, I suppose. Same as last time you asked."

"Happy?"

"Hell, I don't know, Dickie. Me and Stumpy haul hay and work cattle. We don't cuddle up and share feelings. Ask him yourself."

"Yeah, maybe I will."

"Sure you will. For two people who couldn't be separated with a crowbar for so many years, you don't have much to say to each other now."

"God, Heber, we were kids. People change, you know."

"Stumpy hasn't changed all that much far as I can see."

"Maybe that's the problem."

"Well, whatever the problem is, it ain't mine. I gotta be going."

"Thanks for the rock."

That's all I could think to say. Heber nodded and slammed the door of his pickup truck. Up until Mom's death a year or so prior to this visit, all of the communication between Heber and me had gone through a translator. It wasn't that we were mad at each other; we simply didn't speak the same language anymore. Heber was rural; I was city. Heber didn't particularly want to step into my world and I didn't dare take a step back into his. Every once in a while Heber would surprise me with a seemingly small gesture—like the rock—but I never knew how to acknowledge the magnitude of the gift. So we held our ground. And that's where we were firmly planted on the day he died.

FROM DOWNTOWN SALT LAKE CITY, the land begins a gradual climb northeast into the foothills of the Wasatch Mountains. I live in the toenails of the foothills in an area known as "the avenues," made up of closely spaced houses built in the 1850s before driveways were necessary. It's the only old Salt Lake City neighborhood to escape the Mormon-grid addressing system, which allows any stranger to find any address without a map given they start from the center of the grid: Temple Square.

For the first full year after he moved here from Chicago to fill the Ludwig Wittgenstein endowed chair in the philosophy department at the University of Utah, Michael groused about the Mormon grid. He claims that's why he bought a house in the avenues—to be off the grid. But I've always found it amusingly appropriate to force everyone to begin from Temple Square, the precise place the city itself began. If that makes you uncomfortable, it's a sure bet the infusion of church and state will drive you mad; you might as well pack your bags and go.

Having spent all my life in the company of Mormons and having been officially baptized one in my childhood (although the baptism never took), I'm oblivious to both the quirkiness and the ordinariness of Mormons, so I didn't give much thought to being on or off the grid. As it turns out, I moved to the avenues for the same reason the neighborhood managed to stay off the grid in the first place: the slope of the land. It took me a lot of years to admit it, but I moved there because it put me far enough above the city to get a clear view of the Oquirrh Mountains, the range that cleanly splits Salt Lake City from Ganoa County, the range that keeps the past from spilling into the present.

THEY SAY WHEN nerve gas is inhaled, a dose equal to the size of Washington's eye on a quarter can cause hyperexcretion of fluids from the eyes, nose, and mouth along with involuntary urination, muscle spasms, convulsions, and eventually death. That's what they say. I've repeated this myself; in fact, I've put it in print, although I don't really know the truth of it. I figure Heber inhaled a lot more than a speck the size of Washington's eye on a quarter—more like 140 gallons—though those who know for sure aren't talking. They never do.

I never really knew my brother. We went our separate ways as quickly as we could. I ran to a place where the land—the single source to which I attributed all the pain of adolescence—was blanketed with buildings, pavement, and lawns. Heber went deeper into the desert. Even if I were willing to admit Heber's choice made more sense than mine, we were still separated by more than the thirty-mile stretch of the Oquirrh Mountain range that cleanly splits us apart—me on the east side, Heber on the west—and the eighty-eight miles of road between Salt Lake and Clayton. We were divided by just about everything either of us cared about—the food we ate, the music we listened to, the politicians we voted for, the clothing we wore, the lovers we took, and, most notably, the jobs we held. Heber didn't care much for my job with the "liberal press," although how he could construe *The Beehive Banner*, a Mormon Church–owned daily newspaper, as "liberal" I just can't figure. And I plainly thought he'd lost his ever-loving mind taking a job at the Deseret Demilitarization Facility, a benign name for a bomb burner, an incinerator designed to send twenty-five or so million pounds of mustard gas and nerve agent up in smoke. Sure it had been more than thirty years since we had witnessed with our own eyes exactly what nerve gas can do to a living, breathing thing, but that's not something a person can easily set aside. But Heber said he was tired of living with "that shit" and he'd just as soon see it sent skyward as have it underfoot. He meant that literally. Since the 1940s, the feds had been burying cartridges, ton containers, projectiles, rockets, and bombs filled with the stuff in the desert pretty close to where Stumpy and I used to hunt for arrowheads.

Heber claimed that working at the bomb burner fulfilled his civic duty. The proud ranchers of Clayton—Heber included—talked a lot about civic duty. It softened the one truth about Clayton no one ever talked about: it was the federal government, not the land, that kept bellies full over the years. I told Heber he was nothing more than a dupe for the feds. Well, I didn't exactly tell him that. I told Mom and she relayed it to Heber in some fashion. He told Mom that was nothing more than radical liberal propaganda I was spewing and that I didn't know what I was talking about, beings I'd been gone more than thirty years now—even though I'd only gone to the other side of the Oquirrhs. That's not exactly the way Mom passed it on to me, but it's probably a pretty good interpretation.

Most everybody in Ganoa County took Heber's side of this argument—figuring Heber was lucky to still have a job since most of them did not—the notable exception being my father, George Thomas Sinfield. Unlike most of his neighbors, George had the luxury—at least in his mind if not in reality—of never having been sandwiched in that uncomfortable, narrow space the army created in Ganoa County, the slot between misgivings for your children's health and gratitude for your children's health care. But that's not the reason George sided with me instead of Heber. The rudimentary truth is, six years after we moved to Clayton, the United States Army, in one forty-five-minute *routine maneuver*, managed to cleanly extract George's soul from his body, if not in its entirety, at least any part that would allow a person to bow his head in reverence at the grave of a nine-hundred-pound grizzly. A single event can change the curve of a life. That's what happened to George. And a life abruptly shot off course will cut through the curve of every other life it encounters, leaving a small slit that might never entirely close.

CHAPTER TWO

I enjoyed blissful ignorance of the place called Clayton until ten days after my eighth birthday in the late summer of '62, although in the few months since Grandpa Sinfield had died, my life had grown increasingly strange and I had grown increasingly anxious. For one thing, my mother and father often seemed to inhabit each other's body. My father, heretofore reliably short-tempered, loud, and quick with the time-tested child-discipline tool of humiliation, was suddenly tousling my hair, whistling, and inquiring after my well-being. All else being normal, I might have learned to adjust to this, but I took my cues from my mother, who watched him with wariness, informing my suspicion that his uncommonly good nature was nothing to celebrate. Aunt Alma also seemed thrown off her game by Dad's sudden blitheness, as she was used to jumping into Dad's wake with a good story to explain his actions and soothe the turmoil he often left behind. She watched both of my parents from what can only be described as a constant state of readiness. As Dad went about filling the rented corrals with "4-H projects for the kids," which turned out to be three Hereford calves, Mom became somber and sullen. Every once in a while she would put both hands on her hips and say, "George, what is it you think you're doing?" and he would simply smile broadly, put her face between his hands, and kiss her forehead like you would a child, as if that were all the answer she would ever need. Then, undaunted, he simply took one cowboy-booted footstep after another toward his deemed destiny.

I had hoped that what I referred to as my "tragic accident" and what everyone else called my "very short horseback ride" would excuse me from further involvement in Dad's plans, but each day I was summoned to the corrals to halter, groom, and lead my four-legged project in a circle. As the summer wore on, the cute, white-faced calves ate their way to fat, stubborn, curly-faced steers. There was nothing about messing with those steers that I liked, but nobody hated it worse than Annie. It took her away from jacks and away from her two closest friends, who spent their summer riding bikes and running through sprinklers without her. It ate at her like the snails ate Mom's wisteria vines, gnawing at every little bud that emerged.

Dad stood in the middle of the corral like a circus trainer, snapping instructions as we plodded around the outer edges with our steers. "Pull his head up. Keep him moving. Hold your head up. Don't look at the ground. Look like a champion and maybe you'll walk out of the show ring with that purple ribbon."

"Where does he come up with this stuff?" Annie would say when she thought we were out of Dad's earshot. "Is there some sort of parenting book on how to raise your kids into cowpokes?"

Heber would sneer at her; he took the possibility of a purple ribbon very seriously. As one steer would lumber to a lazy stop and pull back against the lead rope, Dad would stride over and twist its tail up around its rump to get it moving again. If that didn't work, he'd slap an old piece of barn slat down on the steer's ribs or hip. Protected by several inches of fat, they mostly ignored the swats, but Annie felt every one. She'd get wild-eyed and red-faced with every crack of a board against a steer.

One day Annie's steer took a swift kick at Dad and caught him in the shin just above his cowboy boot. That pleased Annie until she realized the steer had succeeded in unearthing Dad's old temper. He grabbed the lead rope out of her hand and jerked with all his strength over and over until two red splotches started to spread across the steer's white hair—one where the chain looped under its chin and pinched its jowl and one on the top of its nose where the rope halter dug in.

"I'll teach you to kick me, you son of a bitch!" Dad repeated with every jerk.

When the blood started dripping down the steer's nose and beading in the dirt, Annie started screaming—one long wail.

"Quit your goddamned screaming," Dad said to Annie. He handed the lead rope back to her. "And you quit your goddamned blubbering," he said to me.

Crying had become so second nature to me, I hadn't even realized I was doing it. Annie led her steer to the water trough, pulled what my mother called her "babushka" off her head, dipped it, and slowly dribbled the cool water over the steer's bloody face. Then she reached under the hanging folds of skin at its neck and unhooked the halter. The steer stood still with eyes almost shut, as she dipped the scarf again and again, squeezing water over its nose and wiping its bloody jowl. Then she gently pushed its head away from her, and it plodded under the shed and lay down in the shade.

My steer followed Annie's, oblivious that it was still haltered and attached to me. It put its nose and knees to the ground, dropped its hefty body, and started chewing its cud and flapping its ears at flies. When my yanking on the lead rope went unnoticed, I took four good wraps—squeezing my scrawny hand into the shape of a funnel—and tugged with everything I had. The steer turned toward the fifty-two-pound pest in front of him, shook his fat head a couple of times, cleaned out each nostril with two swift slurps of a thick tongue, and blinked the flies from his eyes. I looked for my father or Heber to help.

Dad approached from the steer's blind side and swatted it on the rump with his leather gloves. As the steer began to lumber to its feet, my father—with a hint of mischief I once wouldn't have thought possible—threw a leg over the steer's back, fancying himself some sort of bull rider. The steer shot up like a sprinter.

Dad landed flat on his back in clean straw, only his elbow dropped into a fresh pile of cow manure, just as my feet left the ground. The steer headed for the only opening in the corral—four fence poles that had been dropped to the ground—leading to a pasture. The wraps I had taken on my hand held tight. The steer jumped the poles, and I bounced over them like an ocean wave crashing over rocks. My ears registered the chug of irrigation sprinklers and Dad's voice hollering at Heber to head off the steer. My eyes registered only a swath of green and an occasional hoof startlingly close to my face. Every time Heber tried to head the steer into a corner, the steer abruptly changed direction, often stepping over me to do so. When the steer sideswiped me on a sprinkler head that stuck about twelve inches out of the ground, my hand popped loose. As I lay in the warm sun, the scent of wet alfalfa in my nostrils, water spraying in all directions from the sprinkler tucked tight against my bruised and scraped belly—that brief moment before Heber and Dad reached me—I was pretty sure I would not make it out of childhood alive.

I had bumps and bruises, huge scrapes, and even a few cuts to show for this episode, henceforth called "Dickie's Dragging." I used them as evidence that my father had gone mad, showing anyone who cared to see it the purplish mass running from just above my right knee to my hip, the raised welt across my stomach, and the skin scraped raw off my right shoulder.

The impact of the episode diminished with the evidence, however, and two weeks later my steer and I attended the Ganoa County Livestock Show, where "Dickie's Dragging" became entertainment for small groups of men leaning against fence posts and women fanning themselves on the second row of makeshift bleachers. I became the "brave little girl," a moniker I despised, and the brave little girl's father became the hero of the story, asked to tell it again and again, which he did with pride. I would have preferred to be known as the "girl whose father nearly killed her."

As I led my steer into the show ring, I spotted my mother on the end of the fifth and last row of bleachers, segregated from the farmers' and ranchers' wives by Aqua Net hairspray, Maybelline lipstick, and several rows of seats. Her brows were pulled tight like the last stitch in a knitted scarf, as if knotting them would keep her life from unraveling. Aunt Alma sat one row down and toward the middle of the bleachers as if she might somehow close the gap between my mother and the others. A man wearing a bolo tie and wielding a clipboard instructed us to lead our freshly washed and combed steers around the circumference of the ring, their ratted and hairsprayed tails swinging like feather dusters, their shaved, pink faces glistening in the sun.

"Square him up," one father called from the side.

"Make him pay attention," another hollered.

"Don't turn your back to the judge."

"Tuck your shirt in."

"Watch where you're steppin! For hell sakes, now you've got shit . . ."

As best we could—there were about fifteen of us—we did as instructed whenever the judge called "line em up," but for the most part, the steers decided when to walk and when to stand in this particular class of red-faced kids under ten. The judge attempted to line us up in a particular order that left me smack in the middle. The first kid in line, a squatty red-haired boy with a severe sunburn, received a purple rosette ribbon. I and everyone else to my left got blue ribbons and everyone to my right got red ribbons. Heber was third from the front and Annie was second from the other end.

"I'm sorry you only got a red, Annie," I said as we left the show ring.

"You think I care, you little dope? I'm just happy this spectacle is over. Maybe now we can get back to a normal life. Come on, Bo."

Annie had taken to calling her steer Bo, short for bovine, and that steer would have followed her whether she had a halter on him or not. I tied my steer in his assigned stall next to Heber's and tracked Annie down at the empty concrete slab by the hoses where kids and steers had crowded before the show to shampoo the steers with Lux Liquid, rub the shit stains from their faces, rat their tails, and backcomb their hides. She ran water up and down Bo's back as he stood squarely on all fours—a stance he refused in the show ring.

"What the sam hell you doing?"

"Better not let Dad hear you talking like that."

"Dad swears all the time; so does Heber, so do you."

"That doesn't mean you can, dopey."

"What the sam hell *are* you doing? You're supposed to wash him before the show, not after."

"He likes this when it's hot."

She shut off the water then rubbed her hand up and down Bo's shaven pink face and kissed him square between the eyes. "Come on, Bo. Let's go home."

"Heber says we ain't takin em back home."

"I swear, Dickie, you are starting to develop a cowboy drawl just like him. Stop talking to him."

"Well, we ain't."

"*Ain't* what?"

"Taking the steers back home with us. Heber says there's an auction tomorrow and we're gonna sell em and they're gonna be slaughtered."

Annie stood perfectly still, staring at me as if I'd lost my mind. Then she yanked the stock-show program out of her back pocket and tore it open to the back page. Tears filled her eyes as the crumbled program dropped to the ground. She yanked the slipknot in the lead rope and led Bo away.

"Annie, wait!"

She marched past the stall where Bo's water bucket stood and right out the gate with the people who were streaming toward their cars. The Ganoa County Stock Show was in Ullsville, a little town west of Ganoa, so if Annie and Bo were headed home, they had about eight miles to walk.

Dad and Heber were watching the sheep judging and I had since lost track of my mother and Alma, so I went back to the stall where my steer stood obliviously chewing and swatting. Heber had tied his blue ribbon onto his steer's halter, so it hung like a floppy third ear.

"You're just a big stupid oaf," I whispered while I tied my ribbon near the steer's ear. "Wear this proudly because tomorrow you're going to be steaks and hamburger. I'm sorry but that's just the way it is. I should be so lucky to get out of my miserable life so easily."

"You ain't supposed to tell em they're gonna be slaughtered," said a voice from the adjacent stall. "Setting that kinda fear into a steer could make the meat tough."

The redheaded kid smiled but did not look at me while he tied his purple ribbon on a nail in the wood above his steer's head. I had been around Heber long enough to know when someone was messing with me, so I initially ignored him. On the other hand, this kid won the purple ribbon and obviously knew what he was talking about. I looked back at my steer chewing his cud.

"He seems okay," I said, rubbing the steer's face just to be sure.

"He must not a heard you clearly," the kid said.

Before I could say anything more, a man in a plaid shirt and jeans brought a bucket of sloshing water into the stall and set it in front of the steer. "Let's get him settled down for the night, Stump, and get going. If we don't get that hay baled this afternoon, I'm afraid it'll get rained on." Then he looked up at me and tipped his cowboy hat. "Miss Sinfield, you did a fine job in the show ring today."

I had never seen the man before in my life, and I wasn't sure how I felt being known to a total stranger—I assumed he'd heard the story of Dickie's Dragging—but he seemed nice enough. In fact, in that brief moment when he spoke to me, his face and voice held more kindness than I realized possible from the male gender. "Thanks," I muttered.

Three hours later, after the sheep and hog judging, Dad went into a rage when he couldn't find Annie and her steer, but it was my mother's fretfulness that induced me to spill my guts. Dad told us to get in the goddamn truck.

"I'll go home with Aunt Alma," I said, looking around for her.

"She wasn't feeling well," Mom said. "She left about an hour ago. Get in the truck, Dickie. You, too, Heber."

We did as ordered, me in my usual spot—being the family member with the least amount of seniority—plastered next to Dad, straddling the gearshift. I didn't particularly like the furnace of my father's body in such close proximity—especially when he was intensely agitated—but I did like the tingle sent up my arm when I rested my hand on the gearshift. Sometimes, when the world seemed to be flowing just right, Dad would cover my hand with his to shift as he drove. Once in a while he'd say, "Go ahead and shift her into second, Dickie," and I knew where all the gears were and could put it where it needed to be. I also knew when to lean back flat against the seat and keep my hands folded in my lap. This was one of those times.

We drove every route between the stock show and the corrals at least twice, but never found Annie. Dad dropped us at the house then went to the corrals to wait for her.

"What's gonna happen to Annie?" I asked. "Should we call Aunt Alma?"

Mom shook her head. "Heber, stay here with your sister," she said, taking the keys to the car.

"Annie's gonna get her ass kicked," Heber said as soon as Mom left the house.

I glared at him then gathered all Mom's knitting needles out of the hall cupboard, went into the bathroom, and locked the door. As far as I know, my mother never knitted. The needles in our house were used exclusively to pick the lock on the bathroom door, usually by me whenever Annie took a bath. Next to playing jacks, Annie liked soaking in the tub more than just about anything. She'd do it in the middle of a hot summer day, first thing in the morning, before bed at night, just about anytime she could arrange it. Mom tried to limit Annie to one bath a day, but she'd usually sneak in another. I happily kept her secret because I loved to sit on the toilet lid and talk to Annie while she soaked. We didn't talk about anything in particular except how stupid we thought Heber was. And we talked about who we would marry. Annie thought she'd end up with the clean-cut and privileged Tod Stiles on *Route* 66 and I was destined for his poor, streetwise friend, Buz Murdock.

I also loved sitting there because Annie's looks captivated me, and I could stare at her endlessly once she had twirled her long, thick brown hair and pinned it up with six or seven bobby pins, closed her eyes, and leaned back against the edge of the tub like Cleopatra. She had Dad's nose—sort of round and big—and Mom's brown eyes with lashes so long they held little beads of water in their curl. Her limbs floated barely beneath the surface, more muscular than my own scrawny set, not a freckle on them anywhere, just a few perfectly placed moles on beige skin.

I was her opposite—thin, stringy blond hair, Mom's long, skinny nose, blue eyes with short stubby lashes. My skin burned and peeled all summer and turned translucent purplish white in the winter. But we both had the same sprinkling of light freckles across our noses.

The skin on my toes had turned white and wrinkly when someone jiggled the doorknob.

"Stay out, Heber!"

"It's me," Annie said. "Let me in."

I scrambled out of the tub to open the door, got back in shivering, and cranked the hot-water tap. She sat on the floor next to the tub. Her face was blotchy and her hands, holding Bo's empty halter, were scratched and bleeding.

"Did he yell at you?"

"Who?"

"Dad!"

"Haven't seen him. Where are they?"

"Down at the corrals. Didn't you see them there?"

"I haven't been down there."

"Where the hell is Bo?"

"If you could keep a secret, you little creep, I'd tell you. But you can't."

"I won't tell, I promise!"

"Dad or Heber will get it out of you; I'm not taking that chance."

"Please tell me!"

She was right—it wouldn't take more than a look from Dad or a twist of an arm from Heber before I'd tell everything I knew and then some.

"No, I'm not telling you." She stood on the toilet lid to look out the high bathroom window. "It's getting dark. You better get out of there and get dressed before Dad shows up and the fireworks start. You don't want to miss anything."

"Maybe he'll be over it when he gets back. Maybe he'll be the new Dad."

"Not this time, not when his buckaroo plans are getting messed with."

We both heard a car in the driveway followed closely by another. I felt sick to my stomach. I quickly dried myself and put on the same dirty jeans and stupid western shirt I had taken off. Annie looked into the mirror, washed her hands—which didn't look all that bad after the dried blood was gone—rinsed her face, ran her hands through her hair, and sat on the toilet lid picking at her nails.

"Annie?" We heard my mother's call first followed in short order by my father's bellowing voice.

"Annie! Get your ass out here! NOW!"

"Showtime," Annie whispered mostly to herself. She picked up the halter and opened the door. Mom had just enough time to give her a quick once-over with hands and eyes before Dad appeared. His sunburned arm shot past Mom and his fingers wrapped around Annie's wrist. He jerked her through the doorway and into the hall.

"That's a neat goddamn trick!" he said, pulling her arm up in front of her face, the halter dangling from her fingers. I was stunned at how violently her hand shook before I realized it was my father trembling, not Annie.

"Isn't it?" she said back to him, her face soft and expressionless as if she had just tumbled out of bed.

Dad looked momentarily stunned, his face red and tight. Annie looked around like everything was new and interesting, as if she wasn't quite sure why her own hand hung quivering in front of her face.

"George."

My mother's tentative voice fell so softly it seemed as if she were fading away. My father heard nothing. He ripped the halter from Annie's hands and starting swinging it at her, keeping one hand on her wrist. Annie woke up. She tried to wrest her hand free, but he held tight. They went round and round in a circle, her trying to get away from him, him coming after her. I had seen this same dance when Dad once took hold of Pug's reins near the bit and used the other end to whip him for not standing still as he was trying to pull a loose shoe off his foot.

In the instant Dad went after Annie, he had not taken the time to free the lead rope from the rest of the halter. He swung the entire thing at her. The chain that loops under the steer's chin jangled and clanked when it hit the wall, but most of the time it made a dull *chunk-thack* sound when it landed soundly on Annie's legs, back, chest, and stomach. Three words tore up through Dad's throat every time he swung the halter: *ignorant little bitch.*

When the chain hit Annie square in the mouth, a steady hiss rumbled up from deep in her body and spewed out of her mouth with saliva and blood.

I dropped to my haunches and buried my head between my knees.

I saw Heber's feet shuffle past me, but I didn't see Mom step in front of Annie, didn't see the chain clip her at the outer edge of her perfectly drawn left eyebrow.

When the silence became unbearable, I pulled my forehead off my knees. Annie leaned against the wall, a nearly inaudible hiss still coming through a thread of snot. Mom stood facing Dad, a single trickle of blood from eyebrow to chin, otherwise beautiful—cheeks flushed, each hair still lacquered to the next.

Dad gasped for air and stood as if his body might pop and crumble into a heap. When the halter slipped from his hand and rattled to the floor, I thought he might follow.

"Ruth, I—"

"Dickie, get me a washcloth," Mom said, never taking her eyes from Dad.

When I came back with a cloth, Mom lifted Annie's hair, wiped her nose, and dabbed her mouth. Then she kissed her on the forehead as if she were simply saying good night.

"Annie, go to your room. Dickie and Heber, you, too."

She picked the halter off the floor and wrapped it around thumb and elbow as if she were winding a skein of yarn, then she pushed Dad toward the kitchen. Annie sat down right where she stood against the wall, and Heber sat down next to her, close enough that their shoulders and legs touched. I moved to my usual place—a corner just past the kitchen door where I could see and hear everything. Dad sat heavily in a chair and Mom sat opposite him.

"Ruthie, I didn't mean . . . my God, your eye . . . you never should have—"

"Shut up, George."

Mom had not wiped the blood from her face; Dad kept his eyes cast down. Her voice was calm and steady and powerful—a voice I couldn't recognize.

"George, I've let you swear at my children, humiliate my children, and scare them half to death. I pray to God every night to forgive me for that. But you have never hit my children. And you will never lay a hand on one of them again."

"I'm sorry, Ruthie. But Annie—"

"Don't say another word, George. Not another damn word."

They sat in silence for several minutes before Mom spoke again.

"I don't want this life . . ."

He raised his eyes to her face, winced, and dropped them again.

". . . this TV western of yours."

Dad looked as if someone had a twisting grip on his intestines. The pain pulled his face down toward his chin, only his eyes rose up to meet hers. I felt as if the floor had started to tilt under my feet and I looked backed for Annie and Heber. They both sat silently against the wall, Annie's head resting against Heber's shoulder. I wanted my father back. Not the one who touched the top of my head when he passed me in the hall, not the one who caused my mother to move through the house in cautious silence. I wanted the predictable father. I wanted to hear profanity cut through the air. I wanted to see my mother stand behind him, roll her eyes, and smile at me while he growled and snarled. I wanted my simple world back—the one where the father roared and the mother soothed and I knew exactly how it all worked.

"Ruthie, you were raised on a farm, for God's sake," Dad said.

"A farm that killed my father, a farm I was damn glad to get off of."

"What are you telling me, Ruth? You want to live your whole life right here between the gutter in front of the house and the ditch bank in the back?"

"Yes, George, that's what I'm telling you. You're acting like a child who's watched too many episodes of *The Lone Ranger*. It's 1962 and you're an educated man. Start acting like it."

With that, Dad straightened in his chair, and his face fully released its pain. He leaned across the table toward my mother and placed both of his hands firmly on top of hers. When she tried to pull her hands away he pressed harder, pinning her to the table. He looked directly into her eyes and formed only his lips into a smile.

"I'm going to check on those steers down at the stockyard, make sure they have feed and water. I don't want them going into the sales ring tomorrow looking gaunt. Heber and Dickie should get a decent price for them."

I didn't see or hear him again until the next morning.

WHEN WE PILED into the pickup for the auction, Annie was still in bed and no one insisted otherwise. There had been no mention of Bo's whereabouts.

"Dickie, you need to keep that goddamn steer moving around the ring so buyers can get a good look at him," Dad said. "Don't let him pull back and stand—they need to see him on the move."

My stomach began to churn; Mom looked dreamily out the window. Seemed all was back to normal.

When my steer balked at the gate to the auction ring, Dad swatted it on the rump with a rolled-up program. It dashed through the gate dragging me with it, the crowd perked up hoping for a rerun of "Dickie's Dragging," and the auctioneer made a joke about "who's leading who" from his platform above one side of the ring. Two men in cowboy hats and snappy white shirts paced inside the ring and stared intently into the crowd, a rolled-up sheaf of papers in one hand.

"Yah!" one of them would yell in response to a nod from a bidder, simultaneously slapping the roll of papers into the palm of his free hand and sending my steer two feet sideways. Unlike Annie, I'd be happy to be rid of the fat thing. But when the bidding stopped and the auctioneer announced the buyer as Allen's Food Town, I felt a little queasy. I didn't care much about the steer's pending demise, but in that moment, I made the correlation between the neatly wrapped packages of ground beef in Allen's Food Town and the steer dragging me out of the ring.

• • •

MY MOTHER NEVER WENT to the grocery store without me; I made sure of that. By her side, life felt dangerous enough. Away from her, I felt like the single pin left standing at the end of the lane waiting for someone to throw a spare.

The grocery store also provided my only glimpse of the outside world. I was enthralled with products she never bought and our family never ate. Taco shells, twelve to a box, were my latest fascination, which I discovered just above the spaghetti sauce in a jar—the prior week's find.

"We don't eat tacos," Mom said when I tried to get her to buy them.

"Why not?"

"Your father doesn't like them."

"Why not?"

"They're messy. Your father won't eat anything messy."

True enough. My father was an eater of neat foods. He didn't mind using his fingers in certain cases but didn't like anything that might drip back onto his plate or onto him. When he ate a hamburger, he garnished it with only a dab of ketchup—no messy tomatoes, pickles, onions—nothing that would slide out of the bun under pressure. No excess sauces—never more ketchup than the bun could absorb. No mustard, no mayonnaise. My father did not eat chicken on the bone, ribs, sloppy joes, or anything with a barbecue sauce on it. Spaghetti and soup were out of the question. Our meals were fairly limited to anything that could be cleanly cut with a knife and carried to the mouth by fork without incident.

The week after the stock show, I caught a glimpse of myself in black and white on the wall just inside the door at Allen's Food Town, where Mr. Allen normally posted the five-rolls-for-a-dollar toilet-paper special. My picture, alongside four others, showed the side of my fat steer standing squarely on all fours. Behind the steer stood Mr. Allen flanked by Miss Ganoa County and her smiling attendants, incongruously dressed in formal gowns and tiaras. I stood stiffly, squinting into the sun, pigtails coming loose, the steer's fat nose in my left ear. The picture made me look little and stupid, like I was someone's 4-H project. The caption above the picture said, "Allen's Food Town supports local beef growers."

Local Beef Grower. My new title. Mom either didn't see the photo or chose to ignore it. I lingered in the meat aisle, studying the contents with new intensity, searching to find the resemblance between the loathsome creature that stole my summer and what I'd always known as raw hamburger. The meat looked neat and orderly—something the steer never was—tiny squiggling rows of red and white rivulets sculpted together. Blood accumulated around the edges and seeped into the creases of plastic wrap underneath the Styrofoam tray, trickling cold onto my palms. I pressed the package with the palm of my hand, making blood ooze out the sides, then stuck a finger into the center until I heard the plastic wrap pop and the meat sucked my finger up to the second knuckle.

In the frozen-foods aisle—separated from the meat by a full run of pallets holding cases of Pepsi in bottles—Mom loaded Swanson chicken pot pies, one of the few things she knew I would eat unconditionally, into her cart. I had the meat aisle to myself except for half-blind Mr. Carver from the post office, who occupied the butcher with a lengthy explanation of how he wanted his whole fryer chicken cut up, each part double-wrapped separately. I moved to the next package of ground beef, popped through the plastic wrap quickly, and sank my finger in as far as it would go, then on to the next, and the next, until every package on the top row had a perfectly neat hole in its middle. I restacked them and started on the second level. By the time I reached the pot roast, I was no longer aware of the exact location of my mother. I dug all my bitten-down nails as deeply into the red mound as possible and dragged them across the top, tearing plastic wrap and more. I pulled my hand up to sniff the blood under my ragged nails just as Mom gasped.

"Dickie! What . . . ?" I froze. She grabbed the pot roast and stuck it in the cart. "Why would you do such a thing? We're going to have to buy this now."

"I wouldn't be so hasty about buying that pot roast, ma'am." A low whispering drawl from a man wearing an army uniform. A full head taller than Mom, he stood so close she had to take a step back before she could smooth her hair without her elbows hitting his chest. I stared mesmerized. An army uniform wasn't a particularly strange sight in the grocery store, but it wasn't all that common either. The only army personnel stationed in Ganoa were the base commanders and their small staffs who watched over several thousand civilian employees. What had me stupefied, though, were shoulders the shape of shoe boxes, eyes the color of juniper berries, and hair the color of mine perfectly cubed around a big head.

"But I have to. Look what she's done!"

"I see that, ma'am. But unless you have a big freezer at home," said army man, pulling the pot roast out of our cart, placing it back with the others, and pointing to more than twenty punctured ground-beef packages, "I'd just put this back, take your little girl, and move away quickly and quietly."

Mom gazed at the circular holes in the ground-beef packages as if they were a phenomenon of nature she had yet to comprehend.

"What on earth . . . ?"

Army man nudged Mom forward with authority, using only two fingertips at the back of her waist, which seemed to bring more attention from Mr. Carver and the butcher than my antics did. But it also seemed to work. She allowed herself to be guided up the aisle, tripping over me because I had positioned myself between her and the cart so her arms would have to reach around me. My shinbones banged against the lower bar of the cart as we moved.

"Finding what you need, Mrs. Sinfield?" asked the butcher as we passed by.

"What?"

"Do you need any help?"

"No," Mom said. "Thank you."

"And how's our main beef supplier doing today?" he said, looking at me. I burned and dropped my head. He chuckled and went back to his conversation.

In this single-line fashion—the cart, me, Mom, and army man—we turned into the next aisle and came to a stop.

"Dickie, for heaven's sake, why did you do that?"

The sting of disappointment in my mother's voice tore at my insides. I had spent a good deal of my relatively short life thus far with my eyes cast down over my cheekbones because I never had answers for the questions adults asked. Never before in my life, though, had I wanted to offer up an answer as badly as I did at that moment. So I lifted my head and looked directly into Mom's eyes. I expected her to know the answer that I had no way of providing. We looked at each other, locked in our anticipation. My heartbeat thudded up inside my neck. I waited for a flood of love and compassion to flow from the woman who promised it by the act of giving birth to me. Instead I saw resignation. She turned to army man.

"I'm sorry for the trouble we've caused you."

"No trouble, ma'am." He stuck out his hand. "Lee Fulmer."

"Well, Mr., I mean, Sergeant . . ."

"It's captain, ma'am. But you can call me Lee."

"Well, Captain Fulmer, my apologies. I can't imagine . . ."

Her words faded as she shook her head in my direction.

"Maybe she just likes the way it feels."

"What?"

"Raw meat. Maybe your little girl just like the way it feels in her hands."

He bent neatly at the knees and brought his big cubed head directly in front of my face.

"Is that it, little girl? Do you just like the way it feels?"

I had no idea what he was talking about. He was the squarest man I'd ever seen. Every part of his head, face, neck, chest, and shoulders began and ended in a right angle. He smelled of Brylcreem and Lucky Strikes, and as far as I was concerned, he was closer to me than any human—except Mom—had a right to be unless we were crammed five into a pickup truck.

"Somehow I don't think that's it," Mom said.

"No? Why not?" he asked, returning to full height but not taking any steps back.

"Well, that's ridiculous. Isn't it?"

"Not necessarily. Touch is the most underutilized and underappreciated of all the senses, don't you think?" he asked as he lightly touched her elbow with two of his fingers.

"I guess I never thought much about it," Mom said, dropping her hand to the top of my head.

"Well, think about it. Do you make meat loaf?"

"Yes . . ."

"And do you mix in egg and bread crumbs with a utensil or with your hands?"

"With my hands, but not because I like the feel of raw meat. Because I can get it mixed better."

Captain Fulmer stepped in a little closer to Mom, although I wouldn't have thought it possible.

"Think about that first moment when you sink your hands into the meat and it slices through your fingers, the power in your hands, the numbing coldness at your fingertips. Tell me you don't linger there just a few minutes beyond the point when eggs and bread crumbs have been entirely absorbed by the meat."

At that moment, Mom did something I had never seen her do before—she threw her head back and laughed just like an actress in a movie. I remember hair falling softly around her face in slow motion, fluttering with the breaths of her laughter. But it couldn't have. Mom wore her hair cut short at her neck, ratted high above her head, and sprayed to hold in the strongest wind. Still, she was ravishing in that moment, beautiful creases forming around brown eyes, flashes of white

teeth seen through slits of fingers held in front of her mouth. That's
the moment I recognized my mother's sadness.

ANNIE HAD BEEN QUIET since the day of the auction, spending most of her time on the back porch playing jacks alone and disappearing on her bike for hours at a time. A few weeks later, Holly and
I packed a lunch and rode our bikes toward the corrals down Cole-
man Street, a dusty dirt road that ran straight west as if it might take
a person all the way to the Pacific Ocean without a turn. Rangy and
Pug stood in one corral swatting flies with their tails; the adjoining
corral that once held steers stood gloriously empty.

"What's down this road?" Holly asked.

"Don't know. Never been any farther than these corrals."

When I caught up to her again, she was leaning against a fence
chewing on a weed as if she'd been there all day. She nodded toward a
lone animal in the middle of a ramshackle grouping of corrals.

"Well, isn't that your sister's steer?"

Sure enough, Bo stood fat and happy in an otherwise empty corral, chewing his cud and slapping his enormous sides with a shit-
stained tail. Before I could speak, Annie clattered down the road on
a pink Schwinn, hay leaves flying from both rear baskets and a burlap
sack tied around the handlebars.

"What are you two doing here?" she asked. She threw the hay over
the fence and emptied the sack of grain into an old tin dish that sat on
the ground next to a water bucket. Bo lumbered over and started eating. "If you tell Dad, you little pest, I'll beat the crap out of you."

"Annie, whose corrals are these?"

"I have no idea. But I think they've been empty for a while. No
fresh signs of animals."

"How did you know about them?"

"I didn't. Turns out this road here comes out at the Highway 81
junction. I guess people stopped using it after the highway between

Ganoa and Ullsville was built. There's a big tree across the road about a mile from here. Seems no one saw any reason for moving it. I put Bo here until I could figure things out, and he's been here ever since. No one ever comes down here."

"He looks like he's going to explode. Are you going to keep feeding him forever?"

"That's the plan."

"Where do you get water?"

"I have to carry it from the ditch." She nodded across the road.

"What about when school starts?"

"I haven't figured that out yet."

"What about in the wintertime? Your bike can't make it down here in the snow!"

"Well"—Holly spoke for the first time since Annie arrived—"Pug can make it down here in the snow, and I can help you."

Annie put both hands on Holly's cheeks and kissed the top of her head.

"Brilliant plan."

Holly's brilliant plan never got implemented. A month before school started, after Dad had been complaining that someone was stealing hay and grain from him and he'd catch the son of a bitch sooner or later, he came home with an old chest freezer in the back of the pickup and had Vern, the next-door neighbor, help him haul it down the basement. They tinkered with it the entire day and finally got it running. When they plugged it in, a steady drone rose up from the basement and filled the kitchen with the sound of a dozen distant chain saws. The same day, Annie rode her bike down to Bo's corral and found it empty. Next thing I knew, the freezer was filled with all cuts of beef wrapped in fine white butcher paper. My father never said a word about it to Annie, and she showed nothing but solemnity.

The following Sunday Mom plopped two pounds of ground beef into a large bowl, added two raw eggs and a bunch of crushed saltines. She dropped her hands into the mixture and the red meat pushed up through large-knuckled fingers—the only part of my mother that wasn't petite. I pushed the front side of my body against her leg and hip and dropped one of my hands into the bowl. She massaged my hand into mixture like it was another ingredient, squishing the raw meat through my fingers entangled with hers.

At dinner, we sat in our usual places, but nothing else felt normal. Our innards vibrated to the buzz of the freezer, Mom and Dad barely acknowledged each other, and Heber ate with manners. Annie never touched a bite of the meat loaf that night or any night thereafter. We didn't know the name for it then, but that's the day Annie became a vegetarian.

EVER SINCE THE STOCK show it seemed like we had less of everything in our house—less yelling, swearing, laughing, humming, arguing, dancing, crying. Less television, music, and conversation. Less noise. Maybe even less food. We sat down to dinner in such polite silence each night, I felt compelled to drip gravy over the edge of my plate or drop a dab of butter onto the tablecloth just to get Dad swearing and get things back to normal, but he barely noticed. It felt as if a belt had been wrapped around the house and each day it got pulled tighter, constricting all movement within.

About three weeks before I was to begin the third grade, Mom stood quietly and watched Dad hammer a "For Sale by Owner" sign into our freshly mown front lawn. I found out years later that at that particular time our family was being held together by the Ganoa eleventh-ward bishop, Aunt Alma, and Mom's two sisters (living two hundred miles away from reality), who were all imploring her—with a barely veiled threat of eternal damnation—to stand by her man. My father, however, was fully aware of this and also fully certain my mother would not risk either her standing in the church or in her family, which is no doubt what compelled him in either an act of defiance or desperation—possibly a combination of both—to sell our

house in Ganoa and buy 150 acres of land in Clayton without my
mother's knowledge. She didn't say a word about the For Sale sign for
days, then at dinner one night she brought it up just as casually as
could be.

"Where are we going to live, George?"

"This is no place for us, Ruth. We've got to have some land."

"A man's gotta have some land," proclaimed Heber in a remarkably good John Wayne voice.

"Hush, Heber! Where are we going to live, George?"

"It's obvious Heber's feeling pent up as a captive bobcat and Annie
screams every time an insect crosses her path. Dickie's so afraid of her
own damn shadow she acts like Chicken Little every time you're out of
her sight. The kids need to get out of this neighborhood, Ruth."

"Where are we going to live, George?"

"They need to know that the west is not rectangular like a lawn
or square like a television screen. They need to make a connection
between chicken pot pies and chickens."

"Where are we going to live, George?"

"They need to stand under a pitch-black sky that isn't gutted by
streetlights and watch a thunderstorm roll over the mountains toward
them. Then they'd be able to find their way in the dark, to understand the way the sun moves and the way the wind blows. If we keep
them here where everything is so damn tidy, where we've covered up
every last inch of the earth, they'll never understand the difference
between real danger and irrational fear. We're snuffing the lives out of
them, Ruth."

I looked at Annie, trying to gauge whether what I felt at that moment was irrational fear or the real danger my father spoke of. She
was arranging her green beans according to length across her plate.

"Where are we going to live, George?"

"They're my kids, too, Ruth."

"Where are we going to live, George?"

"Small ranch out in Clayton."

"How could we afford such a thing on your salary?"

"We can't. You'll have to get a job and pitch in."

In the ensuing silence, Annie picked up a knife and sawed one end off her green beans to make them all the same size. Then she stabbed at them until she got all eleven beans on her fork at once, shoved them in her mouth, and left the table with both cheeks puffed out.

CHAPTER THREE

The light from my own kitchen pulls me out of my thoughts as the sun sinks behind the Oquirrhs. Through the window I see flashes of mixed bright colors moving in my kitchen—assorted scarves of varying lengths and materials—around a long translucent white neck that sits at the bottom of a shaved head covered by a quarter inch of spiky silver hair surrounding a perfectly plain face. All of that tops a wildly beaded torso and bangled limbs. I pull myself off the rock and make my way through the garden to the back door.

"God, don't you have wine or beer in this house?" Dot asks. She puts two coffee cups on the table and pours from the pot she'd just made. Based on the daily advice column Dot Barlow writes for *The Beehive Banner,* she should, in fact, be dowdy, the embodiment of civility and decency, but she doesn't come close.

"What are you doing here?"

"Sit," she instructs. "Charlie told me about Heber. I'm sorry, Dickie."

"Who's Charlie putting on the story?"

"Dunno. Probably Jack."

"That idiot?"

"What other idiot does he have? You would have been the person to cover that story. Charlie's worried about you. That's one reason I'm here."

"Tell him I'm fine. I'll be back in a couple of days."

"Then Michael called me."

"Jesus, the world must be coming to an end."

"That's what I thought. I told him I didn't know any Michael because, as you know, I find a great deal of joy in antagonizing him, but he was so damn worried about you he helped me out by identifying himself as 'Mikey' and he even refrained from calling me a militant dyke. That's when I knew he was serious."

"If you and Michael insist on calling each other names, I wish you'd find some that fit a little better."

"What's wrong with 'Mikey, the gay professor,' and 'Dot, the militant dyke'?"

"For starters, he's not gay and neither are you."

"You know you're only half right about that."

"Michael is not gay."

"The only person who believes that is Michael."

"I believe it."

"You're just playing along for the sake of convenience."

"He wouldn't call you a militant dyke if you'd stop calling him the gay professor."

"Lots of people call me a militant dyke. You've heard the guys at *The Banner*. Comes with the territory."

"What territory?"

"Shaved-head territory."

"I should join you on that one."

"Of course you should; all women should. It's absolute bullshit how much time and money women spend on their hair."

"At least they got the militant part right. How does Harry feel about that moniker?"

"He doesn't care."

"He really doesn't, does he?"

"Nope."

"How does he feel about the shaved head?"

"Never asked him, but I assume he doesn't care about that either."

"What makes you think so?"

"Harry loves me—bald or shaggy—what difference does it make?"

"Oh yeah, I forgot. You guys believe in that kind of love."

She walks behind my chair, leans down, puts both arms around my shoulders, and kisses the top of my head.

"What other kind of love is there, sweetie?" I don't answer. "So how are you holding up?"

"I'm fine. Go home to Harry."

"Why don't I drive out to Clayton with you?"

"What the hell for?"

"Because, Dickie, when a family member dies, families gather."

"Well, there's getting to be damn few of us left to gather."

"All the more reason."

"We'll gather soon enough. As they say in Clayton, we like to *set* with things awhile before making a move."

"What is it about you and Clayton?"

"What do you mean?"

"You treat it like one of those big quicksand pits in the old Tarzan movies."

"Do not."

"Yes, you do. Like if you get too close you'll get sucked in and Tarzan won't be around to pull you out."

"Well, there aren't many Tarzans left in the world today."

Dot leans in close and stares directly into my face. "I get a feeling it's just the opposite." I get up to make another pot of coffee. She follows me into the kitchen. "I get the feeling Tarzan's lurking in Clayton and that's why you never go there. You're afraid he's going to swing down on his rope and swoop you up."

"God, you should write for television."

"I would," she says, releasing me from her gaze, "if they still had couples like Tarzan and Jane."

"You're a hopeless romantic."

"Militant romantic. There's nothing hopeless about it."

"Hmm. Want some cake?" I ask, getting up to retrieve a German chocolate cake.

"Why is it you start talking about food every time we get close to the subject of love?" Dot asks. I ignore her question and set the cake down in front of her.

"That's a damn pretty cake," she says. "If Michael ever gets tired of hanging out with those puffed-up old philosophers at the U, he could open a bakery and do quite well. But you still haven't answered my question."

"What makes you think I didn't bake the cake?"

"They say people use food as a substitution for love. That they're really hungering for something else."

"Who is they?"

"Actually I said it in one of my recent advice columns."

"Then it must be true. Don't you get your advice from Dr. Phil?"

"Pretty much. I feel a kindred spirit with Dr. Phil. We both make a living by stating the obvious. But that's beside the point."

"What is the point exactly?"

"The point is, Dickie, I've known you for a lot of years now. And this is a subject that you refuse to talk about. Don't you believe in love?"

"Of course. Everybody believes in love." I look at her. She looks back at me as if she's waiting for me to continue. I shrug.

"Let's talk about love," she says.

"I thought you came over here to console me."

"That's what I'm doing. Do you want to tell me about Heber?"

"No."

"I didn't think so. But the death of someone close to you brings up all sorts of memories and sentiments. It's good to talk about that stuff. And what more appropriate subject could we start with than the most remarkable of all human emotions?"

"Have another slice of cake," I say, picking up the knife and slicing a large wedge.

"Tell me about your first big love," she says, "the one that took your legs out from under you, the one you thought you'd never recover from."

I begin to lift a bite of cake to my mouth but stop midway when Dot says, "Just say his name." The cake jiggles and drops off the fork onto the table next to the plate.

"Just say his name," she demands quietly.

"Stumpy Nelson," I whisper.

"Stumpy Nelson," she repeats softly. "Perfect. Sounds like the outlaw in a western soap opera. The good, bad outlaw. The one who's capable of killing, but only the bad guys. The brooding one who scares the men and attracts the women."

"I think he'd appreciate the characterization," I say.

"Where is this Stumpy Nelson character now?"

"Right where he's always been. In Clayton."

"Tarzan," she says, pointing a fork at me.

"You know, Dot, you remind me of my mother. She was a romantic like you—although more hopeless than militant."

"I take that as a compliment. I liked your mom. Dickie, why is it we never just hopped in the car and took a ride out to the west desert before?"

"What the hell for?"

"Just to look around. Just so you can show me where you grew up, where you drank your first beer, lost your virginity, and so forth. It would be fun."

"I very much doubt that."

ON A DRY AUGUST DAY in 1962 I followed closely behind my mother as she picked her way along a narrow, crumbled walk through a yard of hard-packed, bare earth without taking her eyes from the stretch of tacked-together materials in front of her. Dad had promised that her new home would be twice the size of our red brick house and he delivered. At its core stood a small white farmhouse that had dried to a shrunken dusty gray, its boards curling on the edges and splitting down the middle. It had been added onto in five different directions—all four points of the compass and upward—and in as many different building materials—wood plank, cinder block, tin sheeting, brown brick, and mud adobe—leaving the original farmhouse looking like a mouse balancing an elephant. At first glance it looked as if something less than one of those storms Dad envisioned rolling over the mountains would bring it to the ground, but upon closer inspection, one could see it had been soldered, nailed, wired, and cemented together in excess.

As we entered, a wooden screen door on rusty springs snapped my heels as if in warning, notifying me that my days of lazing about on green lawns and playing hopscotch on smooth cement were behind me. Mom wandered through the house holding her arms straight out in front of her as if the rooms were tipping, beseeching her eyes to adjust from the soft desert browns outside the door to a shocking array of primary colors covering the walls and floors inside. From the kitchen, she pushed on what we both thought to be a pantry door and exposed Annie on the toilet.

"Privacy! There are no locks on these doors! How is this going to work?"

"Calm down, Annie," Mom said as we both pushed our way in and closed the door behind us.

"Do you mind?" Annie insisted, but we were too involved in our inspection of the only bathroom to acknowledge her protests. In a long, narrow room, fixtures were lined up along one brilliant blue wall like a row of theater seats. Rust stains ran from the drippy faucets down the graying porcelain of both the bathtub and sink to form a ring around the drains.

To show her displeasure at our presence, Annie let the toilet lid drop with a clank, displaying a large daisy on the top, painted the same stark yellow as the kitchen cabinets, its long green stem winding down off the lid and around the bowl, ending where the water pipe stuck up through the wood slats of the floor. Mom smiled for the first time that day. A door opposite the one we'd entered led us to a small bedroom, walls painted pastel pink.

"If we have to live in this godforsaken place," Annie said, "I'll take this room."

Twisting her head in all directions as if she expected snakes to drop from the ceiling, Mom made her way to another door in the adjacent wall. She swung it open, took one step inside, gasped, then stepped all over me as she backed out, holding one hand over her mouth and pulling the door shut with the other. I put my hands on her hips and tried to push her forward.

"Mama, what are you doing?" (As soon as I found out we were moving to "a ranch," I had taken to calling my mother "mama.")

"Back on out of here, Dickie. We can't live here."

"Are we going back to our house in Ganoa?"

"No, it's already been sold. I don't know where we're going, but I have no intention of living here."

"Why, Mama, what's wrong with this house?"

"That's a plainly stupid question," Annie said, pushing past me and Mom into the room we had just backed out of. Then she let out a scream that continued until she was forced to inhale. Most people go their whole lives without really screaming, but to Annie it came as naturally as sleep.

"Must be a huge spider," I said as Mom grabbed Annie's shirt, yanked her back into the pink room, and slammed the door. Annie sucked in a breath then started again—one loud wail without interruption in pitch or tone. I pushed past them both, flung the door open, and froze. The sound—a buzzing as if the room were filled with ten old freezers—registered before the sight. Hundreds of flies disturbed by my sudden intrusion left the walls and windows and flew in a frenzied state around my head and through the open door. The walls of the empty room had been painted the color of a morning summer sky, which made the blood splatters all the more horrifying. A stench similar to that of an open infected wound stirred my gut in the stifling heat.

"Mama, what happened in here?"

"I don't know, Dickie, you'll have to ask your father," Mom said as Dad walked into the room.

"Ask me what?"

"What happened in this room?"

"Yeah, we'll have to clean this place out. Apparently the old guy who lived here used to slaughter pigs in this room. Smells like it, too, doesn't it?"

Dad opened the blood-smeared windows on two sides of the room then walked over the thickly blood-coated concrete floor—sticky in the summer heat, so his boots made a *schlip, schlip, schlip* sound as he walked—and flung another door open. Out the doorway, a narrow path cut through a stand of cedar trees, and a hot summer breeze pushed the clean smell of dirt into the room around us.

"That path leads to the corrals. Apparently whenever old Ira got short on bacon, he'd call Merv Nelson at the next ranch down the road and have him send his grandson, Stumpy, over to run a pig up the path and into this room. Ira would put a bullet in the head as soon as the first hoof crossed the threshold, then cut its throat and butcher it right here. Merv said he was a dead shot; never missed a one."

Dad smiled and laughed in a strange, easy way—the way I'd heard other men laugh—as if his belt had been loosened. He touched the side of my mother's face gently and rested his other hand on the top of my head.

"Don't worry, Ruthie. Heber and I will hose out this room, re-paint it, and put some tile down on the floor. The old shed out there is filled with about twenty cans of paint, old floor tiles, bricks, wood slats, and a bunch of other junk. Looks like old Ira was just getting started with the home-remodeling job."

He looked directly into Mom's eyes and his face fell into a placid smile when she looked back at him. I had never seen that face before. I had never seen my father's brows, eyes, and lips fall loosely around his cheek- and jawbones as they did now. He looked strange, like someone else's father, not mine. Like one of those fathers who thrust their kids in the air and swing them around with ease and a laugh when they arrive home from work in the evening. I didn't know any fathers like that, but I had seen them on TV. He brushed a nonexistent hair away from Mom's forehead and pushed it back behind her left ear. I waited for her to tell him what she'd just told me—that there was no way she would live in this place—but she never did.

After Dad and Heber cleaned and repainted, I slept in the pig room as mandated by Annie, who took the pink room. The pig room was preferred for its outdoor entrance, but in the end Annie swore it still smelled like "death and murder" and couldn't talk herself into sleeping there. That gave me an excuse to go through Annie's room every time I needed to get to any other part of the house unless someone occupied the bathroom, in which case Annie and I had to exit outside through my room and come back in either through the front door or through Heber's room to get to the kitchen.

Heber got the "mud" room, stuck onto the back of the house where the kitchen door once led outside, which suited him fine. His room had another door that led down a path to the first outhouse I'd ever laid eyes on—a three-holer with a window cut into the wood slats on the west so a person could gaze out toward the Onaqui Mountains and, I suppose, receive visitors at the same time. The outhouse seemed well used, the wood around each hole worn shiny and smooth so a person had no worries about slivers. On the north wall, a mounted magazine rack made from four scraps of wood held dog-eared copies of *Western Horseman.* Mom decided it would do us well to have a second bathroom, so she swept out the spiders and their webs, scrubbed the inside with ammonia and vinegar, and hung some cotton lace curtains in the screenless window to billow in the breeze (although they froze up solid in the winter and would smack against the wood in the wind). Then she convinced Heber that real cowboys use outhouses, and except to take a bath under orders, Heber seldom used the inside bathroom.

We fixed the attic room up for Aunt Alma whenever she wanted to stay, but she said she'd just as soon drive back into Ganoa and sleep in her own bed rather than climb the steep ladder that shot directly through the ceiling from the middle of the living room. Mom and Dad's bedroom, at the opposite end of the house from Annie's and mine, was twice the size of the room they shared in our brick house, cinderblock walls painted passion red. Mom, Alma, Annie, and I spent the next week painting every wall in the house white with the exception of Annie's room, which she insisted on keeping pink. We finished up and had all of our furniture moved in with time to spare before school started.

Annie took to her room, her books, and her diary. My father and Heber worked at a frenzied pace—out of the house before the sun came up and seldom back in before the sun set—to get the haying done before Dad was expected back in the classroom. When he and Heber came in for dinner around 9 P.M., sweaty and filthy, Heber looked like someone who'd been badly fooled. He had anticipated trailing cows by day and eating his dinner around a campfire each evening before stretching out on his bedroll under a ceiling of stars. As it was, he could barely get food into his mouth before he'd start nodding off at the table. My father, on the other hand, ate and laughed and joked with frightening manic energy, swatting my mother on the rear every time she got up from the table to retrieve something, never noticing her growing annoyance. But as the first day of school neared, Heber perked up and my father settled down.

I talked to Holly on the phone when I could, although two other families shared our phone line, then I trailed Mom around the house until she finally agreed to drive into Ganoa and collect Holly, who had just returned from her annual summer California vacation, for an overnight stay.

HOLLY TRIPPED OVER the records and coloring books I had carefully laid out on my bedroom floor in anticipation of her visit, tearing one of the coloring books in half with the bottom of her shoe as she twisted away from the window. Before we had moved to Clayton, I loved nothing more than to slip out of my house with my box of sixty-four-color Crayolas—built-in sharpener in back—and scurry up the street to Holly's house, where we could color undisturbed for hours. Holly colored like she did most everything—with intensity. My heart would drop a little when she'd reach for the best crayon in the box, the one that had not yet been used, because it would be only a few minutes before she broke it and passed it along to me. I once reached into the second tier of the Crayolas for a new crayon and Holly's hand slapped down around my wrist faster than an eagle swooping down on a snake. I went back to using the broken pieces and Holly took the crayon I was reaching for.

Holly lived alone with a mother who spent her entire life making up for the fact that Holly had no father and no siblings. Her house seemed like a wonderland to me. She had her own bedroom complete with ruffled canopy bed on which two black cats—Tom and Jerry—lounged. (My father considered people who let animals roam freely in their homes—even in their yards unless it was a barnyard—of inferior ilk.) Another bedroom, at one time intended to house a sibling for Holly, instead held an enormous custom-made Barbie dream house that went around all four walls, so when you stepped inside the door, you were smack in Barbie's living room, which, along with the other six rooms, was filled to capacity with tiny elegant furniture all crafted by an uncle in California. Two years into Barbie's life, the uncle was called upon to build a separate closet large enough to house Barbie's extensive wardrobe, as Mrs. Hamilton made sure Holly's Barbie had every outfit available for purchase then went about sewing what Mattel had not yet dreamed up. Whenever we played there, Mrs. Hamilton tiptoed on slippered feet into Barbie's kitchen to deliver a tray of peanut-butter-and-jelly sandwiches with the crusts neatly cut from all sides and disposed of. (I never had the courage to tell Mrs. Hamilton that the crusts were my favorite part; I sensed that information had the capacity to crush her.)

What lured me most strongly to Holly's house, however, was the single promise of a few noiseless hours. When we played there, even Holly set aside her usual boisterousness, seeming almost sedated inside her surroundings as if there were an unspoken expectation of reverence. A blessed, commotion-free sanctuary. That, more than anything, baffled me about Holly's insistence that we spend the majority of our time immersed in the bluster of my family. Unlike me, Holly held no fear of my father. The first time they met, they didn't say a word, just glared at each other like boxers entering the ring. I thought they might circle like that until Holly's mother called her home for dinner, but eventually Dad grunted and walked out of the room. Holly said, "Well," and that was the end of it. After that, they simply moved around each other without comment or strain, as if each had some sort of exclusive knowledge about the other.

Holly had an ample vocabulary and could string sentences together better than most teachers in our school, but she didn't waste words on anyone she didn't deem worthy of her attention. When she did speak, she began many of her sentences with "well." If she could stop right there, she did, having perfected her various tones to convey almost any emotion—exasperation, expectation, exclamation—with that one word. Holly never missed her father because she never knew him, but she understood his absence perfectly.

One day fat Mr. Oldroyd, the man in charge of Ganoa Municipal Swimming Pool, fed himself into Holly's hands like tape rolling into a cash register. On our walk to the swimming pool that day, we had stopped at Bevan's Drug, scraped a couple of wire-footed stools across the octagonal tile floor to the soda fountain, and spent every last penny we had—after setting aside twenty-five cents each to get into the pool—on sodas and penny candy, ignoring the sound advice to wait three hours after eating before swimming. We then stopped at the construction site of a new house to gather metal slugs before arriving at the pool.

After we swam, Holly pulled one of those slugs out of her pocket and fed it into the candy machine. When her Big Hunk didn't drop, she started banging on the machine. Mr. Oldroyd pulled his large body up off the small stool behind the counter, tugged at his ever-falling pants, and lumbered over saying he had just filled that machine and something must have gotten stuck. Then, without looking down, he pulled a key from the mass of metal that clanked at his side and swung the door of the machine to expose the full neat rows of Butterfingers, Snickers, Bit-O-Honeys, Baby Ruths, and Big Hunks. When he pulled out the coin tray, a single slug jingled at the bottom. He fished it out with one jumbo hand and opened his palm to Holly.

"There's your problem, little girl; this machine catches little thieves."

I wasn't sure if it was the "little girl" or the "little thieves" characterization that tightened Holly's jaw.

"Well, I'd like my Big Hunk, please," Holly said, calm as could be.

"When you produce a dime, little girl, I'll produce your candy bar," said Mr. Oldroyd, carefully enunciating each syllable.

Holly locked in on him. "Well, I put a dime in that candy machine, and now I'd like my Big Hunk, please."

With remarkable agility, Mr. Oldroyd bent forward, resting his huge belly on his thighs, a movement he had perfected to get himself into the faces of misbehaving boys and girls.

"Little girl, it's plain as the nose on my face you put a slug in that candy machine. Now you two get on out of here before I call your fathers."

Bingo. Mr. Oldroyd had given Holly her cue. As soon as the word *father* slipped from his lips, Holly's tears welled up, and with perfect timing, one slid down her cheek as she started into the story.

"Well, it would be nice if you could call my father, Mr. Oldroyd, but you can't. My father's dead."

She paused there for dramatic effect but not long enough for Mr. Oldroyd to respond.

"You see, when my mama was five months pregnant with me, my daddy went to work at the Ganoa smelter just like he'd done every day for most of his life. They say he was the hardest-working man out there."

Mr. Oldroyd straightened up and started to clear his throat, but in a tone that demanded full attention, Holly continued her story without hesitation.

"You might not know this, Mr. Oldroyd, but the smelter had an aerial tramway to transport ore from the mines to the smelter. That tramway was twenty thousand feet long, and each bucket on that tramway ran on a four-inch steel cable and could carry twelve hundred pounds of ore. The buckets were made of heavy steel plate, but some of them were badly rusted. They were spaced two hundred feet apart and traveled at the rate of six hundred feet per minute. When the buckets came into the Ganoa terminal loaded with ore, they would swing out over a receiving bin and the bottom of the bucket would swing open like a gate and empty out the ore."

With this spewing of staggering detail, Mr. Oldroyd—and anybody else who heard it—did as Holly expected: stood mute and dumb in her presence.

"My daddy worked one of the three way stations along that tramway. To get to work each day, he had to climb a seventy-five-foot iron stairway then ride one of the empty ore buckets out to his way station. His way station was the middle one, which was located on the very top of the mountain out there in the Oquirrhs. I don't know if you know this, Mr. Oldroyd, but the top of the mountain was eighteen hundred feet higher than the Ganoa terminal building.

"So one day, when my mama was home all alone and pregnant with me, Mr. Oldroyd, Daddy climbed into one of those rusty old buckets like he had done every day he'd ever worked at that smelter to ride out to his way station at the very top of the mountain. But on this particular day, just after the bucket left the Ganoa terminal seventy-five feet above the ground, *whoosh!* The bottom of the bucket he was riding in swung open and he fell to his death."

At this point, Holly blinked out another timely tear and wrapped up with, "So you see, Mr. Oldroyd, I wish you could call my father, but I'm afraid that's not possible," and we left with our hands full of Big Hunks and Butterfingers. I adored her. And I spent much of my free time trying to guess the precise move that would garner her adoration in return. I was pretty sure my new living arrangements would set me back so far I might never make up the difference, but I was wrong.

Holly pulled my straw cowboy hat off the tip of the dresser mirror and positioned it perfectly on her head, looking in the mirror and taking pains to tuck errant strands of hair behind her ears. She rolled the bottom of her jean shorts up twice to make a cuff about five inches above her knees and propped a foot on my bed to tighten the laces of her Keds.

"Well, let's go."

"Where?"

"Well, to see the ranch!"

"Oh."

Our new house sat a couple of miles directly west of Clayton's town center—defined by the Mormon ward house and a general store that also served as the official U.S. post office—on a dirt road at the foot of the Onaqui Mountains. The ranch spread behind the house— a small grouping of decaying corrals and sheds, a barn with a roof that threatened to come down on any person crazy enough to walk under it, a relatively stable calving shed with a tin roof, and a loading chute leaning so far to the south it went over with one good kick from Heber.

Holly perched herself easy as could be on top of the four-pole fence that enclosed the corrals, elbows planted on knees, breathing deeply and scanning the horizon. I sat next to her, both hands gripping the shaky fence. About a hundred acres of what looked like desert to me, but what Dad called pasture, fanned out from the corrals to the foot of the mountains. A small herd of Hereford cows and one old curly-faced bull dotted the land. Forty fenced acres of alfalfa signaled the end of our property and the beginning of Merv Nelson's ranch to the north. Holly silently scrutinized the scene through watery eyes. I was a little taken aback by her tears but deeply touched. I scooted along the pole so our arms touched.

"We'll still be best friends even though I live clear out here," I assured her.

"That doesn't concern me," she replied.

Heat rose through my cheeks.

"Then what's the matter?"

She shook her head.

"At least you don't have to live out here!"

"Dickie, sometimes you're so stupid."

She pushed herself off the fence, landing soundly on both feet, then ran back toward the house. I carefully climbed down the four poles and ran after her. Mom stood in front of the kitchen counter making bologna sandwiches.

"Holly, how do you like it out here?"

"Well, Mrs. Sinfield, I like it fine. Do you suppose we could wrap our sandwiches up and take them with us? I think we might just walk across the land toward those mountains and see what we find."

"I don't think you're going to find anything more than rabbit brush and cow pies, but sure, I'll pack you a lunch."

"Holly, that field has a bull in it! We can't go out there!"

"Well, Mrs. Sinfield?"

"Check with your dad, Dickie. I think it will be okay."

Holly took the sack lunches and strode toward Dad and Heber, who were unloading hay off a flatbed wagon hitched up to a John Deere tractor.

"Stay out of the way, Dickie," Dad said, eyeing Holly.

"This ain't no place for you little girls to be playin," Heber drawled. "Git on now."

"Heber, for Christ's sake, quit speaking like you're on a movie set," Dad said.

Holly pulled a clean piece of alfalfa out of a bale and started chewing on it. I followed her lead, surprised by the fresh flavor, sweet as peas straight from the pod I'd eaten one summer when Mom took us to visit her sister in Idaho.

"Well, Mr. Sinfield, do you suppose that bull would bother us any if we were to walk out across those fields toward those mountains."

I'd never before heard Holly directly address my father, and by the look on his face, it was a first for him also. He straightened up, pulled his work gloves off, and slapped them together, sending hay leaves into the air.

"No, I don't suppose he'd give you any trouble. Just keep an eye on him."

I followed Holly as she dipped gracefully through two tightly pulled strands of barbed wire and we wound around stubbly, close-to-the-ground sticker bushes that grabbed at our ankles as we stepped over cow pies. The wheatgrass tickled my bare legs and perplexed my mind with its ability to stand upright in dirt that looked as if it hadn't soaked up a raindrop in decades.

"Just keep an eye on him? What the sam hell does that mean? What good does it do to keep an eye on him if he's charging us? Keeping an eye on him isn't going to save us!"

Holly ignored my ranting and stopped to pull yellow flowers off rabbit brush, which she put behind her ears and through buttonholes in her clothing. Then she grabbed a stalk of sagebrush, rubbing the leaves between her hands until they fell apart.

"Well . . ." She sighed then held her hands up to my face. "Smell that."

I obliged her as I always did, but I'd smelled sagebrush before—every time it rained in Ganoa, the whole town smelled of sage. But when she cupped her hands over my nose, the stinging aroma swirled inside my head like a drug, making me swoon.

"Whoa!"

Holly giggled. I tore a stalk of sagebrush, rubbed it hard between my hands, then closed my eyes and inhaled deeply. By the time I opened my eyes again, Holly was near the far fence, heading directly through the cows, although she could have easily skirted them. The bull raised his curly head framed by down-turned horns and swung his enormous body toward Holly. She stopped and turned her body toward him. I caught up with her and tried to drag her in another direction, but she pulled away and continued her steady pace toward the fence line.

"Well, just keep an eye on him," she said.

"Keeping an eye on him is not going to save us! Why am I the only one who seems to understand that?"

"He ain't gonna hurt you none." The voice floated mysteriously at the height of the sagebrush before a chunky red-haired boy stepped out from behind a cedar tree on the far side of the fence.

"Who the hell are you and how the hell do you know?" I asked. "It isn't your bull, it's ours."

"I been here longer than that bull, and I can tell you he'd turn and run if you said 'boo' to him." With that, the boy picked up a stone and pitched it at the bull.

"Go on now, Ruf." The stone arched, landing on the crest between the bull's horns. The bull shook its head then turned and lumbered in the opposite direction. I pulled two strands of barbed wire apart and Holly slipped through. She walked directly to the boy, leaving me to negotiate the barbed wire by myself, which I did with only a small tear on the back of my shirt. They stood face-to-face about a foot apart—Holly a few inches taller—summing each other up. I recognized the boy as the purple ribbon winner at the Ganoa stock show but opted to pretend otherwise, hoping he'd do the same. Holly didn't always like knowing that lives continued to be lived outside of her company.

"Well, why is your face so sunburned?" Holly asked.

"Ain't. It's windburned."

"Well, what's the difference?"

"Not much."

Holly smiled and released her gaze.

"Well, what are you doing out here?"

"I live here." Holly caught his eye again and waited for a better explanation. "That there's my grandpa's land," he said, nodding northward.

"Where?" I demanded.

"Over there and on up the valley," he said.

"Merv Nelson your grandpa?"

"Sure is."

"My dad says your grandpa owns almost this whole side of the valley except our spot here."

"Pretty close—least everything north of here."

"Well," said Holly, smiling sweetly, "Dickie here is your new neighbor. I'm Holly, Dickie's best friend."

"I remember you from the stock show," he said to me. Holly looked at me; I averted my eyes. Then she took a step closer to Stumpy.

"What's your name?" she asked.

"Stumpy Nelson."

"What kind of a name is that?" I asked. "What's your real name?"

"My real name don't much matter. Stumpy suits me just fine.

Sides, you ain't got much room to talk. What kinda name is Dickie for a girl?"

I shrugged. "Where do you go to school?"

"I go to the same school you go to. I've seen you both in the lunchroom."

"What teacher did you have last year?"

"Miss Blanchard."

"Miss Blanchard! You're a year younger than us! No wonder we haven't noticed you!"

Stumpy shoved both hands in his pockets and stared over his grandfather's land.

"I'm the same age as you, but I missed a year a school."

"You flunked first grade?" I asked.

"I didn't flunk! I just missed a year."

"Nobody just *misses* a year of school," I demanded.

"Well, I do believe I've seen you in the lunchroom," Holly jumped in, shooting me a stern look. "You sit at the cold-lunch table."

Stumpy dug the toe of a well-worn cowboy boot into some bunch-grass.

"Well, I think I'll probably be joining you there this coming year," Holly continued. "I told my mom I'm sick of that crappy lunchroom food and want to take my own lunch."

I squinted at Holly. We'd spent the last two years practicing our best expressions of arrogance and disdain for the moment our section of the hot-lunch line marched past the end table scattered with the brown paper bags and Roy Rogers lunch boxes of the kids whose parents were too poor to buy school lunch.

"Your whole family live in that little old house up the road from Dickie's?"

"Just me and Grandpa."

"Where's your mom and dad?" I asked.

"My mom lives in Salt Lake."

"Why don't you live with your mom?"

"I ain't never lived anywhere but here."

"What?" I was astounded. "You could live in the city with your mom! Haven't you ever set foot in Salt Lake City? The streets all have trees running up and down them and shady yards and lots of grass! You're a damn fool to live in this hot, dirty piece of hell!"

Stumpy stooped to pick up a handful of rocks and started pitching them at a boulder about twenty feet away, hitting it every time.

"Where's your dad?" I asked.

"He ain't around."

Holly passed her slim, tanned arm through Stumpy's fleshy sunburned arm and turned him toward the mountains.

"Well, we were just about to head into those mountains to do a little exploring. Care to accompany us?"

I watched them move off arm in arm from where we stood. Tears burned the ridges of my eyes.

"Holly?"

She turned to look at me coldly, impatiently.

"Want to see a cave?" Stumpy asked Holly.

"Well, yes I do. Lead the way."

Holly and Stumpy disappeared into a thick forest of cedar and piñon as the desert climbed into the mountains. Initially, I dropped behind deliberately in a vain effort to extract sympathy from Holly, but I couldn't have stayed with the two of them regardless. Stumpy strode through the desert agilely, his short legs transforming miraculously into long, lean muscles that moved him around sagebrush and over boulders the size of our outhouse with the grace of a ballet dancer. Holly's thin, muscled calves tucked into a sockless pair of Keds followed as if she'd been moving over this land as long as Stumpy had. I stumbled through cactus and stickers that tore at my ankles and let out cries that far exceeded the actual pain involved. Neither of them turned or slowed at all.

I finally gave up and perched myself on a rock partway up the mountainside. I could see our house, but I opted to wait for their return rather than travel alone back through the field that held the bull. I tried to keep a steady stream of tears going—wanting full sympathy and contrition when they showed up—but the sun warmed my back and a single red-tailed hawk played on the currents above my head, shaming me into contentment.

THE SILHOUETTE of the Oquirrh Mountains against the summer sky to the east began to fade before I allowed myself to believe Holly was not coming back for me. The hawk had soared off, and in its place, three turkey vultures bounced on the last remaining thermals of warm air. Worried they had pegged me for supper, I waved my arms and screamed at the vultures, but they paid me no mind. My screams turned into hysterical wailing. Between sobs, I thought I heard mimicking wails from Stumpy and Holly hiding among the rocks at my back. When I quieted down to listen, however, the yips from a pack of coyotes sent me scurrying ten feet down the mountain before I stopped again, realizing darkness had completely engulfed me and I could no longer see where my feet were landing. I plopped down on another rock and waited to be ripped open and dined upon by wild animals. If that didn't happen, I thought my father might kill me.

I'm unsure how long I sat in the dark—might have been an hour, might have been three—but at some point Stumpy simply walked out of the night and sat down quietly on the rock by my side. Our shoulders and legs touched. I moved to separate from him—having never been that close to a boy before in my life—but the small rock we shared didn't allow it, and the heat from his body felt good against mine. I hadn't realized until that moment how badly I was shivering. For a long time neither of us spoke.

"What are you doing here?" I finally said in as nasty a tone as I could summon up, trying to hide the overwhelming relief I felt at seeing him.

"I'm sorry, Dickie. That was a mean thing for us to do."

I wanted more. I didn't know what, I only knew a simple apology from him wasn't enough.

"Everybody's out looking for you. Your mom's fit to be tied."

"Who's out looking?"

"Your dad, your aunt, your brother, and my grandpa. Bev Christensen is at your house with your mom and your sister."

"Where's Holly?"

"Her mom came and picked her up."

"Oh. Who's Bev Christensen?"

"She sort of runs things around Clayton. She owns the Bar C south of here."

"How did you find me?"

"I knew where to look. I tried to tell your dad they should head out this direction, but Holly was pointing him way south a here toward Mule Creek Fork that goes straight west a Bev's place." Stumpy reached down for a few rocks and started pitching them into the darkness. "She has a way a persuading folks, but she has a lousy sense of direction."

"They let you come out here looking for me by yourself?"

"Grandpa knows I can take care a myself out here. He figured he'd better stick with your dad since he hasn't been in these mountains long or we'd have so many folks to find it'd take us a week to round y'all up."

"Aren't you afraid out here by yourself? I'd love to see a streetlight about now."

"Guess this might be the only place I ain't afraid."

"What about coyotes!"

"What about em?"

"There was a whole pack of them here! I could have been eaten!"

Stumpy laughed.

"It's not funny!"

"Yeah, well, this ain't coyotes' normal huntin season. They haven't ripped into a person around these parts for I guess better than five months now."

I glared at him. When he smiled the freckles around his mouth and eyes shifted shapes.

"How long you lived out here?"

"My whole life."

"Did your mom used to live here?"

"My mom dropped me off here when I wasn't any more'n six months old. Don't figure she stayed longer than the time it took to set me on the couch and walk back out the door."

"Who raised you?"

"Grandpa."

"Where's your grandma?"

"Died from pneumonia before I was born."

"How'd your grandpa take care of you all by himself when you were a baby?"

"Bev says he packed me along with him wherever he went. He'd put me up front a him on the horse when he'd gather cows down off the mountain, set me in a playpen out next to the fire at branding time. I suppose Bev helped. I guess they were both pretty happy when I could sit a horse by myself."

"How come you missed a year of school?"

"You're kind of nosy, Dickie Sinfield."

My scalp prickled and I turned away.

"I'm sorry, Dickie. I don't mean to keep hurting your feelings."

"You don't have to tell me. I don't even care."

"The day I was supposed to start the first grade, I was out in the front yard practicing my roping, waiting for Grandpa to drive me to school. A car drove into the driveway and a real pretty lady got out, walked toward me, and hugged me. I screamed my head off then started kicking and cussing at her. Grandpa came running outta the house and introduced me to my mother. Next thing I knew, I was in the car with her and we were heading out to the point a the mountain to pick up my father."

"The prison?"

"Yep. We moved into an apartment in Salt Lake, and my dad started looking for jobs. Mom said I'd go to school as soon as we got settled, but we never did. Dad never found a job, and six months later he was back in jail and I was back here. I'd already missed six months a school, and it was calving time, so I spent the rest of the school year working with Grandpa on the ranch."

"What's your dad in prison for?"

"Never asked."

"Do you visit your mom?"

"Haven't seen her since the day she dropped me off again in front a the house."

"Do you miss her?"

Stumpy began pitching rocks out into the darkness again.

"No. Come on, we'd better get back before Bev gets the whole town out looking for you."

He started toward the lights from the house below us. I began to follow but stumbled directly into a prickly-pear cactus and screamed. Stumpy turned back and took my hand.

"Sorry about that. You'll be picking those things outta your legs for the next two weeks. The good news is you'll probably never step in one again."

I pulled my hand away from his.

"Just stay close on my heels," he said.

"How can you see where you're going?"

"You get so you know the shape a things in the shadows. And, you don't entirely rely on your sight—you have to sorta feel your way out here. You'll get used to it."

"No, I won't," I proclaimed. He didn't reply, just kept moving at a steady pace. I stayed on his heels as directed. We entered the house through my bedroom.

"This your room? This is the slaughter room!" Stumpy roared.

"Shush! They'll hear you!"

"Well, ain't you gonna let em know you're okay?"

"In a minute."

We went through Annie's room into the bathroom, and I inched open the door to the kitchen and looked through the crack. A sturdy woman—like Aunt Alma only younger and taller—sat next to Mom, who had her head resting on her folded arms like she was taking a nap. The woman made small circles on Mom's back with a large, strong hand and brushed her other hand over her own jet-black hair, which hugged her head like a stocking cap. She wore a black tank top, jeans, and work boots, in sharp contrast to my mother's flowered cotton blouse, sunny yellow pedal pushers, and sandals. I couldn't take my eyes off her bare, tan arms; I had never before seen a woman with muscles.

I turned to Stumpy. "Is that Bev Christensen?" I whispered. He nodded.

Mom raised her head and stared at the wall in front of her as if she were straining to read an eye chart. Her face was blotchy and the front of her hair was matted to her forehead. The rest of it was sprayed into perfect order.

"I don't know what we're doing out here, Bev," Mom said. "We don't belong out here."

"That's just fear talking, Ruth."

"Dickie and Annie shouldn't be out here. They should be in Ganoa, where it's safe."

"I mean no offense, Ruth, but that's bullshit. It's perfectly safe out here. Dickie's going to be fine. In my thirty-four years here, we haven't lost a kid yet."

Mom looked quizzically at Bev. "Aren't you the president of the Clayton Ward Relief Society? Should you be swearing like that?"

"Yeah, but I gotta call it bullshit when it is. They mostly just put up with me in church. The bishop gave me that Relief Society job hoping it'd rein me in a little. I took it hoping I could loosen them up a little. Stay tuned."

Mom smiled, as if she'd momentarily forgotten the situation at hand, then fear flooded her face and she dropped her head again.

"Being out here's gonna be good for them girls, Ruth. Hell, look at Merv Nelson's grandkid. Stumpy can do more work in a day than most grown men and can sit a horse better'n anybody in this valley."

I turned to look back at Stumpy, his red face now scarlet.

"Bet you wish you had some rocks to pitch now, don't you?" I whispered, but I had whispered too loudly. When I looked back at the kitchen table, Mom and Bev were both looking straight at me.

"Miss Dickie," Bev said, "why don't you come on out here and prove to your mama that you can survive in the country."

Mom dropped her head to her arms again and started sobbing. I ran to her, wrapped my arms as far around her as I could get them, and joined her.

"Where'd you find her, Stumpy?" Bev asked.

"Right up there where we lost her."

"I'm sorry, Mama."

Mom pulled me into her arms then pulled my head back with her hands in my hair and looked at my face.

"Are you all right?" I nodded. She buried her face in my hair and whispered in my ear, "I'm sorry, Dickie. I'm sorry for all of this."

Whatever reaction my father might have had, being in the company of strangers kept it from breaking through. He snorted through his nose upon seeing me at the kitchen table when he, Alma, Heber, and a man I assumed was Stumpy's grandfather arrived a half hour later.

"Maybe we need to put a leash on you," Dad said.

"Oh, the best way to get to know your way around these mountains is to get lost in em a few times," Merv said. "Isn't it, Stump?"

Stumpy nodded and blushed more. Merv's presence calmed me, the same way it had when he spoke to me at the stock show. His cuffed Levi's, his plaid shirt, and his worn boots calmed me. His bald head covered with an old Case Tractor ball cap, his worn and crinkled face, his deep, quiet voice, and the way he reached out and pulled Stumpy toward him by tugging gently on the neck of his T-shirt sent a warm rush through me. The way Stumpy leaned back naturally against the front of Merv's legs and the way Merv's large, rough hands rested on Stumpy's shoulders made me feel safer than I'd ever felt in my life.

"Come on, boy," Merv said, nudging Stumpy back toward Heber's room. "It's getting late. Bev, you coming?"

"I sure as hell hate getting all of you out here for nothing," Dad said. "I told Merv he didn't need to call folks—"

"Hush," Bev said. "Merv done the right thing calling me. You'll understand the way things work around here soon enough. Ruth, I've put my number on that pad there by the phone. You call me if you need anything, anything at all, you hear?"

Mom stood, but before she could shift her feet, Bev pulled her into a hug, and Mom stumbled into her arms. Bev kept a clasp on her a good long while, leaving Merv and Dad fingering their ball caps and scanning the kitchen with their eyes. Bev released her hug but held Mom by both shoulders.

"I'm just down the road a piece, you hear?"

"We'll call you if we need you," Aunt Alma said, placing one hand on my shoulder and gripping Mom's elbow with the other. Bev looked at Mom, who busied herself by blowing her nose, then nodded at Alma before she, Merv, and Stumpy filed out of the kitchen.

CHAPTER FOUR

 I reach for another slice of cake, and Dot swats my hand away.

"I'm going to fix you a sandwich," she says. "You need to eat some real food."

"What's not real about cake?"

"So what do we do now?"

"You go home to Harry and I go to bed."

"Can't."

"Why not?"

"I trust the gay professor. If he's worried enough to call me, then you must be on the verge of a crack-up. So I'm here to check on you as best friends do."

"You're not my best friend."

"I would be if you allowed such a category, but since you categorically do not, I simply fulfill the duties of one without benefit of title or pay."

"Sorry. I figure a person can only survive one best friendship in a lifetime. Holly already used mine up."

"What the hell did this Holly chick do anyway? Steal your tricycle?"

"Something like that."

"Where is she now? I'll beat the shit out of her for you," Dot says, pushing the cake aside and setting bread, mustard, and ham on the table.

"Fortunately for all involved, I have no idea where she is now, but don't think I don't appreciate the offer."

"When's Heber's service?"

"George won't have one without a body."

"Jesus, that's a little weird."

"Well, no one ever accused George of being normal."

"So how's he doing?"

I shrug. "Haven't talked to him."

"Don't you think you should?"

I shrug again. "Don't know what the hell I'd say to him."

I can count on one hand, maybe even one finger, the times my father and I have had an actual conversation involving an exchange and consideration of thoughts beyond swapping the meager bits of practical information necessary to coexist in a family. Mom always said we'd both have to acknowledge too much of ourselves if we were ever really to talk to each other. I never asked her what she meant by that.

A FEW DAYS BEFORE I was to enter the third grade, at 6:45 in the morning, I plunked my butt down on the yellow daisy that decorated our toilet lid to watch Mom rat her hair, smooth it over, then rat and smooth again. She flipped the gold metallic comb around with nimble fingers and stuck the long end deep into the mound on the top of her head, pulling it upward as she sprayed Aqua Net in great quantities. I sneezed.

"Mama, why do you have to go?" I whined, distraught at the idea of my world without her. Since the day I got lost in the foothills, I had stuck so close to my mother she had to pry me loose to go to the bathroom alone.

"I told you, Dickie, I have a job now."

In the middle of my incessant protest a car honked in front of the house. Mom snatched the blue bottle of Evening in Paris from my hands, put a dab behind each ear and one on my nose, then took one last look in the mirror. She was stunning in a blue three-piece combed-cotton seersucker suit with mock pockets and simulated pearl buttons, which she had ordered from the Sears catalog for $7.84. She and I had driven to the catalog store in Ganoa to pick it up.

"Who do I look like?" she asked.

I shrugged.

"Jackie Kennedy."

"Oh, you do, Mama, you really do!"

She kissed the top of my head and held my face in her hands.

"You'll be fine today, Dickie."

The car out front would take her over Johnson's Pass—which cut west through the mountains at the place where the Onaquis became the Stansburys or vice versa depending on your perspective—and drop her at an office building inside a high wire fence. Although Kress's lunch counter encompassed my mother's entire working history, she had excelled in typing and shorthand in high school and was quickly hired as the secretary to the comptroller at Dugway Proving Grounds. Feeling as if my world had just become a dangerous place, I went into Annie's room and crawled into bed next to her.

"Mama's gone."

"Grow up," Annie said without opening her eyes.

"Will you do something with me today?"

No answer.

"Annie?"

Annie sat up in bed and propped some pillows behind her. I did the same next to her.

"Dickie, listen to me. You have to stop acting like this."

"Like what?"

"Like your world is falling apart every time Mom walks out the door."

"It is!"

"No, it is not. What are you so afraid of?"

"I don't like this place."

"Well, I'm not crazy about it myself, but there's nothing to be afraid of."

"Dad!"

"Why?"

"Because he yells."

"In case you haven't noticed, Dad isn't doing much yelling these days."

"That's what scares me! Remember last year when I had to build that plaster volcano for school? I think Dad's like that—dormant now, but ready to spew hot lava any minute!"

"You're wrong."

"How do you know?"

"Remember your first trail ride with him? Not the one where you fell on your head before it ever got started but after that?"

"Yeah."

"It's like that. Once he got out there in the mountains, you could relax around him."

"Why?"

"I don't know why. I only know that ever since we moved out here, it's like someone stuck a pin in the balloon that surrounded this family and let all the tension out. Now we're all like little kittens whose eyes are just beginning to open."

"Annie, I don't know what the hell you're talking about."

But I did know exactly what she meant. Before we moved to Clayton, Annie had dubbed Dad the "Prophet of Noise," a title he unknowingly embraced. Noise, in fact, followed him like disciples with their leader. Even when he was absolutely still, which was seldom, the air seemed to audibly rustle around him. His slender frame reached no higher than sixty-eight inches, but he came down heavy on the earth. He struck the floor hard with each heel as he walked, and his footsteps on the wooden slats in our hallway sounded like the Lord's gavel on Judgment Day. As soon as I heard the first crack of his heel, I had about five seconds to shove the book I was reading under my bed and jump to my feet before the door swung open. My father liked people to stay busy, stay in motion. Something about stillness disturbed him, as if he were afraid the entire world might suddenly stop moving and life would be over. But as soon as Dad mounted a horse, his sharp edges fell away, as if the reaching branches we rode through pulled the harshness and angst from his body and discarded it along the trail. And it was contagious. I didn't plan on admitting this to anyone, but the few times I had gone riding with him in the canyons around Ganoa, as soon as we got into the mountains, my skin lost its tenseness and settled down over my bones. The movement of the horse rocked me in a way I envisioned my mother might have done when I was a baby, the creaking of the saddle leather not unlike the creaking of a rocker. Inhaling horse sweat mixed with damp earth, leaves, pine, and wildflowers was like inhaling the spices in a soup simmering on the stove.

"All I'm saying is you don't have to be scared of Dad," Annie said. "Just get that in your head and keep it there. Okay?"

"I guess."

"Now, what else are you afraid of?"

But before I could go on to explain that I was afraid of losing my best friend, afraid no one would like me now that I lived in Clayton, afraid of giving up a life of somersaulting and roller-skating—a life I had some aptitude for—for a life of horses and open space—a life I was so obviously incompetent at—Dad's voice bellowed through the house.

"Darlene!"

I looked at Annie. She pushed me off the bed toward the door.

"Just remember what I told you."

"Why isn't he calling you, too?"

But he had given up on Annie the minute she took Bo from the stockyards, and she eliminated all hope every time she passed the plate of beef on to the next person at the table without taking a bite.

Dad sat at the kitchen table eating toast and drinking coffee.

"Put some boots and jeans on; we're gathering cows down off the mountain today."

"Is Annie going?"

"She can come if she wants. Annie?" he hollered.

"No thank you!"

"What horse am I going to ride?"

"You can ride Pug. Heber will ride one of Merv's."

Heber emerged from his bedroom dressed for a guest shot on *The Roy Rogers Show* wearing a pair of fringe-lined chaps and matching vest Aunt Alma had given him shortly after Grandpa died and she had recognized Dad's intentions. He had his hat pulled down so tight his eyebrows crushed his eyelids because, as he had explained to me a number of times, that's how real cowboys wear them.

"There's no way a man could ride a horse with a hat tipped back the way those singing cowboys wear em," Heber said. "How could he keep it on his head?" To prove his point, he would call us into the room whenever *Rawhide* came on to look at Rowdy Yates trailing cows with his hat pulled down so tight it required him to tip his head and peer out from under his hat sideways to see where he was going.

But Aunt Alma had misjudged Heber's growth spurt, so that just six months later, the chaps now pulled at his crotch in a way that made Dad wince and dropped just to the top of his cowboy boots, and the vest cut in so tight around his shoulders he could barely lift his arms to open the refrigerator door. He had been waiting for "roundup" ever since we moved to the ranch and had been sorely disappointed to find out we'd instead moved just in time for haying.

"Heber, I think you might want to take that outfit off before Merv and Stumpy get here. Where's the straw hat I just bought you? Or even a ball cap would be fine."

Heber slunk back to his room.

"I don't really know what to do," I said tentatively.

"Time you learned, then, isn't it?" he said. "You'll do fine, Dickie."

Dad had finished saddling Rangy and Pug and was coiling and tying a rope to his saddle when Merv and Stumpy rode up leading another horse. I looked at Stumpy; he looked at his saddle horn.

"This little mare here's as gentle as they come," Merv said, dismounting and handing the reins to Heber, who took them with a scoff to let Merv know he didn't need "gentle." Merv smiled.

"In fact, she's so gentle, you're probably gonna need these."

He handed Heber a pair of rusty old spurs, which immediately allowed Heber to forgive the prior assumption. He strapped them on and made three full circles around the yard just to hear them jingle.

"You're probably gonna have to let those stirrups down a bit. Stumpy's been using that saddle and we don't call him Stumpy for nothin."

Heber fussed with the stirrup, but it began to look like it might take a while, so Merv nodded at Stumpy, who jumped down to help. In two quick movements, Stumpy had the stirrup lengthened by two holes. He gave it a quick jerk to make sure it was set then went to the other side and did the same. Heber—who had ten years of life experience to Stumpy's eight—stood red-faced. I turned to glare at Stumpy for humiliating Heber, but Stumpy looked equally embarrassed.

The sun broke from behind the Oquirrhs and began to throw heat as we left the corrals. Pug's blondish-red mane shook and shimmered as he stepped out, and my body acquiesced to both the sunlight and the movement. I stopped shivering and felt my muscles drop into the saddle. The sunlight splashed against the Onaquis, opening up the canyons, as we rode toward them. Merv led us through the field of cows Holly and I had walked through the week before, his head and lips moving slightly.

"What's he doing?" I asked Stumpy.

"Counting."

"Why?"

"So he knows how many we still need to bring down. These cows here came off the mountain early by themselves. Sometimes they do that."

I fumbled with my reins, dropped one off the side, and Pug stepped on it, jerking his head toward the ground. Stumpy leaned down the side of his horse, looped the rein back up, and handed it to me.

"Like this," Stumpy said. "Hold em in your left hand."

"But I'm right-handed."

"That's why you want to hold em in the left—so you have your right hand free to rope or whatever else you might need it for. Make sure the reins are even and that you've given Pug enough room to walk out but not so much that the reins are dangling all over the place. Split the reins with your little finger—one rein on top and one on the bottom—then both reins under all your other fingers and over the top a your thumb. That way you can slide your hand up and down the reins without dropping one."

Heber rode on the other side of Stumpy and about half a horse length behind, threading his reins through his left hand. I tensed up when I realized Dad was turned in his saddle watching us, but he just nodded.

"I meant to switch those out to a single rein, Dickie. We can tie a knot in them if you're having trouble," Dad said.

"I think I have it."

"I think you just might," Merv said.

"Heber, get the gate," Dad said as we got to the far end of the field. Heber stomped toward the gate, making his spurs jingle, and tugged on the loop of wire that was slipped over both the fence post and the gatepost.

"Those gates are strung pretty tight," Merv said as he nodded to Stumpy. Stumpy jumped off his horse, swung an arm around both the gatepost and the fence like he was putting it in a headlock, and slipped the wire off.

For every one of Heber's ineptitudes, Stumpy answered with stunning ability. Heber gave his horse a kick with those spurs to head off a cow, and the mare took off on a trot, bouncing Heber all over the saddle. Stumpy started after the same cow, kicking his horse into a full gallop without hesitation. Heber knocked his hat off trying to rope a calf going back up the mountain and had to get down to retrieve it, while Stumpy flung a loop around the calf's neck like he was swirling water in a bathtub.

By the time we had gathered most of the cows and headed toward the corrals, Heber looked like he'd just as soon crawl under one of the boulders we rode around and stay there. Stumpy looked about the same. When a calf got spooked at a creek crossing and turned back, Heber watched it run right past his horse without making a move. Stumpy hesitated for a moment, but the instinct to retrieve the calf was just that—instinct. He couldn't have cut Heber any slack if he'd wanted to.

Dad and Merv rode side by side behind Stumpy and me, Heber a good five minutes ahead, staying right on the last cow's tail, although some of those cows had been coming off the mountain for so many years, they didn't need any of us to do much except signal it was roundup time.

"Your boy's a hell of a hand, Merv," Dad said.

Stumpy stared straight ahead, slumped in the saddle, hands folded casually over the horn.

"He's got a knack for it, that's for sure. Your boy'll get the hang of it. Takes some time. But that young girl a yours is a natural, you know that? I been watching her today."

"Hell, she's scared of everything, Merv. I don't know that she'll ever let go of that saddle horn."

"She lets go of it plenty when you're not watching her. She moves with that horse as if she's part of it. She don't know it yet, but she's comfortable up there."

Stumpy looked at me out of the corner of his eye and grinned.

My face burned. Why do grown-ups think kids are hard of hearing? When we got to the fence line, the cows were already grazing as if they'd been there all summer, and Heber was nowhere in sight.

"Stump, why don't you and Dickie ride on up through that west section above our property and see if you can find those stragglers we didn't get," Merv said. "You have plenty a daylight left."

Stumpy nodded and turned off. I had been about as close to euphoria as a girl could be when I saw the fence, thanking the Lord my cowboying day was coming to an end without incident, but Merv smiled at me in that calming way, so I followed Stumpy back into the mountains.

When we were out of sight, Stumpy kicked his horse into a run. Without prompting from me, Pug lunged into a run and followed closely, winding around boulders and through scrub oak and cedar. I held the reins with my left hand and the saddle horn with my right, my knees tightly squeezing Pug's sides, partly terrified and partly exhilarated. When I caught up to him, Stumpy was already off his horse and sitting on a rock as if he'd been there all day.

"What the sam hell was that all about?" I demanded.

"Just wanted to see if Grandpa was right about you, if you really can ride."

"Well, you didn't leave me much choice, did you?"

"Wanted to see if you'd let go a your saddle horn for a few minutes."

I dismounted and tugged at my jeans along the inside of my thighs. "Go to hell, Stumpy Nelson."

"He's right, you know."

"Who?"

"Grandpa. You actually could ride if you'd relax a little and stop being so scared of it. Just throw the reins over that scrub oak."

I wrapped the reins tightly around a branch and tied a knot in the end while Stumpy watched, stifling a chuckle.

"What's so funny?"

"You've got his head tied so tight to that tree he can't move. You're gonna end up with busted reins," he said, moving to pull them loose.

I sat on a rock about three feet from Stumpy. "I thought we were supposed to be looking for straggles."

"Stragglers," he said, moving to sit next to me. "Grandpa knows there ain't no cows out this direction."

"Then what'd he send us out here for?" I asked through spontaneous tears.

Stumpy sat silently for a bit.

"I sure do make you cry a lot, Dickie. Wish I didn't do that. What's wrong?"

"I hate living out here!"

"Why?"

"It's ugly!"

"No, it ain't! I'm sick a folks saying that!"

"We used to have a front lawn big enough to play Mother-May-I on! We used to have smooth sidewalks and a driveway and a porch to sit on and sprinklers to run through!"

"But we've got thousands a acres out here to play on! We can hunt for arrowheads and catch horny toads and swim in Grandpa's irrigation pond. I even know where some springs are!"

"I don't want to do that stuff, especially not with you! I already have a best friend!"

Stumpy's ears turned red and he took off up the mountain on foot. I sat for a moment and quickly realized the dropping sun left me pretty much in the same spot I'd found myself in not so long ago. I went after him.

"Stumpy! Don't you leave me out here again! Stumpy!"

No way I could catch him. I kept my eye on splashes of his white T-shirt and jeans as he climbed over rocks ahead of me, but eventually I lost him. I climbed on a tall rock in frustration, looking in all four directions.

"Stumpy!" I screamed, panic rising in my gut.

"Stop your screaming already," he said in a voice that seemed to be right next to me.

"Where are you?"

"Down here. You're practically standing on my feet."

I found him tucked into a spot that looked like it had been carved into the rock by a giant ice-cream scoop. Five shiny arrowheads dangled from strings in front of the opening. Along the south wall, a shoulder-height ledge held a rusted horse bit and a braided piece of hair. I started crawling in next to him.

"Stop!" he said. "I never said you could come in."

"Well, can I?"

"I guess."

I crawled forward then turned to look out at the valley from inside the rock. We were high enough that the view was uninterrupted across Clayton, across the highway, and into the Oquirrh Mountains.

"What's this?" I asked.

"Those are genuine arrowheads made from obsidian and that's the bit and a piece a mane from the first horse I ever had. He died three years ago."

"No, I mean what's this place? Is this the cave you showed Holly?"

"Yeah, but I'm sorta wishing I hadn't."

"Why not."

"It's sorta special place."

"Well, Holly's my best friend."

"Yeah, but . . ."

"She won't tell anybody about it."

"I know, but . . . ah, you just don't get it, Dickie."

"Get what?"

"Not just anybody can have this place. I shoulda never showed it to Holly."

"But you're showing it to me."

"Yeah, but I'm not so sure I shoulda done that either."

"Then why did you?"

"Cause you live here now, Dickie. These here are your mountains now, just like they're mine."

"I don't want to live in these damned ugly old mountains! Come on, Stumpy, it's getting dark. Let's go back."

"You can go back if you want; I'm staying here awhile."

"But I can't go back without you! I don't know which way to go!"

"You shoulda paid attention on the way up here."

"How could I? We came up on a dead run!"

"Well, good luck finding your way back."

"Fine. But if I get lost again your grandpa's gonna kick your butt!"

That had him thinking seriously, so I turned and started down the mountain. By the time I reached Pug, he was next to me. Before I had the chance to remember that my father had always lifted me onto Pug's back, knowing the stirrup was too high for me to reach, Stumpy had taken Pug's reins and positioned him next to a boulder. He nodded at me to stand on the boulder, where I could then easily climb onto Pug's back. Although Stumpy was no taller than I, he needed no such assistance. In one smooth movement he apparently had perfected from the time he could stand, his hands grasped the horn and his left foot landed in the stirrup as his right foot left the ground and swung over the horse's rump.

CHAPTER FIVE

The morning sun bounces off the fat, blond body of Big Max. He stretches and purrs. I try to shush him so I can listen to the sound of movement downstairs in the kitchen. I can usually determine identity—Michael or Dot—by sound alone. Michael sounds like a stroll through a British rose garden; Dot sounds like bushwhacking through the rain forest. The fact that someone is in my kitchen at a time of day when I abhor company—a fact well known to both—means they are still worried about me. I'm simultaneously touched and annoyed as hell. I consider sleeping until the sound disappears, but the smell of bacon intrigues me. Michael is a vegetarian, and Dot uses frying pans only to discourage intruders and prop doors open.

As I walk into the kitchen, Aunt Alma puts two plates heaped with bacon, eggs, and fried potatoes on the table.

"Eat before your eggs get cold," she commands. I do as directed. Alma is squat and sturdy at eighty-two—as she's always been—like a five-foot post sunk into three feet of clay. And she lives that way, knowing it will take something big to knock her down. She had been engaged once but never married; her fiancé never returned from WWII. As far as I know, no one ever questioned her about her unmarried status, and come to think of it, she's one of few people who never question me about mine. I've always assumed—and still do—that she remained single by choice, not by lack of opportunity.

Alma had the same capacity as her brother for creating and tolerating noise, and stepping into the middle of one of their conversations felt like playing on the railroad tracks in a deafening wind. After Grandpa Sinfield's funeral, Alma and Dad had held court near the potbellied stove in my grandfather's kitchen.

"It's colder than hell out there," my father started.

"Oh, hell, George, we've had colder days than . . ."

"That's easy to say from your rocking chair . . ."

". . . this for Christ's sake."

". . . next to the stove . . ."

"To listen to you gripe . . ."

". . . with a blanket across your lap . . ."

". . . about the cold, I believe you've . . ."

". . . blocking all the heat, making sure no one else . . ."

". . . become a little soft . . ."

". . . can get anywhere near the stove."

". . . in that school where . . ."

"How about if you get off your ass and go feed that horse out there . . ."

". . . you sit on your ass all day staring out the windows."

". . . and I take your spot in the rocking chair for a while."

"How much you gonna ask for Dad's horse?" Alma had asked him.

"I have no intention of selling that horse," Dad had answered, and I had pictured Rangy grazing on our grass and petunias and drinking out of the sprinkler in our front yard. I wasn't that far off.

Aunt Alma had swung into the spirit of our new cowboy life with gusto. Annie always thought she might be messing with us, but I figured she was just as nuts as Dad. I tried to stay out of the fray by spending as much time as possible at Holly's house, but Holly confoundedly took a great deal of joy in this—as Mom put it—TV-western life of ours, and she found an ally in Aunt Alma.

Dad and Heber had set up a sawhorse on the back lawn to

practice their roping skills, and they could keep themselves content for hours throwing, coiling, swinging, throwing, and recoiling. Holly and Alma liked nothing better than to pour themselves a glass of lemonade and whoop and holler at Dad and Heber.

"Head em up and move em out, boss," Alma would call to my father as she lowered herself the few inches it took to drop her bottom into a lawn chair.

"Watch out, Rowdy," Holly would holler at Heber, "that little dogie is gettin away from you!"

My father seemed to thrive on performing in front of an audience, swinging his rope fast so it sounded like a bee close to your ear, pulling the slack hard when he caught the sawhorse, flinging it through the air. It somehow became my job to retrieve the sawhorse and set it up again, which I did fearlessly until Heber recognized me for an easier target and left a three-inch rope burn from my ear to my shoulder. Dad put a stop to that, but still Heber timed his throw close enough to nick my heels while fooling Dad into thinking he was trying for the sawhorse.

Heber would have preferred to practice alone because every time he swung the rope over his head and sent his cowboy hat flying, Alma and Holly busted apart laughing and slapping each other on the back. "Whoa there, Rowdy! Slow down, cowboy, you're gonna take your own head off!"

In the early sixties, cheap gas, cheap cars, and cheap hotel rooms coalesced into the perfect family vacation for most everybody in Ganoa County. We were no exception. The two summers before Grandpa died, we covered Yellowstone and the Grand Canyon. The year my father decided to be a cowboy we drove straight for the "Daddy of 'em All" rodeo in Cheyenne, Wyoming, with enough single-slice ham-and-mustard sandwiches to get us there with few stops. We started out at 5 A.M., but before long, the sun was beating on the hood of our green-and-white Buick and hot air was blasting through the four open windows, whipping my stringy hair around my face. Annie, Heber, and I fought over space and comic books. Annie slapped my bare thigh every time my knee touched hers, mostly out of fear something might be crawling on her, and Heber gripped my leg above the knee about every fifteen minutes and squeezed until I screamed, which got Dad turned around with one hand on the back of my mother's seat, yelling at us with his full attention. Once an hour or so, Annie let me lean across her legs and stick my head out the window to get my hair all going in the same direction.

My mother, in the middle of the front seat between Dad and Alma, looked dreamily out the window, passing ham sandwiches over the seat as soon as someone started whining about being hungry. We drove eight hours, stopping only for gas, and pulled into the empty parking lot of the Wagon Wheel Motel in Cheyenne late in the afternoon.

"George, are you sure this is the right place?"

"Yep. Rodeo starts tomorrow. You watch. This place will be packed with cowboys."

I didn't care much about seeing real cowboys, but I craned my neck to look out the back window at the giant wagon wheel hanging overhead and took note of the words *swimming pool* next to it. They were faded and barely readable, but they were there and that's all I cared about.

We unloaded the car in a room smelling of mold and cigarettes, and Heber immediately spread his sleeping bag—which he had taken to calling a bedroll—onto the floor. I rummaged through my suitcase to find my swimming suit and nose plugs, and my mother followed me out the door. She opened the gate marked POOL, and we stood at the edge of the largest sandbox I had ever seen in my life.

"Those look kind of fun," Mom said, trying to distract me by pushing me toward two giant rocking horses suspended three feet off the ground on four springs as big around as soup cans attached to concrete slabs. The horses were freshly painted—a black with a red saddle and a white with a green saddle. Mom lifted me onto one, hot against the insides of my bare thighs, the paint still tacky. I slid my flip-flop-clad feet onto the pegs just as Heber, outfitted in the chaps and vest Aunt Alma had given him, ran through the sandbox.

"Yeeeeeeehaaawwww!" Heber flung himself onto the black horse next to me and rode with one hand suspended above his head, shortly figuring that he could come down low enough to get a push off the ground with both feet and fly a good six feet into the air.

"Heber! Slow down!" Mom screamed. Her yelling was so mild compared to my father's that none of us really paid much attention to it, including her. She put no expectation behind the words, just put them out there to alleviate guilt in the case of Heber "cracking his head open," something she seemed convinced he would eventually accomplish. The motel owner walked out of the office toward us, and I figured Heber was in big trouble. With our newly acquired expertise, we pegged him immediately as a city slicker in tan polyester pants that stopped about two inches above the ankles of his new cowboy boots. He wore a shiny belt buckle well hidden under a big belly that looked as if it would give off a thunk like a pumpkin.

"Something, ain't they?" city slicker said to my mother like a proud papa. "Got them just in time for the rodeo. I knew they'd be a big hit with the kids."

He looked at me standing pathetically in my swimming suit.

"Darn pool was costing me a fortune to keep open. I messed with that for about six months then called my brother-in-law, Gib. He works on over at the gravel pit. Best thing I ever did putting these beauties in. Well, have fun," he said, patting me on the head as he turned. I hated him.

THE SCENT OF COW MANURE and fried hamburgers rode on a thick mantle of dust that hovered three feet above the ground as we entered the rodeo grounds through the gate marked GENERAL ADMISSION. So we'd have a good seat, Dad had rushed us out of the motel room hours before the rodeo, but apparently everyone had the same idea. We were forced to the top row of bleachers to find room for a family of six. Dad seemed satisfied, however, that we could look down upon the pens behind us filled with horses and Brahma bulls at the same time we could watch the rodeo in front of us as if he'd planned it that way.

"You'll learn a little about the way rodeos work if you keep an eye on those separating pens," he said, nodding toward two cowboys on horseback cutting one animal at a time out from the group and sending it through an open gate at the same time as they sent a swirl of dust in our direction. Dad pulled the rodeo program from his back pocket, where it had been folded lengthwise, pulled his pen from his shirt pocket, and ran down the list of contestants for the day, putting a star by the names familiar to him.

"There are some guys here to watch." Dad thumped his program with his index finger and spoke loudly. I thought he must be talking to someone five benches away, but he leaned across Heber and Annie and looked at Mom, who sat farthest from Dad next to Alma.

"You know that?" he said when he got no response.

Mom nodded and raised her perfectly sculpted eyebrows.

"Don McLaughlin's been tearing them up in the calf roping and Jim Shoulders is still sitting in first place to win the all-around this year."

When four old guys slurping out of Shasta cans four rows in front of us craned their necks around to look at him, he turned up the volume.

"Jim Shoulders was injured last week, you know that? So I'd be surprised if we see him here. But he's drawn Tornado and that's a damn good bull, so he might try to make it. He'd hate to have to turn that bull out."

"That sure is a good bull," said the father of another family dressed very much like us sitting one row down. He twisted around in his seat and spoke in an excited drawl. "I seen that bull throw a guy clean over that fence there last year. Cleared that top pole without even brushing it, like he had a set a wings."

"The world is full of Dads," Annie murmured.

"Yes sir," Dad said. He thumped his program again in a satisfied manner and talked directly to the man in front of him but still spoke as if trying to draw a crowd into a circus tent. "I'd like to see Jim try to ride him. I'll bet he could do it."

"I know he could," Heber piped in.

My father and the father in front of him—with constant echos from Heber—carried on like this the entire rodeo, giving our section of the bleachers commentary on every cowboy and every animal.

"I think he missed him out," Dad said when the first bareback rider came out of the chute.

"He did! He missed him out!" Heber yelled.

"Settle down, Rowdy," Annie said. "You don't even know what that means."

"What does it mean?" I asked Annie, and she shrugged.

"I do so!" Heber said.

"No," Dad said, "the judges look like they're scoring him."

"I thought maybe he was okay on that one," Heber said.

"Sure, Rowdy," Annie said. "They probably wish you were out there helping with the judging and all since you know so much."

"What does 'missing him out' mean," I whispered to my mother.

"I don't know. You'll have to ask your father."

I really didn't need to know all that badly, but she nudged me to ask just as the announcer informed the crowd that the cowboy would receive a goose egg because he missed him out. The announcer went on to explain that a cowboy is required to "mark" his horse out of the gate by having his spurs over the points of the horse's shoulders on the first jump out. If a spur dropped below that point, he missed him out.

"I thought so," Dad said. He looked as if he'd just won something. "I thought I saw that left foot fall."

"Yeah, I was purdy sure he was making that ride for nothin," said the other father. "You gotta have those spurs dug in on that horse cause he does come flyin outta that gate."

Dad had been waiting all day for Dean Oliver, currently leading the national standings in calf roping, so we all perked up when they announced him as the first to go. Annie watched in horror as a rope around its neck jerked a baby calf off its feet from a full run. It struggled back to its feet in just enough time to be grabbed by the cowboy and thrown down again with enough force to knock the wind out of its belly for a second time. It was then tied by three legs and dragged across the dirt on its side by the rope still around its neck until the cowboy got back to his horse to give it some slack. It struggled against the piggin string then let out a bawl that ought to send a shiver through any warm-blooded person. Annie took one look at Dad and Heber, who were grinning from ear to ear with the performance, and decided she'd seen enough. I wasn't quite sure what I'd just witnessed until I saw the tears well up in her eyes, then I started crying also. She knew better than to let Dad or Heber get a glimpse of us, so she stood on her seat, turned around, and announced that she wanted to watch the separating pens. I quickly joined her.

Below us, horses snorted and played restlessly, strong and healthy with long scraggly manes and heads high. I felt immediately better. But tears still streamed down Annie's face, leaving streaks in the fine covering of dust over her freckles. I followed her gaze to the corner of the far pen, where a lone sorrel horse stood with its head dropped low. Except for this, it looked like any other horse in the pen, but when it came anywhere near the others, they bit and kicked it mercilessly. It retreated back to its corner but tried again and again to join the group of horses, and again they bit and kicked until it retreated, its nose almost dragging in the dust. Finally, it remained in the corner, head down, blond mane hanging between its flattened ears. Annie announced she had to go to the bathroom and took off down the bleachers. I went after her.

"Annie, Annie, wait up!"

I caught up with her and tried to grab her hand. She yanked it away from me and kept going. I followed her to a corner on the back side of the hamburger stand, where she sat down in the dirt and sobbed. The tears also ran down my neck and into the collar of my shirt. I touched her hair, and she slapped my hand away. She cried for a good long time before she looked up at me.

"I hate rodeos," she said.

"Me, too."

"Cowboys are mean and stupid."

"Yeah."

"I hate him."

"Who?"

"Who do you think?"

"Heber?"

"No, you idiot. Dad. I hate Dad."

"You can't hate Dad."

"Why not?"

"Because it's wrong."

"Don't you hate him?"

"No."

"Liar."

"I don't."

"I know you do. I can see it on your face every time he yells at you for some stupid little thing that wasn't your fault, every time he laughs at you like you're dumb, every time he dresses you up in that stupid cowboy outfit you're wearing now. You hate him."

"Do not."

"Say it."

"No."

"Say it. It feels good. I hate Dad. I hate Dad. I hate Dad."

"Stop it!"

"I hate Dad. I hate Dad. I hate Dad." She was almost singing.

"Stop it now!" I started pounding on her back and she started laughing.

"Okay, okay, get your bony fists out of my back, you little shit."

I stepped back and she looked at me with a goofy smile on her face.

"You look ridiculous in that outfit," she said.

"So do you."

"You look like it's Howdy Dowdy time."

"You, too."

"And now your face is all blotchy and your ugly shirt is all wet."

"Yours, too."

"Let's go find a bathroom and get cleaned up," she said, taking my hand. "We have three more days of this rodeo crap, and I have a horrible hunch there's a whole lot more to come when we get home. Time to buck up, as they say in cowboy land."

Dad continued to enlighten the folks in the stands around us for three more days, and Heber continued to confirm everything he said. Mom kept herself busy wiping my face and tucking my shirt in, picking at her nails, or gazing in the opposite direction of anything going on in the arena. Alma kept herself entertained with a book of crossword puzzles and looked up only when she was stumped. Annie attempted to sneak a book in, but Dad shortly confiscated it.

"Watch what's going on in the arena, for Christ's sake. You might learn something."

Annie agreed to watch the bareback riding, the saddle-bronc riding, and the bull riding, events in which she thought cowboy and animal to be on equal footing. But she steadfastly refused to watch calf roping, team roping, steer wrestling, and an event called steer roping, which, according to my father, was not performed in many rodeos except Cheyenne, so we were lucky to be able to see it. The event required a steer running full speed chased by a rider on horseback. If done properly, the cowboy throws his rope in such a way as to catch the steer near the front legs, ripping its legs out from under it and pitching it head over tail into the air. At this point Annie and I both stopped watching; I have no idea how the event ends.

Annie perfected a way of looking over the top of the action in the arena and dropping into a daydream sort of trance as if she were really enjoying it. I tried to copy her but couldn't keep my eyes from dropping down to the arena, and once they did, I couldn't pull them away. Each day I left the rodeo with wobbly knees and a queasy stomach as if I'd just gotten off a roller coaster.

On the last day, we planned to attend the rodeo that afternoon, have a picnic on the grass at our still-empty motel afterward, and get an early start back home the next morning. Dad had become quite comfortable with his running commentary, calling the cowboys by their first names and offering up a little personal information on each. I told Annie I was a little impressed by the amount of knowledge he seemed to pull out of his head, beings we were pretty new to this cowboy thing, and she said I was easily impressed.

Dad directed most of his comments that last day to a man and woman who sat in front and a little to the right of us. The man's jeans were almost worn through on the tops of his thighs and his boots were dull, cracked, and caked with a mixture of mud and manure. He wore a white western shirt, fraying a bit around the collar and thinning at the elbows, but incredibly clean and bright. A felt hat with a faint sweat line around the hatband covered a head of gray hair that hung unevenly on his dark brown neck. Deep crinkles held his eyes in a persistent squint, and lines in his face went diagonally from nose to chin so perfectly spaced they looked drawn on. Annie said he looked like Gil Favor after he'd hit town at the end of a long cattle drive, taken a ten-cent bath at the hotel, and put on a clean shirt.

The woman wore tan slacks with an untucked flowery blouse and what the women in our church called sensible shoes. Her gray hair hung around her head, face, and shoulders as if she hadn't even noticed it was there. She had one of those expressions that might look happy to one person and sad to the next, angry to one and pleasant to the next. Hard to tell. Whenever Dad said a cowboy's name and gave information on him, they both turned politely and nodded but never joined in or spoke a word as others had done previously.

Shortly after the bareback riding, a cowboy—dusty and smiling and still wearing his contestant number—made his way up the stands.

"Here comes Skeeter Hamilton," Dad said.

"Here comes Skeeter Hamilton," echoed Heber.

"He's a good bareback rider, but I believe Jim Shoulders is just a better all-around cowboy."

Skeeter appeared to be headed straight for us, taking the stairs two at a time, and for a moment I think Dad and Heber thought he might be coming to see them. He turned in to the row in front of us and excused himself over ten pairs of knees to get to the man and woman down to our right. The man slapped him on the back and said, "Good ride," and the woman leaned across her husband to touch the cowboy's knee and smile.

"I think I might end up in the money," the cowboy said, grinning. "There's a couple of rerides after the show, but I think that score will hold. I'm starved. You want to get something to eat or do you want to watch the other events?"

"We only came to see you, son," the man said. As they got up and started to make their way to the stairs, the woman turned and patted Heber on the knee.

"You've got a real cute family," she said to my mother.

Dad got real quiet after that and we left immediately following the calf roping, with Heber whining all the way down the stairs because he'd waited all day for the bull riding. When we got back to the motel, my father loaded everything into the car, settled up the bill, and we drove through Wyoming with a cool night breeze filling the car.

CHAPTER SIX

"I like your hair wild like that," Alma says, having finished her breakfast and now watching me push the last of my potatoes around. "Suits you."

"Thanks." I run my hand through the snarled mop. "I'm thinking about shaving it."

"How's Michael?"

"Fine."

"And your friend Dot?"

"Fine, cept both of them are hovering around me like they're on suicide watch. Speaking of which, other than cooking me an excellent breakfast for which I thank you, what are you doing here? And how many others have keys?"

"Didn't need a key; back door was open. Old habits are hard to break, aren't they? I came to talk to you about Heber's funeral."

"Thought you said George didn't want a funeral."

"That's what I came to talk to you about. Have you talked to him?"

"No, I'm getting all my information from you."

"Well, I can't talk any sense into that damn-fool brother of mine."

"And you think I can?"

"No, actually I don't think anyone can now that Ruth's gone. But we need to do something for Heber."

"What's the army saying? Are they going to release Heber's body?"

"Oh, the same thing they always say—not a goddamn thing that makes any sense. It's a matter of public safety or a matter of national security. You and I both know it's a matter of them covering their own ass as usual. One idiot told me the body had been disposed of, if you can imagine that, and the next time I called, a different damn idiot told me the body had been delivered to Bates Funeral Home, but it hasn't. Regardless, we need to have a funeral for Heber."

"It hasn't even been a week; let's wait and see what happens."

"I just don't like seeing George and the army getting into another pissing match. George didn't come out of the last one all that well."

"I wasn't aware he'd come out of it at all."

"Well, that's just my point. We can't let the army do this to us again; we need to move on with our lives."

"Fighting the army is Dad's life."

For the second time in my fifty-two years on earth, I see tears rimming the edges of Aunt Alma's cloudy old eyes. The first was when Mom died. She pulls off her glasses and wipes her eyes with her shirtsleeve.

"Dickie, your dad and I don't have many years left on this earth. God knows it hasn't been an easy life, but I figured once we both turned eighty we could just be blessedly ignored to live out what time we got left to us. Us Sinfields aren't churchgoers, but I didn't think that was too much to ask. I just can't figure this."

"I don't know that there's any figuring to be done, Alma."

"Just seems to me George gets tested in ways that others don't. I don't have any other explanation for it."

Seems to me my father brings on a lot of his own misery, but I didn't say that to Alma. I just know life would have been a whole lot easier had we stayed in Ganoa instead of moving to Clayton.

"Have you talked to Annie?" Alma asks.

"Yeah. She's sort of waiting to find out if we're having a service before she makes any plans to fly home."

"Call her back and tell her to get on the next plane."

"Why?"

"Because she ought to be here."

"Okay."

"Tell her to plan on staying for a week or so. Robert and the kids should come, too, if they want to."

When Annie left Utah, she left it in every way possible. Upon graduation from high school, she packed a VW Bug full of what she considered the essentials—record albums, clothes, and makeup—and drove to Los Angeles to become a model. Instead she got a job at the cosmetics counter at the Broadway Department Store, and five years later was married to Robert, a born-again Baptist preacher ten years her senior. None of us really know the steps that led from lipstick to Christ, but I assume they had something to do with disillusionment, reality, and the search for something in between. Or maybe it was love, as Dot gently pointed out to me when I told her the story.

Shortly after they were married, Robert tried to save the family from what he considered the evil cult of Mormonism. He thought Aunt Alma and Dad would be easy marks since they were both jacks and spent a good amount of their energy complaining about the Mormon Church. He waded into one of their bitching sessions one day and silenced them both in a way I'd never seen done before. In about a minute, they had regrouped and were preaching the gospel of Mormonism like two of the twelve apostles. I thought it unfair of Annie not to warn Robert about the unswerving righteousness that will surge from a jack-Mormon as soon as an outsider jumps into the Mormon-bashing conversation. Letting him wander naively into one of Dad and Alma's bitching sessions was like sending a golden retriever puppy into a pit bull fight. After that, Robert didn't even try to save me, which left me feeling relieved on the one hand and worried on the other.

"I don't think Robert relishes the idea of a week's vacation in Clayton, and Annie's kids are both in college back east now."

"Good for them. Annie has smart kids."

"Yes, she does."

"After you call her, pack your own bag and get your butt out to Clayton."

"I have a few things I need to—"

"Do what you need to do. But if you're not out there by tomorrow night, I'll be back."

EACH PERSON I PASS in the newsroom falls disconcertingly quiet after mumbling a greeting or condolence. I go directly to Charlie's office and close the door. Charlie and I had been hired at the paper within weeks of each other twenty-five years ago, and had gravitated toward each other as outcasts tend to do. I was the most radical apostate the church had ever hired, which they did shortly after the *The Beehive Banner* came under fire for journalistic integrity, its critics questioning whether the newspaper could overcome its Mormon Church ownership and be taken seriously as a major city daily. Charlie was one of about ten African-American Mormons in the entire state at the time and the only one at *The Banner* then and now. He had become my editor fifteen years ago after they offered me the job and I turned it down.

"What the hell's wrong with everybody out there?" I ask. "I can't be the first person to have a death in the family."

"No, but I'm pretty sure you're the first to have one killed by nerve gas."

"That doesn't make me toxic—although growing up in Ganoa County might."

"What are you doing here? I left numerous messages on that turned-off cell phone of yours that I didn't expect to see you for a few weeks."

"What do you know about what happened out there?"

"Official statement from the army—employee error, immediately contained, no danger to the community or the environment—hell, Dickie, you know the story. You could have written it verbatim without ever seeing the press release."

"I don't want to know the official statement, Charlie. I want to know what the hell happened out there."

"Well, nobody's talking. That shouldn't surprise you."

"So that's it? That's the story you're going with?"

"What do you want me to do, Dickie? I'm damn sorry about Heber, but you've worked here as long as I have. You know the capabilities *and* the politics of this newspaper. We're all about giving the fine citizens of Utah what they want. And with the exception of a very few so-called left-wing alarmists like you and me, what Utahns want—here in the middle of probably the most noxious state in the nation—is to feel safe. And that's what we're going to give them."

I sit silently, knowing Charlie is absolutely right. I've seen it before. In fact, I've seen it all my life—the amazing ability of Utahns, particularly Ganoa County residents, to adapt to their surroundings. I suppose all humans do it, but not all humans share their neighborhoods with gas-filled M55 rockets. When the incinerator started operations in 1996, as its members gathered from all over the country to protest at the gates, the Sierra Club called Ganoa County residents apathetic and ignorant. Still trying to distance myself from Ganoa County two decades after leaving, I paid my dues and joined the Sierra Club. But I knew better. Apathy and ignorance did not keep Clayton ranchers on their tractors while the protesters gathered. They were there because they had to be there. They were there because after the protesters would resume their lives a few hundred or thousand miles away from the very thought of nerve gas, there would still be hay to haul and cows to bring in. And mostly they were there because the protesters had shown up fifty years too late.

When Charlie reaches across the desk to touch my hand, I realize I'm crying for the first time since hearing about Heber's death. The tears flow silently and abundantly down my face and onto my ratty leather backpack. Awkwardly, unable to see through the tears, I rummage through the pack and pull out a faded and crumbled copy of a *New York Times Magazine* article entitled "Chemical and Biological Weapons: The Secret Arsenal," written by Seymour M. Hersh in August 1968. I throw it across the desk at Charlie. He already knows what it is; we had discussed it many times over the years.

I was fourteen when Hersh wrote the article after an incident in the west desert threatened Utahns' world of plausible deniability. The army issued their usual report disclaiming all responsibility; Hersh's article said otherwise. I didn't see either the report or the article until a couple of years later. But I did inadvertently find myself in the deep chasm of dissonance between the two when I was called to the principal's office on the first day of school that fall for "causing undue fear and alarm" among my fellow students after I told a few what Stumpy and I had witnessed on a sunny day in 1968, very similar to the day Heber died thirty-nine years later.

"So fuck the truth, Charlie, is that what you're saying?"

"Dickie, listen to me. It's 2007 not 1968. The Patriot Act has trumped the Freedom of Information Act and you work at *The Beehive Banner* not the *New York Times*, not to mention that you live in the reddest state in the nation. That's the reality."

"But—"

"There's one more thing," Charlie says, holding up his hand to stop me. "I know this is hard for you to hear, but there's a good possibility the army's telling the truth on this one—somebody just flubbed up and Heber paid the price."

"Well, you'd kind of like to think the army would have some safeguards in place for such a possibility, wouldn't you?"

"I'm sorry, Dickie. Go to Clayton. Be with your family."

I TURN DOWN the rutted dirt road in Clayton intending to drive directly to the Bar C before facing George, but an army vehicle

parked in front of my childhood home causes me to stop in hopes of
preventing yet another death—that of the young soldier reaching out
to knock on George's front door. According to Alma, they had already sent an army chaplain, who suggested that a service might be
Dad's civic duty; the community needed closure. Dad promptly and
not too gently escorted the young chaplain off his property.

I pull around to the back side of the house and enter through the
makeshift plywood kitchen door my father had put up to cover a hole
he'd cut into the wall with a chain saw in 1969 after my mother had
complained one too many times that "it sure would be nice to sweep
dirt out the door like normal people." As I walk in, Dad slams the
wall phone back into its cradle with precision and force. That phone
had taken a beating over the years and was seemingly indestructible.
I often thought the government should use it in some kind of weapons-
testing program.

"Who was that?"

"Alma. I suppose she sent you out here to talk sense into this
crazy old son of a bitch."

"Yep."

He grunts, grabs a John Deere ball cap off a hook, and pushes
past me out the back door, oblivious to the incessant knocking on the
front door. On the porch I find a young starched and pressed soldier—
must be about nineteen, looks about fourteen. He sticks both arms
straight out toward me holding a tightly taped box, the words *this side
up* upside down on the side facing me.

"Is this the Sinfield residence?" he drawls.

"It is. What's this?"

"Don't rightly know, ma'am. I'm just the delivery boy."

After I sign in five different places, he swings around smartly and
walks away in a perfect straight line, then turns back sharply and
nods before dipping behind the steering wheel of the car. I set the box
on the kitchen table and cut the tape. Inside I find a letter from an
army general—"sorry for your loss . . . matter of public safety . . . sure

you'll understand . . ."—and a smaller box marked HAZARDOUS. DO NOT OPEN, which I promptly open.

I stare into the plastic-lined box. A person's ashes hold absolutely nothing of the person they came from. Missing is the nasal twang Heber had acquired about the same time Dad moved us to the ranch, and perfected, much to my father's vexation, over the next forty years. Missing is the flowered Hawaiian shirt he wore and the Jimmy Buffett CD he listened to when he moved sprinkler pipe. Missing are the two ex-wives and one estranged daughter. Missing is the tune he whistled every time he looked across the west desert to the Onaqui Mountains or caught a whiff of sage and cedar on a spring day as he rode through his herd. The ashes will not satisfy George; he'll doubt their authenticity. But whether or not they're actually Heber's ashes doesn't much matter as far as I can see.

My old bedroom—still called the pig room—holds all of my mother's belongings that hadn't been touched since the day she died. I climb over a stack of boxes to the light switch then rummage around with a specific type of container in mind. My mother never threw anything out; she had to have at least twenty of those decorative tin cans that once held cookies or fudge or divinity, probably all three. After casting aside all Santa and Easter-bunny designs, I find one that seems appropriate enough to hold a person's ashes: peacocks and feathers in blues and greens. The tin can had likely been passed from one woman to another—every time someone was ill, every time someone's daughter had a baby, every time someone had a death in the family—until it had passed through the fingers of every woman in the Clayton Ward Relief Society. That seems fitting for a man who spent his entire life nestled among those women.

As I climb back over some boxes to shut off the light, I notice they have DICKIE scrawled across them in my mother's handwriting. I had never seen them before. Actually I hadn't been in the pig room more than a handful of times since I'd moved away. After Mom got ill, I drove out to Clayton once a week to see her but seldom spent the night. Prior to her illness, I generally avoided Clayton, holding firmly to the adage that one could never go home again. Instead, Mom and Bev spent every other Tuesday in Salt Lake City seeing movies and generally snooping into my life over the dinner they always had prepared and waiting in my kitchen when I got home from work. Even now, on the evening of the second Tuesday of every month, I still find Bev in my kitchen mashing potatoes or slicing a roast when I walk through the door, cleanly eliminating any need I have to be in Clayton.

I had never paid any attention to the accumulating boxes in the pig room because I assumed they held images of my sour little face— on the back of a horse, clinging to the lead rope of a steer, dressed up like a child version of Dale Evans—events I didn't care to experience a second time. I look around for boxes labeled ANNIE. Hers would be worth scavenging. She was one of those kids who took care of her things, and a box of hers would surely hold unscathed treasures of the sixties—troll dolls, Beatle albums, and love beads—but every box within reach has my name on it.

The top "Dickie" box is stuffed beyond capacity, so I nudge the lid aside with my knee. As expected, a scrapbook rests on top, but it unexpectedly does not contain my childhood pictures but instead newspaper articles written by me. Underneath this scrapbook, five more. A note in my mother's handwriting is taped to the front of each one: "Dickie Sinfield: August 12, 1983 through December 28, 1983," and so forth. I knock the lids off four other boxes—all loaded with similar scrapbooks. My mother had apparently cut out every article I'd written since the day I started working at the paper—even back in the beginning when I covered nothing more significant than the grower of the largest pumpkin at the state fair—and pasted them in a scrapbook.

I tip the lid off a sixth box and newspapers spill onto the floor. As my mother's illness progressed, she had clipped the articles but never put them into a scrapbook. I can imagine her at the kitchen table fretting over this unfinished project. During the final year of her illness, she hadn't even clipped the articles—just folded the entire section of newspaper into the box. On top of the stack lay a neat bundle, clipped together—the series I had finished just weeks before her death in the spring of 2005: *The Cowboy Myth: How Romance Destroyed the American West*, a five-part series by Dickie Sinfield.

In the series I wrote about alkali flats created from flood irrigation, about groundwater depletion by more than a half trillion gallons a year, about land sunk thirty or more feet from irrigation pumping, and about massive erosion in national forests from overgrazing, all to satiate the rugged, individualistic western rancher who insists—even after six generations of evidence to the contrary—that the arid west adapt to him instead of the other way around. Before the series was published, I had prepared myself for the fallout, prepared myself to be shunned by the town of Clayton, especially Dad, who would view the articles as nothing short of treason, but it never happened. I assumed then that Mom's illness and death mitigated his resentment, but as I looked at the newspaper in my hand, I was certain Mom made sure he never saw it. The only word I heard from Clayton was an e-mail from Bev—*Read your series about ranching, interesting ideas. You sure can string words together. See you for dinner next week. Bev.* And a later e-mail—*Saw that your ranching series got picked up by the NYTs. Good for you. Bev.* The following week, Bev set before me a T-bone steak the size of my head, a baked potato near as big, and a stack of research and articles published by Utah State Extension Services—byline Bev Christensen—on planting, growing, and grazing imported wheatgrass sustainably in Ganoa County. She fairly gave me the points I'd solidly made in the articles then went about feeding the rest of my words to me with dinner and wine.

I rinse the decorative tin in the kitchen sink, transfer Heber's ashes, and leave it sitting on the table next to the letter from the general and a note telling Dad the ashes had been delivered by the

general himself. I throw the "This Side Up" box in my car along with
the "Hazardous Materials" box and head over to the Bar C.

BEV SITS ON THE TOP STEP of her back porch staring into
the Onaqui Mountains over the chugging sprinklers watering the alfalfa fields. The familiarity of her pose—feet planted firmly on the
lower step, elbows lodged on knees, both hands wrapped around a coffee mug, torso leaning toward the land—tugs at me. At the end of
long summer days when Mom returned from her job at Dugway and
Bev had showered off hay leaves and dust, I often found the two of
them sitting there, shoulders and knees bumping, deep in conversation or laughing until tears streamed. Ruth was everything Bev was
not: Ruth was soft; Bev was hard. Ruth was vulnerable; Bev was im-
penetrable. Ruth cried softly; Bev laughed loudly. From the first day
she walked into our kitchen to comfort my mother the night I got lost
in the foothills, Bev loved Ruth with a fierce and protective obsession.

If Bev were anyone other than Bev Clark Christensen, talk of her
love for Ruth Sinfield would have passed over the bars of every drinking establishment in Ganoa County as regularly as the diluted beer
they served. But because she *was* Bev Christensen, her love for my
mother was simply established, accepted, and taken for granted. Prior
to Bev coming into our lives, it was always Alma's job to console Ruth
when she needed consoling, to commiserate with Ruth when she
needed to vent. When Bev entered the scene, she and Alma got
into a bit of a tug-of-war with my mother, but they knew she was fragile enough to pull apart easily, leaving them tumbling backward. They
both recognized this, but Bev's love involved obsession, so she was unable to back off. Alma's did not, so she let go—or at least loosened her
grip—saving them all. Although Bev was a couple of years younger
than Ruth, for four decades, she hovered over her like a mother cow
with a calf.

Whenever I found them on the back porch, they'd always welcome me, motion me to the bottom step, where I could lean back against their legs, although I sensed the conversation changed when I arrived. I assume they continued this ritual long after I left Clayton, likely up until my mother's death two years ago.

The young woman I first glimpsed through a crack in the door, the woman who mesmerized me with her splendid features of sureness and strength, is still recognizable nearly forty-five years later in Bev's chiseled face. Over the years, Bev and Mom had both aged directly into the beauty they held in their thirties. Mom's radiance was steeped in softness, and in her last years she accumulated it like she'd been dipped in smooth, white chocolate each year of her life. When her hands became crippled, she let her hair go natural and it fell in gentle white swirls around her neck and face, both of which were covered with exquisite skin that yielded to its lines and crevices like a lake yields to its rocky shore. Her breasts and hips both became fuller and softer with every year—her limbs also—all of which seemed applied to her by an artist, exactly right, never disproportional, never clunky or awkward. Yet she never got any bigger; she simply got softer, as if an outer layer were added and an inner layer stripped away at exactly the same moment.

Bev's beauty is carved from stone—hard and certain—each year the edges made darker and deeper by the seasons she knows intimately. Her muscles attach to her bones like lichen to a rock, and her skin easily covers the muscles like a worn pair of one-owner chaps, wrapping around with little coaxing at all. Her gray hair grows protectively over her skull with wiry intensity, stopping just short of her eyes, which have also darkened and deepened each year. She wears a black tank top, jeans, and work boots, exactly what she wore the first time I saw her.

"Sandwich wrapped up in the fridge for you," she says. "Roast beef."

"Rare, I hope."

"Course."

I sit on the step next to her and pull at the wax paper around the sandwich. The sun is strong, but a breeze from the west brings a fine, cooling mist from the sprinklers.

"Sandwich looks fresh," I say.

"I figured you'd show up today."

I nod. The woman has always known me better than I know myself and I've learned to accept it. She hadn't called once since Heber died, knowing I would detest having to indulge well-meaning folks intent on comforting the distraught sister of the deceased, and knowing—with staggering precision—how many days I'd need to drive myself around the point of the Oquirrh Mountains into Ganoa County.

"Seen George?" she asks.

"We passed each other in the kitchen about an hour ago. Didn't have much to say."

"I don't think he's said more'n two sentences to anybody since he got the news. Cept that army chaplain they sent over. I hear he got an earful."

"The army delivered up Heber—least I think it's Heber, although there'll be no convincing George of it."

"Ashes?"

I nod.

"I figured they'd do as much. I'm gonna call the girls and tell em to plan a service," Bev said, referring to the women of the Clayton Ward Relief Society. "George can come or not, but we're gonna give Heber a service. I know Heber wouldn't much care one way or the other, but folks round here need it. In a place this small, one person drops out suddenly, makes you feel like you're walking around with one leg shorter than the other. Folks need to regroup. When's Annie coming?"

"I'm picking her up at the airport tomorrow."

"Good. You talked to Stumpy?"

"No."

"Think you might?"

I shrug.

IN THE TWO YEARS preceding my mother's death, I went to Clayton every Saturday. Mom and I would walk across the fields and lose ourselves in the juniper forest at the foot of the Onaquis. One summer day we started up the hill at the far end of the cow pasture and found a flat rock in the shade at the first plateau. I pulled cheese, apples, and a pocketknife from my pack.

"Bless your heart. I didn't think to bring anything today."

"You feeling all right, Mom?"

"I can't seem to find my breath."

It had been a year since she had been diagnosed with congestive heart failure, ten years since she had been diagnosed with lupus. Our walks had been getting consistently shorter each week.

"We don't need to go any farther," I said. "Let's just sit here awhile."

"You know, Dickie, I'm pretty much done with this life."

"I know you are, Mom."

"I'm not complaining—I've been blessed with a lot in this life—but I think the next one will be much better."

"Yeah, if I believed what you Mos believe, I'd be raring to go. Don't know why any of you want to stick around here with the promised life you have waiting for you."

"You could have it, too, you know."

"Think they'd still take me?"

"I think they might if you repented and prayed real hard—and if Bev intervened on your behalf like she did for me."

"Yeah, but that only gets me as far as the Clayton ward house. Think she has any clout higher up?"

"I wouldn't doubt it."

The hot summer wind blew through her thin, white hair, which had not been sprayed or ratted in the last decade, revealing several bald spots the size of quarters.

"Isn't that a mess?" she said, looking over the valley.

"The incinerator?"

"Well, that, too, but I was talking about our place."

"Oh," I said, gazing down on the slumping barn and patchwork house. "Didn't it always look that way?"

"Pretty much."

She smiled and grew quiet then placed a hand on my knee. Purple veins protruded from the claw bejeweled with a single gold band.

"I'm sorry, Dickie."

"For what?"

"For your life."

"Lordy, Mom, you make it sound like I have the most pathetic life in the world."

"Are you happy?"

"I suppose so."

"That's what I'm sorry for—that I never taught you how to be happy."

"I don't know if that's something you can teach a person, Mom. Maybe we all have to figure it out for ourselves."

"Think you have it figured out?"

"Oh, hell no."

"Think you ever will?"

"I don't know. I suppose I'm as happy as the next person. Were you ever happy?"

"That's what I'm sorry for. That I never figured it out in time to hand the gift down to you."

"And Heber and Annie?"

"Heber and Annie found their way—I always knew they would."

"Mom—"

"It's all about love, you know."

She took a slice of apple and matched it with a slice a cheese before taking a bite. She chewed slowly, nodding slightly as if acknowledging an unseen presence. I watched her closely, having always loved that dreamy quality of hers, the ability to drift away at any given moment in any situation.

"Passionate, crazy, intense, romantic love. That's what it's all about, Dickie. You ever loved anyone or anything that way?"

I shrugged.

"I know you love your job and I know you're good at it, but that's different. Sometimes I think you might be a little too good at it."

"And that's a bad thing?"

"It is when you use it to crowd out every other part of life."

She looked at me, silently challenging the protest she assumed I'd make. I stayed quiet until she gazed over the valley again.

"Well, Michael and I—"

"I know you care about Michael, Dickie, and I know he cares about you. He's a good man. But the two of you—"

I let her struggle with the words, not wanting to hear what I knew she wanted to say.

"Well, never mind," she said. "You and Michael watch out for each other and there's something to be said for that."

I nodded and threw a slice of apple away from us to entice a crow to dip down for it. Mom grabbed my arm as I reached for another slice.

"But, Dickie," Mom said with a sudden note of urgency in her voice, "playing it safe is a shitty way to live a life."

"Mom!" I turned to her, stunned. It had been more than three decades since I'd heard a profane word slip from her lips. She ignored my reaction and continued unabated.

"Ever loved so intensely, Dickie, that it enhanced every one of your senses, changed the way you moved over the earth?"

"I don't know, Mom."

"Oh, you'd know it!" she said, unconsciously rubbing my knee. "See that rotted wood fence we just climbed over?" She pointed back toward the house. "You'd smell that rotting wood long before you reached it; you'd see the way the light holds its shimmering grays and wispy whites like you'd never seen it before."

She took hold of my hand and lightly touched the center of my palm.

"If you'd ever loved that way, Dickie, that old fence post would leave an imprint against the tender skin of your palm, jagged and silky. You'd hear it creak and groan and squeal as you climbed over it. You'd know it, Dickie."

She worked her way through another slice of apple then turned her body toward me, held my chin in her hand, and turned my face so our eyes met.

"Ever loved so deeply that half your body was torn away when that love was gone?"

I pulled my face away from hers.

"They say that isn't love at all," I said. "They say that's obsession or infatuation. It can't last."

"Only those afraid of that kind of love call it something else. It doesn't last because we don't allow it to last. We're scared to death of it. Instead of pouring every last bit of ourselves into it, which is what it demands, we push it away, build protective walls, keep ourselves *safe*. We tell ourselves it's unhealthy, can't be real. What could be more real than loving with everything you have—every emotion, every thought, every heartbeat, every inch of your body? What could be more real than that?"

"What happens when the love isn't returned? How do you protect yourself from that?"

"You don't, Dickie. It doesn't matter. What matters is how *you* love."

She was stunning that day sitting on a rock in Utah's west desert, passion gushing from her seventy-seven-year-old, sagging, impaired body, moisture running through the soft creases in her face. I scooted closer to her, wrapped both arms around her small, hunched shoulders, put my face in her hair, and inhaled her cheap strawberry-scented shampoo. Her hands lay lifeless in her lap, folded into each other as if by accident. I imagined them caressing the top pole of a rotted wood fence; I remembered them sunk deep into a mixture of raw ground beef and cracker crumbs; I knew they had stroked the inside thigh of a lover.

"Why didn't I teach you to love like that?" she said, tears dripping over her top lip.

"What makes you think you didn't?" I whispered.

She broke from my embrace and dug a well-used Kleenex from the pocket of her stretch jeans. Her legs hung over the rock like a child's, ending in a pair of inexpensive pink sneakers.

"You're almost fifty years old, Dickie, and you and Michael have been together for a lot of years. But you don't love him that way."

"That's doesn't mean I'm incapable of that sort of love."

She scrutinized my face, then shifted back around so our shoulders touched and put a craggy hand on my thigh.

"You're right about that. I think you're capable; I just don't think you're willing to let that sort of love flow out of you."

"Makes a person a little bit vulnerable, don't you think?"

"Sure does. That's the beauty of it, Dickie. Loving like that splays you wide open to the universe. Stuff comes gushing in like monsoon rains over slickrock."

"People get killed by flash floods all the time, Mom."

"Open yourself up to the flow, Dickie. You won't drown. I can promise you that."

"Have you ever loved like that, Mom?" I asked, but I already knew the answer. Her hand softened on my leg, her face relaxed, and her body yielded its passion to the desert around us.

CHAPTER SEVEN

When school started up again a few weeks after we moved to Clayton, I made the grim discovery that I had two transportation alternatives: ride to school with Dad or take the bus. At Whittier Elementary (a.k.a. Shittier Elementary), both were prime targets for ridicule from those strolling to school without parental oversight. Heber chose to ride with Dad; Annie chose the bus, so I did the same. Stumpy was already at the bus stop—halfway between his house and ours—when Annie and I arrived.

"Where's everybody else?" I asked.

"The only ranches on this side are yours, ours, and Bev's, and Bev don't have any kids. Everybody else gets picked up on the other side of the valley. Only five of us ride from Clayton—seven now, I guess."

"They run a bus for only seven of us?" Annie asked.

"No, they pick up a bunch more in Warner," Stumpy said.

The town of Warner between Clayton and Ganoa was geographically much smaller than Clayton but held many more families—most of the fathers working at the mines in the Oquirrh Mountains. When the bus stopped and the doors swung open, I was surprised to see Bev Christensen behind the wheel.

"All aboard."

"Hi, Bev," Stumpy said.

"Stumpy. Dickie. Annie." Bev nodded with each pronouncement

of our names as we climbed up the stairs. "Annie and Dickie, how's your mom doing?"

"Fine," Annie said. "She started her new job out at Dugway last week."

"How does she like it?"

"Seems to like it fine," Annie said.

"How are you girls getting along there without her?"

"Just fine," Annie answered.

"Dickie?"

I nodded.

"Well, you tell your mom hello for me. I'll give her a call in a few days and see if she needs anything."

On that first day of school, I set out to do whatever I could to protect my school life, since my home life had been blown to smithereens. I assumed that protection would mostly require shunning Stumpy Nelson—bus rider and cold-lunch eater—in public, and sneaking on and off the bus without drawing attention to myself. I wasn't sure how to do that, but I was quite sure Annie knew how, so I'd just stick close to her.

As we drove in to the school grounds, my heart sank to see Holly walking our old familiar route deep in conversation with Marlene Franklin. Stumpy and Annie both waited for the bus to empty before they got up to leave, so I did the same. Annie flitted away from the proximity of the bus like a sparrow from a cat. I, on the other hand, dropped the three notebooks I carried down the steps of the bus and onto the curb just as Marlene and Holly reached me.

"Oh, you ride the bus now!" Marlene squealed, and bent to help me pick up my papers.

"Stump, help Dickie pick up her stuff," Bev said to Stumpy, who was patiently standing on the bus steps behind me. He bent to help.

"I don't *have* to ride the bus," I informed Marlene. "I *want* to."

Holly stepped around me and Marlene and stuck her head in the bus door.

"Well, hey, Stumpy."

"Hey, Holly."

I reached to pick up the last few papers, one of which was under Holly's left foot.

"Holly, either bend yourself at the waist to help or move on outta the way," Bev said.

Holly and Bev locked eyes. On the night I provoked a search party, it had taken Bev about thirty seconds after Stumpy and I entered the kitchen to figure out that Holly had sent folks out to search for me in every direction except the right one. After that, Bev and Holly developed a healthy wariness of each other, but it didn't concern me one way or the other. Holly spent many weekends and even some school nights at the ranch. She seemed to fit into our family better than I did, dropping into the kitchen to set the table just a split second before Mom called for us and gathering Dad's work gloves from a fence post where he'd forgotten them. Once I recognized Holly's obsession with my new western life, with Clayton, and with Stumpy Nelson, I realized my fears of losing my best friend the same way I had lost my curb-and-gutter life were unfounded, and I made it through the third grade relatively unscathed.

AT THE END OF THE school year after Dad got all his grades turned in, on a sunny spring Saturday, he called upon the entire family for a day of "working the herd." Apparently Annie translated that to mean "going to the beach." She donned culottes and sandals and filled a bag with suntan lotion and books. I expected Mom to put up a protest, pointing out—as she did every time Dad tried to get her to ride out and check the cows with him—that she was doing her part to support this TV western by working at Dugway. Instead, she simply walked outside looking like a freshly painted Easter egg in lavender pedal pushers and a matching polka-dot top, looked up at the blue sky, and said, "You picked a lovely day to burn a few hides, George," then tossed a lawn chair into the bed of the pickup.

That first year at the ranch, I remained stuck somewhere between Ganoa and Clayton, an awkward fusion of cow pasture and rose garden, and it showed in my clothing choices: a sundress pulled on over a pair of jeans or cotton shorts with a long-sleeved snap-button western shirt. That particular day, I emerged from my bedroom in the latter, and was promptly sent back by Dad to trade the shorts for jeans, but Mom took pity on me and snuck the shorts into her bag.

We showed up at the Nelson Ranch at 7 A.M. with two saddled horses and our new Lazy S branding iron. Bev had already unloaded two horses and a load of firewood from her truck and trailer and downed two cups of coffee. Merv kept saying it sure would be fine to have the extra help, but every one of us Sinfields knew that Merv, Bev, and Stumpy could vaccinate, brand, waddle, dehorn, tag, and castrate with about a quarter of the hoopla we produced that day.

Dad, Heber, Merv, Bev, Stumpy, and I were to ride out and gather the cattle. Alma and Holly were assigned to make a pot of sloppy joes and all the fixings, and Annie and Mom were given fire duty. Somehow in the progression of our ranching life, I had been identified as a cowpuncher, and everyone had gotten it into their heads that I should spend a great deal of time on the back of a horse. In the year since we had moved to Clayton, Merv conjured up more duties for me that required horseback riding than I thought possible—checking irrigation ditches, checking on pregnant cows, checking on fences, checking to see if that damn bull had crossed the cattle guard again at the end of his property, riding up on the ridge to make a count of his herd. Sometimes he'd send me out with Stumpy, but lots of times he'd put me on his old mare, Goldie, and send me out alone. He said we made a good pair—Goldie and me—and I guess we did. She was easy and calm and didn't seem to mind that I wasn't. She knew when it was time to turn toward home, and she'd pick her way through sage and cedars to arrive at the corrals a few minutes before sunset. Sometimes I accomplished what Merv sent me out to do and sometimes I didn't. He never yelled or swore at me, never even looked disappointed, just said, "Oh, we'll get it next time" as he met me at the corrals, lifted the saddle and blanket off Goldie in one swoop, and handed me a brush to wipe her down.

Sometimes I'd talk Mom into going along and we'd amble into the mountains, her behind me with her breasts tight against my back so she could wrap her arms around me and hang on to the saddle horn. Once we'd gone far enough for her to relax a little, she'd let go and comb her fingers through my hair, pulling it into a ponytail, twisting it, getting the snarls out, and releasing it again. "I don't know anything about handling a horse, Dickie," she'd tell me. "You're in charge."

Close to seven months had passed since she'd gone to work at Dugway, and she'd been whistling and humming around the house for the last six of them, thumbing through fashion magazines, trying new hairstyles, and acting as if this were exactly the life she had envisioned for herself. As soon as the snow began to melt, she'd sing my name when she walked into the house after work, take me by the hand, and we'd walk as far into the mountains as we could get before darkness fell. She'd tell me the names of plants just beginning to come to life, dropping to her knees to sniff an early blossom or plunge her hands into a cold stream, giggling with joy.

"Don't you miss your rosebushes, Mama?" I'd ask.

She'd smile at me.

"Do you miss Ganoa, Dickie?"

"Don't you?"

"Well, I miss the ladies I used to play canasta with."

"That's all?"

"No, I miss other things. But . . ."

"But what, Mama?"

"But nothing," she'd say, gently tugging on my ponytail. "Come on, I'll race you home."

On branding day, I climbed on Goldie as usual as she stood with her head low, eyes drooping, barely flinching as she registered the weight of my body with only a slight bob of her head. Since Bev had brought two horses, we wound up with an extra. Holly strode forward

declaring that she knew nothing of making sloppy joes and that
Alma could take care of things in the kitchen. Holly'd be put to better use rounding up cattle. Alma, who had a soft spot for Holly, confirmed this fact.

"This little horse hasn't been ridden for a while," Bev said. "I
don't feel comfortable putting him under you, Holly."

"Well, I'm sure I can handle him."

Her fearlessness captivated me but did little to convince Bev.

"Stumpy, why don't you take this horse a mine. Dickie, you take
Ol' Yeller there," Bev said, pointing to the tall, muscular buckskin
Stumpy had just dismounted, "and, Holly, you take Goldie. She's so
damn gentle a two-month-old baby could stay on her."

Holly was none too pleased with the comparison to a baby and I
was none too pleased to get off Goldie and straddle Stumpy's prancing, high-headed horse, but we all moved as directed. Merv winked
at me.

"Ol' Yeller will settle down soon as we get moving," he said quietly. "He's just anxious to get to work."

Although Holly had only been on a horse a few times in her life,
she rode with the same intensity she exhibited for every other activity.
She yanked up the reins, pulled Goldie's head around to the right,
clicked her tongue, and dug her heels into the mare's sides. Goldie
popped her head up and put her ears back. Holly pulled her feet out of
the stirrups so she could get plenty of motion into her kicks and started
whapping both legs against Goldie's sides.

"If you and that horse are gonna fight over who's the boss, Holly,
I'm putting my money on the mare," Bev said. "Put your feet back in
the stirrups and give her her head. She knows how to bring cows in."

Holly glowered at Bev but acquiesced when Goldie started backing
up instead of going forward. Merv paired us off to gather cows so we'd
make a clean sweep around three pastures—Dad with Heber, me with
Stumpy, and Holly with Bev. Merv was on gates. But as we started out,
it became apparent Holly intended to ride with me and Stumpy.

"Bev's gonna need some help bringing cows in from that lower pasture," Stumpy said, and took off at a gallop to catch up with Bev.

"Hey, wait!" I called after him. "We don't even know where we're supposed to go!"

"Well," Holly said, "where's he going?"

"We're supposed to be paired up."

"But I want to ride with you and Stumpy; I want to ride with my best friend."

A minute later Stumpy came back and pulled his horse up next to mine. "Bev says for you to go with her," he growled. "Holly can ride with me."

Holly smiled sweetly again, and I fell back to turn off and join up with Bev, who sat on her motionless horse, both forearms folded over the saddle horn.

"Give him a nudge, Dickie," she hollered. "We've got a lot to get done today."

I kicked Ol' Yeller into a run. He felt different from Goldie, choppy and hard. I grabbed hold of the saddle horn.

"You look good up there, girl," Bev lied when I reached her. I was impressed with Bev Christensen to the point of speechlessness. She occupied her tan, muscular body as if she had never stood in front of a mirror examining herself as I had seen my mother do—lifting her breasts, drawing the loose skin on her belly around to her sides, and pulling her face toward her ears. She seemed oblivious of her situation, as if she had set out to run a ranch the size of the Bar C by herself. She exhibited no fear of the world around her. I couldn't imagine a tear ever rolling down Bev Christensen's perfectly carved face. My mother was a fretter, but when Bev said, "Ain't no use frettin about it," no matter what "it" was, you got the feeling she was probably right.

"So how do you like it out here in Clayton, Dickie?" she asked. I shrugged. "Been getting along okay?" I shrugged again. "Well, this is gonna be a long ride out to the south pasture if I'm the only one talking." She paused. "Course folks around here think I have plenty to say—usually too much—but I'd just as soon have someone responding on the other side. Less, a course, I'm talking to ol Darrel Summers. Then I'd just as soon he'd shut up and listen for a change."

She smiled at me. I wanted to please her, wanted her to like me, wanted some words to come out of my mouth, but none did.

"Damn, Dickie, you do make it hard."

"I'm sorry."

"Lordy, girl, you've got nothing to be sorry for. It'd likely do a girl like you well to strike those two words from her vocabulary for a while. Some folks need to learn those words; other folks need to forget em."

"I don't know what to say," I mumbled.

"Well, folks round here might be right, maybe I do talk too much. There ain't nothing wrong with a little silence from time to time."

We rode in silence until Bev started whistling a tune. Ol' Yeller strode with a purpose and I loosened into the saddle. Without being aware of it, I softly began to sing the words to the tune Bev whistled.

"Come and sit by my side if you love me . . . do not hasten to bid me adieu . . ."

Bev's face broke into a grin and she joined me. "Just remember the Red River Valley . . . and the cowboy who loved you so true."

We stumbled through as many verses as we could then both threw our heads back and sang the chorus big and loud one more time. ". . . just remember the Red River Valleeeey . . . and the cowboy who loved you so truuuue."

"Why, Dickie Sinfield! You don't have aspirations of being a country-western singer, do you?"

"No, Annie says I have the worst singing voice she's ever heard and that even in church I should be singing as quietly as I can so as not to draw attention to myself."

"Well, big sisters are good to have—and I think Annie's a good one—but here's a little piece a news for you: they ain't always right."

"You think I have a good singing voice?"

"I think it don't matter. I think you should sing at the top a your lungs whenever the desire rises to the surface."

"I could never do that."

"You just did. And you did a damn fine job of it."

"Yeah, but that's out here where nobody can hear me."

"That's the beauty a being out here, Dickie. Ain't you figured that out yet?"

I shrugged.

"Lordy, don't start shrugging on me again, girl, or we'll have to sing another song. We don't want to spook them cows and send em stampeding into the mountains."

I shook my head.

"I'm kidding, Dickie. How about we play a game?"

I eyed her suspiciously. "What kind of game?"

"Twenty questions."

"I don't know how to play."

"Well, I really don't either, but here's how you play according to Bev Christensen: we take turns asking each other questions. Anything at all, nothing is too personal, nothing is off-limits, and we have to answer honestly. Game?"

"Okay."

"You start."

"I don't want to."

"Okay. I'll start. Who's your best friend?"

"Gosh, Bev, that's easy. You already know the answer to that. It's Holly."

"Why is Holly your best friend?"

"Because she is! She's always been my best friend since before kindergarten. Isn't it my turn to ask you a question?"

"Right. Forgot. Shoot."

"You ever been in love since your husband died?"

"Whoa, girl, you shoot from the hip, don't you? Don't waste any time with those mealy, pussyfooted questions. You go straight for the jugular."

"Sorry."

"There's that word again! No need to be sorry. I like your style, Dickie Sinfield. I can respect a girl who knows how to be direct. Well, I'm not quite sure how to answer that. Love is a difficult thing. Lots of different ways to love someone, you know."

"You don't have to answer."

"Yes I do. I'm the one that wanted to play this game, you see, that means I have to play by my own rules, which means I have to answer your question. So here goes. The answer is yes. I have, in fact, been in love since my husband died."

"How long ago did he die? Who were you in love with?"

"Whoa, hold on there. I do believe it's my turn to ask a question now."

"Oh yeah."

"Let's see. Okay. I have one. When you gonna cut your dad some slack and stop being mad at him for moving you out to Clayton?"

I wasn't sure how to answer or if she even really wanted an answer.

"Remember the rules," she said. "You have to answer."

"But we were fine in Ganoa! We had a good house with a lawn and a driveway! I don't know why we had to move out here to this place!"

"Dickie, I can't claim to really know your dad, but I do understand a man who needs some earth to walk on, and this basin offers that and then some. You have the Oquirrh Mountains standing guard here in front a you, the Sheeprocks nudging up on your left, the Stansburys snuggling in on your right, and the Onaquis watching your back. Dickie, your dad coulda done a whole lot worse by you kids than moving you out here to live nestled in these mountains, where you can sing at the top a your lungs and there ain't no one to tell you otherwise."

I looked glumly straight ahead as we rode toward a herd of Hereford cattle.

"I don't mean to upset you, Dickie. I just have a hunch you might come to sorta like this place if you give it half a chance. At the very least, do me a favor, will you?"

"What?"

"Get to know this place a little. In fact, that's a good project for you this summer. Get outta your house, get on a horse, and get into the Stansburys and the Onaquis—even out to the Sheeprocks south a my land. Let the place get inside you a little. If you do that and still don't like it, then fine, when you're old enough I'll help you pack your boxes myself and we'll move you back into Ganoa or even all the way into Salt Lake City. Deal?"

"What if I get lost again?"

"Take Goldie or one a my horses. Every one a mine or Merv's horses can find their way out of those mountains and back to the barn in a blinding blizzard."

"I thought you weren't supposed to go up into the mountains alone. In school they taught us we should always let our parents know exactly where we are and not stray too far from our own yards—ever since Austin Rigby got lost and they found his body in the ditch."

"First off, Austin Rigby was three years old and somebody shoulda been watching that boy. Secondly, folks have a tendency to overreact and pass foolish rules every time something like that happens. Third, those rules are for townfolk, Dickie. They don't apply to us. It's that simple."

"But Mom worries about me."

"That she does. Tell you what. You spend some time over at my place this summer, you can ride and explore from there. That way your mama don't have to wonder where you've gone. Better yet, take

Stumpy out with you. He can show you some things and some places that are hiding up in those mountains that none a us old folks have discovered. Ain't no way you'll get lost then."

"I don't want to go with Stumpy."

Bev laughed. "I guess a girl your age needs another girl for a best friend, but Lordy, I do question your judgment on that one. Okay, leave Stumpy home. Might be good for you to spend some time alone anyway. Deal?"

"I guess so. Is it my turn to ask a question now?"

"Shoot."

"Who were you in love with?"

"Sorry, girl, time to work. I'm gonna circle round and pick up that cow and calf over there. You just keep riding right up this fence line and pick up everything as you go."

Before I could protest, Bev turned off and was gone. I rode toward the cattle, worried that I would make a mistake and scatter them in all directions, but I soon realized Ol' Yeller and the cows knew exactly what was going on. I was simply along for the ride.

"LORDY, THAT'S A LOT a smoke for a little brandin fire," Bev said as we met up again and pushed about forty head toward Merv's corrals. "Hope your mama and sister haven't burned Merv's barn down."

I knew Bev was joking, so I tried to look calm, but I'd never seen Mom or Annie build a fire before in my life. Neither of them showed a bit of apprehension this morning as we rode out, though, both prancing around in their colorful spring wardrobes as if they were going to a ladies' luncheon.

From a ways out we could see Mom spread out in a lounge chair just outside the corrals, sandals kicked into the dirt, pedal pushers rolled up above her knees, blouse flapping open in the breeze to reveal a white, lacy bra. Alma sat upright beside her in an aluminum-and-vinyl lawn chair wearing a floppy straw hat, a checkered red-and-white blouse, and jeans cut off just below her knees—"the most fitting outfit I could find for the occasion," she had pronounced. Annie circled the fire, alternately poking it with a long stick and stooping to shoo flies off her calves.

"Looks like your mama's got the right idea," Bev said, smiling. "Don't she look like she belongs in some glossy edition of *Better Homes and Gardens*."

Not really, I thought. I had never seen half-dressed women in any magazine. As we rode up, Mom scrambled to button herself up.

"Don't disturb yourself for our sake, Ruth," Bev said, glancing over her shoulder. "Looks like the guys are gonna be another five minutes or so." Bev eyed the diminished wood pile. "Annie, I think you've got enough wood on there. You just as well stick those irons along the fence into that nice fire you got going."

The morning sun beat down on my jeans and booted feet, and my stomach clutched when I got a whiff of Sea & Ski suntan lotion. Last year this kind of day would have found Holly and me skipping over the lawn sprinkler while Mom basked on the sidelines, blindly rubbing Sea & Ski on her body without removing the soaked cotton balls covering her eyes.

Mom and Alma walked over to greet us as Bev and I pushed the cattle into the holding pen. Mom put her hands around my waist and slid me off Ol' Yeller with a low grunt.

"You're getting too big for me to lift anymore, Dickie," she said, brushing my hair away from my forehead. "When did that happen? How was your ride? Stumpy's horse behave himself?"

"Yep, it was fine."

"Can I get you some lemonade, Bev?" Alma asked.

"Love some, thanks."

"Mama, can I go put some shorts on?"

"Sure, go ahead."

Bev stole Alma's seat, and when I walked out of the house Bev had her right hand resting on Mom's forearm and they both had their heads thrown back, laughing loudly. I'd never witnessed two such oppositely beautiful creatures, and I couldn't comfortably place them both within my limited definition of *woman*. I'd always wanted to be just like my mother until I met Bev. Now I wanted to be just like both of them, but I couldn't fathom how that might work out.

Stumpy and Holly brought more cows in—Holly looking exuberant; Stumpy, glum. White lather glistened between Goldie's hind legs and on top of her withers; her eyes bulged wildly. Holly placed the reins in my outstretched hand as if she were handing Goldie off to a stable boy.

"What happened?" I exclaimed.

"We had a great ride!" she said, grinning. "Didn't we, Stumpy?"

"But . . ." I could feel the tears brimming in my eyes.

"Looks like you two had a helluva ride," Bev said, running her hands over the gelding she had put Stumpy on. "He's got quite a lather going for a short ride over to George's pasture. What the hell happened, Stump?"

"Cows got spooked," Stumpy said somberly.

"What spooked them?" I demanded.

Stumpy shook his head and led the gelding to the shed. I looked to Bev for an answer; she watched Holly fling a log on the fire.

"I get an uneasy feeling about that little girl," Bev said, shaking her head.

"We need to do what we can for her, Bev," Mom said. "She doesn't really have a family, you know."

Bev nodded, still watching Holly.

"Trouble is, I believe she wants this one."

"Well, we'll give her what we can," Mom said.

Bev turned and brushed a speck of dirt from Mom's cheek.

"You do have a streak a goodness runnin through you, Ruth. Dickie, take Goldie over to the shed and brush her down. You know what to do."

"She gonna be okay?"

"Don't she look okay?" Bev said, turning back to watch Holly.

"Goldie will be fine, Dickie," Mom said.

"Oh Lordy yes," Bev said, squeezing my shoulder. "Don't fret your-self over that."

Bev put Holly in charge of tending the fire and making sure the irons stayed hot, but it didn't take Holly long to figure out that Bev had given her the hottest, most miserable job. She soon abandoned the fire for a perch on top of the four-pole fence, where she could watch the festivities in a cool breeze with a glass of lemonade.

Stumpy rode into the holding pen on Merv's horse and cut a cow out from the rest like he was slicing off a pat of butter with a warm knife. Merv ran her up the narrow alley into the squeeze chute, but in his excitement, Heber pulled the head gate closed just a second before she stuck her nose through and she backed down the alley the same time she lifted her tail.

"Goddamn you, old girl!" Merv shouted, scrambling up the fence to get out of her way but not before a stream of runny green shit splat-tered onto his jeans just above his knees. Bev and Stumpy busted out laughing, but Heber looked like he wanted to cry.

"Goddammit, Heber, you're going to have to watch what you're doing," Dad shouted. He was standing next to Bev, both of them holding clipboards.

"Oh, that's bound to happen," Bev said through peels of laughter. "She's a smart old cow—been through that chute too damn many times. Besides, the longest Merv's ever gone without gettin covered in cow shit is only about five cows, ain't it, Stump?"

"Six," Stumpy said. "Last year. Year before that it was two."

"Ever think that might be because you two take the easy jobs?" Merv said, cleaning himself off with a work glove.

"That better not be my glove you're using," Bev said. Merv grinned and slapped the glove on a fence post. "You old son of a bitch."

"Let's try that again, Heber," Merv said, dropping back into the alley behind the cow.

Annie and I had been put in charge of delivering whatever tool Merv called for—syringe, dehorner, irons, or ear tags. The first cow didn't need anything but vaccination, so Annie was refilling the syringe and humming the tune to "Runaround Sue" when Stumpy dragged a small calf out of the corral by a rope around its neck and two dallies around the saddle horn. Merv put one hand on the taut rope about three feet in front of Stumpy's horse, followed it to the end, where the calf fought and bawled for its mother, picked it up by a front leg and a flank, and laid it neatly on the ground with a whomp, knocking the breath out of both the calf and Annie, at which point, Annie vanished.

Merv fell upon the calf and tied three of its legs together with lightning speed. As instructed, Heber held the calf with a knee on its neck while the mother cow paced inside the holding pen, moaning, wild-eyed. When Merv called for the Lazy S branding iron, I panicked, and with shaking legs, delivered up the dehorner.

"Good enough," he said.

Placing the top of the dehorner on the tip of the calf's head next to the ear, Merv pulled the handles apart to snap the cutting edges together, scooping out a chunk, then did the same on the other side.

"I think we got it all the way to the bud," he said as he handed the dehorner back to me. "Hand me that small iron."

I heard him but couldn't find the wherewithal to turn away from the fine stream of blood spurting out of both sides of the calf's head. Bev handed her clipboard off to Dad and pulled a red-hot straight iron out of the fire, touching it to the place where the blood sprayed, stopping it immediately. Bev then handed Merv a full syringe, which he passed back to me after emptying the contents into the calf's neck. I managed to lift my hand and take it. When Merv pressed the Lazy S branding iron into the soft red hair, the calf blew snot into the dust under its nostrils and let out a long, tortured, resigned cry. His

mother met his bawl with one of her own, the most haunting, despairing sound I'd ever heard.

With the smell of burning hair and skin in my nostrils, I bent
forward to study my toes and regain my equilibrium. I straightened
up in time to see Merv fish a pocketknife out of his jeans, loosen the
piggin string around the calf's legs, reach between the two back legs,
and make a cut faster than my brain could register the action. A thin
jet of blood sprayed my bare calves as a small bloody nugget, then
another, popped out from between Merv's fingers and landed near
my left sneaker. I looked at him, alarmed, sure something had gone
horribly wrong. He looked up at me with his usual calm smile and
pulled a plastic squeeze bottle of blood stopper from my limp hand,
although I had no idea I'd been holding it.

"Let er up, Heber," Merv said, slapping Heber on the back. "Good
job." Heber grinned and preened. The calf struggled to its feet, Merv
opened the gate, and the calf staggered back to its mother. I looked
around for my own mother. She lay back in her lawn chair flipping
through a *McCall's* magazine. Alma sat next to her sipping lemonade.
They were both swirling in a haze of heat. I dropped back down to study
my toes, the whir of Stumpy's swinging rope in the air around me.

"Why don't you cut one a our cows out of there, Stump, and give
those branding irons a minute to heat back up," Merv said, eyeing me.

Bev squeezed my shoulders from behind, gently taking the dehorner and syringe from my hands. Then with one hand on my neck,
she got me turned around and walking.

"How you doing, Dickie?"

I didn't answer.

"Why don't you go see if your mom's doing all right."

I looked at Mom, then up at Holly, who surveyed the scene
from her throne atop the fence. Bev and Merv both watched me, a
half-amused and half-worried look on their faces. I'm not sure
which part of that look got to me, but I silently vowed to stay at
my post.

When the sun got high, Mom and Alma set up folding tables under the trees for lunch.

"I'm so hungry I could eat a horse."

"That's a fine spread."

"Hard work sure works up an appetite."

"My breakfast has pretty much wore off."

"I feel like I ain't et fer days."

"Heber, watch your grammar; I'll have some of that potato salad, Alma."

"There's plenty to go around; lots more in the kitchen."

"Dickie, aren't you going to eat something?"

WHEN WE RESUMED work, all had shifted positions inside the corral except me. Heber roped calves and cut cattle out of the herd, which he handled not quite as competently as Stumpy, but well enough to elicit nods of approval from Bev and Merv and eventually from Dad. I watched him sit fully centered in the saddle through every abrupt movement of Merv's cutting horse. Something had changed in him since we moved to the ranch. His face seemed to hold some sort of secret. Stumpy wore that same look—the men they would become already showing behind their transparent boy faces. With Stumpy, the look unnerved me, made me feel like a stupid kid. But when I saw it in Heber while he worked cattle, it comforted me. That's the moment I figured Heber would be all right in our family.

Stumpy helped me with the fire and tools, and Dad took over the branding, dehorning, castrating, and vaccinations. Mom and Alma leaned against the fence, peering into the corral between the third and fourth pole.

"Looks like he's been at that his whole life," Alma said as she watched her brother use the pocketknife Merv offered him to expertly cut a waddle on the right side of a calf's nose before castrating him with the same efficiency. "Seeing George bent over that calf would no doubt bring tears to my father's eyes. He'd likely be crying pride out of one eye and disappointment out of the other, but maybe George was meant for this life after all, Ruth."

Mom didn't respond, just turned her back on the arena and shooed Holly out of her lounge chair.

"This will be the last one for today," Bev said, running a cow into the squeeze chute as the sun dropped behind Stookey Benchmark, the highest point in the Onaquis. "We'll start earlier tomorrow."

I sat on the sole piece of unburned firewood halfway between the hot coals and the chute, leaning against a fence post, feet straight out in front of me like I was in a recliner. My position held high odds of attracting a directive from Dad that I should "move out of the goddamn way," but I was just tired and frazzled enough to risk it. Dad dropped the slats in the squeeze chute, and Stumpy stepped forward with the Lazy S branding iron, red as the sunset at my back. At that point, the sizzle and stench of burning hair and hide barely registered on my brain. Dad handed the iron back to Stumpy. I watched Stumpy take two steps back, watched his left boot come down on the dehorner, watched the dehorner roll under his foot, watched him twist around to catch himself, and watched the branding iron, still hot and sticky with burned cowhide, come down cleanly on the inside of my left calf, which was crossed over my right.

I screamed. Stumpy fell into the dirt. Dad swore. Merv and Heber froze. Bev called Mom's name then picked me up in her arms like she was lifting a puppy. She carried me into Nelson's farmhouse, where she laid me on the bed then rushed to the kitchen. Mom saw the brand on my leg—almost a full S but with the outside edges missing— bubbling up in a rosy lavender on my white skin, going nearly from knee to ankle, and started to sob. Alma pushed her way through the crowd forming at the door, picked a few red cow hairs out of the wound, and pronounced, "Hell, that looks pretty clean, Ruth, she'll be fine. Merv, get me a bowl of warm soapy water, a bowl of cold water, and some baking soda, if you have any."

Merv came in with two bowls, a washcloth floating in one, ice cubes in the other, and a box marked ARM & HAMMER. Mom sat at the top of the bed, my head against her left breast, pulling the hair back away from my eyes as if the wound were on my forehead. Everyone else gathered around the bed as Alma cleaned the burn then dipped the cloth in ice water and placed it over the brand.

"Not much more to be done than that," Alma said. "We'll let it soak awhile with the cold cloth then put some baking soda on it."

Bev came into the room and stood behind Stumpy, her hands on his shoulders. "I boiled some water," she said.

"What for, Bev?" Alma asked.

"I don't know," Bev said, surprised. "I thought you always need boiled water when somebody gets hurt." Then she started laughing and two pink spots appeared on her tan cheeks. That might be the only time in my life I ever saw Bev Christensen flustered.

Stumpy ducked around Bev and went out the back door. She started to follow, but Merv stopped her. "I'll talk to him," he said. "I'm sure he feels like hell about this."

"Oh hell, Merv," Dad said. "It wouldn't have happened if Dickie hadn't been sitting exactly where she shouldn't have been and it wouldn't have happened if she hadn't left the damn dehorner in the dirt and it wouldn't have happened if she had some pants on instead of those goddamn shorts! Tell Stumpy he doesn't have a thing to feel bad about."

"Well, accidents happen," Merv said. "She did a helluva job out there today." He winked and squeezed my toe as he left the room. "You're a natural at this."

Everyone else drifted out except Mom, Alma, and Holly.

"Well, does it hurt much?" Holly asked.

I nodded. "It hurts a lot."

"Well, looks like Stumpy's put his brand on you," she said.

Mom and Alma both chuckled, but Holly wasn't even smiling.

CHAPTER EIGHT

Every summer Holly's mother took her to California to visit Holly's aunt and uncle on her father's side, and every fall she'd fill me with tales of places I dreamed about but would never see—Disneyland, Knottsberry Farm, the San Diego Zoo, Sea World, Hollywood, and, of course, the Pacific Ocean. The summer after we moved to Clayton, the summer Holly and I would both turn nine years old, Holly baffled and thrilled me by proposing that her mother go to California without her. She would stay with us at the ranch. It was all settled when Holly let slip that my mother now had a full-time job—a secret Holly had been guarding carefully. Holly and her bags were on their way to California a week after school ended.

Bev convinced Dad that I ought to spend my summer with her, and Dad readily approved that arrangement. It was unanimously agreed upon for miles that Bev was the most competent woman around, and I suppose Dad figured some of that might rub off on me. It didn't much matter where or how it rubbed off, there were few parts of me that didn't need improving upon. But I wasn't entirely sure how I felt about the deal. On the one hand, I liked Bev a bunch and it would keep me out of the vicinity should Dad's temper ever return. But on the other hand, I was still convinced he would soon give up on me being a cowgirl the same way he had given up on Annie. I'd fallen off a horse, been dragged by a steer, been lost in the mountains, and been branded. Could he possibly need more proof of my unsuitability for the cowboy way of life? Once he wrote me off, I figured that, like Annie, I could spend my summer reading, riding my bike, and talking on the phone, although I had few people to talk to once Holly left town. But on the first Monday after school let out, Bev showed up at the house at 6:15 A.M. to pick me up.

"We're in the bathroom, Bev," Mom called out when she heard footsteps on the porch.

Bev stopped in the kitchen and poured herself a cup of coffee then leaned against the door frame and watched Mom rat and smooth her hair. I sat in my usual place on the toilet lid.

"Do I have any gaping holes back there?" Mom asked, turning the back of her head to Bev.

"Looks good to me, Ruth, but you always look good to me. I don't believe Clayton's ever seen anything quite as pretty as your mama, do you, Dickie?"

"Nope. She looks just like Jackie Kennedy."

"Dickie!"

"I believe she's right, Ruth, but prettier."

"Oh, Bev, really!"

"True, Ruth. You've got every woman in Clayton riled up."

"What?"

"Oh, nothing to fret about. Women round here need to get riled up about every ten years or so. I believe the last time was shortly after Bobby died. These women decided I couldn't run a ranch without a husband, so I held some tryouts, if you know what I mean. If you don't think that threw em into a tizzy. But it did get them off my back about finding myself a new husband."

"What kind of tryouts?" I asked.

"Oh, just to see who could stack hay bales the fastest, that sort a thing," Bev said, winking at Mom.

A car honked in front of the house.

"I have to run. Bev, I can't thank you enough for taking Dickie this summer," Mom said, giving Bev a peck on the cheek. Bev blushed.

"Don't give it a thought, Ruth. She'll be a big help to me."

"Dickie, try to make that true, will you?" Mom said, kissing my head. "I'll see you tonight."

When we got to Bev's house, she filled a cast-iron skillet with bacon.

"What are you cooking bacon for? It's Monday."

"There some kind of religious rule says you can't eat bacon on Mondays?"

"Guess not. I just thought bacon was for weekends."

"What's the menu for Mondays?"

"Cheerios."

"Would you rather have Cheerios?"

"No, I'd rather have bacon."

"Good. Pull a couple of plates down and get the eggs out of the fridge."

After breakfast, Bev asked me if I could saddle a horse.

"I know how, but I can't lift the saddle that high."

"That's what porches were made for," she said, leading the horse up to her back porch, which stood about three feet high. From there I was able to maneuver the saddle onto the horse's back. Bev's intent was to send me back home that afternoon on Plummy, her old roan mare, so I could ride back and forth each day from then on. The next morning, however, I showed up at Bev's riding Plummy bareback, my right hand twisted in her mane.

"We don't have a back porch," I told her when she came out of her house smiling. "Or even a back door."

"Hmm. Didn't think about that. How'd you get up there?"

"I led her up to a fence, then climbed the fence."

She nodded and smiled. "Tell your dad I'll drive over and pick up that saddle later this week. Don't look like you're gonna be needing it."

Combined, Merv and Bev's ranches covered more than 1,900 acres on the west side of Clayton, running north and south along the

Onaqui Mountains, separated only by our 150 acres. Merv had tried for years to buy the land we now owned, but feuds go back a long way in Clayton, and Ira refused to sell it to him on the grounds that Ira's grandfather had won it in some sort of long-forgotten bet from Merv's grandfather. Bev also tried to buy it, but Ira refused to sell to a woman "without no man to run the place" even though Bev ran a ranch more than five times the size of Ira's little place. Regardless, Merv and Bev ranched their lands as a joint venture, very much the same as Merv had done with Bev's mother, then Bev's husband, before Bev took over.

Bev described her family as one destined to be testosterone free. When Bev was thirteen years old, her father, Frank Clark, had a tractor and baler roll over on him while he was trying to get it unstuck from an irrigation ditch in a rainstorm. He was alive and fully conscious when Harold Summers found him. Said he didn't feel a bit of pain, but when Harold crawled under the equipment to take a look, the sight made him lose his potatoes. Harold didn't know how Frank had managed it, but somehow he'd gotten his legs so twisted up in the machinery that although Frank was lying on his back in the ditch, his legs were under there pointed toes to the ground. As soon as Harold hooked some chains up to his own tractor and started pulling the equipment away, Frank screamed like a threatened mountain lion then spewed out a string of profanity that made even Harold blush then dropped his head back in the ditch, dead. Bev's mother, Francine, whose own father had died when she was ten, took over working the ranch, and that's when Merv and Francine decided it would benefit them both to work their ranches as a joint venture. Rumor had it Merv was a little bit in love with Francine, and that contributed to the early demise of Merv's own wife, Elenore, who died of pneumonia at the age of fifty-one.

When Bev married Bobby Christensen, the Ganoa High School quarterback, the summer after they graduated, Francine and Bev were both looking forward to having a strong man around the place, but six years later his neck snapped like a string bean under a load of hay.

During the first summer I worked with Bev and we continued our game of twenty questions until we'd probably asked more like about twenty thousand questions, I told Bev that I'd heard Merv wanted to marry Francine and I asked her if that was true. She looked at me and asked, "Where you getting your information?" then before I could answer she went on to say it wouldn't serve a person well to put too much stock in Clayton rumors.

My information all came from Annie, who had become fast friends with Ella Anderson, a girl a year older than Annie and equally stylish, whom she met on the school bus between Warner and Ganoa. Ella's father was in charge of the gold mine in the Oquirrh Mountains, and Ella hadn't been in Utah longer than a couple of years. But Ella's mother, Catherine Anderson, was the former Cathy Hunsaker of Clayton, Utah, who had "gotten out just in time, thank the Lord," to snag herself an engineering husband from California who had been enticed to Utah by a couple of earnest Mormon missionaries who had converted his entire family. She never thought she'd end up only ten miles from her childhood home, much less in a crappy little mining town like Warner, but it was only temporary, she told herself.

One morning I entertained the idea of spending my summers with Annie and Ella instead of Bev. Annie had escaped the ranching life so cleanly, it left me in a state of awe and bewilderment. How did I, in my mind the most unlikely and resistant cowgirl, find myself on the back of a horse every morning, and how did Annie succeed in living her suburban life uninterrupted as if unaware of her location? What's more, Dad seemed unaware of her location. But one day spent with Annie and Ella in Annie's bedroom, polishing toenails, trying new hairstyles fashioned after pictures in magazines, and writing poems about boys in school left me feeling like my lungs were collapsing. Around the time they started trying on Mom's dresses along with her nylons and heels, I found myself behind the corrals clipping wild asparagus from the ditch banks, sucking air as if I'd been bound in a corset all morning. By 1 P.M. I tracked Bev, Merv, Stumpy, Heber, and Dad down in the middle of a lunch break from hauling hay.

"There she is!" Merv called out as I sheepishly came into the middle of their gathering at the picnic table in Merv's backyard. "You hungry? Grab a plate."

"Eat," Bev said, pushing the last burger and bun toward me. "We have a lot a work to do this afternoon."

After that, as soon as my mother went out the front door to work in the morning, I went out the back. Most Wednesdays during our summers together, unless we were in the middle of haying, Bev disappeared into her house around noon and emerged scrubbed and combed before she drove the pickup over to the Clayton ward house for the Wednesday-afternoon Relief Society quilting bee. While she showered I threw together a green-bean salad based on the directions she hollered from the bathroom. She seemed utterly wrong to me in the role of Relief Society sister, but whenever I mentioned this to her she'd grin and the crinkles would travel down her nose.

"I like those old cows," she'd say, "even if they do get their tails stuck in the air once in a while."

While she was gone I had full run of her house, her garden, her ranch, and the entire range of both the Onaqui and the Sheeprock Mountains, as long as I promised to come home before my mother got off work at 4:30 P.M. Bev's two-bedroom farmhouse held the minimum required furniture to live comfortably and was otherwise stuffed full of bookcases and books. I had been going there four months before I noticed Bev didn't have a television. The house was never terribly dirty but never really clean either; never messy but also not what you'd call straight. Bev said I could take anything off the bookshelves and out into the mountains that I wanted, bring them back or not, she didn't fret much about that. I could do whatever needed doing in the yard or garden or ranch, but she'd just as soon I resist the urge to clean her house if I was so inclined. I told her I wasn't so inclined and she said we'd get along just fine, then, which had turned out to be fact.

Annie told me that after Merv's wife died he told Francine they might just as well get married and officially join their two ranches, but she refused, saying that marrying a Clark woman was like playing chicken with a semi truck out on Highway 36, and she'd just as soon not have that to worry about. About ten years after Bobby's accident, Francine died and Bev was left to run the ranch on her own. Over the years, Frank, Francine, Merv, and Bev had tried many times to buy Ira's 150 acres, but he would never sell.

"I understand that," Bev said to me one day. "That little patch of ground was all Ira ever had. I wouldn't a let go of it either. And it's a nice piece a land, too. Old Ira's granddad knew what he was doing when he took it from Merv's granddad. Ira's cattle all started to look like him—bleary-eyed and belligerent—but that little alfalfa field a his is sunny even on cloudy days and gets rain even when the whole damn valley's dry. On years Merv and I got two crops, Ira always got three, and when we'd get three, Ira'd get four."

"How did our house end up the way it is?" I asked.

"Well, that's another sad story. Poor Ira had arranged with a fourth cousin a his back in Iowa to send her single and not so lovely daughter out to marry him, so he set to building on that house to impress her. He spent two years on it. The cute little white house originally there probably would have impressed her plenty, but the contraption that went up around it—the monstrosity you're living in—scared the beje-sus outta her. An hour after Ira let her outta the car, she was out on Highway 36 thumbing a ride east.

"That's when old Ira started using that back room to slaughter pigs, and that's also when he became nasty and mean and a general pain in the ass. The day she left was the day he put locks on all his gates and 'No Trespassing' signs up on all his fences. Merv and I used to move through his property on horseback all the time, going back and forth to each other's ranches. Then one day he shot some rock salt at Stumpy from only about twenty yards away—took the left eye outta the horse he was riding and coulda done the same to Stumpy. That's about the only time I believe I've seen Merv riled up enough to gut a man. He beat old Ira half to death." Bev started giggling and couldn't stop.

"What's so funny about beating a guy half to death?"

"Absolutely nothing," she said, still giggling. "Stumpy called me in a panic as soon as Merv walked outta the house, said he figured his grandpa was set upon killing Ira—and I believe he was right about that—and could I come and stop him. But when I got there, all my words—yelling and pleading and swearing—trying to pull Merv off Ira weren't landing anywhere near Merv's ears. I finally pulled a cattle prod outta Ira's barn and used that on Merv's backside. After the third time I buzzed him, he shot up off Ira like he'd just heard the bell that ended the round and swung around looking at me like I was his next contender. If I didn't have that cattle prod pointing straight at him, I don't know that he wouldn't a come after me before he figured out who I was."

"Then what happened?"

"Nothing. Merv walked past me outta the house, I checked to make sure Ira was still breathing, then I went on home. I figured they both needed to cool off a little bit before any a us tried to discuss this thing like mature adults."

"Then what happened?"

A small, tight smile spread across Bev's face. "Can you keep a secret?"

"Sure."

"Stumpy snuck over to Ira's after Merv went to bed. He couldn't a been any more than seven years old. Ira had dragged himself to bed, but he was a bloody mess. Stumpy got a pan of soapy water and helped clean him up. I have no idea what was said between the two of them, if anything at all. It was only a few months after that Ira put the place up for sale—he still refused to sell it to me or Merv—and that's where you came along."

"How come your ranch is so big?"

"Well, some piece or other a my mother's family has been on this land more than a hundred and fifty years. Lotsa family members left and went to cities through the decades, but there was always a stubborn one refused to leave no matter how tough it got or how hungry their kids were, and there were some years those kids couldn't a been eatin much more'n worms. That's the line that produced me."

"Did you ever want to leave and go to the city?"

"No, can't say I did. Don't think I'd know how to conduct myself in a town much bigger than Clayton."

"Gosh, Bev, Clayton's hardly even a town."

"Exactly."

"Haven't you ever wanted to go anywhere else?"

"Oh, every once in a while I get a hankerin to jump in the truck and drive straight west through basin and range until I reach the Sierra Nevadas."

"Then what?"

"Then I suppose I'd turn around and come on back home."

"I'll bet my dad wishes he was born into your family. He'd a been the one that stayed no matter what."

Bev nodded and looked at me.

"How come you know so much at your age, Dickie?"

"Cause during the school year I watch him in the mornings before he leaves for work. He drinks his coffee standing at the kitchen window looking at the cows and tugging at his tie. It seems like his tie gets tighter every day and one of these days might just choke him right there at the kitchen sink."

"Sometimes you think too much, girl."

"I also hear him talking to Mom at night in the kitchen about how he wants to stop being a hobby rancher."

"That so."

"Says it's killing him."

"Well, he might be right about that."

"He wants to quit being a teacher and just be a rancher."

"Well, your dad's not alone there. Most a the men in Clayton would ranch full-time if they could make it work. The army bases round here ain't staffed outta patriotism, though folks like to pretend they are."

"He tells Mom he's going to build up the herd and then maybe see if you or Merv will sell him some more land."

"That so. What's your mama say to that?"

"She doesn't say much. Mostly just nods and paints her finger-nails."

"Well, your dad's a natural-born rancher, Dickie. I don't know where he comes by it, but it's in him and it's in him deep. But here in the west—especially here in the basin and range—a rancher's gotta have a lot a land to make a living and it's a meager living at that. Hard to keep a family in shoes."

"Why?"

"Cause this is arid land. We don't get more'n about fifteen inches a rain a year. It's a damn-fool place to set up ranchin, but by the time my kinfolks figured that out they were already dug in."

"Where'd they come from?"

"My great-great-grandfather Larsen and his buddies got per-suaded by Brigham Young's boys to leave their homes in Scotland and come here where God loomed large and the western wheatgrass ran deep as first-crop alfalfa and thick as Stumpy's hair. They figured they'd found the Promised Land."

"But they were wrong?"

"Well, not necessarily. But it took em a lot a years to learn the hard lessons of the desert. They figured the rains would come every year to replenish the grass; that's all they'd ever known. So old Sam Larsen turned loose all his oxen and mules and sheep into that wheatgrass and had this valley turned into goat grass, sage, rabbit-brush and cedar—those goddamn junk trees—in less than fifteen years. It's taken a lot a years and a lot a coaxing to bring back anything a cow would find appetizing and it ain't ever gonna be like it was."

"Do you wish you'd been born in Scotland?"

"No, this is my place here, but I wouldn't mind a few more days a rain every year, if that's what you're asking."

"Me neither. I like rain."

"That doesn't surprise me."

"Why?"

"Because you're a desert rat like me, and desert rats like the rain."

"Why?"

"Well, it's sorta like a hot shower running over the top of your skin when you're cold—makes you feel calm and safe. Except the rain feels like it's running on the inside a your soul."

"How come you call us desert rats? Because we crawl around in this damn desert like rodents?"

"No. Because the desert crawls around in us."

CHAPTER NINE

"Is that what you're wearing to the funeral?" Annie asks, standing before me in a dark blue suit pulled sharply over an aqua silk blouse. Annie still reeks style; she adorns it and it grows on her naturally. Her hair wouldn't dare gray in an ugly patchy manner the way mine has. Her gray settled gradually and evenly into her thick auburn waves like lotion into skin. People's hands flinch when they get near it, like they're making a conscious effort not to reach out as she passes by. Her bangs always hang just over her sculpted eyebrows, which I find perplexing and impressive. Mine are either too short—cut myself out of a practical need to see—or too long. I get only one day of "just right" between the two. She's housed in a soft and compliant body like Mom's, in direct contrast to mine, made of hard and defiant angles.

I drop my eyes down over my own white cotton shirt and faded pair of Levi's 501s drooping around my hips. I had pulled out my newest pair and washed them twice in an effort to dress them up a bit, but that hadn't done much to hide the frayed seams and edges.

"Is that what you're wearing?" I ask her. "Aren't you supposed to be wearing one of those full-skirted flowered dresses with a lace collar? How many wives of Baptist preachers do you know who wear silk blouses?"

"Devotion to the Lord doesn't come with a vow to give up all sense of fashion."

"Could have fooled me. Have you seen those ladies at the ward house setting up lunch? I know you don't think the Mos are really all that devoted to the Lord, but—"

"Why are we having a Mormon service anyway? Heber never went to church."

"Did you forget where you grew up? Because, one, it's the only church in town; two, it's also the only building in town big enough to hold more than ten people; and three, the bishop's the only person in town who knows how to officiate."

"Didn't you bring anything else to wear? Don't the Mormons still require women to wear skirts to church?"

"I'm banking on the sympathy card. You really can't throw the sister of the deceased out of the church. How would that look?"

"I have a skirt you can wear."

"No way. I'm sick of wearing your clothes. I've been going to funerals in one of your old dresses for as long as—"

"My dresses are not old. What else do you have?"

"A different pair of jeans."

"You can't wear jeans to a funeral."

"I hope you don't plan on telling Dad that."

The footsteps of George Sinfield come down with force on the wooden slats in the hallway. I jump up from the table to start rinsing dishes before the footsteps stop then retreat.

"I can't believe you still do that," Annie says.

"Do what?"

"Jump up and get busy the minute you hear him coming, like you were five."

"Yeah, I know. Sound, they say, is the prime trigger of memory. Want a cup of tea?"

"Actually I think they say that about smell, but gosh, Dickie, you'd think four or five decades might cure you of that. Where did that come from?" she asks, pointing to a shiny new kitchen screen door.

"Ronnie McFarland was here putting it in a few days ago when I came back from Bev's. Funny, huh? Mom wanted a kitchen door in this place since the day we moved in here, and now there's finally one there."

Annie shakes her head and pours herself a cup of coffee. "God put Dad on this earth to teach me patience and tolerance. That's the only way I can figure it."

"Annie, how do you think he's doing?"

"Dad?"

"No. God. I'm giving him about a C+." She shoots me a reproving look. "Yeah; Dad. How do you think he's doing?"

"Well, I can't imagine he's doing too well, can you? First Mom, now Heber."

"No, to be honest, I never thought he'd last this long after Mom died. The only thing the man knows how to cook is toast—and maybe Pop-Tarts. I'll bet he might hold the record for living the longest on Wonder Bread alone."

Annie licks her thumb and rubs a sticky spot on the table.

"Is Dad going to be okay out here without Heber?" she asks.

"Was he okay out here with Heber?"

"Well, I assume—"

"How would we know? When's the last time you talked to Heber?"

A horsefly buzzes through the open window and perches on the edge of Annie's coffee cup, crawls around the rim and down toward the dark liquid inside before it swoops up directly at her face. She gasps and swats at the fly then jumps up and dumps her coffee into the sink.

"Annie?"

"I don't remember. I guess it might have been at Mom's funeral."

"Two years ago."

"Had you talked to him recently?"

"A few months ago. I was writing an article about the incinerator, and I called him to ask some questions. Of course he was totally useless—wouldn't give me any information at all. Kept saying, 'I'd tell ya, but then I'd have ta kill ya.'"

"Dickie, what happened at that incinerator anyway?"

"The inevitable. I mean, good God, you've got rockets filled with that deadly shit being wrestled around by a bunch of yahoo cowboys like Heber. What the hell did anybody think would happen?"

"Seriously, Dickie, could you stop being you for a just a minute and tell me what really happened?"

"I don't know what really happened."

"But didn't your newspaper investigate it and write about it?"

"Write about it, yes; investigate it, no. I don't think you could attach the word *investigate* to what the paper did. They reported what the army told them—employee error, nothing to worry about, all is fine. You know the story line, Annie. It hasn't changed in fifty years."

"But you must have some ideas?"

"Near as I could piece things together, someone forgot to replace a washer on a bolt and a hundred and forty gallons of nerve gas spilled out into a room. I'm guessing Heber saw some sort of abnormality on that control panel he watched over, got up, and walked into the next room to holler at one of the guys to check it out. When no one responded, he opened one last door and stuck his head in. That's about it."

"But how could that happen?"

Annie stares at me as if she expects an answer. I shrug.

"I tried to nose around a little, but the guys who were there are closed down tighter than bottled peaches. Ralph Carosella and Danny Miller both ducked their heads and walked away from me like I was a total stranger instead of the girl they spent ten years tormenting on the school bus. What does it matter anyway? The truth about one dead guy isn't going to change a damn thing around here."

"It might raise the awareness level of the dangers—"

"Jesus, Annie, you *have* forgotten where you grew up! Folks here should be studied by psychologists far and wide purely for their ability to comfortably hold tight to cognitive dissonance. We're in the county of Orwellian doublethink. We are nothing if not proficient at forgetting inconvenient facts. If *awareness levels* weren't raised in '68, I doubt this is going to be any more difficult to palliate. The army has already spun it and slapped themselves on the back for preventing a 'catastrophic occurrence.' Heber's nothing but a little mishap. Everything worked as it was supposed to, the danger was contained, but just in case, all employees will go through intensive emergency-procedure refresher courses or some goddamn thing."

Tears fall from Annie's chin to the collar of her silk shirt, seep, and spread. "I hate this place," she says, more to herself than to me.

"You and me both."

I move to get up when Dad's footsteps echo again in the hallway; Annie clamps a hand down on my wrist.

"Sit," she demands. I do as instructed.

Dad looks up with a start as if he's surprised to see us sitting at his kitchen table. He never had much physical mass to begin with, and he's been steadily shrinking the last thirty-nine years, closing tightly in on himself. His cramped expression lies somewhere between misery and anger, and that's the only hint he readily gives away. Most wouldn't notice that his jeans are too clean and his boots too shiny.

With a thud he places a large brown paper sack between us—WAL-MART ALWAYS LOW PRICES *Always*—rolled tightly closed, a dark stain the size of a fist apparent around the roll. He tucks the sleeves on his white snap-button shirt, rolling them under toward his elbows, then turns away from us to tuck his shirt into his jeans. While he does so I unroll the bag and peek in to find the tin can holding Heber's ashes.

"What's that?" Annie asks. Dad swings around and glares at her then at me. I say nothing. He drags a chair across the kitchen floor and sits down heavily.

"Well, that's the goddamned problem. I'm not sure what it is. Could be burned-up charcoal briquettes for all I know."

"Are those Heber's ashes?" Annie asks.

Dad thumps the tips of four fingers on the table and exhales deeply. He looks at Annie and she meets his eyes—something I've never been able to do. He thumps the table some more and drops his eyes, but Annie doesn't drop hers. She never has. She's been meeting him head-on for as long as I can remember. He lifts his eyes to mine and I try to hold his gaze. I'm trapped in unfamiliar territory, unhinged by what I don't see. I've spent most of my life being either afraid of or angry at this man. Looking into his eyes now, I find no justification for either.

"Jesus H. Christ. Where the hell is Alma?" Dad says, pushing his chair back and knocking the kitchen table against the wall. "That woman's been hounding me for two damn weeks about a funeral service and now she's going to make us late."

"Calm down, Dad, we have plenty of time," Annie says, freezing me up solid. All of our lives, Annie has said the exact thing that will set Dad off and then acted surprised when it happened. Telling Dad to calm down when he's agitated is equivalent to placing your lounge chair on the beach to watch the oncoming tidal wave. But today he doesn't respond. He stands at the new kitchen door staring at the empty corrals as if he didn't hear her. I stand in front of the window above the sink and stare out also, knowing exactly what he's seeing but unable to tell him so.

It's been an unusually wet winter and spring. The fields run golden with crested wheat from the edge of the corrals almost to the foot of the Onaqui Mountains, where the wheatgrass loses its footing to the goat and cheatgrass fighting for space with sage and rabbitbrush. Squat, bushy junipers start the climb into the mountains. The Onaquis still wear caps of snow and run the gamut in shades of green from lemon lime on the edges of their slopes to near black in their deepest canyons. Bev and Stumpy had already ridden the fences; the four barbed wires separating one desert pasture from the next are strung tight.

Closer to the house, the barn has lost a few more of its roof slats, its door hangs a little closer to the ground from a single creaky hinge, and the tractor inside turns a bit more of its green body over to rust. The corrals match the barn and tractor—misplaced in the flush of new life around them like a sick old man lying in the middle of a child's birthday party. The cedar fence posts are enshrouded with shaggy bleached bark; even the cow shit in the corral has been left undisturbed long enough to petrify and gray.

On the south fence line of the corrals, near the old water trough, a row of brilliant purple flags bloom next to four rosebushes heavy with buds, which Mom planted for the sole purpose of having flowers to put on graves on Decoration Day. They remain, ironically, the only sign of life near the house.

A 1984 beige Oldsmobile Ninety-Eight clatters up the dirt drive and comes to rest in front of the back door. The seat is shunted forward, allowing Alma's large breasts to rest on the steering wheel. She starts talking before she gets the door open, her voice carrying like a tumbleweed in the wind.

"That road's a damn mess. Doesn't the county grade that in the spring anymore?"

"Yeah, but spring starts sometime in September for those boys," Dad says.

"George, that grass looks good out there. You oughta bring some of Heber's cows over here this weekend and put them in that field."

"Heber's cows are runnin with Bev's, and I already told Stumpy he could put some heifers in there," Dad says. Alma brushes a hand across his cheek as she pushes past him into the kitchen.

"How you doin, George?"

"I'm okay, sis."

She wears chunky black heels and, I swear, the same dark blue dress she wore to her father's funeral forty-five years ago, slightly tighter now, the belt around the waist fraying a bit along the edges. She stands on her toes to kiss me on the cheek and brush the hair out of my eyes. She pulls Annie into a full hug.

"Good to see you, Annie. Wish you didn't live so damn far away. How's the family? They here with you?"

"They're good," Annie says. "No, they couldn't make it."

"Will Stumpy be at the service?" I ask Dad.

"You'd have to ask him."

"Annie, give your sister a skirt to wear," Alma says. "Dickie, go change your clothes. George, hell, I suppose you're going exactly as you are."

"Damn right."

"Fine," says Alma. "Anybody heard from Buffy?"

"She's not coming," I say.

"Well, that's a goddamn fine how-do-you-do," Alma says. "Don't even show up for your own father's funeral."

"I think it's shameful," Annie says. "I never understood what she's so angry about anyway."

"The name for starters," I say. "How would you like to go through life with the name Buffy? We're redneck, not blue blood. What the hell was he thinking?"

"That's enough, Dickie," Alma says. "Go put some decent clothes on—something that will please your mother's friends so they won't be saying 'good thing her mother's not here to see that.'"

I follow Annie out of the kitchen, but Alma's voice can be heard in the next county over.

"What's in the bag, George?" Alma asks as she starts to unroll the top.

"Leave it!"

"For Christ's sake, George! Are those Heber's ashes? You can't take Heber to the church that way!"

But Alma is wrong about that. Dad can and does take Heber to the church that way and never takes his hand off the roll of that brown paper bag.

The small ward-house parking lot is filled beyond capacity—it appears all of Clayton and half of Ganoa are here. Cars and pickups spill off the pavement and well into an adjacent field.

"Those boys are in my parking spot," Alma says, noting an official army pickup in the NO PARKING FIRE ZONE in front of the church. We make several circles around the lot in her Oldsmobile until she tires of it and pulls into the only handicap spot, freshly painted in blue, the result of a push by the Relief Society for the sake of Emma Olsen, who just turned 101 and still drives.

"Aunt Alma, we can't park here," Annie says. "What if someone needs—"

"These are ranch people, Annie," Alma replies. "They'd crawl from the back forty before they'd park in the handicap spot. We'll be fine here."

Alma is right about that. Emma had taken the gesture as an insult and refused to use the parking space. Every Sunday she parks in the last spot of the last row and slowly makes her way up to the church, leaning heavily on every car she comes to, sending about half the congregation out to shut off their car alarms around the time someone stands to offer opening prayer.

I run my thumbs around the waistband of the skirt I'm wearing and tug at the black panty hose, sending a run up the front of my foot. Annie shoves my hands out of the way and dabs the run with clear nail polish.

"Wow. Do you always carry nail polish? How the hell do you wear these things? My legs feel like they're all twisted up and gasping for air."

"Stop being such a drama queen. It won't kill you to wear panty hose for a couple of hours."

"It might."

"Yeah, well, you've thought you were on the verge of dying your whole life."

"Well, as we both know, I came pretty damn close a few times."

Dad twists around in the front seat and looks over the headrest at me as if he wants to comment on my near-death experiences. Instead he shakes his head and tightens his grip on the Wal-Mart bag before opening the car door.

CHAPTER TEN

On a Friday afternoon in October 1965, with school closed for the deer hunt, I crawled along the damp dirt behind Bev, pulling the last of the plump Roma tomatoes off the vines we'd planted that spring. A co-op of sorts had arisen among the Nelsons, the Sinfields, and Bev Christensen. Each family took care of their own financial affairs and kept their own cattle records, but we worked cattle together, we hayed together, and the garden Bev and I grew behind her house provided vegetables for everyone. In a place known for feuds over water rights that could string through generations of families, a place where the debate of whether cattle ought to be fenced out or fenced in had continued unresolved for more than a hundred years, such cooperation was a rare thing. I never heard a cross word or even a discussion about how things would be done among Merv, Bev, and George. Merv and Bev were happy to have the extra help—allowing them to hire fewer local boys for haying and cattle working—and George could be a big-time rancher in the flesh if not on paper. The arrangement seemed to grow as organically as the tomatoes we plucked from the vines.

"Kind of quiet around here today with everyone gone to the auction," Bev said.

"Yep."

"Why didn't you go? I thought you liked staying in hotels."

"Only if they have swimming pools and the one in Spanish Fork doesn't. It's just an old crappy motel. How come you didn't go?"

"Oh, I kinda like the quiet. I like your dad and Heber and Merv and Stumpy well enough, but every once in a while I like the sound a the wind without a man's voice in it. Did Annie go?"

"Nope. She's over to Warner spending the weekend with Ella."

"Lordy, I guess she'll have plenty a gossip to share when she comes back."

"Hope so. Without Annie and Ella, I wouldn't know so much about you."

"You'd know as much as you need to know."

"Don't you have any good gossip about Ella's mom? How come she knows so much about you and you don't know anything about her?"

"For one thing, I mind my own damn business, and for another, there's nothing to know about that woman. She's proper—she follows the rules. Always did, even as a teenager. What's there to say about a woman like that?"

"Don't you follow the rules?"

"I follow the ones that need followin."

"Is that what I should do?"

"Sure, once you're old enough to make a distinction."

"I'm eleven. That's old enough."

"Close to it. You have good instincts, Dickie. You just need to learn to trust em," she said, eyeing me, "stead a trusting the opinions of your friends."

"But Holly's one of the most popular girls in the sixth grade. I'm lucky to be her best friend. If I wasn't, no one would ever talk to me."

Bev raised up from her picking position and stood on her knees. She took three tomatoes from my hand and put them in the basket between us.

"Dickie, it's a hard thing to explain to a girl your age, but that's the biggest load a crap ever to exit your mouth. Trust your instincts. They'll serve you well if you'll let them."

I grabbed at more Romas, feeling Bev's eyes following me; we picked in silence for a while.

"So it's just you and your mom this weekend?" she asked.

"Yep."

"How about we surprise her?"

"How?"

"Let's take a bunch of these tomatoes, clip some oregano, dig up some garlic, and head over to your place while she's still at work this afternoon. I'll make a pasta sauce that she'll smell all the way to Johnson's Pass. It'll be just us girls tonight. How does that sound?"

"Like perfection." And it did. I wasn't ready to admit it yet, but the truth was my summers spent out of the company of Holly and in the company of Bev had soothed something in me I didn't even know needed soothing. Every once in a while I'd stop what I was doing and exhale heavily. When I'd turn around I'd see Bev watching me. She'd nod then go on with her business.

At night in the full-length mirror Mom had hung on the back of the door between the bathroom and Annie's room, I'd study my body, which had started to take on Bev's characteristics—small bulges of muscles where I'd never had them before, my arms, face, and chest darkened from the sun, everything else glaring white, kept hidden under a pair of baggy overalls and work boots, both of which Bev had bought for me at Ganoa Merc.

By the end of my third summer, Bev had taught me how to drive the tractor and the pickup. I knew where the majority of the cows ought to be depending on the month and when it was time to move them. Bev and I could move fifty acres of twenty-foot-three-inch irrigation pipe without any help from the men. I knew how to till and plant a garden that would produce lettuce, spinach, peas, beans, corn, tomatoes, squash, peppers, and every kind of herb a person could want. I knew a field of rabbitbrush and goat grass had to be plowed deep—preferably right before the first snow—before seeding crested wheat the following spring if we wanted the wheat to have a fighting chance.

I knew how to cook bacon and eggs and a pot of chili. What surprised me even more than my own competency was that none of it really felt like work. My longing for those lazy summers spent in Ganoa with Mom and Holly faded with each summer spent in Bev's company.

BECAUSE WE HAD NO KITCHEN DOOR, Bev and I entered the house through Heber's room, which had become standard for anyone entering from the barn or fields—so much so that a scuffed path wore itself right down the middle of the wood floor next to the bed. Heber spent the better part of his life outside and, even when he was in his room, never seemed to mind the company passing through. We dumped the load from the garden onto the kitchen table and got to work. Bev was chopping oregano in an impressive manner and I was peeling tomatoes with far less proficiency when we heard what sounded like one of Annie's spider yowls—only deeper and shorter—come from the direction of my parents' bedroom. We locked eyes for a moment.

"Shit!" Bev said, banging the knife down on the cutting board.

"Mom?" I called, turning toward the sound.

"Dickie, wait!" Bev said, grasping for my arm, but I was already out of her reach.

"Mom!"

I reached the bedroom door just as my mother flung it wide, her robe hanging off one bare shoulder and open down the front of her naked body. She put a hand on the middle of my chest and pushed me backward out of the room. Bev grabbed me from behind at the same time the door shut behind Mom, but not before I glimpsed the perfectly square head and bare chest of Captain Fulmer propped on one elbow in my parents' bed.

With a hand clamped firmly above my elbow, Bev pulled me back up the hallway toward the kitchen while Mom followed, fumbling to tie her robe, muttering something about not feeling well and coming home from work early. Bev also mumbled something about wanting to surprise her but not quite like that. When we got to the kitchen they both fell silent. I stared frozen at the floor. Bev still had hold of my elbow and Mom had taken hold of the other.

"Dickie . . ." they both said simultaneously. I broke from their grasp and ran into the bathroom, slamming the door behind me.

"Let her go, Ruth," I heard Bev say. "I don't think she'd be able to hear you now."

I WASN'T SURE how, but I intended to stay away from the house until Sunday when Dad and Heber returned from the auction. I wasn't even sure I'd go back then. Maybe I'd go directly to Merv and Stumpy's and stay there. Maybe I'd ride Plummy twenty miles into Ganoa and stay with Holly. Or maybe I'd have Stumpy deliver supplies and live in the cave for the rest of my life.

My resolve sank with the sun. By 7 P.M. Plummy was back in the corral and I was in Annie's room trying to hear the kitchen conversation between Bev and Mom, but Bev had heard Rangy's greeting and Plummy's reply when I rode up, so they spoke in whispers. I strode defiantly into the kitchen and got a glass of water. Mom kept her head down, but I knew she'd been crying.

"Dickie, why don't you get a plate and have some pasta," Bev said.

"I'm not hungry," I said as I slammed three doors behind me on my way back to the pig room.

The next day I got up early, crept into the kitchen to pack some food, and went out to saddle Plummy. Bev pulled up before I even got the saddle out of the shed.

"Where you headed?"

I shrugged.

"I'm gonna plow that field a your dad's down next to my pasture today. I could use some help."

"It only takes one person to drive a tractor. You don't need me."

Bev leaned against the fence post watching me struggle to lift the saddle to Plummy's back. On the first try I got it pushed up against Plummy's ribs then pushed it the rest of the way on, but I knocked the saddle blanket off the other side in the process. I yanked the saddle off and dropped it in the dirt, something that would normally get a rise out of Bev, but her hands didn't even come out of the back pockets of her jeans. I hooked the stirrup up over the saddle horn and started over, eventually getting it into place. Bev watched silently while I tightened the cinch by turning my back to the horse and pulling the strap up over my right shoulder.

"Have a good ride," she said as I pulled myself into the saddle. I watched her enter the house through Heber's room then I turned Plummy toward the mountains.

I would have stayed and worked with Bev if she'd tried a little harder to talk me into it. And where was Mom this morning? In reality, I hadn't *crept* into the kitchen at all. I had stomped in and banged around. Not that I wanted to talk about what happened yesterday, but I wanted her to know I had no intention of discussing it.

Before I knew where I was headed, I realized Plummy had taken us toward Big Canyon. We were well into a thicket of piñons on a steep trail before a gunshot sent Plummy sideways off the trail, slamming my right knee into a tree trunk.

"Shit! Deer hunt!" I reached down to pull the reins up tight and stroke Plummy's neck as another shot went off. She swung around a full 180 degrees and caught me in the face with the top of her head. Plummy was normally a levelheaded, hardworking horse, but I had been caught in a thunderstorm with her before and knew that loud, booming noises made her a little crazed. I wasn't too thrilled about them myself, especially when I remembered Merv's comment a few weeks ago.

"We need to bring those cows down off the mountain before the opening of deer hunt," Merv had said, "or we'll have one or two dead cows on our hands. Those hunters will shoot at any goddamn thing that moves out there."

I slid off Plummy and was leading her down the trail—wanting to make a smaller target out of myself and not sure I could stay on her back anyway—when the next shot rang out, louder and closer than the others. Plummy reared back, yanking the reins out of my hands, and knocked me off the trail as she pushed past me down the mountain on a dead run.

"Shit! They're shooting at us!" I said aloud, noting the brown canvas coat I'd put on this morning. I heard two more shots in quick succession and realized they were shooting at Plummy now, thinking she was a running deer.

"Stop shooting! Stop shooting! Stop shooting!" I screamed. When I quit screaming I heard the distant sound of Plummy crashing through trees. Thank God, she's still alive. I stumbled back onto a log. Two men in red plaid shirts and red hats ran up the trail toward me, sweating and gasping for air.

"Are you hurt? Are you all right?" asked the one with the gray beard.

The younger one with blond stubble stared at me wide-eyed. I put my head down on my arms and started sobbing.

"Are you hurt? Are you all right?" graybeard repeated, now nudging my arm. I raised my head and wiped my face with my flannel shirt.

"What are you doing out here all by yourself? Why aren't you wearing red? Do you want to get yourself killed? Don't you know you're supposed to wear red?"

"Don't you know you're supposed to shoot at deer, not horses and kids!" I screamed. "For God's sake, the horse is roan!"

"We must have seen the saddle," he said, dropping onto the log next to me, holding his hand to his chest. "You could have given me a heart attack."

"Good!" I pushed past them down the trail.

By the time I reached the cedars at the foot of Big Canyon about twenty minutes later, I caught sight of Bev coming toward me at a steady trot on Sego, her big white stallion. She jumped off before Sego slowed to a walk and dropped the reins in the dirt.

"What happened? Are you hurt?" Bev said, kneeling on the ground in front of me and tipping my head back with her hands. "Oh God, you are hurt!" she said, pulling me toward Sego.

"I'm fine, what are you talking about?"

She knelt in front of me again and looked more closely.

"You're bleeding from somewhere; you've got blood smeared all over your face."

"Plummy hit me with her head. I must have a bloody nose."

"What happened?"

"Some deer hunters spooked Plummy."

"Shit, I forgot about the damn deer hunt or I wouldn't a let you go this morning. I'm sure Big Canyon is crawling with those jugheads."

"Is Plummy all right?"

"She's fine, just a little frenzied. But I'll tell you, girl, there's not a worse sight in the world than seeing a horse come back to the barn with an empty saddle."

"Is Mom worried?"

"Yes, but not about this. I was out plowing when I saw Plummy go by. Figured I best find you before alarming your mother."

"Then what's she worried about?"

"You."

I felt tears coming back into my eyes and looked at the ground.

"You want to ride or walk?" Bev asked.

"Ride."

Bev got in the saddle and pulled me up behind her. We didn't talk until we got almost to the corral behind our house.

"You know," Bev said, gripping my arm at the elbow while I slid off the horse. "Your mother loves you more than anything in the world. In the end that's all that really matters."

"That's not all that matters," I said, and turned down the path to the pig room.

THE MEN RETURNED from the auction in time for dinner on Saturday night, and I was glad for the company. I had spent the afternoon in my bedroom avoiding my mother, who had spent the afternoon in the kitchen cooking and baking like a woman possessed. The same demon had apparently taken hold of Bev, who showed up about the same time as the guys with a pot of chili, fresh-baked bread, and two pies.

Spirits followed cattle prices, which were high that year. Merv tucked a check into the back pocket of Bev's jeans while she was stirring the pot of chili. She pulled it out and looked at it, put his face between both of her hands, and gave him a big kiss on the mouth. Then she grabbed Stumpy's hat off his head and gave him a big kiss on the forehead. Merv and Stumpy both blushed the exact same color as the red sweater my mother wore. Dad tucked a check down the front of Mom's sweater then danced her around the kitchen singing "We're in the Money." Heber tried to pull me into a similar dance, but I pulled away from him. He shrugged and danced his own jig, following Mom and Dad around the kitchen. Merv and Stumpy each stomped a foot and clapped their hands to keep Mom, Dad, and Heber dancing for a bit, and Bev rested both hands on top of my shoulders. I slid out from under them and got the bowls down from the cupboard. I wished Annie—who thought it best to show restraint and composure when everyone else was acting like fools—were back from Ella's. Then my mood wouldn't have been so obvious to Merv, who never missed a thing.

The seven of us crammed ourselves around a table with room for five while Merv and Dad filled us in on the details of the auction— who was buying and who was selling. Just as Bev passed a piece of bread to Stumpy, Merv said, "So, I hear you all had a little excitement around here this weekend." He was half smiling, half scowling. Stumpy tried to take the bread from Bev's hand, but her fingers didn't release it and it tore in half. Mom seemed to be searching for the bottom of her soup bowl, her face crimson. Bev stared at Merv as if she didn't know the man who'd just spoken. Dad and Heber looked around the table wide-eyed.

"What happened?" Dad asked, looking at me.

I shrugged. "Ask Mom."

"Ruth?"

"Nothing happened," she said abruptly.

The table grew silent.

"This a secret round here?" Merv asked, beginning to blush and looking to Bev for help. "Cause it sure ain't a secret down at Penny's service station; it's all those old boys can talk about."

The color in Mom's face deepened.

"What kind of manure are those idiots spreading now?" Bev demanded, shifting her chair in a way that put Mom behind her back.

"Well, according to the guys leaning against their pickup trucks and slurping Coors, we're lucky Darrel Summers isn't a better shot," Merv said.

"Darrel Summers! Is that who shot at you today?" Bev said, looking at me. "That man is too damn stupid to live. If I'd a known that's who it was—"

"Shot at you?" Mom screamed, her head popping up to look first at me then at Bev.

"She's fine, Ruth," Bev said. "I was gonna tell you, but in the midst of what was going on—"

"What was going on?" Dad asked.

"Just things, George," Bev said, without missing a beat. "I wanted to get that field a yours plowed cause I think we're gonna get an early snow this year."

"Shot at?" Mom said again.

"That just goes to show you what a moron that man is," Bev said.

"Shoots at a little girl on a roan horse thinking she's a deer then doesn't have sense enough to be embarrassed about it. Down at the gas station bragging like he got a six-point."

"Well, I think deer hunting turns most men into fools," Merv said. "A can of beer in one hand and a gun in the other—"

"Anything else happen here this weekend?" Dad asked, turning to Mom.

"Don't look at me," Mom said, composed once again. "I didn't even know this happened."

"What else do you think happened, George?" Bev asked.

"I don't know, Bev. That's what I'm asking. Dickie, why the hell would you ride into the mountains on the opening weekend of deer hunt?"

"I forgot it was deer hunt."

"What happened?" Mom asked.

"Just what Merv said. Some guys thought I was a deer."

"Are you all right?" Mom asked, placing her hand on my arm.

"Fine," I said, pulling my arm away.

"You don't seem fine," Dad said.

"I'm fine," I said, putting my bowl in the sink and retreating through the bathroom.

"She's just a little shook up. Not every day you get shot at," Bev said as I shut the doors behind me. "She'll be fine."

It was the last three words that got to me. The three words I'd been hearing my entire life. Dropped off a horse onto her head. She'll be fine. Dragged by a steer. She'll be fine. Lost in the mountains. She'll be fine. Branded. She'll be fine. Shot at. She'll be fine. At what point, I wondered, do the actions of grown-ups add up to a child who actually won't be fine?

CHAPTER ELEVEN

Men in their cleanest jeans and shined-up boots stand shoulder to shoulder in the church foyer looking for the open casket—some to pay their respects, others just curious. A few tug at too-tight belt lines and inside seams of ill-fitting khakis trying to get them out of their crotches and an inch closer to the tops of their still new but out-of-style loafers. Even Bishop Knowlden—although he dresses this way every Sunday—looks ill at ease in his white, short-sleeved shirt buttoned tight over his belly, the outlines of his temple garments clearly visible underneath, as he stands at the door shaking hands.

The women move with ease among the fidgety men, most of them being regular churchgoers and having the proper attire. (Bishop Knowlden has long since given up on trying to even out the seventy–thirty women-to-men ratio of the Clayton ward.) Some have simply exchanged jeans for calf-length skirts and knee-high hose five minutes before heading over to the church, but many use Sundays, funerals, and weddings as their only occasions to gussy up and they go all out—high heels, earrings, nail polish, the works. The air at nose level reeks of hair spray and Avon Skin So Soft.

I find Bev and pull her off to the side to find out what's going on.

"I forgot to tell Sister Robbins Heber'd been cremated," Bev says.

I doubt Bev's story. The error unquestionably belongs to Sister

Robbins, Clayton's most bossy and befuddled citizen, who had set up the velvet rope line and had spent the morning on the phone in a heated discussion with Bates Mortuary in Ganoa about the nondeliverance of the casket before turning her attention to a public chastisement of Bev, who congenially and quietly shouldered the sin. Before I can protest, Bev moves off to coerce people into the chapel without a viewing. No easy task. Mormons in general and Claytonites in particular like to have a final look at a person, give a declarative nod and grunt, before they completely let go of the possibility of running into him once more down at the post office.

Dot and Harry walk hand in hand through the front door followed closely by Michael and Charlie. Each of them is conspicuously out of place—Dot too wild and bald, Harry too long-haired, Michael too impeccably dressed, and Charlie, one of only two black men in the church (the other wearing an army uniform) and likely in all of Clayton. They cluster together just inside the door, obviously banking on the safety-in-numbers formula. I move to relieve them of their discernible discomfort when I feel a hand on the small of my back and lips close to my ear.

"Nice outfit. Tell Annie I like her style."

My breath takes a few stutter steps, forcing me to push it out in a deep and too-noisy way.

"I'll have you know these are my own clothes."

"You'll go to hell for lying, Dickie, especially in a Mo church. You should know better."

Stumpy's hand slides from my back to my waist, nudging me out of the slow-moving crowd, at the same time as he fingers one of the safety pins Annie has not so discreetly used to make the skirt fit. She has also loaned me a scarlet, silk, scoop-neck sweater that makes me feel like my name should be Sherri or Delila.

I turn and look up the eight-inch differential in our heights into Stumpy's perpetually sunburned face. Like every other guy in the Clayton ward house today, Stumpy looks awkward without a cowboy hat or ball cap, the top two inches of his forehead—white and unlined—shining through thick red hair like a full moon through the trees. The last half of the twentieth century had etched itself deeply into his face, resembling a sandy desert hillside after a heavy runoff, but his blue eyes still hold a little anticipation and a little defiance—same as always. His left hand softly rests on my right hip, which feels at once so familiar and so strange, I'm unsure whether to take a step forward or a step back, so I hold my ground.

"Is Holly coming?" I ask.

His hand drops to his side.

"How would I know?"

"You were married to her."

"*Were* being the operative word. She's been gone more'n a few years now. You know that, Dickie, so stop pretending you don't. Nothing happens in this town you don't know about."

"Well, contrary to what you might think, Stumpy, I don't keep tabs on you and your lovers."

"Obviously not, or you wouldn't throw the word *lover* out there so casually. I'm a fifty-year-old man living in a town with a population of two hundred—most of em older than dirt and most of em men."

"Actually, you're fifty-two."

"So you are keeping tabs on me."

For a moment we simply stand, taking a full, long look at each other. I know he won't fill the silence.

"I'm sorry about your marriage breaking up, Stumpy. I never had the chance to tell you that."

"Oh hell, you've had plenty a chances. But every time you and me get within ten feet of each other or have a conversation that lasts longer than four sentences, you break out with some sorta disease that requires quarantine and go rushing back into Salt Lake. Why is that, Dickie?"

"Haven't the slightest idea what you're talking about, Stump."

"You know damn well what I'm talking about. Can't imagine this time's gonna be any different. Guess you'll be heading back to the city as soon as the service is over."

"Can't see much reason to hang around these parts, can you?"

"Obviously I can—been doing it fifty-two years, as you say."

"Come on, come on! We've already started," Bev says, rushing out of the chapel and tugging at my sleeve. "Hey, Stump, didn't see you come in. How's it going?"

"Good, Bev," Stumpy says, pushing me forward. "Looks like you got em all herded through the gate."

IN THE SECOND ROW of church pews Annie looks like she's in pain. I'm not sure if I've caused that look by walking in late or if Bishop Knowlden has caused it by assigning Heber some divine attributes that have left a group of his buddies in the back pew—Stumpy included—clearing their throats and dropping their heads and casting knowing looks at one another. Aunt Alma nods her head with every statement the bishop makes, although she knows as well as the boys in the back it's mostly bull. Dad keeps a tight grip on the paper bag and, implausibly, seems to be muttering a silent prayer. Dot, sitting in the row behind me with the others, leans forward over the back of the bench.

"I'd have to see him in a loincloth to be sure, but that redheaded cowboy you were talking to looked remarkably like Tarzan," she whispers.

Michael tugs at one of the scarves around her neck and shushes her. He reaches up and squeezes my shoulder. His touch is reassuring.

"Now we're going to hear a few words from George Sinfield, the father of the deceased," says Bishop Knowlden after the congregation sings a church hymn.

Dad's head pops up and he stares at the bishop behind the podium with the same stunned look he had at the kitchen table this morning. Alma nudges his elbow.

"Get up there, George."

Like the rest of the family that still hangs on to shreds of their Mormon roots, Alma rations out her churchgoing to funerals, weddings, and confirmations, so she's careful to get things right once she steps inside the door. She doesn't like to give the Relief Society ladies fodder for the gossip session that takes place during the after-luncheon cleanup.

Dad rises to his feet and Alma attempts to relieve him of the paper bag he's clutching, but he holds tight. She quickly gives up the struggle. He sets the bag on the podium in front of him, the Wal-Mart logo facing the congregation, and stands silently for a good two minutes.

"Have you ever noticed that he looks just like his corrals," I whisper to Annie, "sort of gray and withered, like he's about to fall down."

"What's he doing?" she asks. I shrug.

"I'm not sure we had any choice," Dad starts, "but I believe we made a deal with the devil when we let the U.S. Army take up so much of our lives and our land. I know a lot of you disagree with me, but none of you have given quite as much to those bastards as I have."

Bishop Knowlden flinches. He's not above the use of some colorful speech himself now and then, but he tries to keep it out of the ward house and particularly out of the chapel. Dad waits as if he's addressing a town council meeting and expects a debate to ensue on the pros and cons of life in the clutches of the United States Army. His eyes drop to the end of the pew closest to the exit, to the commander of Dugway Proving Grounds and his young aide. They sit board straight, perfectly still and expressionless in their dress uniforms. Impeccably trained. They will not be intimidated—or even moved—by Dad's remarks or by the fifty or so pairs of eyes now upon them.

When folks begin to turn forward again in their seats, Dad pulls a piece of paper, folded to the size of a quarter, from the front pocket of his jeans. He unfolds it deliberately, pressing out the creases at each stage, and reads the following so quietly the entire congregation leans forward several inches:

Horse sweat and leather
Are the smells that I crave
May they line my casket
When I go to my grave
And maybe a horse
Can be buried with me
To ride in tall grass
That once set me free.

Annie exhales deeply, folds and unfolds her legs several times, and tugs at her skirt. I'm unsure if it's the poem itself, Dad's shaky, barely discernible voice, or just the excruciating slowness of the reading that is making her uncomfortable. Dad pauses at the words *casket*, *grave*, and *buried*, as if he considers making some sort of commentary on those. He continues:

And perhaps some cattle
To graze that grass
Then I'll have somethin to do
When my life has passed
Give me a good woman
To lie down with me
Cause I wouldn't want to be
Without company.

Dad stops reading and looks over the congregation. The veins on either side of his neck pulse. Alma has both hands on the pew in front of her—a far reach for her—as if she's ready to jump up. Annie has uncharacteristically slumped down with her elbows on her knees and her head dropped into her hands. I look back to see Stumpy

nodding toward Dad. Michael and Dot turn and follow my eyes. Dad
waits a few more seconds then clears his throat and reads the last few
lines in a clear, strong voice:

Then send me along
And I'll take the lead
That'd be about all
That I'd really need.

Dad slowly refolds the paper back to its original size, picks up the
Wal-Mart bag, nods to the congregation, and walks back toward us.
Alma jumps up to meet him. He swings an arm around her shoulders
and they sit down next to Annie. Bishop Knowlden steps back up to
the podium, hems and haws a little, obviously worried about ending a
funeral less than fifteen minutes after it started, and asks if anyone
else would like to say a few words. He looks desperate, so I nudge Annie and she nudges me back. A low drone rises from the back row and
finally Stumpy strides up the aisle with his fingers tucked in the front
pockets of his jeans. He clears his throat and my hands start to sweat.
I wipe them across the skirt I'm wearing until Annie gently places her
hand on top of mine.

"Well, I didn't expect to be standin up here today, but I suppose I
could say a few words." He places two scuffed red hands on the front
corners of the podium, puts most of his weight there, and nods at
Bishop Knowlden, who nods back.

"Heber ran a good herd and he always closed the gate after goin
through—that's more'n I can say for a bunch a you here."

Stumpy runs his left hand through his hair, a gesture so painfully
familiar, I have to push and pull my breath to keep it moving through
my lungs. Color has traveled up his face and over the white expanse
of forehead like the sun setting on a lake.

"Oh, hell, Bishop, let's just bring an end to this thing. Heber

never was one for long-winded chats anyway. George, I'm assuming
that was one a Heber's poems you read there?"

Dad nods.

"Well, that says it better than any a us guys could."

Stumpy drops his head for a moment, and when he lifts it again
moisture runs through the gullies in his face.

"Heber, goddammit, we'll miss you, buddy. Have a good ride."

With that, Stumpy strides back down the aisle and straight out
the door. The entire congregation sits quietly listening to Stumpy's
truck door slam and his engine turn over, then Bishop Knowlden
stands to offer the world's shortest closing prayer.

"I DON'T SUPPOSE you four want to stay around for green Jell-O
salad?" I ask Michael, Dot, Harry, and Charlie when we get out of the
chapel. All four shake their heads. Michael takes hold of my elbow
and gently guides me away from the others, who exit through the
glass double doors and stand on the sidewalk in the sun.

"Are you coming home tonight?"

"No, I need to stick around here for a while."

"When should I expect you?"

"I'm not sure, Michael. I just need to be here now."

He nods. "I don't know what to do, Dickie. I don't know how to
help you."

"I'm fine. Go back to Salt Lake and stop worrying about me."

He nods again. "I've just never seen you quite like this."

"Like what?"

He shrugs. "I'm not sure. You just seem different."

"Jesus, Michael, my brother just died."

"I know, Dickie, but—"

"But what?"

"I don't know, Dickie. I've just never seen you so—"

"So what?"

"I don't know, Dickie. It's like you're being held underwater, like you're struggling just to breathe."

Silently I watch the few remaining people leave the chapel and disappear into the gymnasium for lunch.

"I'm okay, Michael. I just need to be here right now."

"Well, I'll be home whenever you get there, Dickie."

He kisses me on the cheek and turns to leave.

"Michael?"

"Yes?"

"Thank you."

Dot comes in through the doors just as Michael goes out.

"You coming home tonight?" she asks.

"Not you, too. I'm fine. Go back to Salt Lake."

"I intend to. I'm just making sure you're not."

"What?"

"Coming home tonight."

"Why not?"

"I think you have some unfinished business here."

"Hell, Dot, everybody has unfinished business with their families."

"Yeah, I know, but I'm not necessarily talking about your family."

"What are you talking about?"

"Go track down your cowboy, Dickie."

"He's not *my* cowboy."

"Well, with the mere mention of him you're flushed from the cleavage of that fancy new sweater you're wearing all the way to your ears, and that happens to be a look I've never seen on you before. I know unfinished business when I see it."

"Save it for your column, will you?"

"Whatever you say, sweetie. Just don't come home till it's finished."

She takes my face between her hands and kisses me on both cheeks and on the lips.

"That last one was for the old ladies peeking around the doorway," she whispers. "Take care, sweetie."

As Dot goes out the door, Charlie comes in.

"Oh, good Lord, would you guys just go back to Salt Lake!"

"Right. Just want to say you should take whatever time you need, Dickie. The paper won't fall apart without you."

"That's what I'm afraid of."

"Right. See you later."

"Thanks for coming, Charlie."

"NICE SERVICE," Alma says. "Damn nice service." We sit around the kitchen table, eight eyes on the Wal-Mart bag in the center. "And those women sure can put on a spread. Wonder if anybody'll do that when I die."

Annie swipes at her eyes; I fidget with my skirt; Dad stares at his hands.

"Well, George, let's get on with it."

Dad looks at Alma questioningly.

"Heber's ashes. I assume he'd want them spread on his little piece of land there."

"Well, first off, I'm not even sure they are Heber's ashes," Dad says. "And second off, how the hell would I know what he wants done with them. He has a burial plot next to his mother—you all do. No one ever talked about ashes. I don't like the idea one damn bit."

"I kind of like the idea," I say. "I think I'd want that, just—"

"The hell you do!" Dad says. "Everybody deserves to have a burial place where folks can come and visit."

"Nobody visits cemeteries anymore," Annie says.

"I do," Dad says, glaring at Annie.

"Well, nobody's going to after you die," she says, looking directly at Dad.

"I think we have to assume they are Heber's ashes," Alma says. "It just doesn't make sense—"

"I don't have to assume any goddamn thing!" Dad says. "Not a damn bit of this makes sense!"

"George?"

A soft knock on the new screen door turns us all toward Stumpy standing on the other side, ball cap in hand.

"Come on in, Stump," Dad says.

"Sorry to interrupt—"

"You're not interrupting a thing. Get you a beer?"

"No thanks. I just wanted to check with you again before I bring those heifers over."

"That pasture's all yours. I'll go over to Heber's and saddle up one of his horses and give you a hand."

"Actually, George, I've got a couple a horses saddled out there. Thought maybe I'd talk Dickie into riding out with me. Doubt she's any good to you folks here."

"Do I look like I'm dressed for cowpoking? It so happens these are the only clothes I brought."

"That's a good idea, Stump," Dad says. "Dickie, go change your clothes and make yourself useful."

I get up to follow my father's instructions as I've always done. Truth be told, I can't wait to get out of the stuffy kitchen and into the foothills of the Onaqui Mountains. Stumpy has positioned himself against the refrigerator, so I have to slide past him on my way out of the room. He doesn't move as I inch my way between him and the chair Aunt Alma occupies. When I get directly in front of him, his body brushes against mine from knees to shoulders. He holds my eyes with his, and a familiar half smile slowly spreads on his face. The flush Dot noticed flares between us like a propane stove.

CHAPTER TWELVE

For three weeks after Darrel Summers mistook me for a deer, I refused to speak to anyone. Apparently I assumed an eleven-year-old's stance of silence would bring about the noble acts of humanity—contrition, absolution, redemption—and just like in the movies an overflow of tears would cleanse us, leaving the Sinfields awash in love and warmth. In reality, the auction-induced good humor hung around for several weeks, Mom soon went back to humming and singing around the house as she had done since starting her job almost a year prior, and the only person who seemed to notice I had stopped speaking was Bev, who saw me each morning on the school bus. She hadn't tried to force a conversation, but I could feel her watching me closely. On a Thursday afternoon—a half day for Ganoa elementary schools—she stopped me and Stumpy before we got down the bus steps in front of his house.

"Stumpy, since we've got some sunshine this afternoon, why don't you and Dickie ride out and see if you can find those three cows we never got off the mountain."

"We ain't gonna find those cows alive," Stumpy grumbled.

"I think you're probably right about that, but dammit, they had good calves on em. We might as well look while we've still got decent weather."

"Sure," Stumpy said.

"Dickie?"

"Okay."

I saddled Pug and met up with Stumpy at the northwest gate between our fields.

"How come you're riding Pug instead of Plummy?" Stumpy asked as we rode out.

"It's a free country."

"What's going on with you?"

"Nothing."

"Well, something is. You been acting mad at the world ever since Darrel mistook you for a deer. Is that what's wrong? Don't like being shot at?"

"Would you like it?"

"No, but hell, it's over and done and you're still breathing."

I push Pug out front and urge him into a trot.

"Come on, Dickie!"

"It's none of your business."

"Well, I'd bet anything in the world Holly Hamilton is somehow involved."

"Well, you'd lose that bet. Where we going anyway?"

"Hell Hole Springs."

"Where's that?"

"South a here."

"You think those cows are there?"

"Hell no. I think those cows are dead."

"Then why are we going to Hell Hole Springs?"

"I have something to show you."

"What?"

"You'll see."

"Stumpy, I'm really not in the mood—"

"You got anything else to do this afternoon?"

"No."

"Then relax and take a ride with me."

I looked at Stumpy and nodded. Fact is I would have been on the back of that horse whether Bev sent us out or not. It was the only thing I could think to do with myself.

"How far is it?"

"A ways."

"Then let's get moving."

We'd ridden about an hour when Stumpy came alongside of me, grabbed my reins, and pulled me to a stop.

"We have to leave the horses here and walk in," he said.

"What the hell for? If we can walk in, they can walk in."

"No, they can't. Trust me on this."

I had learned a few things since moving to the ranch and one was that I could pretty much trust Stumpy Nelson, especially when it came to following him into the mountains. But I soon found myself walking along a trail that could obviously be traveled by horses.

"Stumpy, the damn horses—"

"Ssshhhh! We need to be quiet now."

"What the hell for?"

"Shut up, Dickie!" he whispered, turning around to place a hand over my mouth.

I shoved his hand away.

"Stumpy, what the hell—"

From behind, Stumpy put one arm around my shoulders and clamped his hand over my mouth, his lips right next to my ear.

"Dickie, please stop talking. You'll see why in a minute."

I nodded and he slowly took his hand from my mouth. I followed him silently up the trail through cedars and grasses that grew greener and thicker as we walked toward the spring. Stumpy climbed and wedged himself between two boulders with a clear view of the marshy pond below. I followed quietly. Several times I attempted to clarify what it was we were doing there and several times Stumpy shushed me. I gave up and leaned back against the rocks. We'd somehow been transported out of the dry west desert into a damp forest. The grasses surrounding us were the green of overwatered Ganoa lawns. I had no

idea the desert harbored such lushness, and in the next few silent minutes I worked up some animosity toward Stumpy for keeping Hell Hole
Springs a secret.

I watched him out of the corner of my eye—a serene half smile
on his sunburned face. That was Stumpy's look whenever we were
in those mountains—a look that mesmerized and perplexed me. A
look that held more peace and certainty than I could grasp. A look
I envied. I tipped my head toward the sun, closed my eyes, and listened to water trickling over rocks. I'm unsure how long we sat like
that before Stumpy squeezed my elbow and pointed toward the
spring.

Timidly, a horse stepped into the last splice of sunshine. She
flinched a sturdy mottled-gray body to clear the flies then threw a
thick head flashing a long, black mane. She turned to show off a muscular rump and a tail that almost swept the ground. One at a time
horses emerged from the wooded path behind her, two bays, one roan,
one palamino, one black, another gray, and a sorrel. They lowered
their heavy heads to drink, and nipped and nuzzled one another. I held
my breath and stifled a sneeze. The sorrel twirled out of the mud and
took a few steps in our direction, throwing his head and stomping the
ground. The others raised their heads.

"He knows we're here," Stumpy whispered. "They won't stay long
now. Just stay still."

"Whose horses are they?"

"They're wild."

Stumpy pulled me close to him and whispered next to my cheek.

"The gray horse that came first is the lead mare. The stallion always brings up the rear and will separate himself a little from his
mares if he senses trouble. That's him—the sorrel—and we have him
riled up right now."

The sorrel charged toward us a couple of times, flung his head,
then pulled up but never took his eyes from our location. The others
milled nervously behind him.

"God, he's beautiful," I said, looking at his scarred and filthy body.

"Yeah, he is."

Soon the mare turned and at a trot led the herd back the way they'd come. The stallion stayed behind momentarily, then turned, kicked up his heels, and ran after his herd. We watched until we could no longer see or hear them.

"Can I talk now?" I asked.

"Sure."

"How did they get here? How long have you known about them? How many are there? Why didn't you show me before?"

"Whoa, slow down. I've seen wild horses before but only on the west side a the Onaquis, never over here. I come up here a lot, but I just started seeing the horses about a month ago."

"How come I never knew about this place?"

He shrugged. "Grandpa showed me this place when I was just little, and I've been coming here ever since." He shrugged again. "It's sort of a special place, Dickie. I've never brought anybody up here."

"So why'd you bring me up here?"

"Thought you might like the horses. But you can't tell anyone they're here."

"But I have to bring Holly out."

"No! No one else can know about this place or the horses! You have to swear, Dickie. The fewer people who know about them, the better. Nobody round here cares much for wild horses—don't consider them good for anything but buzzard bait."

"Why?"

"They gotta eat. And so do the cows that run up here."

"Do Merv and Bev know about them?"

"I'm not sure they know they're ranging over on this side."

"Do they think they're only buzzard bait?"

"Not sure. We ran into a herd a few years back when we were bringing cows down off the other side. Bev and Grandpa pulled out their binoculars and watched them for a good long time. When Grandpa started putting his binoculars away, Bev said, 'You have to admit, Merv, there's something right about seeing those goddamn horses out here, just the same way there's something right about hearing a lion scream from the tops of these mountains.'"

"What'd Merv say?"

"Nothing. He just grunted and went back to work. We'd lost quite a few calves to a mountain lion that year, so I'm not so sure he was feeling agreeable."

I climbed down off the rocks to the spring. Water had quickly filled in the large hoofprints left behind in the mud, but a dusty odor lingered in the air.

"Why was that stallion so scarred up?"

"He had to fight other stallions to get his mares."

"Do they stay together for life?"

"Unless another stallion challenges him and beats him."

"What happens when the colts are born? Does the group just keep getting bigger?"

"When his sons and daughters are about two years old, he'll run them off."

"Hmm. Figures."

Stumpy walked around in front of me and looked directly into my face.

"Don't, Stumpy."

"Don't what?"

"Stare at me like that."

"What's bugging you, Dickie?"

"You are."

"Come on. I know something's been eatin at you." I shrugged. "Did Holly say something to make you feel bad?"

"No. Why is everybody always blaming Holly for things?"

"Then what is it? Are you mad at me for something?"

"I'm not mad at you, Stumpy."

I squatted down and sank my hand into a muddy hoofprint. He squatted next to me and sank his hand into the same hole. Our shoulders bumped and he threaded his muddy fingers through mine.

"I wish you weren't so sad, Dickie."

"Do you miss your mom, Stumpy?"

"What?"

"Your mom."

"You can't miss something you never had. I missed Grandpa something horrible when Mom came and got me that one time. Felt like I had a hole in my gut the size of this hoofprint."

"I think my mom's going to leave us."

"What are you talking about?"

"She's going to leave and have a different life without us, a better life."

He gripped my hand and pulled it deeper into the cool mud. "What the hell gives you a damn-fool idea like that?" he whispered.

SHE STAYED FOR THE KIDS. She stayed for me, really, her most fragile and vulnerable child. I don't remember at what point I consciously knew that mine was the load of her resignation, but I do remember the day it happened. On a normal late-fall day, almost a year since Darrel Summers mistook me for a deer, she stood motionless in the kitchen, both hands resting on the empty counter in front of her as if she wanted to prepare dinner but couldn't locate the ingredients. I looked at her and she smiled at me. I quickly buried my face into her belly. How could a smile hold that much sadness? We stood like that until my tears had formed a dark splotch on her pink wool suit and her tears had formed a soggy puddle in the part in my hair.

My mother received love the same way she gave it. Whether she was loved that way by the handsome and charming Captain Fulmer, I can't say. I like to believe she was, but I'm not privy to that information. Others loved her, though, in exactly the way she one day described love to me—with every emotion, every thought, every inch of their bodies.

Bev Christensen picked up all my mother's broken pieces after the army transferred Captain Fulmer from Dugway to Aberdeen Proving Grounds in Maryland. When he left town, Mom resolved to go back to church, which she'd drifted away from and which, she discovered, she loved with almost as much passion as she'd had for him.

Her resolve was so steady that even when most of the town—at least most of the women—tried to dissuade her from attending church based on rapidly circulating anecdotes of glimpsed flirtatious moments between my mother and Captain Fulmer, she simply smiled sweetly and sat in the back row of the Relief Society, stylish and pretty. At least that's how Bev told it to me not long after Mom died. The Clayton Ward Relief Society presidency—sans the actual president, who was Bev—called a special and secret meeting. The group then went en masse to the bishopric, the event of my mother's excommunication as the ultimate goal. The bishopric had it "under advisement" when Bev got wind of it and brought the entire issue to an immediate and final close. I have no idea what was said—I imagine Bev keeps a tally on Clayton folks for just such a purpose—but an inordinate number of Jell-O, cottage cheese, marshmallow, and pineapple salads showed up in our kitchen that week.

SIX MONTHS BEFORE Captain Fulmer left town, on a cold, snowy Saturday afternoon in early March, Dad found me huddled in the pig room reading.

"Darlene, we've got four or five cows ready to calve in the next few days. Let's ride out and bring them into the corrals so we can keep an eye on them."

"Where's Heber?"

"Dress warm. It's colder than hell out here."

He disappeared through the outside door and down the path toward the corrals. By the time I got there he had two horses saddled, although he'd been insisting I saddle my own horse for more than three years now.

"Put this on." He handed me one of Heber's fuzzy caps with earflaps.

"But—"

"Nobody's going to see you. Soon as we ride out of here, you're going to be damn happy you have it."

He was right on both counts. It had snowed through the night and most of the morning, but none of it had a chance to settle; the wind kept it in constant motion. We couldn't see more than a horse length in front of us.

"We'll find those cows huddled by the northwest gate, I believe. Let's follow the fence line."

Dad put me between him and the fence, riding so tight on my left side that our stirrups and knees bumped together.

"Stay close out here today, Dickie. If this wind gets any worse, we won't be able to see our hands in front of our faces."

"Pug and Rangy can find their way back home."

A half smile crossed his face, and I felt my own flush, wondering if I'd said something stupid. He reached out and put a gloved hand on my knee.

"Well, they'd be better at it than we would, but you'd be surprised how fast even Rangy and Pug could become disoriented out here if it gets bad enough."

I nodded and we rode in tense silence for a while. Until that day, I had done my best—and been relatively successful—to never spend time alone with my father. Our entire discourse involved him giving direction and me obediently carrying it out. I believe he tried to be closer to me—and I believe Annie was right years ago when she told me I no longer needed to fear him—but an awkwardness had been established between us early on and neither of us knew how to let it go.

I wrapped the reins around the saddle horn and tucked both of my hands into the curve of the saddle under my butt to keep warm.

"You're pretty comfortable on that horse, Dickie. Seems you've taken to this life."

Did I have a choice? I wanted to ask, but kept quiet.

"You like it out here, don't you?"

"It's okay."

"I think it's done you good."

That seemed to be a common thought among all adults in my life, but I still kept a running tally of all the ways the cowboy life had damaged me physically and emotionally.

"Something's been weighing on you lately," he said, "more than normal."

The snow swirled around his head like someone had just shaken the snow globe we were stuck in, giving me enough cover to steal a glance at him. Crystals stuck to dark eyebrows I'd never actually noticed before. His skin—wet and brownish red—was remarkably smooth, much smoother than Mom's. His shoulders appeared broader than they were under a padded canvas coat covering one or two sweatshirts. Leather chaps covered his legs, and his gloved hands rested, one on top of the other, on the saddle horn. His body swayed gently with the plodding of the horse through snow as if he'd been sitting there since the day he was born.

I met his gaze only briefly. I seldom dared look directly into my father's eyes, but something was different today. It wasn't fear that kept me studying my own saddle horn. The last thing I wanted to feel for him was pity.

"I'm fine," I said.

"Well, you might be, but you seem to carry more load than a girl your age ought to carry. Maybe I've done my share to contribute to that." He pulled the collar of his coat tighter against the cold and flipped the hood of his sweatshirt over his ball cap. "I'll be the first to admit, I don't always know the best thing to do for you, Dickie. Annie and Heber, well, they're a little easier to figure. You're your mother's daughter."

"I'm not like her," I blurted out, immediately sorry.

He peered at me from under the brim of his cap as we reached the corner of the fence line. "Those cows are not where I thought they'd be. Let's keep following the fence. I can't tell if it's snowing again or just blowing. Either way, we won't find them today unless we happen to ride up on them. I don't like the idea of those heifers calving out here in this weather—better this than mud, though."

Without pause, Pug turned south when he found the fence in front of his nose. Dad reached over and pulled us to a stop.

"Dickie, if ever two people needed each other in this life, it's you and your mother. Whatever happened the weekend of the auction, set it aside."

"But she—"

"No," he said, gripping my leg above the knee. "No, please," he said more softly, releasing the grip and patting my knee. "Your mother's just trying to find her way through life—same as everybody else. Set it aside, Dickie."

We sat like that for a frozen moment, the snow swirling thick between us, then he squeezed my leg and pulled his hand away.

"Go back to the house before you freeze."

I nodded but didn't move. He nudged Rangy forward.

"Stay along the fence line—you hear me?" he called back as he faded into the storm.

"Where are you going?" I yelled.

"I'm going to find those cows."

"Do you need help?"

I waited for a few moments for the answer that never came, staring into the swirl of white, then turned back toward the house.

CHAPTER THIRTEEN

"That city's making you soft," Stumpy says, gently pushing me aside after watching me struggle for a while. "Can't even close a gate anymore."

"Why the hell am I getting all the gates anyway?"

"Got me. Thought maybe you had something to prove."

"I counted fifty-six cows. How many are there supposed to be?"

"There's a few stragglers; we'll round em up in the next couple a days."

"Who's the 'we' you're talking about, Stump? Better not include me in there. I'm the hired hand of the church, not the hired hand of the Stumpy Nelson Livestock Company."

"I figured you were in charge at that newspaper by now and could take time off whenever you felt like it."

"I make it a point not to be in charge of anything. Keeps life quiet."

"Come on. Let's go for a ride."

He turns his horse back toward the foothills.

"Where to? It's getting cold out here."

"Come on. Cowboy up a little, will you?"

I turn the mare and nudge her into a run. Stumpy stays close behind. The mare slows to a trot, then comes to a stop. I slide off and fling the reins over the branch of a scrub oak. Stumpy does the same.

"Glad to see you can still ride," he says.

"I see you've spent some time up here in our old cave; that mare came straight here with no prompting from me."

He drops his head and walks toward the cave. I follow. The cave looks significantly smaller than when we were kids, nothing more than an alcove in a rock really. Stumpy pulls a book of matches from his pocket and lights candles scattered throughout, then pulls a scratchy horse blanket from behind a boulder and sits cross-legged. I settle in next to him, my back against the cave wall, but immediately something rises up in my stomach and tears fill my eyes. I scramble to crawl out of the hole.

"Don't leave," he says, grabbing my ankle. "Hell, it's not like I haven't seen you cry before." I sit back down. "Besides, I love that about you. Always have."

"What?"

"The way this place gets to you. The way you pretend it doesn't."

Clayton sits low in the basin, easily overlooked from here, identifiable only by unnatural blocks of green and gold. The sun hangs behind us, partially blocked by the Onaquis, leaving the Oquirrhs splotched in shadows of deep blue and pale lavender. The view from here climbs through my skin and spreads through my insides, making my belly ache with a feeling I can't define and can never assuage. In the city, I hear people describe this desert as barren, godforsaken, hell on earth. The army banks on this perspective, depends on the collective definition of beauty residing in the color green—the color of lawns and golf courses, the color of trees and lush forests, the color of city parks, the color of money. Who would come to the defense of a wasteland such as this? Once the eye scans past the Nelson ranch, beyond Clayton to the other side of the highway, it lands on a plume of smoke rising from the incinerator.

"Why do we put up with that when we know it's killing us?" I ask.

"Because it's the only thing keeping us alive."

"Why do we believe the army when it tells us we're safe when there's so much evidence to the contrary?"

"Because it's the only rational choice."

I can feel his eyes on me.

"I hate this damn place, Stumpy."

"No you don't." He moves closer and puts an arm around me, as if thirty-five years hadn't passed since the last time we'd sat together like this. I pull back assuming he will also, but he simply tightens his hold. "No you don't, Dickie," he whispers repeatedly, his lips barely moving in my hair. I let go of my resistance and sink in to him.

All color disappears from the Oquirrhs before I pull away from Stumpy and wipe my face with the bottom of my tank top.

"I guess you and Holly used to come up here a lot." I feel his body tense up next to me.

"Holly never stepped past the corral after Bret was born, which, as you know, was only three months after we were married."

I nod. I already knew that but wanted to hear him say it. Even though I'd put three decades and eighty miles between us, I'd never been able to disentangle Stumpy Nelson from my life. Mom and Bev made sure of it—keeping me up-to-date on births, deaths, divorces, and anything else of significance that happened to him—and I never tried to stop them. It only now occurred to me that Stumpy might know as much about my life over the past thirty-five years as I know about his.

"She decided pretty quickly after Kip was born the following year that the ranching life was not suitable for *her* children," he continues. "You know Holly, once she gets an idea about something she's stiff-necked as an ornery old mare."

"How are the boys?"

"Fine far as I can tell. I don't see much of them. Kip's in a graduate program at NYU, and Bret lives in Boston with his wife and their two kids."

"And the grandkids?"

"I don't see them much either. When Grandpa was still alive, Bret used to send Justin out for summers. I remember the first time, when he was just little, he was scared of everything. A cow would lift her head and he'd crawl up my leg and into my arms as fast as he could. A couple of years later, he loved everything about this place. Rode a horse like—"

"Like you when you were a kid?"

"Yeah, something like that," he says, grinning. "It wasn't too long after that Bret and his wife decided Justin should go to computer camp or some goddamn thing in the summertime stead a coming out here. They've succeeded in getting as far away from this place as possible. I'm sure that makes Holly happy."

"I'm not sure anything makes Holly happy. Where's she living now, anyway?"

"She's in Salt Lake. I thought she might try to get hold a you."

"Fat chance of that."

"She used to talk about trying to make amends with you."

I look at Stumpy. Certainly he knows by now that Holly's words are pitched at an angle that only indirectly—or sometimes inversely— coincides with her intentions. He stares into the last bit of light and a sun-freckled hand snatches the ball cap off his head. He rubs a full head of red hair and tugs the ball cap back on, adding one more swipe to the two-fingered stain on the brim.

"That sure didn't turn out like I thought it would."

"What?"

"That. My marriage. My kids. My life."

"Yeah, I could have told you it wasn't going to. It took me a lot of painful years to understand one pertinent thing about Holly Hamilton. She only loves what she doesn't have."

Stumpy pitches pebbles at an unseen target in the encroaching darkness.

"What about you, Dickie? Do you only love what you don't have?"

"It's hard to love what you do have, Stumpy, when you don't have a goddamn thing."

"What do you love, Dickie?"

I sit cold with Stumpy's question hanging in front of us. He waits patiently, watching me with pale blue eyes, his left hand—knuckles worn down—playing with the torn edges of my jeans.

"What I'd love right now is some of that leftover tuna casserole Bev sent home with us from the funeral." I pull myself off the ground and brush dirt from my jeans. He grabs my hand.

"When you gonna come clean, Dickie?"

"Come on, I'm freezing and starving." I yank my hand away from him and walk toward the horses.

"For someone who claims to hate this place, you spend an awful lot of time out here."

"What the hell you talking about, Stumpy?"

"I've seen your car up on Johnson's Pass some weekends—lots of weekends—since your mom died."

I stop and turn toward him.

"There are a lot of Subarus like mine in the world, Stump. It's the number-one-selling car in Utah."

"Have it your way, Dickie," he says, waving me off. "You're the same pain in the ass you always were."

I lower myself back down next to him, knowing damn well the better choice is to get back on the mare and ride back to the house.

"How many acres you ranching here now, Stumpy? Seems like you've got cows spread from the Sheeprocks to the Stansburys. Except for that piece Bev broke off and sold to Heber, seems like you're running this entire side of the valley, including the Bar C."

"You know as long as Bev's still breathing, she'll be in charge at the Bar C, and the rest a Clayton for that matter. But the only thing ever separating our ranches was your dad's place, and he hasn't run a herd since—"

"Nineteen sixty-eight."

"Yeah."

"You're a regular cattle baron; no wonder Holly married you."

He stiffens but doesn't respond. Keep your mouth shut, I think to myself. Get back on the horse, get in your car, go back to the city, and pick up your life. It's that easy. But shit, I can never keep my mouth shut.

"The question really is not why Holly married you, Stump, it's why you married her."

"You know why—she was pregnant."

"Ah, yes, that. How handy for you."

"What's that supposed to mean?"

"The perfect opportunity to fulfill your prophecy as the good, responsible boy. Stumpy Nelson—he's always done right by folks."

"Fuck you, Dickie." He strides to his horse, steps into the stirrup, and turns back toward the ranch.

"You just gonna leave me out here again?" I holler, but he's already disappeared down the mountain. I pull the saddle blanket around my shoulders and lean back against the cold rock until the shadows disappear.

I MOVE SLOWLY, unsaddling the mare in light shining brightly through the kitchen door, unsure whether to go in or get back on the horse. Dad still sits at the table in his funeral clothes as if four minutes instead of four hours had passed. His right hand rests on the Wal-Mart bag; Annie and Alma move around him.

I lug the saddle into the shed and fling the saddle pad—sweaty side up—on top. Heat rises from the pad and the musky scent of horse sweat ambushes me. I've tried—and mostly succeeded—to avoid that smell for thirty years, knowing it has the capacity to jerk out pieces of me I'd rather leave buried. I give myself over to it, sitting cross-legged on the wood floor, resting my forehead against the pad.

"What am I doing here?" I whisper, inhaling deeply. "I've got to get away from this place."

I'm unaware of Annie's presence until her arms reach around me from behind and her perfume invades the space. She gently pulls my head from the saddle pad toward her shoulder.

"Shh, shh, shh," she whispers.

It's only then I realize I'm half crying, half mumbling. She holds me for several minutes, neither of us speaking.

"Oh shit, the mare," I say, breaking from Annie's grasp, remembering I'd simply dropped the reins in the dirt thinking she'd stand long enough for me to carry the saddle into the shed.

"I put her in the corral," Annie says. "That's how I knew you were out here—saw her wander past the kitchen window with her reins dragging. Tell me what happened."

"Nothing happened."

"What did you and Stumpy talk about?"

"The only thing we're capable of talking about—nothing at all."

Annie nods. "Are you okay?"

"I'm fine. What's going on in the kitchen?"

"Alma's cooking dinner and worrying about you and Stumpy being out past dark."

"She does know we're in our fifties now, doesn't she?"

"I don't think so. You'd better come in."

"Good, you're back," Alma says when we walk through the door. "We were waiting dinner on you. George, could I touch that damn bag long enough to clear it off the table so we can eat something?"

Dad stuffs Heber's ashes onto the floor between his feet.

"Annie, I stopped at Albertson's and bought you some of these," Alma says, pulling some frozen veggie burgers out of the freezer.

"Thanks, Aunt Alma, but I'll just have—"

Before Annie can finish, Alma slices the package with a knife and plops one of the veggie burgers into the greasy frying pan with four hamburgers.

"—one of those," Annie says. Alma smiles proudly.

"Where's Stumpy?" Alma asks.

I shrug. "Over at his place, I suppose."

"Where's that horse of his you were riding?" Dad asks.

"Out in the corral."

"Unsaddle her already?"

"Yeah, Stumpy's saddle is in the shed if he's looking for it."

"Well, go throw a halter on her and ride on over to Stumpy's place and bring him back here," Dad says.

"What for?"

"Because he's all alone over there," Alma says. "Probably hasn't had a decent hot meal in years. Go get him to come over here and eat with us. And don't dillydally. It's almost ready."

"He's managed to stay alive so far," I say. "I imagine he can feed himself."

"Well, ride over and get him anyway," Dad says.

"Wouldn't it be easier just to call him on the phone?"

"Phone's not working! You gonna ride over and get him or do I have to do every goddamn thing myself around here?"

"I'm going already."

"I'll drive over and get him," Annie says.

I shake my head at her.

"I'll go. Unless somebody's graded that road in the last twenty-four hours, it'll take you a half hour to drive through those mud ruts."

Besides, I figured in the time it took us to get back to the house, Stumpy and I could reestablish our polite-conversation status quo and all would be back to our version of normal.

"What happened to the damn phone?" Alma demands as I leave the house.

Before I remember we'd closed all the gates, I throw a halter on the mare and wipe her down the best I can. By the time I pull myself on and off her three times to open and close gates, I'm covered in horse sweat and hair, wishing I'd put the saddle back on. I walk in the back door of Stumpy's house without knocking. He's standing in the kitchen.

"What do you want?" he asks.

"I can see you're still miffed at me, but you got any pants I can put on? I'm itching like crazy," I say, rubbing the insides of my thighs. He doesn't move. "Come on, Stumpy! I'm itching like hell!"

He nods toward a pair of overalls hanging on the back of the door. I pull them off and go into the bedroom to change. The overalls, still warm from the late-afternoon sun, smell mostly of Tide laundry detergent, but also of the coconut-oil lotion Stumpy special-ordered through the mail when we were in high school, searching for the magic potion to keep his fair, freckled skin from cracking open after long hours of irrigating and hauling hay.

"I'm borrowing a T-shirt, too," I call out as I rummage through a stack of neatly folded T-shirts in his top drawer, searching for one without a logo or saying splashed on the front. When I pull a plain white T-shirt from the bottom of the stack, a newspaper clipping comes out with it. I quickly stick it back in the drawer but turn my head sideways to read the headline—LOCAL JOURNALIST AMONG THOSE ARRESTED AT INCINERATOR PROTEST—above a photo of me being led away in handcuffs. August 22, 1996.

"I see you found a T-shirt," Stumpy says from the doorway.

"I see you read the competitor's paper," I say, closing the drawer.

"Thought you might lose your job over that one."

"I was there covering the story not protesting. Cops were just a little overzealous is all."

"That so. According to Heber, the only ones arrested at that protest were the ones who chained themselves to the gate."

"Well, you know Heber—prone to exaggeration."

"Right. How is it you've been able to keep that damn job so long anyway? Your politics aren't exactly aligned with that of your employer."

"Fifteen years of good behavior followed by ten years of decent writing can get you a pretty good fan base."

"But still—"

"I covered a story about a certain gentleman who occupies a seat in the church hierarchy. I decided his right to privacy trumped the public's right to know. What are you cooking? Smells good."

"Oh shit, I forgot!" Stumpy says, striding back to the kitchen and pulling the lid off a cast-iron frying pan.

I study the contents: green beans, red peppers, mushrooms, onions, and something that looks suspiciously spongy and white.

"Please tell me that's not tofu."

He smiles sheepishly. "Trying to lower my cholesterol."

"Annie would kill to be where I'm standing right now, but George would consider you a mentally unbalanced traitor." I pick a green bean out with my fingers and pop it into my mouth. "Well, I'll be goddamned. You can cook."

I pull the lid off another pan and catch a whiff of basmati rice. He slaps at my hand. "Leave that alone; rice isn't done yet."

"Herbert Nelson, I swear you have never been sexier than you are right now standing over that hot stove."

He smiles and blushes. I momentarily see the face of the kid who came to rescue me forty-four years ago from the rock I sat upon in the dark mountains just outside the door.

"Stop trying to make amends, Dickie. I know your game."

"Me? You're the one who should be apologizing. You're the one who left me alone on the mountain in the dark, yet again. But I'm about to let you make it up to me." I nod toward the food. "How is it I don't know this about you? Who taught you to cook?"

"Grandpa," he says.

"Well, I knew Merv could grill a steak, but I never thought much about it beyond that. Who taught him?"

"He taught himself. After Grandma died, he was living mostly on TV dinners before I came along. But as soon as I was off baby food and looking forward to a few TV dinners of my own, he said that was no way for a kid to eat. We drove into Salt Lake one day and bought a bunch a cookbooks—he didn't want anyone in Clayton or even

Ganoa to know what he was buying—and we just started experimenting."

"How is it no one knew this about you two?"

"It was sorta a special thing for us—just a couple of cowboys cooking up pastas and grilling salmon. Bev knew—we'd invite her to dinner sometimes and she'd invite us over to the Bar C. It was sorta a contest between her and Grandpa who could cook the fanciest meals."

"Well, I'll be damned. I don't know what to say, Stump, except I hope you have an extra plate and some decent wine to go with this."

He pulls a bottle of white wine out of the fridge and gets down two juice glasses. "Me and Grandpa could put a meal together, but we never worried much about settin a table," he says, handing me a fork and a chipped plaster plate that weighs near as much as the lid to the cast-iron frying pan.

"Thank God. If you'd gone too Martha Stewart on me, I'd have to worry about you out here alone with nothing but a few heifers around for company."

"Clayton women don't much take to being called 'heifers,' Dickie. They prefer 'broads.'"

We fill our plates, push a bunch of newspapers and the *Angus Journal* over to one side of the table and sit. There's too much to say and no obvious way to say it. We eat in silence until I can't stand it anymore.

"I'm sorry I never came out for Merv's funeral."

"Well, Grandpa didn't want much, so we mostly just gathered here and said a few words. I never really expected you'd come, but I guess I hoped you would anyway."

"How old was he when he died?"

"Ninety-two."

"I always liked Merv. He made me feel . . . capable."

Stumpy laughs.

"Seriously. I was a messy, scared little kid, but I never felt that way around Merv. He somehow saw a different me."

"Grandpa could yank the best out of the worst," Stumpy says, reaching out and tugging on a piece of my hair.

"Did he die in his sleep?"

"Oh hell no. He was still going strong right up till the day he died. We were trailing cows and he just slipped down off the side a his horse like he was reaching to pick a flower."

"Guess a guy like Merv couldn't ask for a much better way than that—dying in the saddle."

"Damn sure better than going the way Heber did."

I nod.

"I'm sorry about Heber, Dickie."

"Yeah, me, too. Hell, Stump, you knew Heber better than I did. I should be offering you my condolences. It's sad, though. Doesn't seem like Heber had much of a life—two failed marriages, a daughter who never spoke to him, a government job, never been anyplace but this damn valley."

"Well, I'm pissed as hell that Heber is gone—he was a helluva friend—but I don't think we need to spend much time lamenting Heber's days on this earth. He did all right."

"Really? You think he was happy?"

"I know damn well he was happy."

"What makes you say that?"

"Cause I know it when I see it."

"You seem pretty smug about that."

"Everybody's got a place they're supposed to be, Dickie. Most people spend their entire lives trying to find that place. Heber found his right off, that's all I'm saying."

"And you think this damn desert is that place?"

"I'm not saying that, Dickie. I'm not necessarily talking about a geographical place, although that's part of it. All's I'm saying is Heber understood himself as well as any man I'd ever known. And yeah, this valley and these mountains were his place."

"That simple, huh?"

"It ain't simple at all. George, for example, has never found his place in life, and I'm pretty sure he never will. One thing's for sure—"

"Oh shit! I completely forgot! George sent me over here to get you!"

"Must've ripped his phone out again."

"They're all waiting for us! Alma's worried as hell that you're over here eating dog food out of a can for dinner every night—she's got a couple of burgers frying up for you!"

Stumpy starts to clear the plates. I grab one more bite off mine as he takes it away.

"You can come back and finish later, Dickie. But I hate to disappoint your aunt Alma."

"Hell, George must be ranting by now."

"Yeah, sometimes your dad can be a pain in the ass."

"Tell me something I don't know."

"Let's go. We might as well take that mare back over since you dumped my saddle there."

I squinch my face at the thought of pulling the itchy jeans back on.

"You can leave the overalls on," he says. "God, all you Sinfields are a pain in the ass."

STUMPY CLASPS MY left forearm, pulls me onto the mare behind him, and kicks her into a smooth lope. I wrap both arms around his torso and rest my cheek against his back. Somewhere around the ninth grade, Stumpy had outgrown his name. Our legs hang together around the mare's belly—his feet hanging a good six inches longer than mine—the deep muscles of his hamstrings pressing against the insides of my thighs. I press my pelvis against his tailbone, my breasts against his back, and drop my left hand down to the top of his thigh. I catch a whiff of horse sweat mixed with the now unmistakable scent of coconut-oil lotion. I feel his thigh under the tender skin of my palm and hear the snorting of the mare. *Ever loved so intensely*

that it enhanced every one of your senses, changed the way you move
over the earth?

Stumpy pulls the mare up quick to keep her from jarring us by trotting to a stop. The house is dark and Alma's car is gone.

"Shit, I'm going to hear about this tomorrow, if not tonight," I say. "I like the way they worry about me, though, don't you? Dad sends me out on a dark, stormy night on horseback, and when I don't return, they turn out the lights and go to bed."

"There ain't a cloud in the sky and apparently they know you better'n you think. You used to disappear for hours up into those mountains then be upset that your mother was in a tizzy with worry and be mad as hell she'd sent me or Bev out looking for you."

"Well, that was then. I'm a city girl now. You can't send me out on a horse in the dark then go to bed when I don't return. It just don't sit right."

"Where's your editor when you need him?"

"Shit, now I have to sneak into Annie's bedroom and crawl in bed with her. I feel like I'm fifteen again. And I have to go through the kitchen, and I have a sneaking suspicion Dad's still sitting at the kitchen table in the dark with his hand clamped down on that bag."

"Go through the pig room."

"You should see the junk piled up in the pig room. Not even one of Ira's hogs could get through there."

"You do have other options," Stumpy says with a half grin.

"I'm not staying with you, Stumpy, so don't even think about it."

"I wasn't thinking about it. I was going to loan you this old horse and a couple of saddle blankets and send you back up to the cave to sleep. Wouldn't be the first night you'd spent there."

"Funny how a horse blanket doesn't cushion the rocks the same way it did when I was thirteen."

Without any definitive plan we sit until the mare tires of it, swings her rear end to the south and her nose to the north, and steps deliberately toward the Nelson ranch. We don't stop her.

"I remember the first night I ever spent alone in that cave," Stumpy says, twisting his head back toward me. At the slow pace the mare's traveling, I have no good reason to wrap my arms around Stumpy's waist, so I hook my thumbs into his belt loops. "It was a few summers before you moved here. When was that—'62?"

"Yeah, '62, I think."

"So I guess it was '60 or '61; I must a been six or seven years old. Fancied myself Daniel Boone, intended to stay out for a week, trap coon and shoot bear. Had myself a new BB gun. Grandpa just nodded, wished me luck, and helped me pack."

"God, I loved that man," I say, my voice cracking on the last word. Stumpy reaches back with his right hand and squeezes my calf just below the knee.

"I know you did," he says.

"I've got to get the hell out of Clayton; it makes me cry too damn much."

"You've always been a crier."

"Not since I left this place, I'm not."

Stumpy doesn't reply, just squeezes my leg again and goes on with his story. "I packed enough bologna and bread into the saddlebags on Ol' Yeller to last me about a week in the brush. Figured I'd make camp in the cave then hunt from there. I got up there just before dark, just enough time to set some traps, I figured. I'd done my Daniel Boone and Davy Crockett research, ya see."

"Mm-hmm."

"When I got back to the cave, a pack a coyotes were finishing off the bologna and bread. I was too embarrassed to ride back home that night, so I waited for sunrise in the cave. Can't say I got much sleep. When I came back to the house empty-handed, Grandpa said, 'Well, you'll try again, boy, still a bit early. Hills'll be lousy with coons in a month or so.'"

"Funny, Stump, but that's not the way I heard the story from you forty years ago. If I remember right, you came home with so many pelts hanging across Ol' Yeller, he could barely walk out of the mountains."

"You have a lousy memory, Dickie."

The mare stops in front of the gate to the horse corral, patiently waiting to unload her burden for the night. I follow Stumpy back into the kitchen, where the dinner dishes sit on the counter, the pan still on the stove. I pull the recorked bottle of wine out of the fridge and sit at the table. Stumpy starts to clean the kitchen.

"When was the first night you spent alone in the cave?" he asks. "It couldn't a been too soon after you moved here. That scared little girl wouldn't have lasted twenty minutes out there alone." He finishes wiping down the counter and joins me at the table. The scared little girl he speaks of bounces around my insides like a tennis ball spiked with tacks.

"God, wasn't that scared little girl tiresome?" I say, more to myself than to Stumpy.

"No, she was heartbreakingly sweet." He tips my chin up with two fingers so the kitchen light hits my face. "And she's not that far gone," he says.

I push his hand away and pour some wine into one of the juice glasses on the table, aware of the gurgle as the wine leaves the bottle, aware of the clunk as the bottle hits the table, aware of Stumpy's eyes never leaving my face.

CHAPTER FOURTEEN

It was the end of seventh grade when I first spent a night alone in the cave, or at least attempted to. I would turn thirteen that summer, starting to shed the angst of youth and entering the darker anguish of adolescence. I may have always been an anxious girl regardless of my circumstances, but I believed my parents complicated my life in ways that other thirteen-year-old girls couldn't comprehend. I certainly could have mastered life had we stayed in Ganoa, so I meant to hold fast to my rejection of the ranching life in spite of pleasant summers spent in the easy company of Bev, driving tractors, riding horses, working cows, and gardening. I became adept at holding the experience of my summers and the notion of rejection totally separate in my mind. I was, after all, a product of my environment.

The particular incident that caused such distress as to entice me to spend a night alone in the cave may seem to some unrelated to the complexities of my life as a rancher's daughter, but I didn't see it that way. The actions of everyone in my life—my mother, Holly, Annie, Heber, Stumpy—were all intricately entwined, and the main thread led directly to my father's disdain for well-groomed neighborhoods. My mother should have been there for me when I came home from school that day, but she had a job instead. No one noticed that I tore my school clothes off through a fuzz of tears. No one heard the outside door to the pig room slam shut. No one saw me run through the cedars into the foothills.

When the sun fell behind my head, I lit the candles in the cave and settled on top of one horse blanket and under two others. I recognized the melodrama in my actions—disappearing without a note— but I felt alone and thereby justified. My sense of loneliness on that particular day was served up, as it often was, by my best friend, but I was still several years away from implicating Holly for her own actions. In the spring of '67, Holly's actions were, in my mind, still a direct result of George Sinfield's actions, which brought Clayton and Stumpy Nelson into my life—two things that combined to make Holly Hamilton act in inexplicable ways.

That year had been the worst. Starting junior high school initially brought me a great deal of relief because Stumpy—several years ahead of me in maturity, six months ahead in age, but one year behind in academics—would stay back in elementary school and I would have Holly to myself. But it was that damn bus that drove Holly crazy. And it was the way Bev made her rounds picking up and dropping off kids. She dropped off the elementary kids last but picked them up first. So every time that yellow bus swung into the circle in front of the junior high school, Holly would catch sight of Stumpy's red head poking up in a window. I mentioned this problem to Bev, but she just smiled with crinkles forming around her dark brown eyes and edging down the sides of her nose.

"Well, how long does it take you to get home on the bus?" Holly had asked.

"About forty minutes by the time we make all the stops."

"Well, so you and Stumpy spend eighty minutes together every day."

In fact, Stumpy and I spent a great deal more time than that together since our after-school and weekend chores often required a joint effort. I refused to sit by Stumpy on the bus and I told him why.

After that, Stumpy would call my name just as I was stepping on or off the bus and wave hysterically, which always set Bev to laughing like a fool. The two of them had apparently entered into some conspiracy to make my life even more miserable than it already was.

On the last day of school, I jumped off the bus, outwardly prepared to grieve with Holly about our separation for the summer, as we did at the end of each school year, but inwardly—buried as deeply as I could bury it—looking forward to a summer in Clayton with Bev. But Holly and Marlene weren't waiting for me at the bus stop, as they usually did. Stumpy and Bev looked at me then exchanged glances.

"See you this afternoon, Dickie," Bev called after me as I stepped out of the bus. I walked directly to my locker then out the back door of the school, where we hung out before class on sunny days. I found them deep in whispering conversation.

"Well, oh my God, Dickie!" Holly said, pulling me into their huddle. "You poor girl! There's the most awful rumor going around about you!"

I stood mortified, unable to imagine what might come next.

"Well, you tell her, Marlene," Holly instructed. "It's just too awful for me to repeat!"

Excitedly, Marlene relayed the story, literally spitting forth the words, saliva flying from the corners of her mouth and between her teeth. Dickie Sinfield is a slut.

I stood frozen, not entirely understanding what the word or the implications meant, although I'd heard the word slung around plenty since entering Ganoa Junior High School, where the titters of girls in the hallways talking their way around sex and boys was the norm. *She let him feel her up!* one of them would spurt out to be met with squeals of delight and disgust.

The story about Dickie Sinfield, as Marlene relayed it, supplemented with vivid details from Holly, turned out to be much worse than simply letting someone feel her up, which up until that point

I had supposed was the worst a girl could do. The story went like this: Dickie had this cave out behind her house in Clayton and all the boys with driver's licenses knew where it was, and many of them had visited it on more than one occasion. Ralph Carosella, an eighth grader, could confirm this because not only had his older brother, Kenny, been there, but he had, in fact, taken Ralph with him one time!

Dickie would wait for the boys inside the cave, but out in front sat a coffee can into which the boys would drop quarters. And it *had* to be quarters; Dickie insisted on it. If she heard one quarter drop, she'd take her blouse off; two, she'd strip down to panties and bra; three, she'd take her bra off (I didn't even own a bra yet! But since this was a secret I had been carefully guarding from Holly, who was proud of the bra her mother had bought for her to start the seventh grade, I didn't dare use this fact in protest); and four, or if she heard a dollar bill being slipped into the coffee can, she'd strip completely naked! She'd never let the boys go all the way—she wanted to remain a virgin—but she'd let them look and touch all they wanted!

Numbly, I went through my last day of school, the subject of all snickerings in all corners. Holly and Marlene kept their distance at lunchtime because, as Holly had quickly explained between third and fourth periods, Dickie, of course, understood they had to worry about their own reputations. I spent the lunch hour in the last stall of the girls' bathroom. I hoped Annie, who was in the eighth grade, would come and find me, but she had a different lunch hour and I seldom saw her at school.

At the end of the day, Holly looked around to make sure no one was watching then pulled me into a quick hug.

"Well, I do hope you can still have a good summer," she said. "You don't think Stumpy will pay any attention to these awful rumors, do you? No, of course he won't. Well, I hope not anyway!"

I watched Holly and Marlene bump together, walking toward my old neighborhood, giggling and whispering, as I waited for the bus. At one point, Marlene turned and waved wildly. These days Annie rode back and forth to school with Ella, whose mother decided she was "at an age" where bus riding was no longer acceptable. Eileen, Ella's younger sister, approached me as I stood alone at the curb. As far as sisters go, Eileen was about as different from Ella as I was from Annie—neither of us had the flair or the popularity of our older sisters—but Eileen had something none of us had: self-confidence that started deep in her bones, flowed through her blood, pulsated in her muscle tissue, and was wrapped tightly into the strange and wonderful package that was Eileen Anderson, a girl who walked so comfortably through the halls of Ganoa Junior High School, she was almost overlooked. She could be seen talking to the most popular student in the school or the most despised—both were common and either was acceptable for Eileen. So it didn't alarm anyone who was waiting for a bus that day when she sidled up next to the slut.

"I heard that story about you today, Dickie," Eileen said, then continued with the entirety of what she had to say without allowing me comment. "I know it isn't true. I also know who started the story and I think it only fair that you should know. It was Holly."

With that, Eileen wandered away again, sat on the lawn, and opened a book, having said what she needed to with no intention of discussing it further. I stood immobilized, the toes of my saddle shoes hanging off the edge of the curb, one navy-blue kneesock in its proper place, the other bunched around my ankle, an old pair of Annie's wool, plaid culottes—beaded from wear on the behind—hanging unevenly on my hips, thin, blond hair straggling around my face, which was splotched red and swollen from crying all day. I knew Eileen had told me the truth.

That's the way Bev found me when she pulled up. For the most part, I looked the way I did at the end of every school day—awkward, straggly, and disheveled—but my face must have given me away.

"How you doing, Dickie?" Bev said, after watching me climb the stairs without looking at her. She cast a glance at Stumpy, who was in his usual spot behind her; he shrugged and shook his head. I walked past them both and went to the last row in the bus before I remembered that's where the Miller twins usually sat with all the other rowdy boys from Warner. By the time I realized my mistake, it was too late, the Miller twins were already in the aisle headed straight for me. I jumped up and pushed past them to the front. *Here's a quarter, Dickie, show us your titties. Here's a dollar, Dickie, show us your twat. Shit, a quarter? I wouldn't give more than a penny to see those. I've seen better titties on my three-year-old sister!*

As I reached the front of the bus, Stumpy moved over and I slid in next to him. Bev swung the door shut without taking her eyes off the rearview mirror, practically taking Eileen's left hand off in the process as she jumped to get through the closing doors.

"Sorry, Eileen," Bev said, then realized her opportunity for information gathering. "What's going on?"

"Betrayal infused with juvenile idiocy," Eileen answered.

Bev nodded as if she understood completely. She walked three-quarters of the way down the aisle, stopping so her right hand rested on the seat back in front of the Miller twins, and bellowed, "Sit down and shut up!" The bus remained deathly silent all the way to Clayton, making my trip home excruciating.

"Dickie, you want to talk about it," Bev asked, when everyone was off except me and Stumpy. I shook my head.

"Why don't you come help me do some planting this afternoon," Bev said when she stopped to let Stumpy out. I shook my head again, ran down the steps, and disappeared into the fields behind Merv's house.

An hour or so after the desert sky darkened completely and a spray of stars appeared around a crescent moon that hung directly in front of the cave opening, a cold wind picked up. I pushed back deeper against the rock wall. The wind screamed through the cave, extinguishing the candles and masking every other noise around. A shadow rose before me. I screamed.

"It's me, Dickie," Stumpy yelled over the wind.

"You scared the crap out of me. What are you doing here?"

"Thought I'd find you here," he said, crawling under the blankets next to me.

"Well then, would it ever occur to you to give me a little privacy? And next time bring your own blanket."

"As you probably already figured, Bev's at your house, and she and your mom are worked into a frenzy about what happened at your school today."

"How do they know?"

"Oh, I imagine Bev made a phone call or two—can't think it would take her too long to sniff out the story."

"So you heard the story also?"

"Yeah."

"Great. Aren't you worried about tarnishing your reputation with a slut like me?"

"I'm a boy—that sort of thing builds reputations for us," Stumpy said, nudging me. I started crying. "Ah, Dickie, I'm sorry. Please don't cry. At least I know where you get it—your mom's damn near hysterical and crying like crazy. You know she stays calm as long as Bev stays calm, but I don't know that I've ever seen Bev quite this worked up. I can't stand to see grown women crying, so I told your mom I'd come find you."

"I didn't know you were so easily influenced by a tear or two."

"That and seeing Bev so riled up was making me a little nervous. She's having trouble following her 'no-interference' policy on this one."

"Bev has a 'no-interference' policy?"

"She thinks she does. But she wanted to call Holly's mother tonight and have a little chat with her. She talked herself out of it, but she's working at convincing your mother to make that call."

"It's not Holly's fault! It's yours! Yours and Bev's and Dad's!"

"Mine! How do I figure into this? I have nothing to do with the inner workings of Ganoa Junior High School or the evil workings of Holly Hamilton!"

"You have everything to do with it! Don't you see that? If you would just give her the attention she wants, if Bev would just be nicer to her and not upset her, if Dad hadn't moved us out to this horrible place!"

I could just make out Stumpy's raised eyebrows in the light of the moon.

"If you would just ignore me whenever Holly's around, then she wouldn't do this stuff!"

Stumpy's coarse hair stuck straight up to the top of the cave as if it were pushed up by his eyebrows instead of by the wind. He picked up a small rock, pitched it out in front of the cave, and ran his hands lightly over the ground searching for another.

"I don't ever plan on doing that, Dickie, so you're gonna have to figure out another way."

"Figures. You're out to ruin my life. How about if you and I limit our communications to only when Holly isn't present and the rest of the time you just adore her?"

"How about you dump her and find someone else to hang out with?"

"Can't do that. She's been my best friend since I was four, and best friends aren't that easy to come by. You wouldn't know, cause you don't have one."

"Well, if this is what best friends do for each other, I'm pretty happy to be without one."

"You don't have any friends at all, Stumpy, so you don't know what it's like."

"I have one."

IT'S ONLY AFTER Stumpy puts his wine down, disappears into the bathroom, and returns with a box of Kleenex that I realize sometime during the last hour as we reminisced about my days as the junior high slut, my laughter had turned to tears. I take the box from him and he moves behind me, pulling his hands through my hair and rubbing my neck. I don't stop him. All day I've been aware of how naturally our hands reach out for each other, as if our physical contact had never been severed.

"I think maybe you've been repressing your natural affinity for tears too long in that city," he says.

"I'm fine," I say, lifting my head and blowing my nose.

"Sorry to be the one to tell you this, but you don't look fine. In fact, you look very much like you did the night I found you in the cave after Holly made you every thirteen-year-old's fantasy."

"God, Stumpy, why can't we know when we're thirteen how much of life doesn't matter at all? How is it you seemed to know that when we were kids?"

"Hell, I didn't know any more than you did."

"You seemed to. You—and Eileen Anderson—seemed the epitome of calm and confidence. Course Eileen was so much so, she was sort of freaky, but you seemed to maneuver through your childhood with relative ease."

"All a facade."

"Really?"

"Somewhat. I was never really comfortable in school, being older than everyone in my class—you knew that—until I got to high school and got involved in sports. Before that, well, I always knew I'd be coming back here every night and that was enough for me."

"Funny, that was the part of my life that caused the most agony."

"Only because you insisted on it."

"Didn't anything about this place ever leave you feeling anxious or uneasy?"

"Only one thing—you."

"That's great. You live in the middle of twenty million pounds of nerve gas and know with certainty that the army considers this place and the people in it nothing more than potential collateral damage, and the only thing that distresses you is the pathetic, sniveling girl next door."

He walks in front of me and pulls his chair close to mine, putting his knees on the outside of my knees and his palms on the tops of my thighs.

"I had never in my life seen someone so filled with fear and pain as you were, Dickie," he says, a film forming over his pale blue eyes. "It unnerved me from the moment I laid eyes on you being dragged around by that steer at the stock show. And the first day I saw you out here in Clayton, the day you and Holly were cutting across the pasture and you were scared a that old lazy bull."

"Don't, Stumpy," I say, waving through the air between us with my hand and trying to push him back. He pulls both my hands into his.

"Every time I saw you shrink from one a George's outbursts, every time you let Holly manipulate you, every time the tears rolled down your dusty face and the pain lingered in those eyes—you broke my heart, Dickie. I didn't know my heart could be broken by one woman so many times in a lifetime."

"Stop, Stumpy," I say, pulling my hands away.

"You still break my heart," he says, tracing the wrinkles at the corner of my eye with his thumb. "Those eyes still pull at the part of me that wanted to somehow fix you, they still torment the kid who couldn't figure out how to make you stop being scared."

"Well, I'm all fixed now," I say, pushing my chair back and walking to the kitchen sink to rinse my face. "So you don't need to worry about that little girl anymore."

Stumpy puts a hand on the counter on either side of me. I feel his chin near the top of my head, his breath moving my hair, his chest barely touching my back. I'm careful not to react, not wanting to give him the satisfaction of knowing that his closeness unsettles me. I look down at the scuffed hands and see them as they would have looked tangled in my hair.

"Dickie, just because you've fooled the newspaper-reading public doesn't mean you've fooled everyone. Some of us still know you're full of shit."

"Tell me, Stumpy Nelson," I say, turning to face him in the small space between his body and the counter. A lazy smile makes its way through every carved line on his sunburned face and into his eyes, and I hate myself for what I'm about to do. "How is it you were so clear about all things—including the diabolical behavior of Holly Hamilton—up until you turned nineteen? What happened to all that composure and clarity then?"

I expect him to drop his hands and walk away, but he stays. The smile leaves his face and his eyes hold mine in a cold, almost mean, stare. His chest moves up and down under a blue demin work shirt, perspiration rises to the surface—across his eyebrows, on the back of his neck. The tone of his voice matches his eyes.

"Dickie, you and me have been bantering with each other at weddings and funerals at five- or six-year intervals now for more'n thirty years. Maybe that's long enough to go without really talking. How about we open another bottle of wine and finally say some things that need to be said?"

"I don't see any reason not to go another thirty years," I say, trying to push free of him, but his hands tightly grip the counter to keep me where I am. "What the hell is there to say?"

"Let's find out," he says, seizing my right arm just above the elbow, pulling me back to the table.

"Jesus, Stumpy, I feel like the prisoner being led to trial."

"Hmm," Stumpy grunts and pulls a bottle of red wine down from the cupboard as I push myself away from the table and stand.

"Don't fucking move," he commands.

"I have to pee. Can I pee?" He gives permission by throwing his head in the direction of the bathroom. "I promise not to crawl out the bathroom window, boss."

"Leave the door open and make some noise so I know for sure," he says, without even a smirk.

When I come out of the bathroom, Stumpy has lit a bunch of candles, turned out the lights, and poured each of us a glass of wine.

"I thought we were having a hearing not a romantic interlude."

"You know I hate bright lights. Besides, I figured if you're gonna cry some more—and that's a pretty safe bet—you might appreciate some softer light."

"Maybe you're just afraid I'll see you crying—the tough cowboy."

"Dickie, shut up and sit down, will ya?"

I sit and pick up my glass of wine. "To full disclosure."

He clinks my glass. "I hope you mean that and not just being a smart-ass, as usual."

"I mean it," I say, and maybe I really do. Why not? Maybe he's right. Maybe thirty years is too long to let things go unsaid. Then again, maybe it's not long enough. Maybe a lifetime isn't long enough. Maybe some things are best carried to the grave. Or maybe I'm being as melodramatic as that thirteen-year-old girl. Maybe I still can't figure out how much of life really doesn't matter at all—and how much actually does.

We sip wine and look at each other. The crickets rush to fill the silence, and the kitchen faucet drips into the frying pan in the sink. He inhales deeply and exhales slowly and loudly.

"Stumpy, I—"

He holds up his hand to stop me.

"Don't say anything just yet. Let me gather my thoughts."

I wait.

"Fucking Holly Hamilton was the biggest mistake I ever made in my life."

"Jeez, Stump."

"I'm sorry for the crudeness of that statement, but that's the most honest way I can think to put it."

"I don't quite know how to respond to that, other than to agree. Anything else?"

"Come on, Dickie."

"Listen, Stump, I don't really think this is necessary, do you? You have your little life here in Clayton, and I have mine in Salt Lake City. Why do we want to put ourselves through this?"

"Indulge me for a moment in my little life, will ya, Dickie? It's two A.M., you have no place to sleep unless you plan to sleep with me. You want to do something besides talk?"

"Well, if you promise to stay on your side of the bed—"

"I don't have a side; the whole goddamn bed is mine!"

"Okay! Fine! Why did you fuck Holly?"

"Because I was mad at you."

"Ha! God, now you sound like me when I was thirteen and trying to blame Holly's bullshit on you."

"Well, it's the truth. I was mad at you, she made it easy, and that's what nineteen-year-old boys do when they're pissed off."

"What were you mad at me for?"

"Pretty much everything, if I remember right."

"I wasn't even here."

"Precisely."

"Stumpy, I—"

"I never loved her, Dickie. I married her because that's what people did in 1973 when someone was pregnant."

"Not necessarily."

"What do you mean?"

"I mean not everybody who got pregnant in 1973 got married."

"Like who?"

"Like I don't know who! All I'm saying is that you didn't *have* to get married. You didn't *have* to bring her out to the ranch to live. You didn't *have* to move her into this house with Merv. You didn't *have* to have yet another kid after the first one. That's all I'm saying. You act as if there were no other options in 1973 and that explains your whole fucking life! Well, it doesn't. It doesn't explain a fucking thing."

Stumpy stares into the red liquid in his glass, swirling it around and tapping the glass softly on the table. I don't know whether he plans to drink it or fling it at the closest thing, which would be me. The most expressive part of his face—from the eyes upward—flinches and creases. Slowly he lifts his eyes to meet mine.

"I think I damn near broke Grandpa's heart the day I moved her into this house," he says, his voice breaking. "You know Grandpa always did right by everybody. He kept saying to me, 'Boy, I don't know what the right thing is here. I just know in my gut this ain't it. That young girl needs help,' he'd say, 'there's no doubt about that. But it might be beyond our capacity to give her the help she needs.' I didn't listen to him, Dickie. I was all puffed up with the idea of being a man, couldn't see the complexities he was trying to show me. How could I have been so cocky? That old man never gave me a piece of bad advice in my entire life—and I didn't listen to him."

I shake my head and refill our glasses. I want to scream at Stumpy—you're goddamn right you should have listened to him—but I keep my mouth shut.

"Course he loved having the boys around," Stumpy says, "and strangely enough, he and Holly got along fine—the boys sort of acted like a bonding agent between them. Fact, he got along with her better than I ever did. He was smart enough not to fight her when she signed the boys up for tennis lessons and piano lessons and just about any goddamn thing that would keep them away from ranch work."

"Oh Lord, I imagine you were trying to turn them into *real* men?"

"Goddamn right. I kept thinking, 'They're my boys too, goddammit.' Thing was, though, they never were. They were Holly's sons right from the start."

"She never was good at sharing."

"Well, Grandpa knew that and didn't fight it. Kept saying to me, 'There's more than one way to live a life, son,' so he made peace with it a lot sooner than I did. Those boys adored him—me, not so much. I've pretty much gained their animosity forever."

"Well, that might be true, Stumpy. I've never met them, so I can't say. The idea of Holly spawning and rearing members of the human species is more than a little frightening to me, although could be I've got some personal feelings mixed up in that. But your boys are still young enough to be pretty sure about things—right and wrong, love and hate—you know, kind of like you when you married Holly," I say, tugging on his hair. "Give them a few more years to lose all that clarity, they might come around."

His shoulders drop about four inches from where they'd been hunched under his ears.

"Grandpa seemed to like being around them, but there was always something sad about him during those years that would come out whenever the two of us were alone. Sometimes he'd look at me when we were riding next to each other, like he was searching for something he could never find. Seemed like something always went unsaid. Or when we were in the corral working cattle or saddling the horses, he'd touch my back whenever he'd walk past me—so much tenderness under his fingers it'd bout drop me to my knees. God, I hate what I did to that old man," Stumpy says, his voice breaking again and his shoulders drawing back up around his ears.

I walk behind Stumpy and pull my fingers through his hair, pulling his head to my belly. I fight the impulse to lean down and kiss his neck just beneath the collar, where his rough, red skin turns soft and white.

"Stump, you didn't do anything to Merv except rile up his mothering instincts for you. They were always right there barely covered by his skin anyhow. You just never noticed cause you never so blatantly placed yourself in harm's way before."

"The very day we took Kip to the airport to go to college, Holly packed her things in the car and left without a word, without a scene. I watched from the front door. Grandpa walked her to the car and gave her a hug. She clung to him like she never wanted to let go."

"Well, if anybody could draw a little humanity out of Holly, it'd be Merv."

"Finally, he gently pulled her arms from around his neck, opened and closed the car door for her, watched her back out of the driveway, and waved like she was just going to the grocery store. Then he walked back in the house, looked at me, and said, 'Well, that's that,' and the two of us pretty much settled right back into life as if she'd only been here twenty minutes stead a twenty years."

"How old was Merv when she left?"

"Oh, I guess he woulda been around eighty. I can't remember for sure. We had another twelve years together after that. Ranched and lived just like we always had, joined up with Bev and Heber a course."

"How did Bev get along with Holly here?"

"Well, she didn't come over for dinner anymore, if that's what you're asking. In fact, I'm not sure Bev ever stepped foot in this house while Holly lived here. Bev's grudges are as fierce as her loyalties."

Stumpy reaches over his head and grasps both my wrists. He swings me around in front of him and back into my chair. "I think I might be getting a bald spot up there." He rubs his head. "You were yanking pretty hard every time name Holly's name came up."

"How come you never got married again, Stumpy?"

He shrugs, still holding both my wrists. "I don't know. Maybe the same reason you never got married."

"And what would that be?"

"You tell me."

"Oh no. You're doing fine with this confessional. I suggest we stick to the topic at hand."

He shrugs and lets go of my wrists. "Heber tried it a couple of times; it was enough just watching him."

"How is it Heber ended up with that southernmost piece of Bev's land anyway?"

"Well, I'm not really sure I understand that whole thing. I was hoping you could enlighten me on that. Didn't your mom tell you that story?"

"You know Mom always gave the sanitized version—the one that makes all the characters nice. About all I got from her is that Heber wanted to buy some land and Bev was nice enough to sell him some."

"Well, the idea was that Heber would take over your dad's land since your dad hadn't done a damn thing with that land for years anyway. Then Bev would sell him a piece on the north end of her ranch alongside. That piece alone, without your dad's land, wouldn't a been worth much, but with your dad's land, it made a decent little ranch. But George wouldn't sell to him."

"George Sinfield sort of reminds you of old Ira, doesn't he?" I say.

"They do have the same sort of bitterness runnin through em, but George was never near as nasty as Ira. Even after he stopped ranching his land, he let Bev and us have full use of it. We could even talk him into coming out and working with us some days. I like your dad, Dickie. I don't know what eats at him and makes him so miserable or what prevents him from moving past certain events in his life—seems like he just gets stuck and there ain't a tractor in the valley that can pull him free."

"Sometimes I don't really know what people mean by 'getting over' or 'moving past' things, Stumpy. Maybe I take after George that way. Seems like some things are just too damn big to get over. It's like a giant boulder in the road—you can't move it or drive around it, so you take a detour and sometimes you never find your way back. You might cross the old road a few times, but you've detoured so far and long it doesn't look familiar anymore. Except George didn't even take the detour. In the summer of '68 he just sat down next to the boulder, leaned his back against it, and stayed there."

Stumpy nods and stares into his wine. "Is that what happened to us, Dickie? Did we get detoured so far, we couldn't recognize the old road anymore?"

"Maybe."

"I sure as hell never expected to go down the road I ended up on."

"But still you ended up here, Stump. Isn't that what you wanted?"

"Sure, but . . ."

"But what?"

"Well, I just never thought it would be like it was, that's all."

"How did you think it would be?"

"Hell, I don't know, Dickie. I guess for one thing I never pictured this basin without you in it."

I don't respond. The truth is I could never picture this basin without me in it either. Which is exactly why, until my mother's illness brought me back, I made it a point to stay away from Clayton. Visiting exposed the difficult reality that the place was no longer mine. It never occurred to me when I left in 1972 that I was leaving for good; nor had I made plans to return. I simply hadn't thought that far in advance. But it wasn't long after my departure that the permanence of it became clear—December 18, 1973, to be exact. The birth date of Stumpy's first son.

"Remember that summer, Dickie, after we found the cows? So quiet in this valley you could hear every single breath you took. I mean the cows were never here in the summers anyway—they were up on the mountain—but that summer when they weren't anywhere . . . so fucking quiet. You, too, Dickie. You barely spoke that summer; so sad I couldn't stand to leave you alone."

"I remember."

"We made promises to each other that summer, Dickie."

"We were kids, Stumpy. Kids say lots of stupid shit."

"It wasn't stupid; it mattered. What happened that summer changed the lives of every single person we knew. You and me, Dickie . . . well, I don't think two people ever clung to each other tighter. It mattered, that's all I'm saying."

"Stumpy—"

"You can say it was just stupid kid stuff now, Dickie, but you know goddamn well it mattered."

"Well, it doesn't matter anymore, does it?" I say, getting up to put my glass in the sink.

"What the hell does matter to you, Dickie? How about you take a turn disclosing a few things?"

"Ah, Stumpy, the wine's gone, and it'll be light soon. I'm exhausted. No doubt somebody will be hunting for us in a few hours. How about I take my turn another time?"

"We're not finished here, Dickie. Don't think I'm gonna let you off the hook."

"Oh Lord, no, why would I ever think that? I need to lie down a minute." I walk toward what used to be Merv's bedroom.

"Well, you're gonna have to lie down in here." He pulls me toward his bedroom. "I turned that room into a study after Grandpa died."

"A study? What the hell do you study, Stump? There's an item that didn't get disclosed."

"Just shut up and lie down with me a minute, Dickie."

Too exhausted to argue, I follow him into his bedroom and begin to collapse on the bed.

"Not so fast," he says, grasping both of my forearms and pulling me back up. "Not in those overalls; they're covered in horsehair."

"They're not, Martha," I whine, slumping on the edge of the bed. "I would have felt it; it would have made me itch. You just want me to take my pants off. You haven't changed a bit."

"Mm-hmm."

"When did you change clothes?" I ask, staring at strong calf muscles below a pair of gray athletic shorts.

"When you were in the bathroom."

"I guess I couldn't be allowed the same sort of privacy? Oh, I'm too old and tired to give a shit," I say, pulling the overalls off and collapsing on the bed in my underwear.

I feel his weight at the foot of the bed, then, for a moment, nothing more. I glide toward the mist of sleep surrounded by the sound of deep breathing. His? Mine? I can't force the answer through the haze.

He strokes the inside of my left calf, tracing the S-shaped scar, so lightly, so tenderly, my skin reaches out to meet his fingertips. He circles the scar with light kisses, then outlines it with his tongue. I'm pulled in two directions—inward to the dream, outward to the physical world. I find him in both places. *You're still wearing my brand*, he whispers.

CHAPTER FIFTEEN

On the first day of summer 1968, the sun fell hot on my left arm and leg as I rode south to Bev's. At the same time, the last of the cold mountain air swirled along my right side from the Onaquis, leaving me feeling like a pancake that never gets flipped. Bev already had Sego saddled when I arrived and had my saddle and blankets thrown over a fence rail waiting to be thrown on Plummy.

"Glad you're here early," Bev said. "It'll take us most the day to drive those cows up over the mountain and into that new allotment on the west side. You see George and Heber?"

"Yep, they already had the horses saddled when I left."

"Good enough."

We trailed the cows down the highway through Johnson's Pass shortly after the government workers had made their way to Dugway Proving Grounds. Only one car passed through the herd, a honeymoon couple from California in a cherry-red GTO convertible with romantic notions of driving the old Lincoln Highway from San Francisco to New York, according to the driver, who rambled the entire story to Merv before he asked for confirmation that they were on the right road. They had just come across Nevada—apparently expecting slightly more commerce than they found—and were overjoyed at the sight of us, honking and snapping pictures and sending cows running off both sides of the highway.

"Hey, buckaroos!" the guy kept yelling.

"Look! A little buckarette!" the woman squealed as Plummy plodded past her door. She removed the scarf that had been tied snugly under her chin and shook out hair the color of root beer. Then she popped up onto the back of her seat to snap pictures, perched with an arched back to accentuate her bare midriff and pert breasts. She was perfectly painted—lips, cheeks, fingernails, toenails—everything matching the car. I had to stare at her a long time because at first glance, it was my mother in that white leather seat, her head thrown back, her long neck visible, painted nails lightly touching her parted lips, laughing the way she did with Captain Fulmer the day we met him in the grocery store.

A few weeks later, on a brilliantly sunny Saturday, Merv, Dad, Heber, and Bev moved irrigation pipe while Stumpy and I loaded two horses into the trailer and drove back over Johnson's Pass. Stumpy was fourteen at the time, but had been driving Merv's truck and trailer since he was twelve. Most Clayton kids started driving as soon as their services were needed without much regard to licenses and laws. Gene Vogul, a Ganoa County sheriff's deputy and the only lawman in Clayton, knew this, so he just gave us the Clayton one-finger wave when we passed him on the county road. Our assignment, as handed out early that morning by Merv, was to ride all day to make sure the cattle guards were in good repair and the gates were closed. Both Mom and Merv had packed us a lunch, so our saddlebags were stuffed with food and cans of soda pop.

Stumpy had been a little sulky lately, having recently found himself the butt of some jokes that should have—but didn't—end when school let out. He was also sore at himself because the jokes took him by surprise and he figured he should have seen it coming. Since Stumpy and I had spent a good portion of our waking hours from the age of eight in the company of each other, it never occurred to us that our friendship would suddenly attract the attentions of testosterone-hyped country boys like a porn magazine hidden behind the haystack.

If the jokes had never started, I'm not sure Stumpy and I would have yet noticed the other was the opposite sex. And even if we did notice, we certainly wouldn't have acknowledged it. Now it was impossible to avoid. Stumpy tried to arrange for Heber to make this all-day trip with him, but since I was more useful on the back of a horse than I was moving irrigation pipe, Merv just smiled and said, "Take Dickie."

We bumped over a dirt road with far too much speed and silence before we got to the clearing that would allow us room to turn the truck and trailer. I barely had Plummy out of the trailer before Stumpy had already tightened the cinch on Ol' Yeller and ridden halfway up the trail.

"Hey, wait up!" I kicked Plummy into a begrudging trot to catch him. "You gonna be this way all day?"

"What way?"

"Not talking to me."

"Just don't have anything to say. Got a problem with that?"

"Oh, hell no. In fact, it'll be pleasant for a change not listening to you singing that damn song you sing every time you put your butt in a saddle."

"I didn't say I wasn't gonna sing. I said I wasn't gonna talk."

"Oh, for hell sakes, Stumpy. It's just us out here. We're on the other side of the mountain from any of those stupid boys."

"Well, how would you like it?"

"Ha! Apparently you've forgotten who you're talking to. I've been putting up with it for so damn long, I barely notice it anymore. Besides, if they're saying stuff about you, what the hell do you think they're saying about me? I barely started shedding my reputation as the slut of Ganoa Junior High School and now this."

Stumpy rode in front of me on the narrow trail in silence, a thatch of red hair sticking out from under his ball cap, covering his already sunburned neck.

"Fine. We won't talk. See if I care."

"Well, that's exactly what's bothering me, Dickie."

"What?"

"What they're saying about you."

"What are they saying about me?"

"That you and me are doing stuff."

"What kinda stuff?"

"God, Dickie, what kinda stuff do you think?"

"Stumpy, remember last year when I felt so bad about being the slut of Ganoa Junior High? Remember what you said?"

"What?"

"You said, 'What do you care what those people think; they're all idiots anyway.'"

"And did that make you feel better?"

"No, didn't make a bit of difference. I felt like crap—still do. But my point is you and me have been friends a long time. And our only option is to stop being friends, which isn't going to be too easy unless we can convince Merv and Bev that this somehow benefits them also and they should no longer send us out on these kinds of jobs together."

"I don't see that happening."

"Me neither. So our only option is to ignore those idiots."

"Have you learned to ignore them?"

"No. But I'm me, Stumpy. Dickie Sinfield. I can't ignore stuff like that. It's not part of my makeup. But you're you. Stumpy Nelson. It's exactly who you are. I don't know why you're letting this get to you."

Stumpy slowed on the trail and waited for me to ride up next to him. There wasn't really room for two horses, so we sat with our legs pressed hard against each other's between the horses' bellies.

"But that's just it, Dickie," he said, looking out from under a red ball cap clashing with his hair and face. "I could ignore it if you could. But I can't stand that you can't ignore it. I can't stand that it hurts you."

I kicked my horse ahead of his on the trail, uncomfortable with the way he was looking at me.

"Stumpy, you can't stop things from hurting me," I said, leaning back with one elbow resting on Plummy's rump, my head tipped to where I could see Ol' Yeller's ears. "Just ask my mother; she's been trying to figure out how to do that for years. I'm an emotional sponge moving across the counter of life. I soak up every stinky mess I come across. But you, Stumpy, you're one of those cheap waxy napkins that come enclosed in plastic with a cheap fork. You skim over the mess without absorbing anything at all. You just—"

"What the fuck . . . ?"

Something in his voice pulled me straight up in the saddle. I twisted to look at him, but he was looking past me up the trail. About fifteen feet ahead of us a cow and calf pair made their way toward us. The calf was bleating alongside its mother as she staggered on the trail, dropped to her front knees, struggled up again, staggered some more, all the time bellowing as if she were being strangled. Her spine was arched—as cows do when they urinate—but contorted, twisting her hindquarters bizarrely off to the right, her neck stiffened and bent around to meet the Lazy S brand on her right hip. A steady flow of green shit and urine streamed from under the tail that rose in the air behind her as if it had a live electric line running through it. She dropped again just as Stumpy and I got to her. Her purple tongue hung from her mouth, swollen and heavy as a church bell, dragging a greenish gluey stream of snot and saliva down the front of her and over the ground. She bellowed steadily, as if she were being gutted alive. Her low groans mixed with the despairing bawl of her clean red-and-white calf, sticking by her left side on its spindly legs.

"Somebody must a shot her," Stumpy said, jumping off his horse. But before he could reach the cow, she dropped over and rolled hideously off the low side of the trail, rolling three times over, huge belly, full bag, and swollen teats colliding grotesquely with stiffened legs flung out helplessly, crashing into the brush, between cedars, still bellowing and struggling uselessly to get back on her feet. The calf ran blindly, stumbling down the hill after her. I followed. Stumpy had me by the shoulders. I saw his red intense face just inches from mine, his chapped lips moving for what seemed like a long time before the words came into focus.

"Dickie! Dickie! Stop it!" he yelled. Then I heard another voice screeching *oh God oh God oh God oh God*. I realized it was my own.

"Dickie! Stop!"

I shut my mouth but couldn't stop moving, my body seemed to be flailing, searching for equilibrium. I let out a wail, just enough to obstruct the cow's strangled cries and the calf's desperate squalling. Stumpy wrapped both arms around me and pulled me so tight against him, I could barely take in air.

"Stop, stop, stop," he whispered, his fingers wrapped tight in my hair. Then suddenly he pushed me away from him and held me at arm's length. The look in his face set my body to thrashing again.

"Jesus Christ, do you hear that?"

"What is it, what is it, what is it . . ." I rocked and moaned, matching the bawling of the calf.

"Dickie, I need you to listen to me." He dug his fingertips into my shoulders, his voice as stiff as his arms. "Something's really wrong here. Get on your horse and ride back to the truck."

"But we can't leave the calf," I wailed.

"We'll come back for it. I promise. But I'm hearing something up ahead on the trail that sounds like it's coming from Marsh Meadow. That's where we expected most a the cows would be. I have a real bad feeling about this, Dickie. I'm going to check it out, but I need you to get back on Plummy and ride back to the truck. Wait for me there. I'll pick the calf up on my way back. I promise."

"No, no, no, no, no. Stumpy, I can't. I have to go with you. Please. I have to go with you!"

"Listen, Dickie, I'm afraid a what we're going to see up there. I'd feel a whole lot better if you'd ride in the opposite direction right now."

"No, no, no!"

"Okay, Dickie, okay." Stumpy pulled me into his chest one more time. "Okay, come on."

He helped me back on Plummy, remounted Ol' Yeller, and took off down the trail at a trot. He reached Marsh Meadow a few seconds before me, jumped off his horse while it was still moving, and ran back toward me. I was screaming again when he pulled me off Plummy.

"Shh, shh, shh, shh," he said, but I had to keep my own scream running through my head. I had to block out the guttural moans of a few hundred distorted cattle, staggering and dying in the meadow in front of us. I had to block out the nasal-y wail of the calves.

I don't remember riding back along the trail to the truck. I remember sitting on my horse at the place where we first saw the mother cow—now dead, eyes open, tongue lolling to one side, legs already stiffened out from her large belly—and watching Stumpy gather the calf up in his arms before he placed it on my saddle in front of me, its legs dangling over my own. I remember Stumpy positioning my arms around the soft red hair of the calf before prying open my clenched hands and closing them on the saddle horn.

"Like that," I think he said. "Hang on like that."

He took Plummy's reins in his right hand, remounted his horse, and led us out of the trees. When we got back to the truck, Stumpy put me and the calf in the cab while he unhooked the trailer and tied both horses to it. I buried my face in the calf's hair. It stepped all over my feet trying to find firm ground. It smelled sour like its dying mother and fresh like the leaves on a cottonwood tree. It shook and moaned lowly and quietly; I did the same.

Stumpy drove like a madman over the steep, narrow road of Johnson's Pass with one hand on the steering wheel and the other on the back of my neck, letting go only long enough to shift gears. I bent over the calf, pulling it tightly against my convulsing stomach. As soon as Stumpy caught sight of the others moving sprinkler pipe, he laid on the horn. Merv didn't hesitate a moment before he dropped his end of pipe and started running toward us from the field, the others close behind. I pulled my head up to see Mom, Aunt Alma, and Annie running down the dirt road—a festival of spring colors. Strange, I remember thinking, how everyone knows immediately when something dreadful happens.

EVERYONE WENT BACK out to Marsh Meadow except me and Mom. Stumpy tried to talk Annie out of going, but for some reason I couldn't grasp, she insisted. Later I found out she had heard Stumpy tell Merv all the calves were still alive.

Mom took me and the calf into the kitchen, put a blanket around me, and fixed me a cup of hot chocolate even though it was eighty-five degrees and sunny outside. I kept the calf between my knees, stroking it and cooing. Mom didn't ask questions. She mixed calf manna with warm water in a two-quart bottle with a nipple the size of a fat man's middle finger and handed it to me. The sweet scent of vanilla drifted through the kitchen. The calf sucked hard, almost pulling the bottle out of my hands, seeking appeasement for its trauma. Its tail switched back and forth as it sucked, oblivious to its own impolite slurping, bubbles and foam collecting at the corners of its mouth and dripping off its chin.

Bev, Merv, Dad, and the others literally scooped up all the calves, put them in several trailers, and brought them back to Merv's corrals. It took them all day and numerous trips. At night, the bawling of those calves traveled through the west side of the valley, carried on the cool night breeze in and out of open windows, in and out of our collective consciousness. A wailing of grief with no possibility of deliverance settled over the basin, trapped between the Oquirrhs and the Onaquis like a high-pressure system, letting nothing out and nothing in.

• • •

THE TALLY AND STORY behind the scene went like this: The day before Stumpy and I rode upon the dying cow and her calf, the army set out to test two new high-pressure nerve-gas dispensers. At 5:30 P.M., a low-flying jet left Dugway Proving Grounds headed for a specified testing zone, where it dropped low and released 320 gallons of VX nerve agent into thirty-five-mile-an-hour winds that blew from the west—from Dugway toward the Onaqui Mountains. The winds were of little concern to army researchers who had access to high-tech meteorological equipment, allowing them to closely predict the distribution of the gas. What they did not predict was the malfunction of the dispensers, which did not close as planned, allowing nerve gas to spray beyond the test area.

The day after Stumpy and I made our gruesome discovery, a U.S. Army spokesman from Dugway issued the following statement, which ran in every Utah newspaper: *Tests at Dugway Proving Grounds are definitely NOT responsible for the deaths of the livestock. Since we were first contacted by local veterinarians in the area, we checked and found we had not been running any tests that would cause this.*

It took about a week for the truth to leak that the army had in fact been conducting nerve-gas tests in the area on the day in question. At that point, the army issued another statement saying its spokesman had been misunderstood. What the spokesman actually meant was that although tests had been run, *the aerial spray tests conducted at Dugway in no way contributed to the death of livestock in the surrounding area,* and the spokesman went on to suggest the livestock died from a mysterious poisonous plant found in Skull Valley. The army stuck with this story for fifteen months. At the end of fifteen months, the army agreed to reimburse the ranchers and sheepherders for their losses, but refused to admit responsibility, saying only that the overwhelming evidence—brought to them by their own large assembly of veterinarians, pathologists, nutritionists, and other scientists who examined the dead animals and plants in the area—was inconclusive.

The scientists determined that the cattle and sheep drowned in an excess of acetylcholine. In other words, the nerve agent did exactly what it is designed to do. It disrupted the enzyme that removes secretions from nerve endings. The livestock drowned in their own nerve liquids. Calves and lambs were spared because they were still feeding on their mothers—they were not grazing on the contaminated grasses.

FOR ALMOST A FULL WEEK after the discovery of the cows, a couple hundred stunned, motherless calves mollified our own anguish by demanding we pay attention to theirs. Merv rigged a way to wire bottles to the second-from-the-bottom fence post so we could line up forty calves at time. Aunt Alma started sleeping at our house to help out, and even Mom took a week's leave from her job to be part of the assembly line it took to mix and hang bottles and record ear-tag numbers. Around 1 P.M. each day, Mom and Alma would set up lunch at Merv's picnic table and we would eat in numbed silence to the background moaning of the unappeasable calves.

At the end of five days, only six calves had died, the others were beginning to quiet down, and among the nine of us, an occasional smile could be seen fluttering through tired eyes. On Friday, the sixth day of tending to the calves, a small but palpable elevation in the mood settled over a large pot of vegetable beef soup and several loaves of fresh-baked bread at the picnic table. Merv was telling Annie that we'd likely get through a feeding session a little faster if she wasn't inclined to hug every calf and kiss the top of its head as she read off ear-tag numbers when he stopped midsentence. When he didn't continue, each of us, in our own time, looked up to see the foreboding in his eyes. A semi truck pulling a stock trailer had stopped on the county road, then backed up and turned down the dirt road toward us. Two army vehicles and Gene Vogul in a Ganoa County sheriff's car led the truck directly down the lane that ran alongside Merv's property. The truck chugged to a dusty stop about thirty feet from where we sat.

"What are they doing?" Annie demanded, wild-eyed, when the semi truck starting backing toward the loading chute.

"That's what I aim to find out," Bev said. "Gene, want to tell us what the hell's going on here?"

"I'm sorry, Bev," Gene said, tipping his hat. "I sure as hell hate to be the one to tell y'all this, but these boys are here to pick up your calves."

Bev turned toward Merv, who was studying a piece of paper handed to him by one of the three men in uniform—the one with first lieutenant's insignia on his shirt and without an M-14 slung over his shoulder. He handed the paper to Bev.

"What's it say?" she asked, taking it from him.

"Just what Gene said. They're taking the calves."

"Like hell they are," Bev said. "Gene, there must be—"

No one except George had noticed the truck driver exit his truck. He was just climbing over the fence to herd the calves up the loading chute when George caught him by the back of his jeans and swung him around, slamming him first into a fence post, then to the ground. By the time the truck driver had staggered to his feet, blood pouring from his nose, George was pinned against the fence with two M-14s pointed at his chest. Annie was sobbing and Mom and Alma were hanging on to Heber, who apparently intended to join the melee with the truck driver. Stumpy went to stand next to Merv and I stayed at frozen to my seat at the table.

"Gene, you call those boys off right now," Merv said.

"Merv, we don't want any trouble here," Gene said. "But you—"

Merv held a hand up to Gene. "We ain't gonna discuss this any further, Gene, until those guns are pointed at the ground."

"Drop those rifles," the lieutenant said. When they lowered their guns, George lowered his head and stalked off through the field in the direction of our house. Mom released Heber and he ran after him. The lieutenant turned to address Merv and Bev.

"I sure don't want to do this to you folks, but I'm following orders here. You'll be reimbursed top price for those calves. I give you my personal guarantee."

"Well, that really ain't the point, now is it?" Bev said. "The army's denying any responsibility for this mess, so what do they want with these calves?"

"I don't know anything about that, ma'am. Like I said, I'm just following orders. I don't have any more information than that, ma'am. But I will remind you folks that during wartime, civilians are sometimes called upon—"

"Son, we don't need to be reminded that the country is at war," Merv said, although, in fact, I had remained mostly oblivious of the Vietnam War thus far. "And we don't need you telling us what our patriotic duty entails," Merv continued. "We've pretty much given our entire livelihoods to the so-called war effort, and there ain't a person here's gonna buy that bullshit right now."

The lieutenant nodded. Bev and Merv looked at each other then at Gene, who lifted his hands in a helpless gesture.

"Bev, unless we want to get our own rifles and have a shoot-out here," Merv said, "I don't know that we can do much to stop this." Merv looked toward the picnic table, where Alma sat with both arms wrapped around the still-sobbing Annie, and Mom had pulled me in tight against her side. He turned back to address the lieutenant. "I understand orders, young man, I followed them myself once. But you picked a helluva way to go about this. A heads-up would have been the right thing to do here," he said, nodding toward us. "You do what you gotta do, but you'll get no help from us." Merv put an arm around Bev's shoulder and turned her toward us. "I think the damage has been done, but let's get those kids outta here."

Mom and Alma packed up the food and we ended up in our kitchen, where we found George and Heber sitting silently at the table. Annie retreated to her bedroom and the rest of us leaned against counters and slumped around the table. Mom futilely pulled the windows shut but could not block out the unmistakable moans of calves still shaky on their legs as they were pushed into the darkness of the truck. There was nothing for us to do but listen. When the bawling ended, we listened to the truck shift gears up the dirt road. When it reached the county road and faded out of earshot, we sat in excruciating silence.

BEV CHRISTENSEN, Merv Nelson, and George Sinfield lost a combined total of 692 cows in addition to the calves. Sheepherders in Skull Valley, on the west side of the Stansbury and Onaqui Mountains, lost 6,293 sheep. The time Dad, Merv, and Bev would have spent mending fences and riding the mountain that year were instead spent in tedious meetings with lawyers and army officials, and even flights to Washington, D.C., on a couple of occasions to testify at hearings. The anger that had been steadily seeping out of Dad over the last six years returned, increasing with each meeting he attended. Around the house his rage flew out unpredictably and indiscriminately, eradicating any comfort level any of us had attained with him since moving to the ranch. Heber got the worst of it, either because he was the oldest—starting his senior year the next fall—or because he was the only son, a constant reminder of the dead legacy. He and Dad got themselves twisted in a downward spiral they couldn't stop. Dad picked at everything Heber did, and Heber gave him more and bigger things to pick at. Soon Heber was sluffing school, drinking heavily, and wrecking cars, which in time led to a fistfight in the backyard that took Merv and Stumpy to pull apart after I summoned them by phone. I might have let Dad and Heber pummel each other for a while had I not seen the sorrow in my mother's face and heard the misery in her voice. My mother's resignation turned to deep sadness in the summer of '68, which clawed at my insides. Bev came over the night Dad and Heber fought, took one look at Mom sitting slack and red-eyed at the kitchen table, grabbed my father by the neck of his shirt, and pulled him through the living room and out the front door with enough force to rip his shirt cleanly down the side seams. He never touched Heber, or any of us, again—in anger or affection.

I rode over to Bev's every morning that summer, searching for refuge in routine, but instead I'd find her still in bed. Jarred and marooned by her sorrow, I'd climb to the top of the haystack and sit facing the Onaquis with my back to the sun until Stumpy showed up, which he invariably did each morning. He'd sit with me for a while, sharing the hard-boiled eggs and cold toast he brought wrapped in a bandanna, and then he'd wordlessly coax me down with a nudge and a look and we'd ride deep into the Onaquis with the disconcerting knowledge that we could stay away all day. No chores, no expectations. By late afternoon, we often found ourselves at Hell Hole Springs searching for signs of life—our own and that of the wild horses.

"They're gone," I said one day, sitting on the same rock Stumpy and I had shared the first day he took me there. "Dead."

"They'll be back," he said.

"What makes you think so?"

"I just feel it. They're not dead."

"I can't feel a damn thing." I left the rock and walked down to the pond, crouching to run my hand over the smooth mud banks that once held their hoofprints, longing for their musky scent in the clean air. I tugged off boots and socks, sank my feet into the mud up to my ankles, and stood with my eyes closed. Following instincts working to dislodge the desolation that had worked its way deep inside me, I was barely aware of the remaining articles of clothing I pulled from my body. But I did feel the cold springwater inch its way up my skin as my feet seemed to glide over the muddy bottom to the middle of the pond. With my feet firmly buried in mud up to midcalf, the water tickled my chin. I floated back, face tipped to the sun, ears submerged, the sound of my own breath tearing through my body.

Without lifting my head or opening my eyes, I knew Stumpy was near. I put both hands out, and he took hold of my right hand, intertwining his fingers through mine. When, eventually, he tugged on my hand I stood up to face him. His white shoulders, muscled from hauling hay practically since he was old enough to walk, were hunched up above the water toward his ears—a posture he unknowingly held whenever he was worried. I rested my hands on his shoulders in an effort to get him to relax, but when my hands touched his skin, hot from the sun, I started shivering uncontrollably. I looked toward my clothes, strewn on the bank haphazardly, as if flung in desperation. He took my hand and began moving toward them. I pulled back. He caught my eyes with his.

"It's okay, Dickie," he said. And I knew he was right. I knew things were okay, that I was okay. I didn't know if anything would be okay tomorrow or the next day, but right there in that moment, holding Stumpy's hand, naked and shivering in the middle of Hell Hole Springs, I knew without a doubt, I was okay.

STUMPY AND I spent the rest of the summer at Hell Hole Springs wrapped in its lush desert existence—a place that matched our vulnerability with its own. We immersed ourselves in mud and water and leaves and sun, needing to feel them on our bare skin as if we couldn't get close enough to the land, feeling as if this place we'd taken for granted might suddenly vanish, leaving us afloat in emptiness. Stumpy didn't say much that summer; I said even less. Stumpy's messages came to me through touch and eye contact. At times his sky-blue eyes seemed laden with the burden. How I communicated to Stumpy, I have no idea. I only know how little was asked of me. The few words that passed between us—promises we would not keep—were uttered in pure sanctity.

About three months after the cattle died, just before school started again, I arrived at Bev's one morning to find her up and dressed with a half pot of coffee already consumed. Tears immediately welled up in my eyes when I walked in the back door and saw her scrambling eggs. She pulled me into a rare hug.

"That's what I couldn't stand not seeing anymore," she said to me. "I woke up this morning with you on my mind and said, 'By damn, I haven't seen a tear fall outta that girl's eye since the day she found those cows dying.'"

She was right. My insides felt dried up and my skin felt hard and heavy and rusted, like one of her cast-iron pans left outside all winter.

"Isn't that a good thing?" I said, wiping my eyes.

"Not with you, it ain't." She placed a full plate of bacon and eggs in front of me. "Eat."

"Are things gonna be all right again?"

"Things will be okay. That I can promise. Things won't be the same, but things will be okay."

"What do you mean?"

"Well, Dickie, ranchers can put up with a lot—drought, freezes, forest fires, mud, heat—you name it. It don't rain all year, then as soon as you get your hay cut and laying in the field, you get a damn downpour. That's just the way a things. You can trust that the universe is gonna mess with you just to remind you who's in charge. Nothing wrong with that. You might be calving in mud one year and the next the land is so damn dry the cheatgrass and cedars start gaining on you. But you can always walk out across the land and know it will hold your weight, if you know what I mean. That's all changed now."

"How?"

"This land never promises an easy ride, but it does promise to take care a you as long as you take care of it. It's sorta like a contract."

"And the contract's been broken."

"It sure as hell has."

"So now what?"

"Well, I'm not really sure. I guess we just walk outside and see what feels right."

And that's what we did. At first we spent a lot of time on our hands and knees in the garden that had been planted then mostly ignored all summer, digging potatoes, gathering the last of the squash and tomatoes. I asked Bev if we were going to bottle the tomatoes but she said she couldn't spend one more day inside the walls of her house, so I took them over to Mom. Once we cleaned up the vines and stalks and put straw down, Bev turned her attention to the fences, which she went after like a madwoman, as if she expected the cows to be coming down off the mountain any day. In the past, I considered mending fences to be one of the most tedious jobs on the ranch, but that year I found solace in the mere act of holding a wire taut with a wrecking bar while Bev stapled it to the post.

In the early fall, on a day that the heat disappeared with the sun, Stumpy and I sat on our rock at Hell Hole Springs and silently watched six mares and a stallion dip their heads to drink.

CHAPTER SIXTEEN

Awakened by a sprinkle of sunlight through lace curtains, I struggle under the weight of Stumpy's right arm and leg, turning over to face him.

"Turn over on your other side," I whisper. He complies without opening his eyes as if it's a typical request. I press the front of my body flat against his back, loop my arm under his, my fingers finding the thick gray hair of his chest. "I just need to hang on to you for a few minutes," I say, before falling back to sleep.

When I wake again, I'm alone in bed. Voices and the spatter of frying bacon reach me from the kitchen. In bold red, the clock reads 10:34. Jesus, George has probably sent out the army, I think, then chuckle at the irony of my own joke. I stumble out wearing Stumpy's sweats and T-shirt. Annie sits at the kitchen table sipping coffee and looking as if she fell down a rabbit hole into a day spa located magically under Nelson's south pasture. She's waxed, coiffed, and polished. White capri pants cover three-fourths of her perfectly smooth, tan legs, and leather sandals wind around deep burgundy toenails. Gold bracelets and earrings jingle in harmony.

"Do you ever wear your own clothes?" she asks, causing Stumpy to chortle as he flips bacon.

"What's going on?" I pour myself a cup of coffee and elbow Stumpy in the back. "Why didn't somebody wake me up? Aren't we expected to be somewhere?"

"Bev's called a big meeting at our place at noon," Annie says. "We have time for breakfast."

"That looks good to me, Stump, but you might want to heat up some of that tofu from last night for Annie."

"Oh, shit, Annie. I forgot. Why didn't you stop me?"

"Just enjoying my coffee, Stumpy, and enjoying watching you cook. Don't get to see that much."

"What is it with you Sinfield women? You act like you've never seen a man moving around a kitchen before."

"We haven't," Annie and I respond in unison.

"Not with a spatula anyway," I add. "Maybe with a chain saw."

A hint of guilt squirts through my abdomen as a likeness of Michael in his lemon-yellow personalized Williams-Sonoma apron forms in my head. I shake my head to push the image away.

"Got some fly spray in the barn," Stumpy says, watching me. "What can I get you, Annie?"

"Nothing, Stumpy, I'm fine. I think I have a granola bar in my purse."

"I can do you one better than that," Stumpy says. He pulls a large Tupperware container out of the cupboard and sets it on the table in front of Annie.

"Granola?" Annie asks, peering inside.

"Make it myself," Stumpy says, grinning.

"If you pull soy milk out of that fridge, I'm walking out of here," I say.

"Well, I'll be darned," Annie says as Stumpy sets out strawberries and bananas.

"Yeah, Stumpy's divulging all sorts of secrets about himself this weekend," I say.

"How about you?" Annie asks. "Sharing any of your own?"

"Can't really think of anything particularly relevant or even mildly amusing."

"Oh, we're not done sharing," Stumpy says. "Dickie's promised full disclosure."

"That'll be the day," Annie says.

"GOOD GOD, I thought we had the service yesterday," I say, noting several vehicles parked in the dirt behind the house. "What's everybody doing here? Who around here drives a Lexus?"

Alma and Dad sit at the kitchen table, still arguing over the contents of the Wal-Mart bag.

"They're starting to creep me out," I say to Annie and Stumpy, both of whom nod.

"Hi, Stumpy, missed you for dinner last night," Alma says.

"Sorry about that, Alma. Hate to miss your good cooking."

Alma looks at me through narrowing eyes. "Nice outfit, Dickie. Ever wear your own clothes?"

"What's going on?"

"We're just biding our time waiting for you and Stumpy to join us," Dad says. "What's it been, sixteen hours now since I sent you over there?"

"Starting to feel sorta like sixteen days. Whose car is that? Where's Bev?"

"She's in the living room drinking coffee with Bishop Knowlden," Alma says.

"Drinking coffee with the bishop. Bet you don't often hear that around this state," I say.

"Well, Bev's drinking coffee," Alma says. "I think the bishop's drinking ice water."

"What's going on?"

"My damn-fool brother here has decided he's going to take Heber's ashes to some lab to have them DNA tested."

"For what?" Annie asks, clearly appalled.

"To see if they really are Heber's ashes!" Dad says.

"Can they even do that?" I ask Stumpy. "Test ashes?" He shrugs. "Is that why we've all been summoned? Are we taking a vote? Why's the bishop here? In case there's a tie?"

"No, we're not taking a goddamn vote!" Dad says. "None of this has anything to do with why the bishop is here—the bishop isn't here!"

"I thought Alma just said—"

"What I mean, if you'll give me a goddamn minute to explain, is that Pete Knowlden is here in his capacity as attorney-at-law, not in his capacity as bishop."

"In that case, he probably is having a cup of coffee," I say. "What do we need a lawyer for?"

"'Cause we're gonna read Heber's will," Dad says.

"Heber had a will? People like us don't have wills. Shouldn't Buffy be here?"

"She should have been here yesterday," Alma says.

"Doesn't matter," Dad says. "We can contact her later. Let's go into the living room."

"Buffy'd likely be willing to sell that land to you or Bev real cheap, Stump," I say. "Want me to try to soften her up for you?"

He puts a hard knuckle into the middle of my back and pushes me forward.

"Let's get started, Pete," Dad says.

"Well, I've pretty much gone through the will, and there's not a whole lot here's goin' to surprise anybody," Bishop Knowlden says like a country lawyer on *The Dukes of Hazzard*. I see Bev's eyebrows lift a bit as she and Stumpy lock eyes. I know that look too well. I saw it every time Bev or Merv devised some little plan designed to boost my character or draw me out a little or teach me there was nothing to be afraid of. I don't trust that look. I study Stumpy's face. He drives his knuckle deeper into my back and nods toward Bishop Knowlden.

"It's all pretty normal stuff," continues Bishop Knowlden, "so why don't I just sumrize it stead a reading all this legal mumbo jumbo to y'all."

Bishop Knowlden is wrong—a bunch of stuff in Heber's will surprises everyone except Bev. For one thing, Heber had managed to squirrel away a decent chunk of change, which he kept in mutual funds in Buffy's name.

"Dirty money," Dad scoffs. He'd been mad at Heber ever since he'd gone "to work for the enemy." That might be one of the few things that Dad and I could agree on, although I don't imagine Heber had much choice. I always thought that was the reason—although Mom never confirmed it—Dad refused to give or sell his land to Heber.

Bishop Knowlden goes through a bunch of Heber's personal property, most of which he left to either Bev or Stumpy. He tells Stumpy that he now owns Heber's two horses.

"That's damn thoughtful a Heber," Stumpy says. "I always liked that little brown mare a his. She's the best cow horse we've had out here in years. But that buckskin—"

"Oh, right," says Bishop Knowlden, "that reminds me." He flips several pages to the back of the document. "I'm supposed to read this little addendum. You ladies'll excuse me if I just read it straight out like Heber wrote it."

"I imagine we've heard worse, Bishop," Bev says.

Bishop Knowlden reads, " 'If that ornery old buckskin has managed to outlive me, then I figure that son of a bitch has earned his keep. Course, I couldn't hold a grudge, old friend, if he was to slip his halter somewhere up around Hell Hole Springs.' "

Stumpy smiles and catches my eye.

Heber left his collection of country-western record albums to Aunt Alma, which causes her to tip her head back in laughter.

"Hell, he borrowed most of those from me anyway. I've been wondering when he was going to return them."

The room is silent enough to hear a car downshift in the first curve on the county road when Bishop Knowlden informs Dad that Heber left him thirty-six cows and a bull—the exact number of cattle he lost in 1968—along with four unpublished manuscripts of cowboy poetry.

"Well, I'll be goddamned. What the hell did he do that for?" Dad says softy, as if addressing the question only to himself. He runs a wrinkled hand over his bald head, hugs the Wal-Mart bag to his belly, and staggers to the arm of the overstuffed chair holding Bev. She puts a hand on his knee, and for a frightening moment, I think he's going to cry. I've come to depend on my father's anger—it's the only shape of him I know how to love. In any other form, he can break a person's heart.

"Go on, Bishop," Bev says.

Wiping his brow with a red calico handkerchief, Bishop Knowlden then says, "And a course y'all know about the arrangement with the land. Dickie, you'll need to go into First Security Title there in Ganoa Monday mornin and Millie will have all the papers ready for you to sign. I guess one a you will be gettin in touch with Heber's daughter and let her know all this. Tell her she can give me a call if she has any questions."

"Bishop, could you go over that last part one more time?" I ask.

"I say, have Buffy give me a call—"

"No, the part before that—the part where I'm supposed to go see Millie Allen tomorrow morning."

"Oh, yeah, well, she'll have the papers drawn up for you to sign to make you the rightful owner a Heber's house and land. She'll go over with ya all the restrictions on you sellin the land and so forth."

"Still confused," I say.

Bishop Knowlden looks helplessly toward Bev. "I was under the impression everybody already knew about this arrangement. It was done years ago."

I look to Stumpy to see if he's as confused as I am. He clearly is

not. Nor is Bev. Nor is Dad. Alma and Annie are looking as perplexed as me. I walk through the room and take the chair next to Bev
that Bishop Knowlden has vacated in search of more water.

"Bev?"

"Apparently Heber left his land to you," Bev says, boring into me
with her eyes.

"Somehow I don't think it's all that simple," I say, returning her
stare. "I'll be the first to admit I didn't know my brother all that well,
so I don't know what might have been going through his mind. But
the Heber I knew never would have left his ranch to a radical liberal
Democrat feminist environmentalist journalist."

"When you put it that way, it does sound pretty bad," Stumpy says.

"And if I thought for a minute, I'm sure I could add a few more
'ists' to that list that Heber would strenuously object to," I say, ignoring Annie's giggling. "What's more, what the hell is a guy like Heber
doing with a will anyway? He was in good shape, midfifties, not a
Rockefeller or a Kennedy, and had a healthy sense of denial about the
risks of working at that damn incinerator. What possesses a guy like
that to drive on over to Pete Knowlden's law office one day and set
down his intentions in a will?"

"Maybe it was that newspaper article you wrote on funerals and
wills," Alma says. "It sure gave me pause about getting my own affairs
in order."

"Somehow I don't think so." I look at Pete Knowlden, who is now
leaning in the doorway between the kitchen and the living room, sipping a cup of black coffee. "Bishop, care to enlighten us?"

"No, I believe I'll leave this one go. Fact, I'm bout all finished
here. I'll leave you folks to discuss the particulars. Call me if you need
me," he says, backing out into the kitchen. The room remains silent
until we hear the kitchen door close.

"Bev? What's the 'arrangement' the bishop referred to? I know it
couldn't involve you because you have that no-interference rule about
things."

"Oh, hell, I threw that rule out about the time your mama came into my life," Bev says. She walks to the window; we all wait silently for her to continue. "Hell, Stump, we've got cows wandering down the road. They must be outta that pasture next to Heber's—I mean Dickie's," she says, almost sneering at me. "Sure as hell that damn bull has pulled that fence down again right there where the ditch goes under. I guess we're gonna have to move him outta there. In the meantime, we better saddle a couple a horses and get those cows in before they reach the county road."

"I'll get em, Bev," Stumpy says, pulling his ball cap off, running his hand through his hair, and plopping it back on his head as he turns to go. "Don't go disappearing back into the city before I get back," he says to me. "You and me aren't finished yet."

"I'll give you a hand, Stump," Dad says, jumping up.

Bev stands quietly while they go, waiting until she hears the snap of the kitchen door before turning her back to the window.

"Wish cows were as predictable as men. I pushed those damn cows through that hole in the fence before I drove over here—thought they'd be here twenty minutes ago." Annie, Alma, and I exchange glances. "Oh, hell, I just thought this would be a little easier without those two here—one, because men just complicate things, and two, because George complicates things more'n most men, and three, because now we don't have to talk around certain things we all know to be true but never talk about."

Annie and Alma both nod with a little too much enthusiasm for me.

"All we really need to talk about—"

"Dammit, Dickie." Bev cuts me short. "You've got the worst parts a both your mother and your father in you. Let's all just take a seat and have ourselves a talk. Annie, you mind making a fresh pot a coffee?"

"Sure," Annie says. "But don't start until I get back. I don't want to miss anything."

"Let's move into the kitchen," Alma says. "I could use a sandwich. Bev?"

"Love one, Alma."

Alma snatches the Wal-Mart bag George has left on the table and sets it on top of the fridge. We settle ourselves around the table with tuna sandwiches and coffee: Bev, serious; me, sullen; Alma, content; and Annie, expectant. We sip and eat for a minute while everyone gets comfortable—all understanding that Bev is in charge and that Bev will speak when she's ready.

"Dickie," she starts, "you have your mother's softness in you. Over the years you've buried it pretty well under humor and intellect, but every one a us sitting at this table knows you. Now that ain't necessarily a bad thing—Lord knows I loved that about Ruth—but it does mean you often step aside when you ought to be stepping up. Now sometimes that don't much matter in the larger scheme of things, but sometimes that changes the whole trajectory of a life."

Alma and Annie nod in agreement.

"This feels a little bit like an intervention," I say.

"But you also have your dad's stubborn streak runnin through you," Bev continues. "I'll bet you weren't more'n seven years old when you decided to hate this ranching life. Annie made the same decision. Thing is, I believe it came naturally to Annie. It don't come naturally to you, Dickie, but still you set about creating yourself a life to fit that hatred."

The kitchen grew quiet. In the distance we heard the melancholy notes of Stumpy's herding song penetrate cleanly through the chirping of sparrows and the shrieks of crows. Since he was five years old, Merv once told me, every time Stumpy trails cattle on a horse, you're gonna hear the same song in the same crystal-clear voice—Hank Williams's "I'm So Lonesome I Could Cry." Until Alma pushes a box of Kleenex across the table toward me, I'm unaware of the tears rolling down my cheeks.

"Here's the thing," Bev says, reaching out and running a callused old hand up and down my forearm. "I been watching you pretty close now for forty-some-odd years. You and me, well, we've spent a lot of hours together over all those years. I know the look a you, Dickie, when you're happy, and I know the look a you when you're not. By damn, I know you'll never own up to this, but there's only one place I've ever seen you happy. So I made a deal with Heber when I sold him that land."

"I can't be a rancher, Bev."

"I'm not saying you have to be a rancher. Hell, I don't care if you ever run a cow or grow a piece a alfalfa on that place—though Lord knows Stumpy and I could use another good hand. You can hook up your computer over there and keep on writing for that damn newspaper about how us ranchers are ruining the world if you want to."

"Bev's right, Dickie," Annie says. "The only time I ever saw the anxiety leave you the entire time we were kids was during the summers you ranched with Bev. Since you moved away from here, you're as messed up as you were when you were seven. Look at your fingernails!" she exclaims, pulling my bitten, jagged nails out in front of me.

"Shit, Annie," I say, pulling my hands back. "Perfectly groomed nails don't necessarily equal happiness." She starts picking at her own manicured nails. "Well, maybe in your world they do."

"Annie, I hope you're okay with all a this," Bev says. "I don't mean to cut you outta things, but you never took to this place or this life, and I knew that was sincere in you. I've left you a little something in my will—"

"That's not really necessary," Annie says.

Bev holds up a hand. "I know it ain't necessary but just to equal things out a little. You Sinfields . . ." Bev drops her head and rocks back and forth a moment. "Well, you Sinfields needed me. I mean no disrespect to you, Alma, but if ever there was a family that needed all the help they could get from every direction, this was it. And goddammit, I didn't know it, but I needed to be needed. Before you came along, I convinced myself that Stumpy needed me, but he didn't.

Merv was all he ever needed; they simply folded me into their family outta pure kindness. But you guys . . . well, that's where I found my place. Now I sure as hell never expected it'd come up this soon," Bev continues after several minutes of silence. "In fact, I expected you young folks'd be having this discussion over my will."

"Are we in for more surprises there?" I ask.

"Well, I figured by the time you'd be hearing Pete read over the particulars of a will, Dickie, that you mighta come to know yourself in a way that would let you come to terms with the pain you nurture so well and carry around like a precious stone. But it didn't happen that way. This might sound sorta crazy coming from an old jack-Mormon like me, but I have to think maybe there's some divine intervention going on here—maybe this is the way it was supposed to happen, I mean, with Heber and all."

"What?"

"Well, they say God moves in mysterious—"

"Jesus, Bev, Heber sucked in nerve gas! If you can wrap a godly story around that—"

"God has a plan for all of us—"

"How the hell can you say that, Annie? Heber walked into a shit-load of nerve gas! Now, I've never seen a person die from nerve gas, but I have seen a cow die from it. Every one of us sitting here has witnessed that. Think about that for a minute. Think about those cows wallowing and gagging on their own fluids with their bodies all twisted up before they dropped dead. Then try to tell me Heber's death is some kind of fucking design by any entity besides the federal government!" I scream through a mess of tears, mucus, and saliva.

Annie sits stiff, ignoring the tears that spot her tightly folded hands. Alma blows her nose and wipes her eyes. Bev stands to the side of me and wraps both arms around my head, pulling the side of my face into her hard belly.

"Girl, girl, girl," she whispers.

"I can't come back here," I say, gently pulling Bev's arms off me and pushing her back to her seat. "You're all wrong about this. This place carries too damn much sadness. I can't get more'n ten steps from my car out here before tears start running from my eyes like I'm ten years old."

"It ain't this basin that holds the pain in," Bev says. "The place is just what it is. It's indifferent. That's the beauty of it."

"Bev, I'm not—"

"I don't know what Stumpy was talking about a few minutes ago when he said you and him ain't finished yet," Bev said, cutting me off, "but there's more goddamn truth in that statement than either a you are willing to admit. It's nigh time for you two to get untwisted with each other."

"Is that what this is about—this land stuff? Are Stumpy and I getting fixed up? Sort of an expensive way to do it, don't you think? You might have just bought us a pair of movie tickets or sent us on an errand and arranged for his truck to run out of gas."

"Dickie, stop it!" Annie says. "Bev's right and you know it."

I look around the table; the three of them look back at me. I love these three women, but I can't stand the looks on their faces—that look of pity mixed with knowledge. I've seen that look on people's faces my entire life and I'm sick to death of it. And I realize, at this moment, there has only ever been one person in my life who has never looked at me that way—Michael Wilson. I push my chair back and stand up.

"I'm going home," I say. "Do what you want with Heber's land, Bev. I'm not signing those papers."

I throw my bag into the back of my car and walk around to the driver's side. I hesitate as I reach for the door handle when the notes of a distant song reach me. "I'm So Lonesome I Could Cry." I close the door and start the car.

CHAPTER SEVENTEEN

It took a solid year or more after the feds took the calves before things began falling into place again. Not that things would ever be what you might call normal, but normal is a relative and elusive thing. Whatever Merv felt during that time, he never let it show. As he had always done without anyone noticing, he assumed the job of holding us all together while simultaneously letting us individually wallow in our own anguish. The moment it looked like one of us might be floundering in the deep end, Merv was there with a line of chores that needed doing. That seemed to work on everyone but George, who each day went from the house to his job at school to the kitchen table in the evenings, where he sat rubbing his forehead and staring into a pile of "evidence" against the army he'd gathered from various sources—usually the army's own. Fifteen months to the day after Stumpy and I found the dying cows, Merv and Bev both accepted a check from the federal government and spent the next year restocking their herds. George refused the check and spent the next thirty-nine years attempting to get the army to publicly admit full responsibility for the dead livestock.

Heber graduated from high school the next spring with a draft lottery number of 358. That let all of us breathe a little easier since several small fracases had already occurred over Dad making plans for Heber to move to Canada. Merv lined up a job for Heber with a sheepherding outfit operating out of Skull Valley, said it would do him good to get away from George for a while, and Heber readily agreed. Merv also figured it might be good for Heber to get away from easy access to liquor and cars. Heber took the job before he understood he'd be spending six months at a time alone in sheep camp deep in the west desert with no transportation faster than a horse.

I didn't see Heber much after that except once when Merv got wind of some trouble between Heber and the owner—concerning the owner's daughter—and sent me and Stumpy on an all-day car trip over dirt roads to check on Heber and gather facts. Our camp location information was a day old, however, and it took us two tries, over the course of two separate weekends, to find him. By the time we did, the owner's daughter was in Montana living with an uncle, and Heber and the owner had reached an accord. Heber fixed us some mutton stew before we turned around and drove seven hours back to Clayton.

Heber ended up liking the solitude and kept the job three years, until he showed up in Clayton one day with a pregnant wife in tow. The girl had run away from Santa Barbara and on her way across the country found Heber occupying a stool at Red's Bar in Delta, Utah, during the one-week furlough he was allowed every six months. Apparently a slow-talking cowboy with a sheepish grin offered the perfect antidote to her seemingly oppressive life of college scholarships and parental expectations. I was gone by then, but Mom and Bev said it took less than a month after Buffy was born for the cure to become the ailment. Shortly thereafter, a red Mercedes sedan caused a stir by rolling through Clayton with darkened windows and "foreign" license plates before it stopped in front of Bev's house—the temporary residence of Heber and his bride—whereupon a well-groomed couple emerged, scooped up their daughter and granddaughter, and blew a rush of indignation through Clayton when they left "without even settin down for a meal."

I ENTERED HIGH SCHOOL still numb from the summer of 1968 and immediately sought Holly in our agreed-upon meeting place the first day. It had never occurred to me to confront Holly about the slut story or any of her other devious machinations, assuming always that I had much more to lose than she did if our friendship dissolved. I was anxious to tell her the story of the gassed cows, seeking some sort of acknowledgment for the enormity of the trauma I'd suffered. I had envisioned a scene whereby Holly would spread news of my horrible story with the same efficiency she'd spread news of my sluttiness. I'd then be inundated with inquiries and pity from all sides, the way Linda Carboni had been when both her parents and her little brother were killed when they dazedly drove over the railroad tracks on the highway between Ganoa and Ullsville and were hit by one of sixteen Union Pacific daily trains that roared past the west side of Ganoa. When, instead, Holly shrugged and pattered on about the boys she met on the beach in California— turning her full attention to Marlene, who she hoped might be sophisticated enough to understand such things—I gave it one more try, this time with gory details of gasping cows and bawling calves. She looked at me in stunned silence. Then she puckered her lips and said, "Oh, little Bow Pows has lost her cows and don't know where to find them," as she tapped the top of my head. It was then I realized that something inside me had shifted acutely during those quiet days at the spring with Stumpy. My obsession with Holly's friendship had vanished.

When I later told Bev about it she said, "Can't say that I'm sorry to hear that."

But the truth was I missed my obsession, didn't quite know how to operate without it. "I just want things to be back the way they were before," I told Bev.

"Don't think that's the way to go about it," she said.

"Why not?"

"Well, when things happen in your life, Dickie—especially big things—runnin around like a dog with fits trying to get everything back the way it was ain't always the right thing."

"What is the right thing?"

"Well, we all laugh about the slow-moving folks here in Clayton who like to *set* with things awhile, but there's something to be said for that. It's all those separate incidents—big and small—that make up a life. You got to find a way to fold em in."

Still I walked dazed through the halls of high school that first year, trying to find a way to fold what felt like zillions of disparate parts of me into the receptacle of skin draped on bones. I felt as though I was streaming tiny pebbles wherever I went, and I suppressed a frantic urge to follow myself with a broom, to sweep them all up so I didn't lose a vital piece.

At first I kept trying what had never really worked for me thus far, which was to take my cues from Annie. In junior high that didn't require much except combing my hair and cleaning the dirt from under my fingernails. In high school all that changed. As soon as Annie arrived, she tried out for the Ganoa Spinnakers—an exclusive sixteen-member drill team that entertained the school with over-the-head kicks and jump splits—and was unanimously accepted by a panel of independent judges (former Spinnakers now working at Ganoa Army Depot). The following year, I tried the same thing and was unanimously rejected. I didn't feel too bad about it. The idea of all those hours of summer practice inside a smelly gym next to the thought of Bev, Merv, and Stumpy working the ranch without me sort of made my stomach clutch. But when Annie became a cheerleader, I couldn't think of what else to do but follow. Fortunately for me, when I mentioned to Annie my intentions to be part of a contest that took place in front of the entire Ganoa High School student body, she enlisted the help of Mom and Bev to save me from that humiliation.

As the tryout date loomed, Mom, Bev, and Annie found me standing in front of the full-length mirror in Annie's room wearing her cheerleading outfit—a snug white ribbed turtleneck and a pair of purple hot pants. Mom and Annie both propped themselves on the bed, and Bev turned a straight-back chair backward and straddled it, her arms folded to hold her chin.

"How do those fit?" Bev asked.

"Okay, I guess."

"Look again," she said.

I looked in the mirror and jutted my hipbones forward in an effort to keep the hot pants from sliding down.

"They comfortable?" Bev asked.

"Not really." I tugged at the skintight turtleneck that flattened out my small breasts.

"Know why?"

"Not really."

"Cause they ain't your clothes."

"But—"

"It's that simple, Dickie."

"But I've been wearing Annie's clothes my entire life!"

"I'm not talking about wearing hand-me-downs, girl. I'm talking about wearing your own skin."

"Bev's right, Dickie," Mom said.

"Mm-hmm," Annie murmured as she flipped through a magazine.

Bev walked behind me, placed both hands on my shoulders, and turned me toward the mirror. "Take a good look at that girl," she said. "Far as I can see there ain't a damn thing wrong with her." She turned me toward the bed. "Ruth?"

"She looks good to me, Bev."

"Annie?"

"Fine."

Bev bent to pick up the jeans and T-shirt I'd dropped to the floor and handed them to me. Then she brushed my hair out of my eyes and in a low voice said, "You know her, Dickie. Let her be who she wants to be."

CLASSROOMS WERE MY refuge. Once I settled into a desk, all my streaming pebbles gathered around me like BBs to a magnet. I consumed geometric angles and compound sentences. And it was there in the classroom that I first learned about the geological exceptionality of the basin and range, where I came to attach intellectual justification to the emotions that seeped through me like I was made of honeycomb whenever I allowed myself to nestle deeply into the basin between the Oquirrh and Onaqui ranges. While most mountain ranges in the world came about as a result of compression, those in the basin and range—five hundred miles stretching (literally) from the Wasatch to the Sierras—did not. Instead, the land was pulled tight in an east–west heave until it was actually torn apart, resulting in massive wedges of earth running north and south that tilted as if reaching for the moon. As the high edge of one wedge met the low edge of another, a basin formed. And that's where I lived, in the stretch mark between the two wedges that formed the Oquirrhs and the Onaqui.

The knowledge that each wedge had found its equilibrium some 8 million years ago, a perfect angle of repose after violent upheaval, surely meant that I held the same possibility. And that's how I navigated the lunchroom and hallways of high school—with a crust 8 million years strong. I understood that in finding such stability each enormous wedge had exposed its deeply buried secrets of the last 550 million years, but I also knew that represented only an eighth of the earth's full life. That's, no doubt, where I first pondered the idea that one could find balance without full disclosure.

In addition to my local geology course, as I entered my second year in high school, two things happened to nudge me toward basin- and rangelike equilibrium. The first was when Miss Smith, my English teacher, insisted that I join the school newspaper staff, thinking I'd fit perfectly into the small gathering of articulate social misfits. She was right. It is still unclear to me whether it was by accident or design that I ran across the *New York Times Magazine* article by Seymour M. Hersh that discussed Dugway's open-air testing of chemical weapons and the dead livestock. Miss Smith, the newspaper's adviser and self-proclaimed feminist (a description with no meaning to me at the time although she eventually lent me her dog-eared copy of *The Feminine Mystique*), had assigned me the task of studying the content and style of a yellowing stack of the *New York Times,* which she brought from home and left in the corner of her office specifically for that purpose. She no doubt knew I would become engrossed in articles covering the Vietnam War—articles that exposed secret bombings, lying government officials, antiwar demonstrations, and draft-card burnings. And she no doubt hoped I would begin to fully understand the hum of patriotism that necessarily permeated Ganoa County, rendering mute any underlying voice of dissent. It was in that stack that I also recognized the smallness of my own experience. By Hersh's own admission, it took less than a month for the national press to lose interest in the poisoned livestock of Ganoa County even while they were vocalizing their objections to the Vietnam War and, with that, the war weapons we Ganoa residents produced and protected with pride.

Whether it was Miss Smith's intention to ignite a sense of righteous anger within me, I'm not sure, but once it was sparked, she picked up her fan. In October of my sophomore year, she nearly lost her job when she pulled me and three other "news reporters" out of school and drove us into Salt Lake City to cover a daylong antiwar demonstration attended by more than four thousand people and headlined by Country Joe & the Fish. That the protest happened at about the same time the army silently reimbursed ranchers for gassing their livestock went unnoticed by pretty much everyone but me. In my mind they became indisputably linked. The war protests seemed the only sensible reaction to a loss I couldn't specify, a loss I wasn't sure I had a right to. From that day forward, I watched my father disintegrate into wretchedness, but a piece of me understood George's actions perfectly. The mere act of accepting cash for the dead cows seemed to leave the matter grossly unappreciated.

So when I suggested to Miss Smith that the school newspaper publish a series of articles devoted to the biological testing being done at Dugway's Baker Laboratory, she wholeheartedly agreed. How either

one of us assumed we'd succeed at doing what the largest news organizations in the country had not—garner information from one of the
most insulated and secretive little spots in the nation, located smack
in the middle of 1 million fenced acres of desert, the 210-mile bor-
der patrolled by air and signed with warnings of authorized deadly
force, considered off-limits even to most military personnel stationed
at Dugway—I'm not sure. Possibly I assumed my mother, a lowly Dugway secretary, might be entrusted with the military's ugliest secrets.
Nonetheless, the idea was quickly squelched by Principal Irvine after I
wrote an editorial introducing the series and describing in agonizing
detail just exactly how well chemical weapons work. Miss Smith and I
were both admonished (my second time; probably a higher number for
Miss Smith) for causing "unrest" among the students, most of whom
picked up the school newspaper only for swatting classmates and deco-
rating homecoming floats. That put Principal Irvine in a bind when
that very editorial ended up winning me a first-year college scholarship in the journalism program at the University of Utah. College
scholarships were such an anomaly at Ganoa High School, they were
usually welcomed with pomp and circumstance, the recipient trotted
out at halftime during the basketball game for a hip-hip-hooray led by
the cheerleading squad. Mine didn't receive such attention. Principal
Irvine did call me into his office, however, to personally congratulate
me, and I left feeling like I'd been reprimanded again.

Outside of class, the school newspaper office became my home. I
studied there, ate lunch there, and used the private small bathroom
in the back to avoid all public restrooms. At one time the newspaper
office was accessible from the main hall outside the lunchroom, but
when the administration decided to put benches in that hall, the main
door got blocked and permanently locked, forcing anyone who wanted
to get to our offices to cut a path through the sewing room of the
home-economics class. Its inaccessibility to most students was something I loved about it.

The second thing that calmed me in my second year was the one

thing I'd come to count on in my life—Stumpy Nelson. Once he entered high school, a year after me, his mere presence brought with it
the stillness of our summer at Hell Hole Springs. By the time Stumpy
hit high school, his nickname had become a mystery and he excelled
in every sport offered. That, along with a body made of ranch work
and a shy demeanor, made him wildly popular with girls, something
he seemed damn near oblivious of.

Stumpy's schedule mostly kept him in the general vicinity of
the boys' gym and practice fields, so we seldom saw each other in
the course of a day. If we did happen to pass, Stumpy would greet
me with a broad grin and gentle squeeze of my arm just above the
elbow. But at four-thirty each afternoon, I'd find him waiting in the
hallway outside the home-ec room after football practice, painfully
entertaining two or three cheerleaders who gathered around him, a
smile of relief flashing through his entire face when I walked out to
rescue him.

Holly Hamilton, who took great pride and ownership in the fact
that she'd known Stumpy since they were kids, was often among that
group of cheerleaders. Turns out, she was the one who could and did
follow precisely in Annie's footsteps—excelling in drill team, cheerleading, and garnering the attention of boys. I saw less and less of her
as she scurried from one practice to the next, arms casually linked
with those of one or more guys wearing letterman's jackets. But her
interest in Stumpy grew exponentially with his aloofness toward her.
Both of those things stymied me—Stumpy's lack of interest in argu-
ably the most popular girl in school and Holly's stubbornness, preventing her from simply moving on to the next boy panting in line.
Both of them seemed to expect that I should do something to sway
the dynamic in favor of their particular leanings, but I wasn't so inclined. For the first time in my life, I understood that any mention
from me that Holly set her sights elsewhere would have the effect of
shaking rolled oats in a pan in the horse corral—she'd stretch out her
neck and come on full stride. Which is why Stumpy should have been

fully prepared two weeks before the girls'-day dance when Holly found
him leaning against the doorjamb outside the home-ec room, but he
wasn't. So when Holly suggested he would go to the dance with
her—just as I walked out the door to retrieve him—the only thing he
could think to stammer was, "Dickie already asked me."

Holly turned toward me the same way she had turned toward
the bull in the field so many years ago, the day Stumpy stepped out
from behind a juniper.

"Is that true?" she asked. It was really more of a threat than a
question. I started to deny it—my only interest in the girls'-day dance
being how much room the announcement would eat up in the school
newspaper—but out of the corner of my eye I caught sight of Stumpy
looking like a big puppy left chained in the backyard too long.

"Afraid so," I said, and, unknowingly, with those two words, entered into a high-stakes poker game—the low bid being Stumpy
Nelson.

When she strode away I turned on Stumpy. "What the hell did
you say that for? Now we're going to have to go to that damn dance!"

"Could that be so terrible?" he asked, grinning.

As it turned out, the answer was yes, it could be quite terrible.
Stumpy and I were stiff as barn slats the night of the dance—him in
the suit Heber had worn to the same dance three years prior and me
in one of Annie's dresses (of course), a boldly geometrically striped
tent dress that, according to Annie, would make me look just like
Twiggy. I didn't look like Twiggy. But after Mom rolled my hair in
empty frozen orange-juice cans and Annie applied thick black eye-
liner and shimmering green eye shadow, I also didn't look like
Dickie.

When the first notes of "Nights in White Satin" rang out, Stumpy
and I shuffled to the dance floor and attempted to move our rigid
bodies together. The physical ease we had found with each other at
Hell Hole Springs—and had comfortably nurtured since—eluded us.
So close we had to maneuver around them, Holly danced—with ef-

fortless grace—with Randy Hunt, the starting quarterback. As they glided by, Stumpy and I simultaneously saw ourselves as we looked to Holly—satisfyingly ridiculous. For the first time that night, we looked directly into each other's eyes and recognized ourselves. I dropped my forehead to his chest just below his chin; he put his right arm around my shoulders and wrapped his left hand in my hair. And like that, both of us quietly laughing but otherwise barely moving, we finished out the song.

Before the next song ended, Stumpy and I had changed into the jeans we'd left in his pickup and were on our way back to Clayton. Without rousing anyone but Merv—who nodded once from behind the kitchen curtain—we traded four wheels for four legs and set out for the cave. On the bare back of Ol' Yeller, our bodies lost their stiffness and relaxed into familiar terrain.

EVEN WITH MY NEWFOUND INDIGNATION, I retreated back to Clayton, back to the Bar C, every summer until I graduated from high school. I set my intentions otherwise, thinking I would spend my summers reading, writing, and protesting, but no more than a week would pass before the tranquil promise of ranch work pulled me onto Plummy's back as the sun came up and set me plodding toward Bev's. Bev didn't mind that I showed up with peace signs hand-painted on my overalls. She said other folks around Ganoa County might be put off by it, but she couldn't find much fault in advocating peace. I told her about the rally I'd gone to in Salt Lake City and she said if she hadn't needed to get that southernmost field plowed before it snowed, she might have gone with me. I showed her the article I'd copied from the New York Times that mentioned the dead cows, but I was immediately sorry. As soon as she sat down at the kitchen table to read it, a heaviness pulled her face down toward her neck, the same way it had the day they came for the calves, and she remained quiet the rest of the day.

For my sixteenth birthday, Bev gave me a subscription to the *New York Times* (which she kept after I left), but because they didn't deliver in Clayton or Ganoa, the paper arrived almost a week late through the postal service. By the time I'd get it, Bev had already read every section and was ready with her own opinions on every editorial written. We discussed the war, the Cambodia bombings, the My Lai massacre, the Kent State shootings. Bev listened and let me ramble as if I were the authority I fancied myself to be.

In Stumpy's company, however, my commentary evoked nothing but silence. The summer before my senior year, Merv and Bev put cattle on the mountain again for the first time since 1968. Stumpy and I spent most of our time riding the range, checking fences, and moving the cows from one allotment to the next on the east side of the Onaqui. (It would be another fifteen years before Merv and Bev felt okay about putting cows on the west side again.)

On a sunny July day in 1971, Stumpy and I sat on a dead log in the shade of a cottonwood eating cold meatloaf sandwiches Bev had made for us.

"Dry as hell this year," Stumpy said. "I imagine we'll have a few forest fires before the summer's over."

"Probably," I replied. "Stumpy, did you know more than fifty thousand Americans have died in Vietnam?" Bev and I had been reading about the Pentagon papers in the *Times* and I was itching to talk about it.

"Dickie, could we please not talk about the war today? Do you have any other topics available to you anymore?"

"What do you want to talk about?"

"Pretty much anything else."

"Well, ignoring it isn't going to make it go away."

"And you think talking about it will?"

"You have to be willing to take a stand, Stumpy."

"Just because a person isn't vocalizing his opinions all the time doesn't mean he doesn't have any, Dickie."

"Why not vocalize them? Why not make your voice heard?"

"Silence is golden, don't you know?"

"Come on, Stump, what do you think about the war? You're not in favor of it, are you? Is that why you refuse to talk about it with me?"

"No, Dickie, that's not why."

"Then what?"

"Sometimes there's only so much a person can let into their lives, you know?"

"What do you mean?"

"Sometimes letting all the misery of the world into every single day can just wear a person down, makes it hard to just saddle a horse and go for ride."

"You can't just choose to live in ignorance."

"That's not what I'm saying."

"Then what are you saying?"

"I'm saying there's an unlimited number a miseries in this world, but the human mind can only handle so much at a time. A person has to make a choice about what to let in and what to keep out just to move through a day and still be able to sit down to dinner in the evening."

"But the war affects every single one of us—especially here. God, Stumpy, if you and me had gone out to check those cows the day before we did, we would have been gassed! The feds could have done some real live testing. After all, that's what that shit is for—to murder people. We don't have the luxury of choosing to keep that out of our lives!"

Without looking down, Stumpy brushed the ground with his left hand and picked up small rocks to pitch at a boulder in front of us. He stayed quiet for several minutes and something about the stillness of his eyes silenced me also. He pulled his ball cap off, brushed a hand through his hair, and repositioned the cap.

"I'm scared, Dickie. I don't want to talk about the war because it scares the hell outta me."

I started to respond and then stopped. What was there to say? I had somehow missed that. I had removed myself such a distance from the very personal emotions of the war, and I was jarred and suddenly embarrassed by my detached rantings. I had never until that moment considered the idea that Stumpy might be drafted, and when I did consider it, it scared the hell out of me also. I moved closer to him on the log so that the left side of his body aligned perfectly with the right side of mine.

"You know I've never been anyplace in my entire life except this valley," he said. "If you took me outta here, I'm not even sure I'd know how to recognize myself, much less how to think and act."

"You'd be fine, Stumpy."

"You know that's bullshit. You just got done telling me about fifty thousand guys who aren't fine at all. But dying ain't really what scares me. Not directly."

"Then what the hell does?"

"Grandpa."

"Why?"

"He's a tough old man, Dickie. Came through World War Two without a scratch, lost both his wife and his true love, Francine, his only child never speaks to him, is barely fazed when his entire herd gets wiped out. There's only one thing in the world could take that man down. Losing me." Tears streamed down Stumpy's face. "I can't stand the idea of doing that to him."

I put both arms around Stumpy and leaned my head against his arm. He turned to straddle the log and pulled me in, wrapping his arms around my shoulders and chest so tightly I could barely breathe. I could feel his tears on the back of my neck.

"I'll take care of Merv if you have to go, Stumpy."

"What about your college scholarship? What about your desire to get the hell away from this place?"

"I'll take care of Merv if you have to go."

"Promise?"

"Yes."

• • •

STUMPY AND I never really defined ourselves; maybe that was our unraveling. It didn't seem necessary. We were simply who we'd always been since we found ourselves riding next to each other at eight years of age. From that point forward, every moment in our lives got folded into "us." The summer of dead cows, as we had come to call it, had fused us—initially through the violence to which we bore witness, and later through the gentle balm of mud, water, and sun. I must have actually believed then that the fusion was permanent, that we were melded by organic matter. I think Stumpy believed it also. It didn't occur to us to interpret and protect it. Maybe that kind of purity can't hold anyway. Maybe we should have known that. At the time I thought what Stumpy and I had was so simple, so obvious, that defining it seemed almost superfluous. When I look back on it now I see that what we shared wasn't simple at all. Our union was so intricate it proved irreducible to the terminology available to us. We couldn't save it because we didn't have the vocabulary.

I've reduced it now to adolescent silliness, a definition that allows me to shrug it off dispassionately and file it under "childhood." It's the only way I can think about it without crumbling under the immensity of the loss.

I can outline the details of our estrangement—chronologically or, as any good journalist, in order of importance—but I can't interpret or clarify them. Nor can I maintain objectivity.

I convinced myself that leaving Clayton was not a choice but a necessity. I simply didn't know how to stay. Heber had been gone a couple of years, Annie left the year prior, and the air in our small household was dangerously heavy—damn near unbreathable. The draft ended the year Stumpy graduated from high school; my promise to him was never tested.

Stumpy never fully understood my reasons for leaving, and because I didn't either, we never discussed it. Once it was done, the

distance between my college dorm and the Nelson ranch grew exponentially with the turn of every season. Less than a year after Stumpy
graduated from high school, he and Holly were married with a baby
on the way. I never heard or asked for details of their courtship—Bev
was reticent on the topic—although it wasn't hard for me to fill in
the blanks. A place like Ganoa County has a way of pairing up those
who remain.

CHAPTER EIGHTEEN

I'm home less than an hour before Michael lets himself in the front door, drops Big Max to the floor, and walks immediately to the kitchen to search for a lint roller. Upon the sight of them I feel as if my life is coming back into focus.

"Hey, big boy, I missed you," I say.

"I assume you're talking to the cat," Michael calls from the kitchen.

"Thought I could address you both at the same time—save on unnecessary words."

"Actually, Dickie," he says, walking in from the kitchen while rolling blond cat hairs from the front of his slacks, "the only words you and I ever exchange are the unnecessary ones."

"That's what makes us so special, Michael."

We position ourselves at opposite ends of the couch, as usual. Big Max circles twice then gets comfortable on my lap and starts purring.

"I suppose that's true," Michael says. "We might, in fact, be the only couple together twelve years without ever having discussed the nature of our relationship or even our feelings for each other."

"Please don't tell me we're going to start now."

"Yes, I think we might."

"Why, for God's sake?"

"Can you think of a better time?"

"Yes, I can. How about never?"

"I've been thinking about this for more than a week now, Dickie, and I don't think that's going to work anymore."

"Well, then could we at least exchange some meaningless pleas-antries first? Like gosh, your hair's getting long. Are those new slacks you're wearing? Did you trim your sideburns? Are we out of cat food? Anything at all? Surely the all-Mormon, all-white, all-male, all-knowing state legislature passed a few moral imperatives while I was gone. Catch me up, Michael. Do Utah women still have the right to wear pants in public? We have lots of things to cover! We can't just abruptly abandon them in favor of . . . in favor of what? In favor of 'how do you *feel* about me?'"

"We not only can, Dickie, we must."

"What the hell for?"

"Because I've seen too much now. Up until this point I only ever saw the Salt Lake Dickie. The only glimpse I ever had into the Clay-ton Dickie was running into your mom and Bev over here every once in a while."

"So what?"

"Well, the so what of it is that the Salt Lake Dickie has always pretended the Clayton Dickie no longer existed."

"She doesn't."

"Oh, but she does. I've seen her."

"Michael—"

"Ever wondered why I've never taken you back to Chicago with me, Dickie?"

"No."

"Exactly. Because you've never really wanted to know any more about me than what you see right here in front of you. And I've never wanted you to. And I've never wanted to know any more about you either. We've stayed clear of all that messy stuff. That's the way our relationship worked."

"And it still does."

"Alas, I don't think so."

"Why not?"

"I've seen too much."

"You keep saying that. What the hell does that mean, Michael? You were in Clayton for the duration of Heber's funeral, which lasted all of fifteen minutes."

"I wish it were that simple, Dickie, don't you? That everything—pain and happiness and love and passion and heartbreak—could all be neatly measured in units of time."

"Are you speaking philosophically or personally?"

"Both, I guess."

"So what is it you think you saw, Michael?"

"Everything."

"Like what?"

"I can't tell you what; there are no facts to be listed. It would be a futile attempt to speak about what cannot be said."

"No, don't give me that Wittgenstein bullshit."

Michael's eyebrows lift. "Certain things simply transcend the limits of human language. 'Whereof one cannot speak, thereof one must be silent.'"

"If one were going to choose to be silent, one should not have spoken in the first place, don't you think?"

"Dickie, I don't mean to be evasive; I don't want to play games with you. I don't know how to explain it. I saw you—more you than I've ever seen in my life. And it wasn't just at Heber's funeral. Ever since you heard about Heber's death, I've been watching you. And it's been there."

"What's been there, for God's sake?"

"Everything. Every little thing. Your whole life. Past and present. Fear, pain, love, vulnerability. Stuff you've never shown me. Stuff we nonverbally agreed to never show each other."

"I promise to never show it again. There. Now can we talk about something else?"

"No, we cannot."

"So what are you saying, Michael?"

"I'm saying we can't pretend anymore."

"Sure we can. We're so good at it."

"Won't work anymore. It's like wine—once the bottle is open, it's time to drink it."

"Well, my purist friend, lots of people recork wine."

"Yes, but it's never really as good again, is it? What's been let in will cause deterioration."

"You seem awfully certain about this."

"I am, Dickie."

"So what does that mean?"

"It means we have to be honest with each other. Worse yet, it means we have to be honest with ourselves."

"We've never really lied to each other, Michael."

"Of course not. Lies are not necessary when there's nothing at stake."

"Are we going to talk about our pasts and our feelings and all that crap?"

"We are."

"Do you really think that's going to work for us?"

"Define *work*. I think it will just be whatever it turns out to be."

"Do we have to start today?"

"When would you suggest? Should we make an appointment three weeks from today so we have time to study?"

"Sounds good to me."

"That's our problem, Dickie. We don't allow anything to grow organically between us."

"You don't like organic, Michael. Organic is messy. Everything comes up—weeds and all. You've spent your entire life keeping weeds out. Why would you want to change that now?"

"Because watching the Clayton Dickie made me realize a few things."

"Like what?"

"Even weeds flower."

"God, have you been watching *Oprah* while I was gone?"

"Say what you will, Dickie, but the fact remains, we have buried ourselves in this relationship."

"Exactly. I thought that was the point."

"I suppose it was. But like I said, things are different now."

"Really?"

"Really."

"You're sure about this?"

"I am."

"Well then, Michael, let's begin, shall we?"

"Why not?"

"I'll go first."

"Fine."

"Do you miss Chicago?"

"Immensely."

"What do you miss about it?"

"The way it smelled on hot summer nights when I was eight years old. A hundred different smells mixed together—beer, curry, garlic, cigarette smoke, mint, bread, chocolate, rotting meat, stale blood."

"Stale blood?"

"Slaughterhouses."

"Is that why you don't eat meat?"

"My father worked in one until it closed down in 1959. He came home stinking of blood. My mother couldn't stand it. She never allowed meat in the house."

"So you never knew what you were missing."

"On the contrary. My father used to sneak my brother and me out to eat steaks. Raw and juicy—that's the way he liked them. But my mother caught on. So she'd fix a big meal of pasta and we'd have to sit down and eat as if we hadn't eaten all day. I got sick one night and brought up both meals right next to my bed. My father was already gone to work, but my mother wouldn't touch it. She insisted we leave it for Dad to clean up when he got home. That's when I stopped eating meat."

"That's disgusting."

"Exactly. Now you know more about me than most anyone outside my family."

"Are you telling me that no one else in the world knows that Dr. Michael Wilson once threw up two meals at once?"

"That's what I'm telling you." Michael moves to the middle of the couch, so he's uncomfortably close. It's not that we necessarily avoid physical contact, but we are both "hands talkers" and we usually sit apart to avoid clocking each other as our arms flail to exhibit incredulity or outrage. "Now you, Dickie. Tell me what you miss about Clayton."

"Absolutely nothing."

Michael reaches out to tip my chin up and force me to look at him. That's when I see it—pity mixed with knowledge. I knock his hand away.

"I really don't think all this sharing is going to work for us, Michael."

"You might be right." He stands.

"Good. So we can go back to normal."

"No, I don't think we can, Dickie."

"What are you saying?"

"I'm saying we can't go back to the way things were."

"What are the options? You want to break up with me?"

"And what exactly would that mean, Dickie? Us breaking up."

"What do you mean what would it mean?"

"I don't think you can *break* something this pliable. We have nothing to break. I learned something from watching you these last couple of weeks, Dickie."

"Besides the fact that weeds flower?"

"I learned that I'd like to have something breakable in my life. Maybe even shatterable."

"But, Michael, we—"

"Think about that, Dickie. How long has it been since you lived with something you loved so much that the loss of it would shatter you into thousands of tiny pebbles?"

"Not long enough," I say, a little jarred at the accuracy of his analogy.

"Don't you want that, Dickie?"

"No, Michael, I don't."

Michael sits back down next to me. "I don't believe you."

"Well, you're in good company."

We sit silently for a moment. "You should go home, Michael," I say.

"I don't think so. I think we just need to sit with this for a bit."

"Good God, you're in Clayton a half hour and you're already adopting their ways."

"I'm going to make some coffee," he says, getting up to go into the kitchen.

"I'll help," I say, getting up to follow.

"No," he says. "Just sit here quietly for a minute, Dickie."

"Jeez, I feel like I'm being given a time-out to think about my actions."

"Try to use it to your advantage."

He comes back carrying a serving tray with coffee, cream, and almond cookies and sets it on the coffee table. It's the small golden rounds with a perfectly placed almond in the center of each—which he had apparently made while I was gone and left in my kitchen to be discovered upon my return—that cause me to weep. Michael takes note but says nothing as he pours coffee and mixes cream before settling back on the couch next to me. He puts an arm around my shoulder and pulls me close. I bury my face in his shirt, an act he would normally barely tolerate as it holds high risks of messing up a perfectly clean shirt. This time he doesn't stop me. He is the cleanest-smelling man I've ever encountered. Soap and water.

"Why would anyone want to live with that much potential for pain, Michael?"

"What are you afraid of, Dickie?" he whispers.

"Shattering into a thousand tiny pebbles," I say.

"Me, too," he says. "How about if we make a pact? How about if we agree that if it happens to one of us, the other will come along with a broom and clean up the mess."

"Oh, Michael, nobody actually keeps those promises. Those pacts never work."

"Hush, cynical girl. They serve their purpose if you let them. They give you just the right false sense of security."

AFTER MICHAEL LEAVES I wander searchingly around my house, looking for what, I don't know. In the late eighties, Dot and I used to watch a television show called *thirtysomething* and howl with laughter when a character began to cry because the act would invariably involve leaning against a wall and sliding slowly to the floor as the tears fell. But that's exactly what I feel like doing this very moment; only the television image of it stops me. Michael had straightened and cleaned while I was gone. In twelve years, I've been unable to communicate to him how intrusive that simple act of kindness feels to me. Books are gone from the floor around my favorite chair and back on bookshelves; smudgy fingerprints are gone from the front door as if no one had ever come through it with an armload of the cedar firewood I keep stacked on the porch.

I call Charlie and tell him I need more time before returning to work. When he asks how I plan on spending it, I tell him what he wants to hear—that I'll hike and relax, get some fresh air, maybe drive out to Clayton again and hang out with my family. I spend upward of fifteen hours a day in front of my computer and on the phone researching Heber's death. At the end of two weeks I know nothing more about the accident than what Charlie told me in his office before Heber's funeral. Somebody messed up and Heber died. When Charlie arrives at my front door, I momentarily consider not letting him in.

"I know you're in there, Dickie," he hollers from the porch. "Open the damn door."

I let him in. He looks around the living room scattered with books and papers, my laptop sitting open in the middle of the mess.

"I like what the fresh air has done for you," he says, looking me up and down. "You look worse than your living room."

"Nice to see you, too, Charlie. What are you doing here?"

"Came to see what you found out about Heber's death."

"Exactly what you knew I'd find out—nothing at all."

"Then I came to talk to you about work."

"I'll be back tomorrow. Nothing about Heber's death, but a secretary I talked to at Dugway did let slip a small lead I'd like to follow."

"That's what else I came to talk to you about, Dickie."

"What?"

"You're being reassigned."

"What are you talking about?"

"Arts and entertainment."

"No fucking way."

"Dickie—"

"Charlie, listen, Dugway is reopening the Baker Lab—and expanding it."

"They just closed that lab in '98 when they opened the level-three lab."

"Exactly. And when I started nosing around about it, everyone shut down and started throwing out the usual crap like 'potential terrorist attacks' and 'post-9/11' and 'top secret.' Of course it's top secret since, as you know, offensive testing of biological weapons is prohibited by international agreement. But what the hell else would they be doing renovating the Baker Lab with twenty-five new biological testing areas?"

"They'll claim they're only doing defensive testing."

"Of course they will."

"I'll have Jack check in out."

"Jack! This is my story, Charlie."

"Not anymore it's not. Not unless they're putting an art gallery in the Baker Lab."

"Come on, Charlie, you can't be serious. The ramifications of this in the middle of all the Iran and China stuff could be huge. Who do you have who knows as much as me about what goes on out there?"

"Unfortunately, that's just the point, Dickie. This isn't my decision. The newspaper's new editor thinks you're a little too close and understandably a little too hurt and a little too angry to be objective about any of this."

"That's bullshit and you know it. Hell, it doesn't take objectivity to report on the feds. You just assume the bastards are lying and you'll be right ninety-nine percent of the time."

"Case in point. Dickie, if it were up to me, you know damn well I'd give you all the rope you need to hang yourself. I hate like hell losing a reporter like you. Far as I'm concerned, we use objectivity as an excuse for apathy around the newsroom a little too often. But it's not up to me. Mary Beckstead is your new boss. Report to her first thing Monday morning."

"Honestly, Charlie, can you envision me writing feature stories on the new quilting shop that just opened up in Sugarhouse?"

"Not really."

"You have to talk to them."

"I've tried to no avail."

"Try again."

"I don't know what to tell you, Dickie. Go into Tom's office Monday morning. Pitch the Baker Lab story. See if you can change his mind."

"Think it will make a difference?"

"Not a chance in hell."

"What's going on, Charlie?"

"Exactly what you suspect is going on. New editor wants to take things 'in a new direction,' as if this damn paper could get any more conservative. You're too radical, Dickie. The older you get, the more radical you get. It's that simple. They saw their opening and they're taking it."

"They can't do that."

"They can and they have."

"Well, shit."

"I'm sorry, Dickie."

"Oh hell, Charlie, to be honest with you it actually took them longer than I thought it would. I didn't think you and I would last longer than five years when we started there."

"Speak for yourself. I was the model Mormon when I started there. It's your influence that corrupted me."

"Thanks, Charlie, that's kind of you to say. How about you? You feeling okay with this new editor?"

"I'm not crazy about working for him, but I don't worry about my job if that's what you're asking. Who else would the church trot out to show diversity when Gladys Knight or Thurl Bailey's not available? I'm their number three man."

"You've got a point there."

"It won't be so bad, Dickie. I don't know how they intend to use you in arts, but it'll give you a much-needed break. You'll be working normal hours and who knows what you'll dig up. I'm sure you can sniff out some misuse of public funds or something like that."

"Sure. Do me a favor, Charlie?"

"What?"

"Don't assign anyone to the Baker Lab story."

"What do you intend to do?"

"Not sure. But give me some time to think about it?"

"No problem. I'd have to fight to run it anyway."

"Thanks for coming here to tell me, Charlie."

"I'll see you Monday?"

"Sure. See you then."

AT 7 A.M. ON MONDAY MORNING I put the teapot on, shower, dress for work, and eat breakfast in exactly the order I have done so for twenty-five years. I keep waiting for my body to reach for the keys and exit through the back door, but it never does. Around 10 A.M. I gather firewood from the front porch. It's sunny and warm, but the weather seems unrelated to the act of building a fire. Many of the logs from the last load of cedar Heber delivered are charred, trees scavenged off BLM land after being split apart by lightning, and I leave four lovely smudges on white paint as I close the door.

I'm sitting in a dark living room with the blinds closed feeding logs into the fire when Dot arrives. She lets herself in through the back door and sits on the floor, her back against the couch, next to me.

"I've left you alone now for almost three weeks as requested," she says. "That's long enough. I'm not leaving even if you want me to."

"I don't want you to."

"Good."

"Unless you've come to tell me we can't be friends anymore."

"Why would I tell you that?"

"I've lost my brother, my boyfriend, and my job in less than a month. The only thing left to lose is my best friend."

"I'm sorry about your brother. Michael was never really your boyfriend in any true sense of the word. And fuck the job."

"You're an excellent best friend, Dot."

"And I intend to remain such."

"You don't find me too radical?"

"There's no such thing."

"Or too emotionally closed off?"

"I've never been fooled by your bullshit bravado."

"You just went along with it?"

"That's the beauty of having a best friend."

"I never knew that."

"You're a slow learner." She gets up and throws another log on the fire. "I like a nice fire on a summer day."

"Happens to be something I'm quite good at."

"I can see that."

"Ever want to just fill your life with things you're good at and abandon everything else? Like I'm not really all that good at brushing my teeth. My dentist says I'm too intense, strip the enamel right off. Maybe I should just give it up."

"Interesting concept," Dot says.

"I was good at my job. I would have kept that given the choice."

"Too good. That's why you don't have it anymore. Never learned the fine art of mediocrity."

"I could keep my garden. Might as well give up cleaning the house altogether. I'm good at stacking hay and moving irrigation pipe. I can also castrate a calf if there's a need."

"Good to know."

"I should abandon my car and go everywhere by horseback."

"There's an idea."

"What are you really good at, Dot?"

"Fucking. I could fill my life with that."

"Don't you already?"

"Yep, so that goes on the 'stay' list."

"Wonder if I'm any good at that."

"Might want to find out before you put it in the 'abandon' column."

"I'd like to."

"What are you waiting for?"

"A good offer."

"Wise. It's all in the partnership." She looks at me out of the corner of her eye. I look straight into the fire.

"You're good at giving advice," I say. "Guess you could keep your job."

"I appreciate that. Can I offer you any?"

"Ever feel like your life just showed up in its entirety, fully formed? Sort of like buying a fully furnished double-wide, all you do is move in and buy groceries. Then one day you're in your little kitchen with the fluttering yellow curtains you've always loved and you look out the window and realize that your double-wide is parked in the middle of a busy intersection. And you realize that you put it there and at the time it seemed like a good idea, but now you're not so sure. Got any advice for that?"

"Secure your breakables and move your double-wide."

"What if you don't have enough Styrofoam peanuts to secure your breakables?"

"Take the risk."

We sit silently watching the fire, our backs against the couch, our shoulders and knees touching.

"You know what I miss about Clayton, Dot?"

"Tell me."

"Everything. Every goddamn little thing."

"Be more specific."

"I miss the smell of fresh-cut alfalfa and sage coming through open windows on a sheaf of dust. I miss silence. I miss desert rain, especially those first few drops that plop into a patch of alkali and bounce chalk into the air. I miss falling to sleep to the rhythmic chug of irrigation sprinklers and being awakened in the middle of the night by a pack of yipping coyotes. I miss turkey vultures circling over my head, diving down every once in a while to see if I'm dead. I miss dark skies, skies not shattered by streetlights. I fucking hate streetlights. Did I ever tell you that?"

"No."

"I miss moon shadows. I miss knowing how to walk in the night, knowing how to feel the shapes and shadows of darkness. I miss the smell of horse sweat and cow shit. Do you like those smells, Dot?"

"Can't say."

"I miss my animal body, the one that knew hard physical work, the one that wallowed in the smooth brown mud of Hell Hole Springs. I miss being tucked into craggy mountains balanced at a perfect angle. I don't mind being here between the Wasatch and the Oquirrhs, but there's so much shit in here with us, it's hard to get the feel for the land itself."

"I concur with that."

"More than anything I miss an old woman who knows me better than I know myself."

"And the cowboy?"

"The ache has never left me."

CHAPTER NINETEEN

Dad balances a cup of coffee on a fence post and throws a wedge of alfalfa hay into the manger at his knees, then retrieves his coffee and rests his elbows between the top two horizontal poles. He cocks his head only slightly when he hears me coming up the drive. Silently, I place a ratty sandal on the lowest pole next to his cowboy boot. A 2,300-pound black Simmental bull throws his head and snorts as he strides toward us to reach the manger. We are all a little wary of one another—the bull of us, us of him, Dad and I of each other.

"Nice bull," I say. The bull raises his enormous head from the manger to keep an eye on us, spewing hay leaves into the wind as he chews methodically. Dad pulls a piece of alfalfa out of the manger and chews on one end. I do the same. The bull blows snot in our direction.

"That's a damn good bull," Dad says.

He lifts his eyes and looks past the bull to the Onaquis, still in shadow, resisting the early-morning sun.

"That's a pretty sight," he says after a long period of silence.

"Yeah, it is."

Without speaking we watch the sun spread.

"I don't know what I'm supposed to say to you, Dickie. I feel like there's something I ought to say, but I don't know what it is."

"I don't either, Dad."

He walks into the house with the same stride he had forty years ago, striking packed dirt hard with the heel of his boot. He shortly reemerges with the Wal-Mart bag, which he holds out to me. I take it.

"What should I do with them?"

He positions himself back toward the bull without answering.

"I want you to take Heber's cows and this bull, too. I just brought him in for a few days because I sort of like the feel and the smell of him out here behind the house."

"But Dad, I don't—"

"I'm eighty-three years old, Dickie. Every morning for the last week I've poured myself a cup of coffee and walked out here to throw some hay over the fence. Seeing this bull standing in this old corral waiting to be fed is about the most beautiful sight a crazy old son of a bitch like me can imagine. But I get right here where we're standing now and I don't know whether to laugh or cry—most mornings I end up doing both."

He starts toward the house then stops and makes a full turn with the tips of his fingers stuffed into his front pockets, looking first north toward the Nelson ranch then south toward the Bar C.

"Gonna be a nice day, Dickie," he says, then continues toward the door. He stops again just as his hand touches the door handle and without turning says, "Hope those aren't the only shoes you own."

AFTER SEARCHING HER HOUSE, barn, garden, and fields, I find Bev at Heber's house.

"I packed a lunch," she says when I walk in the front door. "Let's go out back." We settle into two Adirondack chairs that face west. "I been coming over here every day trying to go through Heber's stuff and get this house cleaned out. Can't say I'm making much headway."

"Need some help?"

"I wouldn't turn it down."

"How bad is it?" I ask.

"Not near as bad as you'd expect for an old bachelor. Heber was a bit of a neatnik."

I turn to look at the log-cabin structure behind us.

"It's a nice little place," I say.

"That it is. Heber and Stumpy did a fine job building this place."

"Whose idea was the solar panels? Never thought of Heber as an environmentalist."

"No, but you did know he was cheap, didn't you? He ran this entire house with those panels. He's completely off the grid."

"I'll be damned."

"I sure do miss hearing Heber's voice under those ceilings. Can't shake the feeling that I somehow let that boy down."

"What are you talking about?"

"Well, I'm not sure really. It's just a feeling. But maybe I shoulda done more to keep him off the army's payroll."

"From what I got from Heber, he liked that damn job. Far as he was concerned, it was the perfect thing—nice paycheck, close to home, good retirement package. Course that part of it didn't work out so well for him."

"Well, that's what I'm feeling bad about."

"I feel bad about that, too, Bev, but how can you figure that's your fault?"

"Sometimes I wonder if I shouldn't a done a little more fighting in my younger days," Bev says.

"What do you mean?"

"Well, maybe if me and Merv hadn't been so quick to accept the army's cash apology back then, we coulda changed some things around here. Maybe things woulda turned out different for Heber."

"That's a bit of a stretch, Bev. You taking money that was rightfully coming to you didn't kill Heber."

"Well, I know there's no direct cause and effect, but maybe we shoulda all made a bigger stink over what the army was doing out here."

"Maybe we should all make one now," I say.

"You might be right about that."

"Or maybe we could all fight like hell and make a big stink and refuse to budge and end up just like George," I say.

"Well, that's the narrow space we're living in, isn't it? A person can spend a goddamn good portion a their lives capitulating one little piece at a time just so that tomorrow looks okay, and you get to the end and realize you've sacrificed too damn much. On the other hand, you can refuse to budge and exhaust yourself in the process and end up miserable as hell. Where does either one a those things leave you?"

"Ganoa County."

"That's about right. I guess it's up to each of us to find some sorta balance in there, but there's not much room to maneuver."

"Doesn't seem like it."

"You know, I like those activist types, though, the ones that really make change happen. I appreciate what they do even when I don't agree with them. I always sorta wished I could be one, muster up that much passion for something I really believe in. I like the idea a that."

"I never knew that about you, Bev."

"But it's just not who I am. Ranching's pretty much the only thing I know how to do with any sorta consistency."

"Well, you're damn good at it."

"That's the truth of it. A person has to live the life they're suited for, I guess. And I got no complaints about it. I do like the work."

She pulls herself up to the edge of her chair and plants her elbows on her knees. "Listen, Dickie, you do what you want to do with this place. As soon as I get this house cleaned out, you can put the place up for sale if you want. No strings attached. It's time for me to mind my own damn business for a change."

"Shit, Bev, who are you kidding? You've tried that no-interference thing before. You're just no good at it."

"Well, I'm not quite eighty yet; maybe I'm still young enough to learn."

"You don't actually believe that, do you?"

"I'm gonna give it a try."

"Okay."

"Okay. I'm proud a you, Dickie. I don't ever want you to think otherwise. I love picking up the paper and seeing your byline. Makes me smile every damn morning. And it finally occurred to me—this mighta taken me a bit longer than it should have—that you're a big girl and you can decide for yourself where and how to live your life."

"Thanks, Bev, I appreciate that."

"You're a good writer, Dickie. You should never stop writing."

"I don't intend to."

"It also occurred to me—and this realization mighta taken me longer than it should have also—that my insisting you need to move back out here to Clayton might just a been the rantings of a lonely old woman who's outlived too many people and is looking for some good company."

"That so?"

"No doubt."

"And did it ever occur to you that maybe you're right about me? That I'm very near the edge of living life in the abyss between my mother's sadness and my father's stubbornness?"

"Yeah, that occurs to me all the time."

"So do you really think this is a wise time to invoke that no-interference rule again?"

"I'm here when you need me, girl."

"I could use your help right now to get my stuff out of the car."

"How much you got?"

"Enough for a few nights. Thought I'd see how this little cabin feels."

• • •

STUMPY JUMPS when he walks out of the sunlight into the darkness of his kitchen and sees a movement in the shadow.

"God, you scared the hell outta me! What are you doing here?"

"Waiting for you. Take a ride with me?"

We get in my car and drive through Johnson's Pass to the west side of the Onaquis.

"I wasn't sure when I'd see you again," Stumpy says.

"But you were sure you *would* see me again?"

"Yeah, but I was afraid I'd have to wait for another funeral."

"Well, here's something you probably didn't know—the road between here and Salt Lake City actually runs both directions."

"Yeah, Bev told me. She tried to talk me into driving into Salt Lake to see you."

"Oh, I see. Her definition of noninterference is to delegate the assignment."

"Pretty much."

"She wasn't too persuasive, was she?"

Stumpy doesn't answer; we ride the rest of the way in silence. I park the car in the same place the truck and trailer sat on that day in 1968, and we hike the trail to Marsh Meadow. I walk out a ways and sit in tall grass. Stumpy follows me silently.

"You been back here since that day?" he asks.

"No. I've never been able to get my car to go farther than the top of the pass. Seems to chug to a stop there. You?"

"Yeah. You know Heber used to come up here all the time." I nod my head. I don't know how I know that but I do. "He thought this was the prettiest place in the world—said he wasn't about to let the army take that away from him."

"Good for him. Hate to let those bastards have everything."

"That's what Heber said."

Stumpy pitches rocks into the meadow and I dig into the dirt with a stick. The shade creeps up on our backs.

"This is the same time of year we found the cows out here," I say.

"I remember this same kind of day, the same warm wind, the same smell of grasses and piñon in the air."

I start shivering. I get up and stride deeper into the meadow, seeking sun. Stumpy catches me and pulls me to a stop.

"I can't get warm, Stumpy. It must be eighty degrees out here and I can't get warm."

"Shh," he says, pulling me in to his chest and wrapping both arms around me.

"I never asked you what it was like when you came back out here that day."

"Hush," he says, squeezing me tighter. He's wearing a T-shirt and I can feel the sun's heat on his bare arms wrapped around my back and the heat from his chest on the side of my face.

"Tell me, Stumpy," I say, burrowing into his shoulder. "I need you to tell me."

He buries one hand in my hair. That movement—his hand cradling my head to his chest, winding my hair around his fingers—has the same effect on me at age fifty-two as it did at age fifteen. It makes me feel safe. I've never told him that, but somehow he's always known it.

"It was about this time of day, when we made the last trip," he says quietly. "The shadows are all exactly the same. It took several trips to get all the calves. The cows were mostly dead by the time we got back here the first time. I was glad for that. The calves were easy to gather up; they seemed too stunned to run. Annie was a mess, sobbing so hard she could barely see, but she helped get the calves down the trail just like everybody else. Bev and Grandpa seemed business as usual until we got back to the trucks, then Bev walked into the trees and started puking and crying. Everybody was just sort of dazed. But your dad was the worst. I could hardly stand to look at him. I can't explain it, but you could just see it in his face. I knew he was finished, not for that day or year, Dickie, but for the rest of his life."

Stumpy walks me out into the sun again and gently pulls me

down into the grass, never releasing his hold on me. He sits behind me, his long legs wrapped around me, and draws me in to his chest. He wipes my wet face with the bottom of his T-shirt, like he would a child, then buries his face in my hair, his lips resting on the bare skin between my neck and shoulder. We stay like this, entangled in western wheatgrass and each other, until the sun is completely gone.

"I'm sorry, Dickie," he whispers.

"What do you have to be sorry for, Stump?" I ask through tears.

"I'm not sure." He pauses and presses his lips harder against my skin. "Maybe I'm just feeling sorry for myself. I'm sorry that you've been away from me for thirty years. And I'm sorry I never figured out a way to keep that from happening."

I want to respond but can't seem to pull myself together enough to do so.

"This place has never been quite right since you left," he says. "I haven't been quite right." He pulls his arms away from me, takes me by the shoulders, and twists me around so we're face-to-face. "Listen, Dickie, I know you have a life and a job and a relationship and all that in Salt Lake, and I know I have no right—"

I press my fingers to his lips. "Shut up with all of that, will you, Stumpy? Just say what you want to say."

"I want you back here, Dickie."

"That's all you have to say, Stumpy. That's all you ever had to say."

I turn back toward the Oquirrhs. He pulls me tight against his chest, lifts my hair away from my neck, and kisses me lightly.

"Remember the way we were at Hell Hole Springs?" he asks softly. "Wild and free. Just following our bodies like every other animal out here."

"I remember."

"It's still there, Dickie, that physical pull. My body to yours and yours to mine. It's the one thing between us we haven't fucked up."

"I know."

We both fall silent and stay this way until we lose all shadows to the night.

"Come on. You're going to freeze to death out here," he says.

"I have one more thing to do." I pull the decorative tin out of my pack.

"Heber?" he asks. I nod and pour half the ashes into Stumpy's cupped hand and half into mine. "Seems like the right place," he says. "I'm sure Heber's much obliged."

"Do you miss him, Stump?"

"I sure as hell do."

"Yeah, me, too. Isn't that weird? I didn't see him more'n once a year, but I sure miss knowing he's out here."

We both pause for a moment with our heads down, then at the same instant, we open our palms and toss the contents into the wind. We start back to the car in the total darkness. Stumpy offers his hand, but I refuse it, imploring my diminished instincts for navigating in desert darkness to kick in. I stumble a few times on tree roots along the trail. I can't see Stumpy's face in the darkness, but I know it holds an amused half grin.

A WEEK LATER I borrow a horse from Bev and ride toward Hell Hole Springs. A ways out, I tie the horse to a piñon and walk the last mile. The clothing that covers my body drops as it becomes increasingly foreign—almost profane—in the verdant desert wildness. And here's another thing I've been missing about Clayton: the way a place can remain undeniably mine, seemingly untouched year after year, as if I were such a vital piece, my absence stills it like a photograph.

and has shared with me his expansive knowledge of the deserts and mountains of Utah. He has read a ridiculous number of drafts of this book, each time offering beautifully insightful feedback. Sharing a life—and the remote backcountry—with him makes all things possible. Without him, there would be no book.

ACKNOWLEDGMENTS

There can be no greater gift to a writer than an editor who sees what's there before it's actually there, and I am the lucky recipient of such a gift. I am enormously grateful to Marjorie Braman for her wisdom and guidance throughout the editing and publishing process. Much gratitude also to Doug Stewart—who is fabulously good at his job—for working tirelessly on my behalf, soothing my neurosis, and fielding a lot of stupid questions. What more could a person ask for in an agent?

Thanks to Peggy Hageman for a great title and for her kind competence; thanks to Lyn McCarter for her great feedback on an early draft; and thanks to Brad Richman for his input on ranching in the arid basin and range, and for his contribution of cowboy poetry.

I offer my thanks to all of those people in my life who inadvertently provide the seed of a scene or the twitch of a character, which I shamelessly appropriate, exploit, and distort to fit my fictional needs—particularly my sister, Sue Armstrong, who quietly acquiesces to finding stolen moments of her life in the pages of my work. Thanks to my mother, Darlene Richman, who fostered my appreciation of silence, and to my father, Reese Richman, who made me a true westerner.

Steve Defa has taken me deeper into the geography of the west